01/19

D0716112

Wи)

This book should be returned/renewed by the latest date shown above. Overdue items incur charges which prevent self-service renewals. Please contact the library.

**Wandsworth Libraries
24 hour Renewal Hotline
01159 293388
www.wandsworth.gov.uk**

Wandsworth

RUTH FRANCES LONG is a lifelong fan of fantasy and romance. She studied English Literature, History of Religions, and Celtic Civilisation in college and now works in a specialised library of rare and unusual books. But they don't talk to her that often. Ruth Frances Long is also the author of *The Treachery of Beautiful Things*.

A CRACK IN EVERYTHING

welcome to the other side

RUTH FRANCES LONG

THE O'BRIEN PRESS
DUBLIN

First published 2014 by The O'Brien Press Ltd,
12 Terenure Road East, Rathgar, Dublin 6, Ireland.
Tel: +353 1 4923333; Fax: +353 1 4922777
E-mail: books@obrien.ie
Website: www.obrien.ie

ISBN: 978-1-84717-635-6

10 9 8 7 6 5 4 3 2 1
19 18 17 16 15 14

Cover image courtesy of iStockphoto
Printed and bound by CPI Group (UK) Ltd, Croydon, CR0 4YY
The paper in this book is produced using pulp from managed forests.

The O'Brien Press receives financial assistance from

To Pat, Diarmuid and Emily.

So many people helped make this book happen, this crazy story that didn't seem to fit in anywhere. I can never thank all of them, but if you have had a hand in this, thank you! More specifically, I have a few people to thank in particular.

Whoever painted the angel graffiti on South William Street, first of all, because that was the spark of this story; my wonderful and ever-supportive Shiny Shiny Critique group for all the … oooh, shiny!; my agent, Sallyanne Sweeney, for her faith in me; the lovely Celine Kiernan for an inspired suggestion; everyone at The O'Brien Press and my editor, Helen, for really getting the world and its inhabitants in a way few others did.

And most of all my ever-patient friends and family. Especially Pat, Diarmuid and Emily. Here's to a lifetime of trips to the wishing stone and saying our (carefully respectful) hellos to Brí.

CHAPTER ONE

Stepping Sideways

Izzy had only just pushed down the lever on the toaster when it exploded with an audible pop. Sparks flared up like fireworks and pungent black smoke filled the kitchen.

Dad cursed loudly – words he seriously wasn't meant to say in front of her – and jumped up from the kitchen table.

'Stand back from the bloody thing,' he said and ripped the plug from the wall. 'Are you okay, Izzy?'

She nodded, trying not to inhale the acrid fumes. 'Fine, Dad. I'm fine.' He looked comical standing there with the cord swinging from his hand like a pendulum, glaring at the toaster as if he had a lifelong grudge against it.

It wasn't like this was the first time. She knew the drill. She punched the switch on the extractor fan and opened the windows while Dad prodded the toaster suspiciously, waiting for it to attack again.

A deathly silence settled over the kitchen until Mum rustled the paper. 'The technological curse is definitely hereditary then, is it?'

Izzy grinned, aware from her mother's voice that she was stifling laughter. She couldn't help herself. It was funny.

Dad gave an affronted huff. 'Your daughter wasn't hurt, since you're so concerned.'

'Oh, good. That's a relief, as always. What item is going to suffer the wrath of the two of you next?'

She folded up the paper, poured herself the last cup of coffee and winked at Izzy, who leaned on the counter and suppressed a giggle. Dad picked up the toaster, crossed to the back door and tossed it onto the patio. It clattered onto the stones and he slammed the door after it.

'There, all gone. And good riddance. Better use the grill, Izzy.'

'You aren't leaving that out there,' Mum protested. 'It's a garden, not a dump!'

'The toaster's dead, love. Let it rest in peace. I'll take it to the recycling centre later.' He put the jug under the coffee machine and hit the red button. It gurgled away happily.

'Careful!' said Mum. Of all the machines in the house, Izzy thought, they couldn't afford to lose that one. Neither of her parents would be able to function. She went to the fridge and got a yogurt instead. Far safer. She and Dad had an uncanny way with electrical items. Mainly with destroying them.

'I won't break it,' Dad argued. 'I've never broken the coffee machine! The coffee machine *loves* me.'

God, they were embarrassing.

'Just stay away from my laptop, David,' Mum warned him. 'I'm not sure I could take another *I've-never-seen-that-before* helpline conversation.' That made Dad grimace dramatically. Izzy rolled her eyes to heaven, because next thing she knew they were kissing in a way that ought to be strictly forbidden to anyone over twenty-one.

But at least they were happy together. Not coldly ignoring each other or getting divorced like the parents of half her classmates. They were happy, and she was happy for them.

Even if they were mortifying.

'Better get dressed,' Dad said. 'Izzy, do you want a lift? I'm heading out by the Temple of Mammon.'

She winced. The enormous shopping centre in Dundrum didn't call itself a 'shopping centre', but rather a 'Town Centre'. And Dad didn't even call it that. He had opinions about shopping centres. Opinions with capital letters, quotes, underlines and italics. Probably why he barely had enough business to get by these days. You'd think in a recession, an architect would be a bit more circumspect about whose buildings he was criticising. But that was Dad, through and through.

Problem was, she agreed with him. She was the only teenage girl she knew who hated the place.

'No, thanks. I thought I'd head into town later on. Dylan's band have a gig this afternoon.'

Town wasn't something man-made, or designed. Town was

the centre of Dublin, an unwritten but perfectly understood area that had created itself, grown organically, carelessly — a grubby, worn-at-the-seams paradise divided by a river. A place of narrow lanes left over from the Viking settlement and the stately Georgian avenues of the Wide Street Commissioners.

Izzy loved Dublin, loved just mooching about, down laneways or around the iron-railed squares, listening to buskers, looking at street art and window shopping. It was a place to just generally hang out, sometimes meeting friends, sometimes on her own. Summer was heaven for that.

She should have known the city centre like the back of her hand at this stage, and yet she always found something new in it. That was its magic, the maze that was Town, a hodge-podge of public and secret places from countless eras, squished together over the course of a thousand years, always new, always old.

'Oh, where are they playing?' asked Mum eagerly. Too eagerly.

Izzy was still living down the last time they turned up to one of Dylan's gigs. Marianne loved bringing that one up. Izzy had known Dylan so long her parents seemed to think of him as their own kid rather than Izzy's friend.

'Just a promo thing. No biggie. Anyway, you're at work. It's in the afternoon.' The words came out in a quick rush and she took the opportunity to escape before they could ask any more details like exactly when and where.

The DART rattled along the tracks, green and ugly. The train was a lifeline for anyone living on the outskirts of the city, a way to get out of the suburban seaside and swing around the sweep of the bay right into the heart of town. Izzy gazed out the window instead of listening to music or playing with her phone like her fellow passengers. The treacherous sand flats of Sandymount Strand, beloved of Joyce, stretched out beyond the wall, the sea rushing in on them with white horses in the waves, breaking off the submerged sandbars. The wind was getting up, but the sky was still clear and blue. Summer wasn't always so beautiful. Usually it was notable for the extra rain, but not this year. This year it was golden and beautiful, like a childhood memory of summers past. It transformed the whole place.

Izzy pushed her way off the train at Pearse Station and joined the crowds streaming down the steep slope to street level. She wandered around the edge of Trinity College, dodging tourists clustered around their coaches and beggars holding paper coffee cups.

'Spare change, bud?' someone mumbled from the level of her knees and she saw a flash of yellow teeth in a grimy face. Gimlet eyes met hers, stopping her in her tracks. Breath caught in her throat, but she couldn't move, not right away. It felt like someone was holding the back of her neck in an iron grip. 'Spare change, love?' he said again, his grin even wider now.

Someone pushed between them, breaking the contact, and Izzy could move again. She jerked away, crossing the road and trying not to look as if she was running. There was nothing to run from. Just an old guy looking for money. But her heart hammered against the inside of her ribs.

It didn't calm until she'd reached Grafton Street, where she paused outside the bank among the shoppers and foreign language students watching a fairly crusty busker playing the guitar like a Spanish master. And here she was, getting freaked out. Stupid, really. She knew better than to let her imagination run away with her. Dad always told her that things were what they were. No one needed to imagine anything worse. Just an old beggar and her overactive imagination.

Izzy let herself breathe more calmly and the noise and conversation, the laughter and shouts, swept over her. The street was full of colour everywhere, and sound like a physical force. She lingered at the shop windows without going inside. It wasn't a day for shopping, even if she had any money to spare. This was just a day for herself. The school holidays weren't the same when you got older. She worked every hour she could get in the coffee shop down the road from her house, while most of her friends were content to waste the summer away. Well, maybe that wasn't fair. Part-time jobs and summer work were tough to come by these days.

Still, Marianne, Dylan's sister and Izzy's classmate and co-worker, could be less of a prima donna about it all.

She was looking in the window of the camera shop, lusting

after an SLR she couldn't ever hope to afford, when in the reflection she caught a glimpse of the beggar again, on the far side of the road, sitting in a doorway surrounded by cardboard and a ratty-looking blanket. The same man. She was sure of it. Her spine stiffened in alarm. He didn't move, still as one of those fake statue people further down the road, just staring at her with eyes that caught the light in a weirdly metallic way. He wasn't painted gold or silver though. If he had a colour it would be 'grime'.

He *was* the one she'd seen earlier on Nassau Street. He grinned the same way, held her gaze as if to hypnotise her and hold her there. Like a cobra with its prey.

The street cleaning truck rumbled by, breaking the spell. Izzy shuddered and turned with a start, able to move again in an instant. He was gone. As if he'd never been there. No sign of him at all. Just an empty doorway, a tangle of blanket and some ragged ends of cardboard. No one was there at all.

Izzy shook her head. She'd imagined it, seen some sort of trick of the light in the reflection. There was nothing there.

But at the top of the street, she thought she saw him again, lurking by the vast grey arch of the gates to St Stephen's Green. Izzy turned away, wincing and wishing there was a cop around. The creep was shadowing her.

She jumped as her phone rang in her pocket. As she fished it out, her hands were shaking so hard she almost dropped it. She glanced over her shoulder. He was gone again and a loud group of tourists stood there instead, comparing brightly coloured maps.

'Let me guess.' Dylan's voice sounded deep with amusement. 'You're sightseeing.'

Seeing something. Not sights. Not good ones.

She looked around, half expecting the beggar to be back, half dreading catching sight of him again.

Her voice shook. 'How can I sightsee here? I've seen it.'

Dylan didn't notice her tone. He laughed. 'Yeah, sure. You can sightsee anywhere, Izzy. Especially here. I know you. Okay, you're wandering around town looking at the buildings and pretending you're window shopping?'

Busted.

Or at least that was what she *had* been doing, before she'd acquired a potential stalker.

'You in town?' she asked, deliberately not answering his question. That amused him even more. She could hear it in his voice.

'Just got in. So are you coming?'

'Now?' She couldn't check the time and talk at the same time. She tried to balance the phone against her shoulder and twist her wrist around to look at the watch. After two. Shit, how had that happened?

Mari's voice sounded in the background, saying something about Izzy always being late – which was a lie if she was talking about work – and then she laughed. Izzy knew that laugh. It was the flirty, *I'm-so-gorgeous-aren't-you-just-sick* laugh she reserved for those guys she fancied beyond reason. Like the bass player in Dylan's band.

'Soon,' said Dylan. 'You'll come though, won't you?' He broke off before she could answer, said something she couldn't quite make out to the others and then he was back. 'I've got to go. Soundcheck's starting. Look, this thing won't even take the whole afternoon. We're going to grab a bite to eat and maybe go clubbing later?'

Izzy frowned. Like she could afford that. She'd love to, though. It had been so long since she'd been out with Dylan. With the guys from the band they'd get in wherever. That was probably what Mari was counting on. Dylan was two years older than both his sister and Izzy, finished school and starting university. Hanging around with him – embarrassing nerd-muso brother or not – opened up a world of possibilities for Mari.

'I've kind of got to go home,' she muttered, wishing she could just blithely say 'yes' and not think about the consequences. 'I've work in the morning and I promised Mum and Dad. But I'm on my way now. Be there soon.'

It wasn't far to Exchequer Street. She could make it with plenty of time. All she had to do was cut down by the side of the shopping centre, past the theatre and head down South William Street. Ten minutes max.

She was only halfway there when the phone rang again.

She tried to juggle fishing her ringing phone out of her pocket and avoiding the crowds of afternoon shoppers who would probably just trample her to the ground and keep going if she stopped. Stumbling out of the way of three suits on lunch break and some tourists who were clearly lost and flapping brightly coloured maps around like sails, she hopped up onto the steps leading to a design shop.

'Where *are* you?' Marianne barked, before even a hello or anything.

'I'm on the way.'

'I'm standing here on my own. They're all up there fiddling with the sound system and making a racket. Hurry up!'

Chills ran spiny fingers down her back again, like a trickle of sweat, bringing with it once more the feeling that she was being watched. She glanced around, but couldn't see anyone. No sign of creepy guy. Where was he now?

'I'll be there in a minute or two.' Surely Mari could stand to be on her own and not the centre of attention for five minutes. Or maybe not. That was Mari all over.

'Come on, Izzy. I don't know anyone else. Hurry *up*. Oh, they're getting ready to start.'

The line went dead and Izzy rolled her eyes.

I promised Dylan I'd be there.

At the best of times Marianne could be a bit of a bitch. She couldn't help it, she always said. It was just the way she was. A handy excuse, but at the same time, Izzy couldn't recall a time when she didn't know Mari and Dylan, or when Mari hadn't been the centre of all attention. Though they were in the same class in school, they only associated because they'd known each other forever. They just didn't have a lot else in common. Mari was boy-mad these days and Izzy never found anything so very amazing about the boys Mari obsessed over. If the truth was told, Izzy was far closer to Dylan than Mari. And sister or not, often enough even Dylan pretended he didn't know Mari. Most of the time Izzy could follow suit. Mari certainly didn't want to know her at school. Mari was ... well, Mari.

Izzy slid her phone into her pocket and looked up to find a gap in the sea of people into which she could slot. Her eyes fell on the graffiti on the alleyway wall.

It was right next to her, cut off by railings from this side and a massive bin from the other. About ten feet high, starkly drawn in black and white. An angel. The figure crouched there, her hands clasped nervously before her, balancing on the tips of her toes with her wings outspread behind her, as if at any moment she might take off. She looked over her shoulder, right at Izzy. The eyes ate into her soul.

When Izzy looked closer, the face was smudged, a smear of morning-after mascara, half on the pillows and half on the cheeks. She looked as if she'd been crying. Worse, she looked afraid.

Captivated by the image, Izzy stepped down and dodged through the other pedestrians until she could slip into the alley itself. She squeezed past the bin, trying neither to inhale nor imagine what she might be getting on her clothes. Even Mum and Dad might ask some questions when she'd only had this jacket a couple of weeks.

Her boot scuffed on something as she stepped closer to the wall, a mound of ash, as if a pile of newspapers had been allowed to burn right down there. Izzy bent closer and touched it. A shiver ran up her fingers, along her arm. The angel gazed down, with a Mona Lisa air. She did the eyes thing, her gaze following Izzy wherever she stood.

Izzy stepped away, alarm snaking around her spine, all the way down, crashing against the wheeled bin and sending it skittering out onto the path.

Someone yelled at her, cursed and kicked it back in before they carried on their way. She dug out her phone and switched it to camera. It made that overly loud, false camera shutter noise as she took the picture.

Something hard slammed into the small of her back, pitching her forward, off balance and flailing. She crashed face first against the wall, the black and white graffiti blurring before her eyes. The same something snatched her phone right out of her hand. Pain lanced down her arm, like wires beneath her skin. Without thinking, she launched herself up and after the shambling figure retreating down the alleyway.

The creep.

She couldn't lose the phone. She just couldn't. The stupid thing cost too much.

He turned back towards her, giving the impression of a dirt-lined face like crumpled newspaper. The same guy she had seen earlier, the old beggar who'd been following her, waiting for a moment like this.

He stopped dead in his tracks and turned side on, still look-ing at her. And grinned again. A horrible yellow-toothed grin, far too big for his face.

His image flickered like ancient film, newsreel from a bygone age. Vanishing. Izzy blinked, her mouth dropping open as he started to fade from his head down.

Vanishing, right there, in front of her eyes.

No way!

Izzy dived towards him, grabbing at the place he had been and her fingers closed on the tattered edges of a filthy wool overcoat just before the shimmer of invisibility claimed it too. She felt herself yanked forwards, her feet jerking out from beneath her and she tumbled after him into the alley.

CHAPTER TWO

Jinx

A blast of hot air struck Izzy's whole body, coming out of nowhere, as if she'd just walked under a shop-door fan. But this air stank of burnt paper and ashes. It sucked the breath from her lungs. Her vision flared, inverting the colours around her and pounding distorted images into her brain like a migraine.

She slammed onto cobbles. The alley, which had looked like no more than a dead end, opened out ahead of her, lit only in patches by a flickering light, the walls and stones slick with a substance that gave them a rainbow sheen. It twisted in and out of sight and it was all wrong …

Her bag spilled from her shoulder, half her things skittering over the alley floor. The old man spoke in a lyric tongue she didn't understand, trying to yank his coat free of her hand. By his tone and the look on his face, he had to be cursing.

Rage returned Izzy's voice to her, forced her into action again.

'Give it back!' she yelled.

He aimed a kick at her face, but it never connected. He jerked back suddenly, as if something in the darkness grabbed him by the back of the neck and shook him hard. It was dark here, the place thick with shadows that shouldn't exist on a summer's afternoon. Izzy's vision swam and a high-pitched whine cut through her head. Through it she could hear words.

'What in all the seven hells' names do you think you're doing, Mistle? Did you bring her through?'

'I didn't mean any harm, Jinx. She came after me.'

A low growl rippled through the air. It shivered against Izzy's skin, made her stomach dip inside her and then leap up. She let go of the coat, pulled herself up onto her knees. Her brain reeled around inside her skull, lurching sickeningly as she moved.

Concussion? It could be. She'd hit the wall hard enough.

Not to mention seeing him vanish. Had to be a concussion. Her stomach twisted and sweetness filled her mouth. She was going to throw up.

Dear God, she couldn't. Bile burned the back of her throat, but she forced it down and pulled herself up to stand.

'Get out of here, you fool,' said the voice called Jinx.

Was he behind her? How had he got behind her? Was he calling her a *fool*? No, he was talking to the old man. 'Don't prey around here. You've been warned enough times. You—'

'My phone,' Izzy said, before it was too late. 'He took my phone.'

There was a pause. She tried to focus on Jinx, but he stood in shadows – and here, in the narrow alley she'd never known existed, the shadows were very dark indeed. They were wrapped around him, hiding him from view. 'Give it back.'

'But it's mine. I did what I had to. It's pretty. It's mine.'

'Give it back,' Jinx's voice rippled with menace, like the growl of a tiger on the edge of a nightmare. Even Izzy took a step back.

With an inarticulate roar belying the fawning behaviour of a second earlier, Mistle flung the phone at her. It crashed onto the cobbles, shattering into too many pieces to count.

Mistle didn't give her a second glance. He just ran, darting through the shadows and down the twisting alleyway, out of sight. His footsteps fell away. In the distance a car horn blared.

Then everything else fell away to silence.

And the sound of the gentle rise and fall of someone else's breath.

'You shouldn't be here either,' said the voice called Jinx. Strangely melodic a voice. So deep it resonated through her. But not kind. In no way could anyone call it kind.

Izzy's temper bristled. No, *are you okay?* No, *did he hurt you?* She scowled, searching for him in the shadows. Her vision drifted back towards normality. She could see again, almost. Blinking hard, she tried to focus on him.

'I'm just fine, thanks,' she snapped. 'No harm done.'

Liar. She hurt all over. Not to mention the wound to her pride. What had she been thinking? Everyone knew not to chase thieves down alleys. Instinct was one thing, but what if he'd had a knife? What if he'd had friends?

A vague outline that had to be Jinx loomed over her. Big, broad. And scary, her instincts told her, a little too late to be of any use. This was *so* not the place to be.

Dropping to her knees she made an attempt to gather her belongings. There was some sort of sludge covering her note-book. She tried to wipe it off, but it clung on stubbornly. Scraping it didn't work, neither did the crumpled tissue that she found with it.

The sob that tore its way out of her came as a complete surprise. Fat drops of water fell from her eyes and splashed amid the rubbish. Her things tumbled from her shaking hands, even as she tried to scoop them into her bag.

'Here,' Jinx said quietly, surprisingly gentle. She looked up to see a pair of long-fingered hands cupped in front of her. Masculine hands, but elegant, like an artist's. They cradled the broken remains of her mobile phone. 'It's banjaxed.'

The apologetic tone made her look up sharply and the first things she saw were his eyes. Sharp as nails, one might say, and the same colour. Bright, shining steel piercing through the darkness. And not quite ... normal ...

His head tilted to one side, he was studying her as closely as she was studying him. She blinked and the world seemed to contract abruptly around her. The illusion shifted, like the shimmer of a heat haze in high summer and suddenly his eyes were grey instead of steel. His pale skin was framed by strands of long black hair, silken and glossy. Her fingers itched to brush against his face.

His eyes tilted slightly, cat-like, smudges of guyliner giving their grey that curious metallic illusion. No, not a liner. Shadows around his eyes, cast by thick black lashes. Tattoos covered the right side of his neck, kissed the underside of his jaw and vanished beneath the tight black t-shirt he wore. They emerged again, trailing down his arms and she wondered where else they went. The thought of what lay beneath his clothes made her blush furiously. A nose stud winked at her, a silver ring pinched around one high and elegant eyebrow and a line of earrings ran right up the side of one pointed ear.

Not human, not real, she thought once more, like one of those crazy alien things in the films Dylan watched, or something inspired by her manga collection, like a stylised sketch, and the image shifted, normalising again.

Shock was making her see things. That was all. Or that concussion she probably had.

Or maybe just the potentially fatal attack of stupid that seemed to be overwhelming her all of a sudden.

Still pierced, still tattooed, still unbearably handsome, but less … alien? She shook her head, desperate to clear it. Taking a deep breath didn't help. She closed her eyes, tried again and found her heart pounding in her chest. She breathed past it, felt it calm and looked back at him. Normal. Everything was normal. Or as normal as it got when you were kneeling in a piss-stinking alley with a tattooed stranger.

All the same she didn't take the pieces of the phone. If shock was making her see things, that was bad enough, but she was still on her knees with a guy who would give her mother apoplexy.

'Take it,' he said. His voice carried a sort of lilt she knew she should recognise. It was an old accent, one she couldn't place. Not local. And yet ... not from far away either. She *should* know it. 'Maybe you can get it fixed?'

Fixed. Yeah, right. Had he actually looked at it? She tried to shrug. 'It's just a phone. I ... I can get another.' There didn't look to be enough of it left worth fixing, to be honest. 'Banjaxed' was an understatement. Thanks to the effect she and her dad had on electronics, she'd seen enough to recognise when something was totally borked. All the same, she held out her bag and he dropped the pieces inside.

Jinx got to his feet, towering over her. Broad-shouldered, slim-hipped, perfectly proportioned.

'I'm Izzy,' she said, and immediately regretted it.

He gave her a baffled look, staring at her for a long moment as if he could see inside her. 'Jinx,' he said at last. 'Are you okay?'

That was when Izzy realised she was still crouching on the ground at his feet. Something jerked inside her and she leaped up so quickly part of her was surprised she didn't hear a string snap. Her head swam and that same peculiar glow she had felt touching the angel surged within her.

'Yes, I'm ... I'm fine ...'

The world blurred. Her skin stretched too tight over her bones and her chest caught in a vice. She felt the ground tip and then a hand caught her arm. Strong, but gentle. Careful, but reluctant.

'Steady. You got up too fast.'

Izzy could only stare at him as if she was an idiot. Any words she might want to say died in her throat. Normally she could come up with a line in a second, something easy and nonchalant, sometimes even funny. Not now though. Jinx released her, his hand still hovering there to catch her again if needs be. But he moved like he didn't want to touch her for any longer than was absolutely necessary.

Oh my God, pull yourself together, her brain tried to tell the rest of her. *You don't just stand here, some kind of moron ogling the hot guy! You do something, say something, anything!*

'Yeah, I ... thanks. I ...' *Smooth, Izzy. Really smooth.* The sense of uneasiness didn't pass though. She looked around, half expecting to see creepy old Mistle sneaking up on her again.

'Maybe you should sit down,' he said with a wariness that belied the macho image. Probably afraid she'd collapse at his feet. Or throw up on him, she thought, as her stomach gave an ominous heave.

'Not sure what the coffee's like here but the seating doesn't look the greatest.' She tried to laugh. The sound came out false and twisted. She could see the hardening in his eyes.

God, did he think she was flirting with him? A noise like real laughter floated through the back of her mind, mocking her.

Was she?

'Can I call someone for you?' Jinx asked. 'A parent or a friend?'

A parent? Oh, thank you SO much. 'No. Really. I'm meeting some friends.'

He frowned, bit back a comment and then nodded. 'I'll walk you there.'

Before she knew what was happening, he slipped his hand around her arm in a supremely old-fashioned manner and escorted her out of the alley, only releasing her to let her get by the bin.

That odd shiver in the air passed over her again and the sunlight was brighter as they passed through it. Her skin drank in the warmth with unexpected relief.

Out on the street, the crowd seemed to melt out of Jinx's way. Or perhaps everyone just avoided him. In the sunlight he didn't look half as ferocious. She'd been an idiot, panic and her imagination painting a wild image of him. Still, the long hair, piercings and tattoos didn't exactly cast him as a conformist.

She glanced at his arm while he marched her down South William Street, his feet alternating between the narrow pave-ment and the road itself, stepping on and off the kerb as needed, completely at peace with his place in the world. His tattoos weren't black, as she had thought, but a deep indigo blue. Whorls and spirals covered his skin in some sort of tribal design mixed with Celtic knots. It was intricate and beautiful, contrasting strongly with the porcelain smoothness of his skin and the taut muscles beneath it.

'Where did you get them done?' she asked.

He frowned, then followed her gaze and snorted briefly, dismissively, as if they were not something to be admired. 'Got them a long time ago. There are few left who can do those right these days.' He sounded almost relieved.

Izzy tripped over a rising cobble and he had to catch her again before she fell. His touch made her shiver all over and made the warm spark of whatever it was that had invaded her rise again. But it wasn't comfortable. It made her want to pull away, to rub at her skin where he had touched her until it was raw. Irritated with herself and with his reticent hero routine, she shook herself free.

'I'm fine, really. You don't have to come with me.'

Jinx stopped right there in the path and stared down at her. The other pedestrians flowed around the two of them, like water round a rock, their conversations muted and dim. Even the hum of traffic faded when she looked at him. All she could hear was breath, in and out, and the thundering noise of her own heart.

'Where were you going?' he asked, the edge rubbing off his patience. He lifted his hand to the nape of his neck, massaging the tight muscles there.

'Music shop on Exchequer Street. Denzion are playing at ...'

She glanced at her watch. 'Or at least they *were* playing at two.'

Jinx laughed, the same dismissive snort that set Izzy's hackles rising. '*Denzion*, right? Well, maybe you really did have a lucky escape then.'

She'd love to see Mari's face if she heard that one. Dylan's band were all she talked about these days. Not for her brother's sake, of course. She had a thing about the bass player and was determined enough to hook up with him that they all ended up dragged along to every gig and public appearance the band did. Not that Izzy minded.

'Not a fan, huh?' She felt a little guilty. But Dylan would understand, wouldn't he? Or not. Probably not. Guy-pride would see to that. But apart from him the band were pretty bloody awful. Especially the bass-dork. What was his name again? Jeez, Marianne said it often enough.

'Not as such,' Jinx said, although his voice softened, and genuine humour inflected it. 'That guitarist of theirs can play,' he offered after another moment or two. Izzy's breath evened out. Dylan, he was talking about Dylan. That assuaged her guilt a little.

'He can. The others though ...' She shrugged.

'At least you seem to have some taste to replace your lack of sense. What were you doing in the alley to begin with?'

As if she didn't feel ashamed enough of her foolishness. She should have known better, even in daylight, in the middle of a city. But with the angel there, she hadn't thought. Instead she'd had images of art projects at school, of recreating it somehow.

All she'd wanted was a photo. Source material and all that. It was such a stupid reason when she thought about it now.

'I wanted to see the angel,' she whispered, mortified.

'An angel?' His face grew serious. 'Well, angels are something else little girls should stay away from.'

'*Little* ... ?' But Jinx smiled, a broad wide smile, and she realised to her greater embarrassment and outrage that he was teasing her. 'Oh ...' She wanted to stamp her foot and storm away, but that would just confirm it to him, wouldn't it? That she was just a kid getting into trouble by herself? 'Very funny!' she snarled at him and held her ground. 'What is the angel, anyway?'

Jinx frowned at her, his glower intimidating.

Someone can only intimidate you if you let them, Isabel.

That was what Mum always said. Although the business suits, the multiple degrees and the MBA probably helped. Didn't matter. Izzy held her ground.

'Well?' she asked again, her hands jerking up to her hips so her elbows stuck out at either side. He wasn't going to answer.

'Aren't you already late?'

She could try a different tack. '*What* is Mistle?'

At the sound of the tramp's name, the corner of Jinx's upper lip drew up into a sneer. '*That* is someone you *definitely* don't want to see again. At best, he's a petty thief. Back away, Izzy. Mistle and his kind are scum.'

'And what about *your* kind?'

Jinx snorted and set off again, striding down the narrow

street. Izzy hurried after him, struggling to keep up with his long-legged stride. For a freaking Goth, he moved fast. And here she thought they were all emo vampire wannabes.

He stopped at the junction of Exchequer Street, with the black-painted façade of the music shop on the other side of the road. The city swirled around them, cars, pedestrians, bicycles, all those lives whirling by.

'Well, there you are. Enjoy.'

A slightly discordant clash of drums and guitars burst out of the doorway and Izzy winced. Jinx's chuckle made her look up at him.

'Are you an expert or something?'

To her surprise a smile flickered over his lips. 'Something,' he replied. 'You take care now. I'd best be going.'

She nodded and pursed her lips together. 'Thank you,' she whispered and his eyes widened in surprise

Jinx's face hardened again almost as quickly. 'You're welcome,' he grunted. 'Go on. They'll be worried about you.'

That would be the day.

She waited a moment longer, staring up into his sculpted face. His eyes stared deeply into hers, unwavering, and for a moment she wondered if he would lean forward and kiss her. It wasn't far. If she stood up on her toes she'd be within reach. He'd only have to bend his head, curve his long neck.

His lips parted and before she knew what she was doing, she let her eyelids flutter closed, tilting her face up towards him.

But he didn't kiss her. Instead he gave the smallest sigh. 'I've got to go.'

Shock and shame flooded through her like icy water. She turned away and crossed the street, head down as she aimed for the door and tried to staunch the sting of mortification.

Jinx's voice drifted across the sound of traffic and pedestrians. 'Goodbye, Izzy.'

She turned around as she stepped up onto the pavement and caught a final glimpse of him out of the corner of her eye. He stood there, without moving, staring at her. Only for another moment before he turned sideways. The sunlight flared behind him, blinding her, and then he was gone.

CHAPTER THREE

Old Blood

Jinx let Izzy go reluctantly. She crossed the road, a little slip of a thing with shoulder-length red hair that, illuminated by the sun, seemed too bright to be entirely natural, darting through the traffic and other people. By the time she reached the far side and glanced over her shoulder, he had already pulled the glamour around him, turning sideways to the sun so as to be invisible to human eyes. The girl paused in the doorway of the music shop, gazing back almost as if she could – well, not see him, but still sense him, perhaps? Could that be it? A touch of old blood, perhaps? It had looked like she could see through his glamour, just for a moment or two. But that wasn't possible in this day and age when fae and humans rarely mixed anymore, let alone interbred. The old blood had largely died out.

His instincts stirred, the deep-seated ancient knowledge of

33

hunter and hunted, intuitive and primal. Standing still as a statue, the late afternoon crowds flowed around him. Light broke through a far off gap in the clouds and fell on her. She glowed with it – special. He couldn't shake the sense that she was special. And that discomfited him more than he could say. Mistle had already noticed her, after all, and it took something mighty special to get him to crawl out of whatever bottle he was currently drowning himself in.

Even Jinx's glamour hadn't worked as fully on her as it should have. Mortal girls blushed and flushed, begging him for attention from the moment he touched them. A fae could always make a human's blood run hot. It was the way of things.

But she'd fought it. She'd fought so hard. For all appearances, it had barely affected her at all … well, right up until the end.

Why hadn't he taken advantage of that moment? He breathed out slowly, forcing his body to unwind. She'd looked like something else, something much greater than she was. Old blood, old soul, old and powerful. But she wasn't. She was just a girl.

Jinx waited until she sighed and turned away. She vanished inside. The sun slid behind the clouds and his world seemed a darker and colder place.

Coincidence, he told himself. Nothing more.

But that was a human excuse. The problem was that in the world of synchronisations all the fae inhabited, there was rarely any such thing.

Unsettled, he headed back home, subtly moulding a path through the crowd of pedestrians who could not see him. A small trick, easily crafted, but one that made life so much easier. Just a case of turning their attention to something – anything – else but him while at the same time making them loath to walk too close to him. Just enough to get them out of his way. From the alleyway it was a short step into the Sídhe-space comprising his home, part of the larger network of Sídhe-ways which made up Dubh Linn. The fae city existed slightly to the left of the human one, overlaid upon it, lurking in the shadows and the forgotten places, the points of intersection where the two converged and all the places stolen away by his people over the centuries. It was grubby and glorious, full of things that never were, the half-dreams of a drink-sodden night. If the gilt had rubbed off it in places, that was only to be expected. Dubh Linn was not for the unwary.

He was suddenly glad he'd shown her the way out.

The club was almost deserted. With all the lights on, it lost its mystery and took on a shabby air. A far cry from the hollows of old, the elders were fond of saying, his matriarch Holly most dismissively of all. Jinx didn't know and didn't really want to know. Life in a hole in the ground, miles from the arse end of nowhere, didn't appeal. He'd always lived in the city, as had most of the fae he knew. Times had changed, another favourite quote among his elders, but in this he was glad of it.

A sound at the open door made him turn. The Magpies stood there, side by side, blocking any chance of escape. They looked alike, dressed as always in pristine black and white, their sharp eyes focused on him and on him alone.

'Well, now, there he is,' said Mags, smoothing back his glossy black hair from his forehead.

'A hard man to track, our Jinx,' Pie agreed.

'What do you want?' he asked, shifting nervously and failing to hide it. 'Silver's not here. Club's not open until later.' And if Silver found them muscling their way into her domain without permission, she'd have their hides. She was in charge of this hollow.

Mags cocked his head to one side and smiled that heartless smile. 'Oh, we're not after a social life. Not yet, anyway. The council's meeting for a parlay in the Casino. You're wanted.'

He froze, staring at them. It couldn't be a lie. Not even the Magpies would risk that. The council operated on a level of mutual distrust and loathing – enemies under a painfully fragile truce – that somehow worked to maintain equilibrium between all the different kiths. Their word was law – or as close to an actual law any of his people would obey. So the council, gathered together, demanding his presence specifically… that couldn't be good. The Magpies served just one member of the council, the Amadán, and Jinx owed no allegiance to him, a fact for which he was eternally grateful. But a summons from the council … What they want? What did *Holly* want? As matriarch of his kith, she wasn't the patient kind. It would bend her nose right out of joint if he shamed her in front of the other members. Especially if Brí was there.

It was no secret the two of them loathed each other. And no secret that Jinx had been born in Brí's hollow and handed over to Holly after the fact. Brí had marked him as surely as Holly, giving a geis to ensnare his destiny instead of tattoos and piercings. They always left their mark, the matriarchs.

He had no choice but to attend. Shame Holly and he might as well hide for the rest of his short and miserable life.

'Well, we wouldn't want to keep them waiting, would we?' he said, as if it didn't bother him at all.

Mags laughed as Jinx pushed by him, shoulder nudging shoulder, neither of them wanting to give way.

'There's a good dog,' Pie murmured with a snide tone as they followed him out of the hollow. At the back of his neck, Jinx felt his hackles rise.

The Sídhe-ways wound between the human world and the fae one, part of neither and intrinsic to both, in and out of time and space, borrowing minutes here and paying them back whenever. It made travel faster, but it could also mess with time, making an hour seem like a day or a week appear to be no more than an hour. Travellers had to know what they were doing, and even then, Jinx thought as they stepped out of a shimmering heat haze to evening sunlight instead of afternoon, it was too easy to slip up.

Pie cursed and checked his watch, the hands of which were

whirling around to catch up with reality. 'Come on, we're late.'

Jinx didn't hurry his gait as they headed across the lawns to the small neo-classical house built in the eighteenth century and quickly assimilated by the Aes Sídhe council so that it dwelt in a neutral area of Sídhe space. Stolen, some might say, or borrowed. Snatched out of one world and into another, but not gone. Not really. It transcended here and there, balanced precariously between the two. The Aes Sídhe loved all things beautiful and deceptive, and it fitted that description. The Casino was only fifty feet square but contained sixteen rooms, and myriad tricks of the eye. Most people translated the name as 'Little House' when 'House of Pleasure' was nearer the mark. It had never been used for gambling. Well, not for money.

The three of them passed unseen by the thin trickle of unwary tourists heading down the steps to the reception – who barely noticed them, let alone anything strange about their surroundings – and climbed the steps on the northern side to the enormous weathered oak door. Set inside the panels was the actual door, of a more normal size, and it opened to them at a touch. In the main hall, they crossed the highly decorated floor and Pie opened the central of three polished mahogany doors. The air shimmered like a heat haze. Jinx followed Pie, Mags taking up the rear, and they entered through a portal built into the fabric of the house. But like this place built entirely of illusions, the door led elsewhere. The world shifted subtly, shivering like a dog with a flea on its back, and the Casino changed with it, still resplendent and ornate, but now eternally new, gold instead of gilt and dazzling in its beauty. *This* Casino, on the fae side of the worlds, glittered and the space stretched to accommodate a banqueting hall far greater than possible in the building outside Dubh Linn.

But inside, anything was possible.

Lights hovered beneath a mirrored ceiling, revolving around one another, illuminating the chamber and the table dominating the centre, its surface inlaid with rare woods in intricate, delicate patterns that defied the eye. The three figures sitting around it remained oblivious to the finery of their surroundings. Beside each of them was an empty chair, demarcating the boundaries and distances between them. The largest chair of all, right at the end of the table, was similarly unoccupied.

The Magpies fell behind Jinx as he entered the room. Silver smiled from her place by the silk-lined wall, her hair iridescent in the moving light, her pale grey eyes darting warily to Holly. Their matriarch didn't deign to notice Jinx yet. She was feeding scraps of fragrant meat to the fae sitting at her feet. She teased him, dangling the food over him before allowing him to take it with his mouth.

He was one of the Aes Sídhe too, the higher nobility of the fae, but that didn't spare him. Stripes of red scored his back from her crop and he shuddered with a mixture of humiliation and despair as she fed him. His hands remained pressed hard on the polished parquet floor. It was hard to feel any sympathy. Most of the Aes Sídhe who'd ever paid Jinx a scrap of attention in the past had mocked and ridiculed him. But that didn't make it any better to see one of them so broken now. It just reminded him of the things Holly had put him through over the years. She loved to show her power over those she ruled, especially those who crossed her. She wielded her power like a scalpel. Or a cudgel, when it suited her.

He wondered what this poor sap had done. He didn't want to know.

Jinx fought to keep the scowl off his face as he watched, waiting for her to notice him. She was his matriarch. Until she did that, he didn't exist for anyone else in the room. He used the time to study the other members of the council sitting today. Only three members had come, the three who hated each other more than the rest. Yet still they came, and met. Mainly to show they didn't fear each other. Even if they did. Jinx suspected it made no more sense to them than it did to him.

Brí's riotous red hair was a marked contrast to Holly's sleek blonde bob. She was shuffling through some papers, looking anywhere but at Jinx. Brí was as beautiful and terrible as any one of the Aes Sídhe, but normally reclusive.

For a moment she looked so very familiar that something inside him ached and he wanted nothing more than to go to her, to serve her. He'd been born to be her creature, and the blood ran true. His father had died torn between her and the family he should never have even tried to have. And even when Brí had given Jinx to Holly in payment for honour broken, she'd cursed him at the same moment, giving him a geis that made him walk on a knife's edge in everything he did, one that could see him enslaved or dead in a moment. An *obligation*. That was the polite term for it. When the Sídhe deigned to be polite.

Her dog. Always. Even when he wasn't anymore. The urge was too strong. *The blood ran true.* That was what happened to any pack animal, any hound. And though Holly owned him, though her charms and sigils bound him more firmly to his Aes Sídhe form, the dog would not be silenced completely. It wanted out. Always.

The only other person seated at the table was Amadán himself, an aged man in appearance, but nothing so vulnerable in reality. He ruled alone, without a matriarch, and his followers, like the Magpies, were to be feared.

There was no sign of Donn, naturally, but he never came anymore. Jinx couldn't remember a time when he had. They kept his place though – wouldn't dare not to. Donn was the most powerful of them, or so the lore said, the oldest and the most obscure, the dweller in the dark. Jinx had never laid eyes on him. He didn't know many who had.

Íde, the matriarch of the mountains, hadn't come in years. Not since her lover, Wild, died right there, at the table, poisoned by an unknown hand. They hadn't replaced Wild because Íde would never allow it.

And the Seanchaí, the Storyteller as she was sometimes known, was no longer part of the council. She wouldn't leave her hall, content to sit there and dwell on the future and the past, instead of the now. Her seat at the head of the table would never be used again.

So half the council made up what was left of the council. They governed all the fae in Dubh Linn, of every kind, from the highest to the lowliest, maintaining a fragile peace. Sometimes their hand weighed heavily, and at other times it could not be felt at all.

They were not friends, not even in convenience. This gathering was about the only thing keeping them from all-out war and though it had served this purpose for more years than he could tell, it still didn't make the atmosphere any more comfortable. No one held a grudge like one of the Aes Sídhe, the nobility of the fae. Hot or cold, they were still at war, and that meant subterfuge, espionage and a variety of colourful assassination attempts were all on the cards. Of course they were. Wild's death had shown that. It was the way of the Aes Sídhe, as old as time. But equally that didn't mean they couldn't meet and be coolly civil. Well, almost civil. Barbed words and one-upmanship were just more weapons in this most lethal of games.

'Well,' Holly said at last. 'It's about time you got here.'

Jinx bowed his head respectfully. 'It's wonderful to see you, grandmother.' He even sounded like he meant it.

Holly wasn't fooled though. She glowered at him. 'Probably a good idea to claim that relationship, Jinx.'

'Then again,' Brí interrupted, her clear, bright voice ringing around the room, 'maybe not. Given that he's the child of a traitorous mother.'

'The product of a traitor and an assassin,' Amadán said with a chuckle. 'Such a remarkable pedigree for a by-blow.'

Ah yes, his mother the traitor and his father the killer. It always came back to them. Jinx fought to quell the rush of anger inside him. He hadn't even known his parents, but lived every day with their legacy and the machinations of the very council he faced now.

'Just so long as he never comes calling at my door.' Brí poured herself another glass of wine. 'Blood will out. In more ways than one.'

They all knew about blood. About the spilling of it anyway.

Holly growled something like a curse and stood up, kicking her kneeling slave out of her way. He landed heavily, his face smacking noisily off the parquet floor and lay still, trying to stifle sobs.

They ignored him. It was a kindness that was somewhat unexpected. Clearly his humiliation wasn't that important to anyone there but Holly.

She stalked towards Jinx and he almost managed not to flinch as she stopped in front of him and slapped his face so hard it snapped his head to one side and left his skin stinging.

Jinx raised his head, but kept his eyes carefully averted from hers. Deferential. Servile.

'I have a job for you,' she said.

'As you command, grandmother.'

She raised her hand again, flexing he fingers as if to unsheathe claws. 'Be careful boy, or this could quickly become very tiresome. Blood kin or not, I owe you nothing. My sources tell me an angel fell today, very close to Silver's hollow. Maybe even right at the door. We want the spark left behind, Jinx. It'll empower the touchstones for a decade or more. Quick as you can now.'

A spark? Well, they'd all be hungry for that. A taste of power, a sniff of the divine ... that would make every single one of the Aes Sídhe ravenous as wolves. The power that could be drawn from one, the things that could be done, the magic it allowed the skilled and ruthless hand to wield ... But that wasn't up to him. He didn't have a touchstone or anything like that to put it into. He wouldn't know what to do with a spark in the first place.

But they did. Each hollow held a touchstone and they were central to the power of the Aes Sídhe. Even Silver had one, though it wasn't as powerful as her mother's. Holly would never allow that. They needed to be fed. That was the problem. Dreams, terror, the million emotions that could be wrung from a human were the most usual energy poured into them – but the light from an angel was the most powerful thing of all.

'No problem.' He didn't even try to keep the relief from his voice. And he'd thought she wanted something difficult. If all he had to do was pick up the sorry remains of a fallen angel and—

The girl had mentioned an angel. Jinx's breath caught like a lump in his throat. She'd glowed. That was what he'd thought as he left her. She'd *glowed* and that had snared his attention, but what if that wasn't all? He hadn't looked any closer. Had he missed a spark in her? She had seemed normal enough. Apart from that wretched glow. An angel wouldn't cause that, spark or no spark.

But she'd said it … *'I wanted to see the angel.'*

Holly's eyes darkened in suspicion. 'What is it, Jinx?'

He had to cover, and quickly. Then he had to find the girl. 'Nothing, grandmother. I'll go right away.'

'See that you do.' She leaned in close and for a moment he thought she was going to kiss his cheek. His whole body stiffened in alarm and shock, but Holly's lips barely brushed his skin. Instead, she whispered in his ear. 'And don't let that red-headed bitch or the old bastard get there first, understand? No one else, understand? Bring it to me and me alone. I'm not planning on sharing such power with them.'

Angels were her thing. He'd seen her in action once, torturing the creature, ripping its spark from it and leaving it no more than a ghostly mark on the walls of her hollow. She'd destroyed not one but hundreds.

Holly glared right into his eyes, a reminder of all the things she had visited on others in the past, things she had made him endure. The silver piercings chilled against his skin and the tattoos coiled tighter.

'As you command.'

Amadán coughed loudly, clearing his throat with a rattle of phlegm. 'Something else you should remember, boy. There's a Grigori resident in Dublin. They don't take kindly to us messing with their shit, you know what I mean?'

'He's just one man.' Holly glowered at the interruption. 'And even he can't be everywhere. We'll take what we want and he'll just send another impotent warning.'

'Not this time,' Amadán told her. 'You've been greedy of late. They notice. He'll notice. You don't want to make a Grigori angry.'

'*He's* not going to interfere,' Brí said. 'And if he does, I'll deal with him.'

The Old Man laughed. The sound made Jinx shudder as if he was suddenly unclean. 'Well, you should know. You interfered with him often enough. Or is that long over now?'

Brí knocked back the glass of wine. 'Maybe I should interfere with you, Amadán.'

'No thank you, my dear. I have standards.'

Her lemon-sucking expression tightened still further. 'All I'm saying is he has other things to concern him just now. Life can be difficult for a family man. Especially when times are hard and money is tight. As I said, if needs be, I will deal with him.'

Holly beamed her most false and barracuda-like smile. 'There we are then. All settled. Go on.'

Jinx bowed and backed away, keeping his whole demeanour studiously reverent. As he reached the door, slipping past the grinning Magpies, he allowed himself to breathe again and turned to escape.

Footsteps rapped on the shining parquet flooring, something that would never be allowed in the human building, where it was covered to prevent damage. But this was not that world and no one was going to say a word to deny anyone in that room. Not if they wanted to live.

'Jinx?'

Silver caught up with him, slipped her arm through his and smiled, leaning against him. Her scent, elderflower and hawthorn, drifted around him. To a human, it would be intoxicating and even Jinx, young by Sídhe standards, had trouble shaking it off. Silver was so much older than him, despite her appearance, and so much more powerful, the prime example of everything an Aes Sídhe should be, a princess among them. One of the most powerful of all the Sídhe except the matriarchs and the council. Why she put up with their petty rulings and restrictions and subjugated herself to them, he didn't know. Loyalty wasn't a natural fae trait. But she was also one of the few who had ever been kind to him, the only one who took him into her hollow and made him part of her life; she indulged him, kept him safe, misfit that he was in his own world. She was everything he wasn't. He owed her more than he could ever repay.

'Are you okay?'

'Yes. I – I should be going.'

'Run along then,' she teased, but when he didn't laugh, she

paused, examining his face closely. 'Whatever did she say to upset you so?'

'It's Holly.' That ought to have been explanation enough for her, but Silver kept staring at him, waiting. 'It doesn't matter.'

'Well, don't be late tonight. Big crowd coming in from Cork. Tour group or something. Should be fun.'

Jinx winced. Out of town fae on the razz were notoriously out of control and Silver's definition of fun usually included a few broken limbs among the bystanders. The club had a way of cleaning up after itself and fae of all kinds could take a lot more punishment than any mortals. Still, it could get ... violent. And messy.

'Whatever. I'll be there. A gig's a gig.'

He started for the door again, but Silver's voice called him, not so brash now, not teasing any more. She almost sounded concerned.

'Jinx?'

He glanced over his shoulder. 'Yeah?'

'Be careful.'

It didn't take long to get back to the alley where he'd met Izzy. Where he'd stopped her from getting any more lost in Dubh Linn. Rescued her, even if she didn't know it at the time.

Rescued her. That was a joke. What sort of knight in shining armour would he make? Particularly as the armour would most likely kill him. Man-made metals burned. There was no other word for it. Not like flames. Like acid. Even those he wore every day. He had never got used to their touch, but they kept him in the desired form and his mind focused on his duty and obligations. They served their purpose. Much as he did.

The first thing to strike him was how quiet it was. Like a tunnel, one of the very old parts of the old city that wound its way in and out of worlds, real and unreal. Cobbles, and high curbs, each stone carefully shaped and worn with age, a certain elegance that was lost to the modern human world, and rapidly deteriorating even in Dubh Linn. His world. One of secrets and shadows, of mysteries that no one could fathom, and really wouldn't care to know if they could. For just a moment she had crossed a threshold best left alone and he'd done her a kindness in seeing her out of it again. And all for a phone. Mistle's desire for it was understandable enough to Jinx. Anything shiny and bright, anything clever and cunning, always attracted their kind. But why would Izzy come after it when she could just walk into another shop and get a brand new one, even shinier? Humans were strange creatures, and Izzy was stranger still. But his life would now be a sight easier if he hadn't seen her out, if he'd kept her close. She'd mentioned an angel and he'd paid her no heed at the time. But even if she hadn't seen it fall, she must have been here almost immediately afterwards. While the image still glowed between worlds.

There was no sign of anything untoward now. Dirt and ashes, stinking rubbish, smears of something akin to old paint on the wall.

The ghost of Izzy's presence lingered on. He toyed with it, letting it run through him, examining it. Not a scent, not really. Rather a *sense*, a ripple in reality caused by her passing through it. But if he closed his eyes and tried, he could have followed her like a bloodhound.

And something else. A crackle of lightning, ozone fizzing on the air, mounting expectation making the hairs on his arms stand to attention.

Damnation, he knew that feeling, dreaded it. All the fae did. He'd never get away in time and glamour wouldn't work. Besides, if he ran—

Never run, he'd been taught from childhood. *If you run, they can't help but chase you.*

No one wanted to be that fox.

Jinx backed away, seeking the darkest corner to pull the shadows around him, a place to hide from the oncoming storm.

Wind burst through the alley, not from either end, but from its centre. Scraps of newspaper and crisp packets took wing, swirling around like demented butterflies.

Two men stood in the eye of this localised hurricane.

No, not men. Only on a first glance would anyone mistake them for men.

The nearer stepped closer to the wall, pressed a pale and slender hand to the stones and closed his eyes. For a moment all was still. Then he shook his head. His hair glistened like gold.

The second, a near mirror image of his brother but for his darker colouring, glanced at Jinx with pale, opal eyes. They'd seen him. Of course they'd seen him.

'Where is the spark?' His voice rumbled through the air and the earth, shaking everything in between.

'It's gone.' Jinx wasn't sure where he found his own voice. It sounded pitiful after the other, and that galled him. He clenched his fists at his side until his fingernails bit into his palms. He had nothing to fear here. He had done nothing wrong. Other than be what he was. And be here when they arrived. 'It was gone when I got here.' He said the words with more force than he meant to.

The first figure hadn't said a word or opened his mouth and for that Jinx was grateful. It did no good to hear some voices. But the second stood very still as if listening to him. Then he spoke again, his voice winding its way around Jinx, tightening like a python's coils.

'If you know where it is, you must tell us, faeling. Time is short.'

Jinx scowled at them. *Must.* It was always *must* with the likes of them. He kicked a can aside and the first one flicked his eyes after it like a cat following a fly.

'Right now?' He forced his face into a smile that never

went beyond his upper lip. 'Right now, I have no idea where it is. Am I free to go?'

The second one spat out a curse in a language Jinx couldn't hope to comprehend. It sounded like music defiled by anger. He knew its name though. Once, the elders taught, his people had spoken it as well.

'We're finished here. But I warn you, we shall be tracking the spark. We will bring it home. It came with one of our brethren and it belongs to the Holy Court. The Word has spoken it. If we see you again, faeling, it will go worse for you. Far worse.'

In another whirl of wind and debris, they were gone and Jinx stood alone in the alley. He gritted his teeth and allowed himself to relax. Only slowly though. He was too wound up.

Izzy had the spark, the divine spark that could be left behind in the after-image when one of these sanctimonious cretins fell from grace. And they'd been sent to get it. Nothing would stop them, and nothing would stand before them. They were always right. That was the problem. Even if they weren't.

They'd kill her. They'd do worse than kill her, they'd damn her as well. And for them, that really meant something.

Angels were all the same.

CHAPTER FOUR

Small Lies

I t was after seven when Izzy got home. Apart from the beeps of the alarm looking for its deactivation code, the house was still and silent. She kicked off her shoes in the hall, dropped her bag and coat under the stairs and padded down to the kitchen. No sign of anyone.

Not unusual, of course, not these days. Since the bankers had shot the Celtic Tiger, her parents spent every hour God sent at work, struggling to keep their architecture business afloat.

At least the house was safe, because it was Gran's and even her folks hadn't been mental enough to drag Gran into their finances. Izzy's grandmother didn't like the city, she said, and preferred to live in the mountains near Glendalough, the middle of absolutely nowhere as far as Izzy was concerned. But that didn't mean Gran couldn't own any number of properties – the ultimate absentee landlord, especially as she was currently on one of her many world cruises.

Izzy opened the fridge and blinked in the garishly bright light. She grabbed the milk and a packet of ham slices before kicking the door closed behind her.

Nothing beats ham sandwiches and a glass of ice cold milk for dinner, she told herself. The false bravado didn't convince her stomach.

She flicked on the TV in the lounge, found a rom-com and curled up on the sofa. The knot that had twisted itself tight inside her slowly began to unwind. Her arm burned, and the back of her neck. Crap, maybe she had caught something off the weirdo in the alley. Or maybe – more likely, her rational mind assured her – she was going into shock. The TV picture blurred, images melting and reforming until the twist in her gut returned with a vengeance.

Izzy shook her head, tried to get up, but her legs had turned to jelly.

'Damn,' she told herself. 'Bedtime.' How to get there was going to be another matter.

Except it wasn't that late. It wasn't even dark outside. Not really. The shadows in the garden stretched out towards the French windows like fingers. Izzy heaved herself onto her feet and wobbled a little. She leaned on the arm of the sofa, staring outside.

The shadows darkened, like someone messing with the contrast control. Even as she watched, they crept onwards, brushing the glass. But they didn't come through. They crossed the pool of light that fell onto the patio, but they didn't venture inside the house. They stopped, impossibly, and crawled up the glass.

A hard, heavy rhythm filled her ears, surging like waves on shingle. Izzy watched the shadows twist and turn, looking for a gap, a chink, some sort of way inside. Tendrils of darkness probed at the gap between the doors, tapped on the window-panes.

The handle rattled, shaken by unseen hands.

'Ward yourself,' said a whisper in the back of her mind. *'You must ward yourself.'*

Izzy slid head on into full-blown panic.

'Stop it!' she shouted, and her voice surged from her, louder than it should have been, shaking the air itself. 'Stop it right now!'

In a moment the garden fell still, and everything snapped back to normal. A summer's evening. Too still. Too quiet.

Izzy fled, tearing from the room and up the stairs. She slammed her bedroom door and wedged the chair in front of it. Her chest heaved, and she stood there with balled fists at her side, waiting, listening.

Nothing moved inside the house. No glass broke, nothing crashed over, nothing. She hadn't reset the alarm though. If anything had followed her inside, she'd never hear it.

A wave of nausea hit her and she lurched towards the en-suite as her stomach brought up everything in it. Shivering with sweat, her throat burning, she sat on the icy cold tiles next to the basket of spare toilet rolls.

Tears poured down Izzy's cheeks, salty on her lips. She was too hot, far too bloody hot. And probably in shock.

Jesus, *shock*! Was that her answer for everything? But she'd heard it could do this, set in much later, make you throw up and shake. And see things.

She should have reported the attack, but maybe it was just as well she hadn't now that she was hallucinating.

Because that was what it had to be. Right? Shadows didn't move that way. They certainly didn't make attempts at breaking and entering.

The shivers passed, leaving only a burning sensation akin to itching below the back of her neck, right at the top of her spine. She tried to rub it with a weak hand, but that just aggravated the sensation.

Using her legs as leverage, Izzy slid her body up the wall. The marble tiles felt gloriously cool on her burning neck. She bunched up her hair and tried to check out the most painful point in the mirror. When she couldn't do that, she remembered the small dressing table mirror Gran had given her.

Heavy silver, a relic from another age, she hardly ever touched it. She had to rummage through the jumble of ephemera on her dressing table even to find it, under some scarves and a couple of perfume boxes she hadn't moved since she got them at Christmas.

She twisted the mirror this way and that as she stood with

her back to the dressing table mirror, until she could see the top of her collar in it.

And the dark blue marks that peeked out above it, etched into her skin.

Izzy almost dropped the mirror in shock. She pulled off her shirt, knotted her hair up with a clip and looked again.

Like filigree, like Celtic knotwork, like an intricate design from untold ages ago, the lines twisted in on themselves. She couldn't tell if they were many, or just one, eternally wrapped around itself. Overall it formed a circle with a cross running through it, the top of a Celtic cross, but with every glance the patterns inside it changed, twisting and turning, becoming ever more intricate. The chain of her silver necklace stood out like a line of moonlight against the indigo of the new tattoo.

On her skin. *In* her skin.

Marking her.

Oh God, Mum was going to freak. Never mind that Izzy didn't know where it had come from, how she had got it or when. That just made everything worse.

The mirror slipped from her numb fingers and thudded onto the carpet.

Jinx. He'd know. The marks covering his skin had been the same colour, the same sort of details. He had to know.

Izzy had already pulled on a black polo neck and was half-way down the stairs when she remembered the shadows in the garden. What if they were in the front garden as well, waiting for her? What if—

The front door opened with a clatter and Izzy choked on a scream.

Mum stepped inside. Just her mum.

On a glance she was sleek and elegant as ever, perfectly groomed, her golden hair swept up in a chignon, the consummate professional. You had to look closely to see the shadows under her eyes, or the slump in her shoulders.

'Sweetheart?' Mum gasped. 'You look like you've seen a ghost.'

The urge to tell her what she had seen gripped Izzy in its jaws. But she couldn't. Tell her one thing and she'd have to tell her everything. And she looked so tired.

Izzy forced a smile. 'You startled me. That's all. Are you okay?'

'I tried to ring you, to let you know I'd be late, but it went to voicemail.'

Shit, the phone. 'I— I'm sorry Mum. I dropped the mobile and it broke.'

A flicker of something more than disappointment crossed her mother's face. Izzy knew the look, was becoming all too familiar with it – another stress, another expense, another worry none of them needed.

But Mum swallowed it down, hid it under a veneer of coping. It made Izzy's guilt burn all the hotter.

'I'll let you have some cash to get a new one tomorrow, okay?' Mum kicked off her shoes and nudged them under the stairs next to Izzy's. She dropped her bag beside them.

'Where's Dad?'

'He stayed on, going over the contract with the lawyer. Did you eat?' Izzy nodded and then her mum took in the jacket and the bag Izzy carried. 'Were you going out? At this hour?'

'I was just … just going over to Clodagh's.'

It was a small lie and those were okay, weren't they? Her parents both told enough of them.

'Not tonight, Isabel, and certainly not so late.'

'But it's only—' She checked the hall clock. Only just after nine. But the tone of Mum's voice said it all. No arguments. Arguments would lead to questions and Izzy wasn't sure she could handle many of those. She had to make sure Mum didn't find out about the tattoo, or whatever the hell it was. That would be a miserable conversation.

'Okay. I'll turn in then.'

Mum just stared at her. 'Did you do something with your hair?'

She couldn't know. She couldn't possibly know. Izzy moved her hand self-consciously to her head, where the claw clip still held her hair up in an unruly knot. The back of her neck tingled.

'No.'

Mum made a bemused sound, not quite belief, not quite disbelief. As if she sensed a change. Izzy didn't like it. Not at all.

'Maybe it's the top. Really brings out your colouring. You look different. *Good* different.' Mum smiled and held out her arms. Izzy descended the last few steps into a warm embrace. 'Sleep tight, mouse. It won't be like this forever. Promise.'

'I know.' Small lies? Maybe. Izzy closed her eyes and tried to pretend she hadn't thought that. 'Are you going to get some dinner?'

'I'll have something while I wait for your dad. Night night.'

Izzy climbed the stairs and waited, checking the shadows through the chink in the curtain. Nothing moved. Nothing at all. Not until a car turned at the top of the road, its headlights sweeping across the street. It picked out a figure on the other side. He wore a long black coat and Izzy couldn't make out much more than that before he vanished into the darkness.

She blinked. Nothing there. Had she imagined it?

A chill ran through her, like ants under her skin. Not fear. Not this time. It was more like a warning. A premonition. Like the voice that had whispered to her. But of what, she didn't know. She crept out onto the landing again, down the stairs, carefully avoiding the squeaky floorboard. She heard the chink of a bottle on the rim of a glass, and the glugging sound of a drink being poured out like a heavy dose of medicine.

Izzy slipped on her shoes. Her breath hitched in her throat as she drew back the latch and pulled the door open. She'd never done anything like this. God, there had never been a need. Nothing had ever felt as urgent. But she needed to see Jinx. She needed to find out what was going on.

CHAPTER FIVE

Along the Sidhe-ways

Jinx checked the amp again and played a couple of chords, listening intently to the layers of sound that only one of the fae – or perhaps a mortal who carried a drop of fae blood somewhere deep inside them, or whose musical ability transcended the mundane – could hear.

The tone was everything. It set the whole energy of the night. Silver had taught him that and she'd learned it from the Dagda himself. And no one played like the Dagda. It didn't matter that Jinx didn't play the harp. The guitar was a modern equivalent, and in his hands it sang with magic almost as potent as Dagda's golden harp, *Daurdabla*.

Tonight, the tone was tight and sharp – tense, irritating. He clenched his jaw and made the necessary adjustments. He knew where the undercurrent of annoyance came from. He'd managed to follow the girl's trail as far as the train station on

Westland Row but then he lost her. No way to tell which direction she'd gone or where she had got off. She might as well have vanished on a breeze. Ironic really. His people were meant to do that, not humans. Even immortals – the angels and demons above and below – left some sort of trace. Izzy had left nothing.

And yet, somehow, he knew she was out there. Knew it deep inside himself, where nothing usually touched him, and he wished with all his heart that he didn't. He had a job to do and he would find her. He didn't like it, but he had no choice but to do it. Find her. Bring her to Holly. And to whatever fate befell her there. The Market wasn't a place for humankind to wander. It wasn't a place for anyone with half a brain. Only Brí's domain was more dangerous. As someone who'd had reason to endure both, Jinx wanted to stay clear of them from now on. And that made him angry.

Aggression had no part in his music. The results, if transmitted to an audience, could wreck the place. But longing could be just as dangerous. The fae, especially those of the Sídhe tribes who remembered the War, knew all about longing. Even those, like him, who had only heard the stories of the fall could feel the ghost of the bliss before, could see it lingering in their elders' eyes, sapping away their joy. Longing reminded them what they had lost, and that was dangerous indeed.

Perhaps that was why the fae, all the fae, celebrated their joys so very hard. Only that could drive the memories away

– drink, drugs, sex, partying hard as could be – if only for a little while.

'Get this into you,' said Sage. The drummer handed him a beer. Ice cold, dripping with moisture. Better than any fairy brew. Jinx knocked it back. Too late, he saw Silver's warning glare. She didn't like them to drink before a show. Pity about that. He drained the bottle with a satisfied growl.

'It's showtime.' She reached out her hands to take his right and Sage's left, and the others followed suit until they stood in a ring. Jinx hated this part, but there was no telling her. Silver was about as old-fashioned as they came. 'Dagda guide our music.' Her voice was a murmur, a rising cadence that shivered through his body, stimulating every nerve. He'd seen warriors weep at her laments, seen their passions rise with her love songs. No one made music like Silver. Her voice was a weapon, even when all she did was speak. 'Ancestors guide our muse. Bring the fire of truth to our songs.'

Her prayer done, Silver relaxed again and light flooded through her. It filled them all. Without her prayer, Jinx didn't even know if they could play, not in the way they would play now anyway. Expertise and practice would let them make music, but it wouldn't be what it could be. What it would be now. It didn't matter though. While she couldn't say 'thank you', her geis demanded that thanks be given, and that was her way. No different from human superstitions, he supposed. The old gods had left them, the Creator was far away. And geis bound all of the Sídhe, himself included, though his had yet to manifest — *No hand but your own can save you, or it will hold you fast.*

When Brí handed down a geis, no one got a chance to ask what the hell it meant. She delighted in making them as obtuse as possible. You figured them out at your peril. And you ignored them to your doom.

Silver gave a shimmy, the thin gauze of her dress hiding only the bare essentials, and the stage lights came on in the same instant.

Jinx pulled out the pick from its home amid the strings on the neck of the guitar and began to play, pouring himself into his music, where he could finally forget what he was.

The city centre heaved with its usual Saturday night hordes of revellers, from the fine diners to the stag and hen nights. Recession nothing, Izzy thought bitterly. Her parents seemed to be the only ones affected tonight. Or perhaps partying hard was a way to avoid what everyone knew, to hide from the inevitable.

Off the main thoroughfares, South William Street took on a seedier aspect by night. The arse-end of restaurants and basement sex shops dominated once the other places had shut.

The alley was empty. It smelled not of piss now, but something like battery acid. Izzy stood there, the entrance like a mouth around her, staring at the place where the angel should have been. All that remained of the stunning image was a smear of paint amid the shadows clinging to the fringes of the night.

It was gone.

Disappointment twisted her stomach. How could it be gone already? And without her phone she couldn't even check for the picture.

'Izzy? Is that you?'

Izzy turned around sharply, only to see Dylan. He was standing at the entrance to the alley, with Marianne and Clodagh trailing along behind him, bemused by the sight of Izzy standing in a filthy alley.

'What on earth are you doing here?' Dylan asked, starting forward, reaching out to her. 'We thought you had to go home earlier.'

'I was just ... just ...' She sighed. What was the point? If she told them they'd never believe her, not the angel, nor the shadows. They probably wouldn't even think it possible she'd sneak out of home like she just had. She wouldn't have believed it of herself. They stopped awkwardly, and Dylan let his hands fall to his side. She smiled at him as if she hadn't a care in the world. 'What are you guys up to?'

Marianne frowned, suspicion making her perfectly-made-up eyes just a little too beady, but she didn't ask another question. 'Clubbing. We're meeting the band and Dylan'll get us in. You coming?'

Dylan rolled his eyes and offered her an apologetic grin. Yeah, Izzy could tell how much he was looking forward to the evening with his sister and her friend. 'Come on, Izzy, you can keep me sane.'

Last thing Izzy wanted was to head off to some nightclub and pretend to be someone she wasn't for the night, but she rolled her shoulders nonchalantly. She wasn't dressed for it. Not like Mari and Clo, in their sparkling high heels and skirts that were completely hidden by their short jackets.

She didn't glitter. Never had. Never wanted to. Even as a kid, pink and sparkles had looked blatantly ridiculous on her. But the clothes she wore now felt like rags. Even Dylan in his black t-shirt, jacket and jeans looked like he was dressed to the nines while she felt like a bag lady.

'Whatever,' Mari drawled, her thin patience tearing. 'We aren't going to get in if we leave it much later. Come on.'

'Quit being a bitch, Mari,' said Dylan in that warning tone he always used with her when she got like this. 'No one's impressed.' Marianne stuck her tongue out at him. 'Do you want to come with me or not? I can just as easily stick you in a taxi and let you explain to Mum why, as you persuade her to pay the fare.'

Marianne raised her hands in mock defeat. 'All right, all right, I'll be the picture of charm.'

Dylan looked far from convinced, but gave her his easy grin. 'Coming, Izzy? Since you're here.' Izzy closed her eyes and reached out to touch the wall. It felt cold and sticky. The mark on her neck tingled and squirmed beneath her skin as if it recognised where it had come from.

And then she heard it. Music. The most amazing music.

Her eyes snapped open and she could still hear it. It echoed down the alley, from the maze of narrow streets and narrower lanes beyond it.

'Can you hear that?' Izzy whispered. If it wasn't real, if she was hearing things or imagining it, she wanted to know right away.

Dylan stepped up beside her, ignoring Marianne's renewed complaints. His eyes darkened with desire, the pupils dilating, and his face filled with such longing. The music just brushed against Izzy's senses, but as she looked at Dylan, she saw it consume him.

'What is it?' His voice sounded different, strained but at the same time deeper, darker. His whole body tensed with expectation and Izzy felt the urge to touch him, an unexpected, forbidden need. To kiss him.

Cold disgust knotted in her stomach. Dylan? God, he was like a brother. She'd known him all her life.

Clodagh cleared her throat like she had something sharp lodged there.

Izzy glanced over her shoulder and met with Clodagh's most adversarial glare. She knew that look, saw it whenever Dylan wanted to talk books or music and Clo didn't have a clue what he was on about.

'Can't you hear it?' she asked.

'Hear what?' Marianne said in stubborn tones. But her eyes flickered with the same light as Dylan's. Izzy frowned. She had to be able to hear it. Why pretend she couldn't?

She remembered the look on Dylan's face when she'd told him about the alley, Mistle, Jinx and her phone earlier. He'd urged her to call the cops, but what could she tell them that wouldn't sound insane? And that was before all the real craziness had kicked off at home. She couldn't tell them about that now.

'The music.' Like a man under a spell, Dylan started forwards into the alley. 'I can hear music, can't you? Come on. It's amazing. We have to find it.'

Izzy's feet could barely keep up with her headlong rush down the alley. All fear fell away as she and Dylan pursued the music echoing off the stone walls. Mari and Clodagh followed behind, but Izzy barely heard their complaints. Relief surged through her, wild and desperate relief. Dylan could hear it too. She wasn't going mad.

And at the same time, it felt like they both were.

The music. That was all that mattered. It called her. More, it commanded her to follow it.

Lost in a maze of narrow lanes, she turned this way and that, heedless of direction. Lanes widened to streets, to squares and open spaces. The rational part of her mind veered close to panic. There was no area like this in any part of the city. It looked more like a fever dream of Dickensian London than modern-day Dublin. There was no litter, no chip wrappers, no cans or ripped flyers, but everything felt tattered, dusty, as if it was mostly unused. There were cobbles underfoot, everywhere, and high curbstones lined the edges. The deep gutters glistened with some kind of pungent oily sludge she didn't want to investigate too closely. The doors they passed were closed, faceless things that gave away nothing. Elaborate fanlights with coloured glass stood over them, unfurled like a peacock's tail. There were no shops, no neon or chrome, and no sign of anything twenty-first century. It was like stepping back in time. What light there was flickered, orange and uncertain.

And yet it was also like the Dublin she knew, the narrow, forgotten bits of Dublin, the ratty and forgotten corners that wound in and out of the modern city. It was like the type of places Dad showed her, hidden beneath the new world, an older one of magic and wonder, where you could find sculpture, gardens, or murals, or crenellated rooftops, gothic spires and bronze domes. Where stone mice ran around the base of a pillar and stone monkeys played the clarinet. Hidden places. Right in the middle of places she thought she knew.

Admittedly Dad never brought her down alleys that were quite so grim and miserable as this. He would never drag her down here. She ran past buildings which carried echoes of the elaborate red façade of George's Street , or the grey front of St Ann's, hints of the hodge-podge of building squashed into the grounds of the Castle painted with the wrong colours, glimpses of jewel-bright stained glass that would have made Harry Clarke's students weep.

It was beautiful, and terrible, because in that beauty was

the constant reminder that none of this should be here. And neither should she.

And then there was a light.

Izzy came to a halt as if she had slammed into a wall made of glass. Dylan swore, his arm lashing out in front of her to stop her if she continued. Mari and Clodagh crashed into them from behind.

'Where the hell are we?' Marianne peered past them. 'It's weird here.' She lifted her shoe, examined the sole. 'Ugh, God.'

A wrought iron Victorian gas-lamp hung over an open doorway, only it had been wired for electricity at some point. Wired poorly. The blub flickered and faded to brown, offering a stuttering illumination. The door beneath it was like a hole into darkness, the top curved in the same manner as the arched sign overhead. Rainbows had long ago been painted along the edges but the paint had faded and flaked away like old dry skin. She could still see the remains of the pattern though, like an after-image on the inside of closed eyelids.

The words had faded too, but once, judging by their edges and the flaked residue around them, they'd been made of gold – 'The Hollow'.

An inner door opened and the music spilled out louder into the night, its rhythm harder now, more insistent, but less compelling. As if it knew they were there now, as if it didn't have to call any more. It was more of an enticement, perhaps a flirtation.

Izzy swallowed hard. They would follow the music. That

was inevitable. The music called. Dylan felt it too. She knew it. He stood beside her, her best friend, and she reached out her hand, fumbling as her fingers closed on his sleeve.

A tall figure emerged from the darkness inside, lean and hard, piercings studding his face and ears catching the light. Izzy's mouth dropped open. For a split second until she blinked he didn't look ... human. Just as Jinx hadn't.

But she'd imagined that, hadn't she?

'Oh, for the love of God.' Marianne pushed by Izzy and Dylan. 'You've got us here now.' She made directly for the door, her most confident air radiating from her. And no one could look like she belonged anywhere so well as Marianne. 'Hi!'

The doorman studied her approach with eyes just a touch too dark for anyone Izzy had ever seen.

'Mari—' Instinct thrummed at the base of Izzy's brain. Something dangerous, something other. The back of her neck had gone icy cold. She just wanted to run. 'Mari, maybe we should just go and—'

Not to be outdone – especially not in front of Dylan – Clodagh tottered across to join Mari at the door, smiling her brightest, most vacant smile. Izzy glanced at Dylan. His eyes were closed as he listened to the music, transfixed, like a prince in a fairytale ensnared by a spell. Maybe she was the only one who didn't feel called anymore. She felt warned. The same warning she'd felt back in the house. This was a bad idea. A really bad idea.

'Who's playing?' Dylan asked. Though his voice was soft, it carried in the night air. He sounded like he was high as a kite, which was impossible. Dylan didn't mess around with any of that. But he sounded it.

The doorman gave a brief laugh. 'Silver and her band. Same as ever.' He nodded at the door. 'Go on in then, if that's why you're here. Anything like a weapon on you?'

'Only my looks.' Mari's laugh was bright as a bell, but the doorman didn't return it. Izzy couldn't shake the feeling that he was about to offer them something so they didn't go in there unarmed.

'Walk away. This place is dangerous.' The shock of the sudden whisper from nowhere sent her stumbling forwards, against her will, through the doorway, the music twisting around her again.

But Dylan had already gone inside. Dylan, Mari and Clodagh.

She could hardly let them go in without her, not when everything in her was certain that this way led to answers. Pushing aside a heavy velvet curtain, she stepped into the heaving noise of the nightclub.

CHAPTER SIX

In Silver's Hollow

The decor ran from baroque to Goth, and the music filled the air, driving, thrilling, working its way inside Izzy's body until it married with her heart. She passed by a couple of riotous groups who looked like nothing she'd ever seen. Metal, leather, velvet, brocade – from the sumptuous to the barbaric seethed around her, coupled with laughter and the excited chatter of people celebrating. She couldn't see the band, though the music was all-encompassing. The rhythm pounded through her, through everyone. It drowned out voices, real and imaginary, which right now was a blessed relief. Chambers spread out like another maze, intimate spaces and huge rooms. She followed Mari's confident march through the strange club, wondering what sort of fetishist group they'd just stumbled upon. The mark at the back of her neck was tingling again. Not uncomfortable. Just *there*. Almost as if it too was worried, or at least aware.

'Bar!' Mari pointed wildly to the left and mimed knocking back a drink. Izzy just nodded and looked around for Dylan. She caught sight of him on the far side of a knot of women who could have wandered straight out of a music video, heading for the next room. She pointed towards him, looking for Clodagh and Mari, but they'd already gone.

And like that they had separated.

Genius, she told herself. *Not only are you here on your own, now they are too.* Cursing under her breath, she headed after Dylan, hoping that the girls would find them.

Worst mistake ever. She had to force herself through a heaving crowd on the other side of the inner doorway. Dancing, allegedly, but it was closer to some kind of orgy. All she could see were bodies, writhing, grinding against each other. The music swept over them and they moved with it – eyes closed, faces lifted as if in worship, mesmerised.

It was all screaming guitars and penetrating drums – the type of music that reached inside your cold, still heart, administered electro-shock and dragged you onto the dance floor to writhe and gyrate like a pagan. It was the type of music people got lost in and Dylan was no different. He stood amid the dancers, untouched and untouchable, watching the stage where a woman with impossibly long white-blonde hair dominated the performance. Her voice rose over the music, high and glorious, the sound like magic itself.

The singer reached the end of the verse and a guitar solo

kicked in, notes wrung out of the instrument like nothing she had ever heard before. Izzy knew her music, the commercial bands at least and a good amount of alternative stuff too. Up-and-coming, underground, garage, whatever. Nothing compared. Even the classic rock stuff her dad obsessed on about – Clapton, Gallagher, Hendrix ... Jesus, only a few of them. The guitar sang as beautifully as the woman. It reached into her heart and made it pulse with a new rhythm.

And then she saw him, Jinx. The guitar resonated for him, his long and elegant hands coaxing out those lush notes. No wonder talk of bands like Denzion had not impressed him. He left them in the dust.

Izzy pushed her way towards the stage, drawn by the music, lured there by the musician creating it. She'd never imagined Jinx could make music like that.

A hand on her shoulder stopped her and the mark on her neck flared so sharply she gave a yelp of pain.

Two figures loomed over her, almost identical mirror images, patched with black and white. Their beady eyes fixed on her and something malicious seeped into their smiles. They wore black leather coats over snow-white shirts and their hair was just as slick and dark. The effect was seamless.

'*Magpies,*' her mind filled in for her, and she couldn't shake the irrational thought. Or the fear it engendered. Fear of them eclipsed the fear of the voice in her mind. She couldn't focus on that. Hearing voices was a really bad sign. Listening to them was even worse! She knew magpies, knew their vicious ways and petty cruelty. They haunted the estate where she lived, terrorising cats and dogs, a plague to smaller birds.

'We're going to take a little break,' the singer's compelling voice flowed around the room, 'but we'll be with you again shortly. Don't go anywhere.' She sounded either amused or bored, or maybe an equal part of both.

Music kicked in on the soundsystem, a pale imitation of music in comparison to what had filled the club before.

The thoughts dawdled through the inner labyrinth of her mind, there, but hardly important, not when facing these two.

'Maybe we should take a break ourselves, love.' The right-hand one leaned towards her and Izzy shied away from him.

The left one's smile thinned out, but didn't fade for a moment. 'I don't think she likes you, brother. I think maybe she's more my type.'

She tried to take a step backwards and collided with something like a brick wall. Only it was warm. It was a body.

'I think she has more taste than to choose either of you.' Jinx's voice rippled through her and around her. In a moment she felt safe again. Impossibly, perfectly safe. Even though all reason told her she shouldn't.

The mark on her neck throbbed. Not with pain this time, nor with the cold. Warm and wicked, like a surge of joy repeating and repeating, a lick of flame deep in her abdomen.

The twins' smiles evaporated.

'Ah, come on, Jinx boy. That's no way to play.'

'Silver's rules.' He didn't touch her, but she could feel him right behind her, as clearly as if his body was pressed against hers. His body heat seemed to reach out and caress her. 'No one messes with anyone unwilling on the premises. You know the score. Break them and you're never coming in here again. That is, if you manage to get out.'

The left one shrugged and then nodded to the bar. The right one gave one final leer at Izzy and then they both strode away through the crowd. It seemed to part for them, as if no one wanted to get in their way. Hell, no one wanted to get close enough to get in their way.

'Magpies,' Jinx muttered in the same tone as he might use to describe shit. Izzy turned, a smile spreading over her mouth. A smile that froze when she caught sight of the ferocity of his glare. 'How did you get in here?'

'I just ... I heard the music.'

His eyes narrowed to silver slits and before she knew what was happening he'd caught her arm in a vice-like grip and pulled her over to the side of the dance floor. The alcove was dark and secluded. She suddenly felt very exposed.

'*Heard* the music? From where?'

She shook herself free of him. 'Outside on the street, where the angel was. I wasn't the only one. Dylan heard it too. Mari and Clo followed us and they got us in past the bouncer, but ...'

His handsome face twisted with confusion as the words tumbled out of her mouth. 'You couldn't have heard the music, not from out there. Neither could— Where are your friends anyway?'

Good question. Dylan had been right in front of the stage. The girls hadn't returned from the bar yet. A sudden cold block of fear formed in her stomach and Izzy strained around, trying to catch a glimpse of them through the heaving mass of people. Hadn't this club ever heard of fire safety regs? Hadn't they—

'Hey!' Jinx snapped his fingers in front of her face and she flinched so hard her head glanced off the wall. 'What age are you?'

'I need to go.' Her voice came out in a breathy rush. 'I need to find them.'

'Get away from him,' the voice whispered. She closed her eyes, trying to push the errant thought away. *'He's dangerous.'*

'You aren't going anywhere.'

Izzy ducked under his arm and sped across the room, sliding between bodies and twisting out of the way as others bore down on her. She wasn't even aware how she was doing it, but she moved with the innate ability of a small person in a big crowd to keep the hell out of the way.

And then she saw Dylan. He leaned nonchalantly against a wall, talking to the blonde singer from the band. The pose screamed 'nothing's happening here', but his eyes were locked onto her face and his attention never wavered for a moment.

Izzy skidded to a halt and stared. The mark on her neck was icy cold now, the sensation she was starting to recognise as a warning.

'Yeah,' said Clodagh, her voice impassive with suppressed

anger. 'He's been doing that for ten minutes.' She handed Izzy a bottle of brightly coloured liquid. Izzy took a mouthful and almost spat it out. It was syrupy like boiled sweets and laced with vodka. She coughed violently and almost dropped it.

'Jeez, way to do stylish, Izzy.' Marianne grinned at her, and Izzy felt her face heat. 'Are you okay?'

'We ought to go,' she wheezed out when she could speak again.

Marianne laughed. 'Go? They didn't check ID, the drink is cheap and hey ... hot guy checking you out back there.'

Izzy shuddered, not even risking a glance. She knew he was watching her, could feel it, and the thought frightened her. He wasn't going to help her. He'd protected her, sure, then and just now, but not through concern for her.

She wasn't even sure how she knew this, but she did, as surely as she knew her own name.

Jinx was dangerous.

'More dangerous than you know.'

The voice came out of nowhere, a whisper, as if someone leaned over her shoulder. But, even as she turned around to face this new threat, she knew there was no one there. She'd heard it, clearly and vividly, and yet there was nothing there. She hadn't imagined it. And yet I couldn't be real.

Most worrying of all, even unreal it was still talking more sense than anyone else here.

'Weren't you going somewhere? Meeting Dylan's band?' It was one last desperate plea, but both Mari and Clo barely heard it. Or if they did they chose to ignore her. Nothing strange there. They might be her own age, but they weren't exactly what you could call friends. It wasn't like she was suddenly one of the cool kids. She'd got them to the club, but Mari had got them in.

'I need some air,' she tried at last. Okay, so she couldn't leave them here. She'd get her head straight, try to work out what the hell was going on and then ... she'd come back in and try to get them to leave.

The problem was the feeling that she would fail.

'Well, *you're* new,' said the woman, shaking her white-blonde hair back over her shoulders. As Dylan stared at her she did a pirouette. 'Finished? Or will I do another turn for you? I'm Silver, by the way. And you are?'

'Dylan.' To his horror, Dylan felt his face heat. 'I'm sorry.'

She raised her eyebrows. 'Why? I'm not.'

The music changed, a mix of plainchant, chords and a heavy rhythm, and the mood changed with it. Sexy, seductive, mysterious. But it was nothing like the music Silver had been making. It was just mortal, mundane.

'I heard your music,' he blurted out. 'From the street. So we followed it.'

The song on the speakers reached a bridge. The dancers undulated on the dance floor, moving closer, pairing off.

Silver leaned in towards him.

'Did you now? You followed my music?'

'Izzy and I did.' Izzy – he felt a small barb of panic. Where was she? Where were the girls? He was meant to be keeping an eye out for them. From the moment he'd stepped into the alley he hadn't given anyone but Silver and her music another thought. That wasn't like him.

'And who's Izzy?'

Dylan scanned the crowd and then saw her, Silver's guitarist at her side. Body language said it all. He read the protective stance, the way she leaned into him. Those big eyes that didn't notice anything else in the room. Izzy was smitten. She'd never let just anyone stand that close. If Dylan tried to act so alpha around her he'd end up with a knee in his balls.

'Ah,' Silver sighed. 'The girl with Jinx.'

After the gig that afternoon she'd mentioned his name. Dylan had barely heard it, he was so concerned about her attack, about the fact she wouldn't report it, but he should have known by the way she spoke of him. Suddenly it was all clear, why Izzy was here, why she'd been in town when she'd never been a rule-breaker. Not to meet up with them. No change of heart there. Jinx was the one she'd come looking for, the guy who had rescued her earlier. It all suddenly made perfect sense.

'Yeah. Figures.' A surge of jealousy took him by surprise. Izzy was a friend, that was all. But she'd been in danger and Jinx had swept to the rescue and all the while Dylan had been playing a lousy afternoon promo gig in a music store for a band that was probably never going anywhere. Brilliant. Marianne had laughed and told him he'd missed his hero moment. Not that he was interested. It would be too weird. Izzy was a friend, a good friend, and more like another little sister. One he was probably closer to than his real sister.

Silver slipped her hand into his. Her touch was very cold, but delicately seductive, the touch of new snowflakes at midnight.

'So you're a musician as well?' She stepped into his line of vision, blocking Izzy and Jinx from view. All thought of them fell away. His mind fumbled after them for a moment, and then gave up as the music in Silver's voice wrapped itself around him. She smiled and all he could think was that he wanted to see that smile every day. Every minute of every day.

'Guitar,' he told her. The smile broadened. Her teeth were astonishingly white and a little too sharp. 'I mean, I play the guitar.' He didn't tell her about Denzion. The band seemed a paltry thing next to her.

'And you heard my music,' she said, twining her fingers with his and then she pulled him after her as she set off across the room towards a VIP section, heedless of the crowd. Indeed the crowd just seemed to melt out of her way. 'That makes you special right from the start. You're what, seventeen, eighteen?'

He bristled, just as anyone would when faced with that sort of question. 'Eighteen.'

'Just left school? At a loose end? Watching it all change right in front of you?' She laughed, turning back to look at him with a gleam of delight in her eye. It was one of the most dangerous things he'd ever seen.

'Something like that,' he admitted. Because she seemed to be peering into his head and reading his thoughts. All his parents talked about were exam results, college applications and courses. 'They want me to study law. I mean how many guitar-playing lawyers do you know?'

'One or two,' she replied with a smile. 'But I see what you mean. Come and play for me, Dylan. Let me hear you. Maybe I can offer you something special in return. A little deal?'

'A ... a deal?' He stumbled as he followed her, but when she glanced back he forgot his confusion. It felt like magic. Like being in the right place at the right time for once. Like he'd just walked into a dream.

'Yes. I'm Leanán Sídhe. Do you know what that means?' He shook his head. He recognised the words as Irish, but he didn't know them. Silver gave a wriggle of something like excitement. 'So innocent. Come on.'

Innocent? Great. That was what she thought? Before he had a chance to protest, she pushed the heavy velvet curtain aside and he was drawn into her lair.

The room beyond was deserted, luxurious and dominated by a white tree. Like some kind of willow made of marble, the branches trailed down to the ground. But this was no thing carved from stone. Vitality and power radiated from it. It was slim, like Silver, full of grace and beauty, just like her. And so very alive.

The curtain fell behind him with a heavy sigh and he forgot his fears. Thoughts of the future, law and everything else fell away.

Dylan stared. It couldn't be real and yet he knew it was. The gap between knowing what he was seeing and knowing what reality said he could see lurched even wider. *Sídhe*, Silver had said. Like Banshees? Like *fairies*?

Before he could argue, or accuse her of winding him up, Silver spoke again and his protests were forgotten.

'Great musicians aren't born,' Silver said. She settled herself on the edge of a divan and drew him closer. 'They're made. You can practise all night and day, have all the natural talent you could want and be born under the luckiest star imaginable, but that won't make you great. It won't make you a legend.'

She leaned forward, her lips parting in a sensual smile.

'But I can.'

Dylan slid to his knees in front of her, lifted his face so he could look into her wondrous eyes. If he was that good, if there was any way he could get that good, he wouldn't have to set his music aside like his parents insisted was inevitable. 'How?'

'I'm Leanán Sídhe, just like I told you. Some people would call me … a muse. And I can offer you a deal.'

He knew she wasn't lying, knew it in his beating heart. Knew that somehow he had stumbled into a dream. One where he could choose his own path in life for once. In the same way he had known to follow the music. It scared him. But he couldn't back away from it.

'What kind of deal?' He leaned in closer.

'Will you give me anything?' she asked, her eyes filled with laughter, with promises. 'Even if I ask for a piece of your soul? Even if you know I'd drink down your essence like sweet lilac wine?'

'Maybe. But what sort of deal?' He wasn't sure why he was asking all these stupid questions when all he wanted to do was kiss her. He'd never wanted anyone this way. He couldn't think of anyone or anything that had ever seemed so important to him in his life, except for his music. And yet there he went, asking questions.

Luckily it didn't faze Silver. If anything, it appeared to amuse her. She tapped his nose with one delicate fingertip. 'Three times three.' Her eyes glittered with something other than playfulness. Her breath played against his lips, as cold as her touch. 'Three kisses, three times three years of fame, of mega-stardom fame, of talent, of creation and adoration, of some of the greatest music mankind has ever heard. Music to speak to people's hearts. Music to change lives. Music to change the world. And then – are you listening, Dylan? – then it's over. Then you're mine and mine alone. If you survive it.'

'Nine years?'

'Give or take. You'd be, what? Twenty-seven?'

'Are you talking about the 'twenty-sevens'?' Musicians so

talented that they were doomed to die, whether from bad luck, suicide, drugs or the sheer reckless speed at which they lived their lives. Musical legends and urban legends. Whispered stories no one quite believed. Not really. 'I thought they were a myth.'

Silver smiled her enigmatic smile. 'So am I, Dylan.' She was offering him all his dreams, and the downside? To spend the rest of his life with someone like her?

'And what do you get?'

She sighed, her body stretching out like a cat, brushing her fingers through the leaves of the tree, along the smooth bark. 'Life.'

'Life?'

'Everything needs something to sustain life. I have my tree, my touchstone, the heart of this hollow. If I didn't have this…' She sighed. 'Well, no one can hold a hollow without a touchstone.'

'Would you die? If something happened to the tree?'

She eyed him curiously, studying him. 'What a strange thing to ask …' She didn't sound amused all of a sudden. Her voice suddenly held an edge of danger.

Izzy would have talked sense into him, he knew that. But here, beneath a tree growing in a basement nightclub, in another world, kneeling in front of the most beautiful and talented woman he'd ever met, sense was a rare commodity. He felt drunk on her company, high on just being with her.

And besides, Izzy was getting her own offers of dreams

come true in the form of Jinx. The one she'd come here to find.

'What happens afterwards?' he asked, reaching out for the tree as well. 'To me, I mean. I'm yours, but what does that mean? I don't see a load of aging musicians skulking around here. All I see is this tree.'

Silver bared her teeth. It might have been a smile, but it looked more like a snarl. Just for a moment. The moment he mentioned that creepy-looking tree.

Dylan's sense of his own body contracted, as if his skin had abruptly shrunk to be smaller than the body it contained. It stretched across his bones too tightly and his head throbbed in sudden pain. A primal sense of alarm shot through him. He shouldn't be here. He shouldn't even be having this conversation. She was more dangerous than he could imagine and this deal … this deal was not a good deal. Drink, drugs, speed or disappearance … something always finished off the twenty-sevens in dramatic style. They were all dead.

Pulling free of Silver, he struggled to stand up. 'I'm sorry,' he muttered, not even sure if the words would clear. 'I need to find my friends.'

Anyone else would have taken it as an insult, he was sure. But it just seemed to slide off Silver. She smiled, getting to her feet.

'Sometimes it takes time to accept these things, even if you know they're true, even if you know they're what you want. Take whatever time you need, Dylan. I'll be here. And you'll be able to find me. You're special, Dylan, something in your blood, something in your soul, your quintessence. The music inside you. You heard my music and came to me. That's the path you're meant to follow. I'll be keeping a very close eye on you.'

CHAPTER SEVEN

Magpies

Damnation, the girl was off again. Jinx suppressed a growl and forced his way through the crowd. It was only when he was almost at Izzy's side that he noticed Silver blithely reeling in the only human male in the whole club. Izzy's female friends looked on in irritation. Their obnoxious pouts faded to interest as Jinx approached.

But he didn't have a moment to spare for them. All his attention was locked on the girl he had saved twice now – Izzy, his intended quarry.

Prey.

She still glowed. Not a light he could see, but something he felt bone-deep. For a moment he wondered if the rest of the club and its inhabitants had blurred, or if she just stood out even sharper to his eyes.

It could be that way, Holly had told him. Sometimes when

Cú Sídhe hunted, the quarry was more defined than anything else around them.

But he wasn't sure. There was something about her that went beyond prey, or the spark. Something ... something striking he couldn't name.

She was brighter and clearer than anything around her. It was as if some other sense he didn't know about was picking it up, something beyond even his heightened fae senses.

Her shoulders stiffened as if she felt him watching her. She lifted her chin, the elegant curve of her neck captivating him. Her fists balled tightly at her side. A fighter then. Normally he would see it as a challenge, but here – now – it was just tragic, pathetic, even. There was no way she could fight him. No way she could fight Holly when he brought her in. But she'd try. Of course she'd try.

And fail.

That was the tragedy.

Angels had fallen to Holly. Their broken images lined the walls of her Market. The shattered images she made of them before the end. Angelic sparks filled the core of her touchstone, fuelling her magic, making her more powerful than any of the other Aes Sídhe, Brí and Amadán included. Always willing to go further in pursuit of power than anyone else. That was Holly all over.

With a jerk Izzy was off, striding towards the door before he realised that she was just going. Leaving the girls who didn't care a fig for her right now. Leaving the boy who probably wasn't aware she existed at the moment, not with Silver's full attention on him.

Jinx marched after her. If she was going outside, she was just going to make this easy. And if she was determined to make it easy, he was more than happy to oblige.

The night called him, as it always did. The moon overhead – even distant and marred by city smoke – set his blood pounding. Ancient blood, with its own memories. The narrow lanes of Dubh Linn stretched out like a maze, part of the human city and yet not, interwoven, transposed on top of the everyday world.

He knew them well. Every cobble, every alcove, every nook and cranny.

But Izzy didn't have a clue. She turned the first corner, realised it wasn't the way to the alley through which she'd come, and froze, gazing around herself at old brickwork, the faded rags of posters, intricately crafted grilles on the windows and set into the ground.

'Lost?' he asked.

At the sound of his voice, she jumped and turned, twisting like a little cat, ready for the fight. This wasn't the girl of earlier today. Not quite. Something had changed her. The glow flickered with uncertainty.

The spark. He wanted to slap himself on the forehead. The spark was already permeating her system. Of course it would change her. It changed everything for good and ill.

'I came looking for you. I wanted answers.'

Jinx folded his arms across his chest and her eyes followed the flex of his muscles, the lines of his tattoos moulding around them. Deep blue eyes, afraid but not helplessly so. She shouldn't intrigue him so. Shouldn't attract him at all. She was prey. That was all. Just prey. He waited until her eyes returned to his face. 'Answers to what?'

'There's a mark on my neck. A tattoo. Like yours. How did it get there?'

This easy? Really? He smiled, barely listening to her now she was willing to go with him. A mark on her neck? Sure. How on earth could she have got a tattoo like his?

'Come with me. I know someone who can explain.' Lies fell easily from a honeyed tongue to eager ears. Usually.

Suspicion hardened her face. 'Who?'

He laughed. It was almost too ridiculous. 'My grandmother.' With a step forward he reached out to her. 'Look, you shouldn't be here. Neither you nor your friends, but we can overlook that. The Sídhe-ways aren't for humans, but some of you still stray from time to time.'

'*Sídhe-ways?*' She forced herself to breathe, a deliberate effort on her part to stay calm. 'Do you mean *fairies*? The Tuatha dé Danann? They're stories my gran tells.'

'We were the first on this island, if that's what you mean. We're not human. And these pathways are part of our world. Sídhe-ways. And they aren't safe, but if you want I'll make sure your friends are shown the way home.'

She gazed at his hand as if it might bite. 'But not me?' A

question, but delivered in a toneless voice. She already knew what his reply to that would be.

'You want answers.'

Her lips tightened as she thought it through. 'All right.'

A brave little tragedy.

The click of boot heel on stone brought Jinx around in irritation – to find the Magpie twins standing behind him.

'Well, now, what a coincidence,' said Mags. 'Just the girl we were looking for.'

Pie, on the other hand, just pulled out the ugliest looking knife and smiled as he ran the flat of it across his black sleeve. It didn't glint, which told Jinx it was cold iron, probably with a natural handle so it didn't burn the skin right off his hand. Jinx knew Pie was rumoured to have one, but he'd never set much store by rumour.

Kind of a pity now.

'So, what's it going to be, dog?' asked Mags with a sneer. 'You going to roll over or sit up and beg? Or just run off with your tail between your legs?' Dismissing Jinx, Mags gazed past him to Izzy. 'Come here, love. Let's not make this difficult.'

'Didn't anyone teach you about poaching?' Jinx stepped carefully to one side, to put them off guard, he hoped. Izzy gave a gasp of dismay, but he ignored that. She thought he was betraying her. Well, she'd need to get used to that feeling anyway. Ignoring the feeling of shame, he let them step forward, saw Izzy close her eyes in fear and then tore himself free of the tight control Holly's wards and charms continually maintained on his form. It hurt. Her spells made sure it hurt every time, but he had to do it. He slipped his shape and the bonds holding him.

There was a soft whoosh, a burst of air from nowhere. Izzy's hair flew back from her face and shoulders, and the scent of cinnamon and sugar melted together surrounded her. Just for a moment. It sent her stumbling back as she inhaled it, a mesmerising smell, intoxicating. Her eyes opened.

Instead of grabbing her, the twins cursed and spun around to face the spot where Jinx had been standing. One gave a low chuckle, a dangerous sound which set her skin prickling.

Where was Jinx?

A creature stood in his place, the size of a wolfhound, but whip thin and sleek as a greyhound, a blue-green silken fur covering its body marked with unnaturally curved and twisted indigo stripes. Like Jinx's tattoos. The whole creature might have been made from Jinx's tattoos. Points of silver flashed in the dim light, little rings on the long pointed ears, tapered back as if they flowed from its head. Studs glinted along its muzzle. Equally silver eyes opened, narrow slits, so dark in the centre. As she watched, it stretched its body out like molten metal. Claws slid from paws as broad as a human face.

As elegant as his hands.

Even as she struggled with the logic of it, reality reasserted itself, reminding her of the situation. Her heart thundered, pounding on her ribs until they ached. Her rapid breath sounded frightened even to her and her skin tightened around her frame. A metallic tang filled her throat and all around her was the creature's scent, its sweet beguiling scent.

The twins changed their stances, shifting to something anticipating a threat for the first time. The creature stalked around Izzy, placing itself between her and them. She looked up its length, from the twitching whip of its tail, along the coiled body, the strength in those tense muscles to the great head.

A growl rippled from the creature, like the voice of a tiger. It couldn't be. It *couldn't* be.

'About time you showed some form, Jinxy-boy.' Mags drew back his upper lip as he spoke. 'Thought Holly made sure it hurt too much to change on a whim, so this must be important. You think you can take us both? Bad doggy.'

Pie laughed, although without mirth.

Another long, low growl came from the creature – from Jinx – one which sent a shiver of fear through her, even though she knew she was not the object of the aggression. The message was clear enough and it got through, judging from the agitation on the twins' faces.

'We just want the girl, Jinx,' said Pie. 'The old man sent us personal. You know how this goes down.'

And then they moved, so fast she saw only a blur. Black and

white streaks that raced towards her. Jinx leapt to intercept them.

'*Run!*'

Not listening to the voice that couldn't exist be damned! Izzy bolted down the alleyway, heedless of her path, moving faster than she could ever remember being able to run before. Terror did that to you, they said. The mark on the back of her neck was cold as ice, warning her of danger. It was too dark ahead and the narrow streets wound left and right. Footsteps echoed behind her and ahead of her. She flung herself around a corner and into a dead end.

With a cry of dismay, she turned around to see Pie bearing down on her, that vicious blade in his hand.

'You're fast, I'll give you that. But it takes more than a mortal to escape us, even with the puppy running interference for you. Now hold still, I've work to do.'

'Stay away from me.' She tried to edge her way along the wall, hoping to dart by him given half a chance. Her foot caught on something, wood, but it scraped like metal on the cobbles beneath.

'*Pick it up,*' said the voice. '*Defend yourself.*' As if she actually needed telling.

She grabbed it, a length of wood all right, but with some nasty looking rusty nails poking from the end. She swept it in front of her, hoping to ward him off.

Pie didn't even flinch. 'Here now, you've got something we want. While my brother's dealing with the puppy, you're going to come with me. We can do that easily or I can make it pretty painful. Understand?'

It was the alley all over again, under the eye of the graffiti angel. The moment her life had turned insane. The moment shadows had started to whisper and move, the moment dis-embodied voices tried to tell her what to do, the moment Jinx had entered her life.

'What is it you people think I have?' She couldn't keep her voice from trembling and hated the way his smile broadened at the sound, white teeth gleaming.

'You don't even know? Oh, that's rich. Now, come here. Put the stick down, little girl.' She tightened her grip, glaring at him. Jinx, where was he? What had Mags done to him? He could have been here by now, couldn't he? She must have glanced over Pie's shoulder looking for him. 'Jinx? You think he's coming to your rescue? You're human. He's Cú Sídhe. A hound, set on a trail by his mistress. All he's going to do is drag you in front of her instead. And you don't want to face Holly, little girl.' He passed the knife from one hand to the other. It danced in front of his face, hypnotic, terrifying. 'Holly's *nasty*.'

Before she could react, Pie's arm swiped the piece of wood from her hand. It clattered against the wall and she screamed, staggering back, her hand flung out before her.

Fire burst from her fingertips. Just for a moment. Long enough to make him shy back in surprise. Before she could take it in, believe it had happened, the tiny flames were gone.

A blue-green shape burst through her field of vision, taking

Pie down in a ball of snarls and curses. He gave an inarticulate shout and Jinx yelped.

As suddenly as it had begun it was over. Pie lurched to his feet, clutching the ragged remains of his arm. With a hateful glance at Izzy, he took off down the alley, his long black coat fluttering behind him and a trail of blood in his wake. The hound stood his ground in front of her, snarling, his chest heaving.

Cú Sídhe, Pie had called him. Like you'd speak of a beast, a monster. She knew what it meant. Fairy hound. Dog of the Sídhe. And with his teeth bared, his fur bristling, he looked like a monster indeed.

And then, with a whine, he sank to the ground, worrying at his shoulder.

Izzy looked back to her hand, still shaking, but there were no flames now. There was nothing at all. Had she imagined it? But then what had the Magpie seen?

The hound turned his head, great silver eyes regarding her mournfully, and gave a whimper that was still more than half a growl.

Izzy's heart lurched. Edging forward, terrified lest she startle him, she laid her hand tentatively on his neck. His pulse hammered beneath the fur. His whine faded and the harsh sound of his breath replaced it. She closed her eyes, waiting for him to turn on her. A wounded animal would attack. She knew that. But she didn't pull back.

Nothing happened.

She took two shaky breaths of her own and ventured another look. He was still watching her over his shoulder and her fingers curled, caressing the fur. More like a cat's fur than any dog she knew. Sensual as silk, but warm, alive, and the skin beneath rippling with strength.

It *was* Jinx.

Izzy jerked her hand away rapidly. The silver eyes understood far too much. They closed in marked despair, and he whimpered again, shifting around.

That was when she saw the knife – Pie's knife. The bone-white hilt jutted from the gash on Jinx's shoulder, which meant the blade was buried deep inside.

Izzy hissed a curse. She had to get it out. It was an ugly thing, and it was going to kill him. He watched her, patient, enduring the pain.

As her hand edged towards the hilt he started to growl.

'Jesus, Jinx, I don't like any of this either, but we've got to get that thing out of you, no matter what shape you're in.'

He bent his head, licking at the wound, trying to get at the knife himself. But he couldn't reach. And even if he could get a grip on the hilt, she doubted he'd be able to pull it out.

She reached out again and the growl turned even more threatening.

'Bad dog,' she told him. 'Stupid dog, in fact. Stupid, rude, ridiculous dog who's going to die in a gutter if you don't let me help.'

The mark on the back of her neck sizzled as she touched

the hilt and Jinx yelped. She grabbed hold of it, didn't think or hesitate, even as his jaws opened and made for her arm. But he shied away at the last minute, the teeth snapping closed in front of her instead of tearing into her flesh. She needed his help, any information he could provide, needed him whole and well. No matter what sort of mythical creature he had turned out to be. Besides, she wasn't the kind to leave any sort of animal in pain, was she? Not even one so … so …

Izzy yanked the knife free and the howl of rage and pain became a voice, a voice screaming in agony and despair.

The air shimmered, moved, and Jinx sprawled on the wet, blood-spattered cobbles before her. Izzy stared at him, realising that yes, the tattoos really did go all over his body. His head thudded against the cobblestones and his voice choked to silence.

'Are you okay? Jinx?' She couldn't make her fingers release the knife. It shook violently.

He struggled to push himself up from the ground, but slumped down again. He was still bleeding, his body trembling all over now. Shock, perhaps. Or grief.

'My clothes,' he said at last, his voice strained and weak. Defeated, but not in pain.

'I don't know. What's wrong with you?' Stupid question to ask a man who'd just had half a foot of iron in his body. She touched his shoulder delicately, but found the wound gone. Just a smear of blood remained. 'Jinx?'

'What do you want of me?' He pushed himself up on his

elbows and glared at her, dipping his head to do so. His dark hair snaked across his face and his eyes were more alien than ever before. Cú Sídhe indeed. Every legend, every nightmare made form. The fairy dog, the hunter, the hell hound.

Old stories like Gran would tell, stories Dad liked to spin as well. Things that had made her laugh or shiver in the darkness. Things she'd never believed in. Not until now.

Hard to not believe in something you'd just seen with your own eyes. Hard to not believe in something when it was hunting you down and brandishing a knife. Or when it saved you.

Not real, her rational brain was still trying to scream at her. *Not real!*

But it was. Her stomach sickened every second she acknowledged that.

'I just ... I just want to go home.'

If she went home everything would go back to normal, wouldn't it? Home was safe. Home was mundane and quiet. Normal. Mum and Dad, the TV, a quiet shift in the coffee shop tomorrow morning. She wanted that. Not *this*.

'Very well.' Just like that. 'But could you find my clothes first? I don't think walking around like this in either your world or mine will go down particularly well.'

'No. Probably not.' Her face heated and she tried to look anywhere but at him. The naked tattooed man who had been a huge, supernatural dog *thing*, and had saved her from a lunatic with a knife.

She closed her eyes, screwed up her face as if she could

make it happen just by willing it to happen. Normal, she wanted normal.

And the world had just taken another lurch deeper into the bizarre.

Because he hadn't argued. He hadn't insisted he needed to take her to his grandmother, however dangerous that was, and he hadn't done anything to hurt her.

Despite what the Magpie twins has said.

Jinx had just agreed to her going home without any sort of argument and that worried her most of all.

CHAPTER EIGHT

Leaving Dubh Linn

The clothes lay strewn on the ground where the Magpie twins had cornered them. Thankfully no one had come by so Jinx took them and quickly pulled on his jeans. One indignity dealt with, thanks be. Izzy was desperately trying to look anywhere but at his torso. Her face had turned scarlet, her eyes too large.

Just a girl, really, when you came down to it. He had to keep reminding himself of that. Not much younger than him, but she'd seen nothing in her short life – nothing like the blood and betrayals he'd seen. She was just a girl.

The iron blade should have killed him. Even had he been able to pull it out – unlikely in his hound shape and the iron would have prevented him sliding into Aes Sídhe form too – even then, the traces of its poison should have remained to destroy him.

A slow agonising death. Just the kind the Magpies loved to gloat over.

But Izzy had pulled the knife free and everything had gone with it. She was a healer of some kind, perhaps, with a fairy doctor in her lineage, or a wise woman with healing hands. Something had to explain it. The spark alone, powerful as it was, wouldn't be enough. Old blood perhaps, just a drop of it would be enough to let her hear the music and follow it. Or just gifted in some way, the type of way liable to attract the attention of the fae world. That could still happen in the modern world. Something like that, anything.

Because he didn't want to think about what else it could mean.

She had pulled iron from his body. She'd saved his miserable life.

Why? Because she'd wanted to? No one did something like that without a sound reason.

He didn't believe in pity. Nor in kindness.

He pulled his boots on, tugging them so sharply Izzy winced, reading his anger. She was a smart one, intuitive, a fighter. She'd been trying to take on Pie when he'd got there.

'Who's the Old Man?' she asked.

Jinx looked up. 'Someone you don't want to be anywhere near.'

'You keep saying helpful things like that.'

Ah yes, sarcasm. She was fine if she was taking that tone with him again.

He struggled into the t-shirt. 'It's the truth. Why did you come here? Sídhe-space, especially Dubh Linn, isn't safe for someone like you.' Especially not for someone like her – with a divine spark attached to her. Her healing ability could be natural, but if it was, the spark amplified it. All of which made her a target. And the something else. Her solidity in his world. That glow he'd seen from the first time he'd met her. What *was* she?

'Dubh Linn?' she asked, making it sound like English – Dove-Linn – rooting the magic of the words themselves in mundanity. 'What's that?'

'It's here,' he replied. 'You're looking at it. The world of the Sídhe lies alongside yours, like a ghost image, there and not there at the same time, two layers so close that they touch in places, like pages in a book. We live on the horizontal, as opposed to heaven and hell on the vertical. Once, our two worlds were one, when we first came here, before the humans, but the Milesian tricksters split them into two when they promised to share with my people, and banished us from their world to ours. Parts of your world drift here, parts of ours drift into yours. One can't exist without the other. Humans and fae stand on the same horizontal plane, which is why you can travel from one world to the other. Stepping from one to another can take a moment, or a hundred years. Dubh Linn is its heart, locked in position here, the anchor between worlds. The centre of everything.'

'Town,' she whispered. 'You're talking about town.' She

sensed it then, the places where the two worlds locked together, where their touches overlapped. Many did. Normally though they had no idea what that meant.

'Why are you here?' he asked again.

To his surprise, she turned her back on him and pulled her hair up on top of her head. With her other hand she jerked down the neck of her sweater.

The mark stood out, starkly beautiful on the pale skin of her slender neck. The silver chain she wore and the small bumps of her upper vertebrae just accentuated the ancient, living wonder of it.

'Where did you—?' He was on his feet, reaching out, and only just managed to stop himself before he touched her skin. His hand hovered there, above it. He could snap her neck in a moment, overpower her and drag her to Holly, or even just … just run his fingers over that cool, smooth flesh until she sighed for him. With a little touch of glamour she could be his entirely, begging for him. She didn't even know how to defend herself against fae wiles. Just a touch of skin on skin and a human would be spellbound. A glamour was a Sídhe's spell of choice when it came to humans, a cross between a disguise and an enchantment. It was so easy. But it hadn't worked on her before, had it?

'It just appeared,' she said in a rush. 'When I got home. And all the shadows were moving like something alive. But they stopped. When I told them to, they stopped. And then I …'

She dropped her hands and turned to him, so quickly she

almost ended up in his arms.

Stepping back was his only option and the hardest thing he had ever done. She wasn't for him. Couldn't be. He had to get her to Holly and that was that. He had to get her out of his life.

She'd pulled iron from his body, his geis screamed at him. She had saved his life, asking for nothing in return. Yet he was her enemy. The man who would give her over to his psychotic matriarch. Holly would do unspeakable things to her in order to claim the spark. Any of the council would, any of the Sídhe. And Izzy didn't know, didn't understand. She had no idea.

'What's your name?' Jinx asked. 'Your *true* name?' There had to be a reason. *Had* to be. For her being here, for the way she fascinated him, for her getting the spark when she didn't even know what it was. If he could gain her true name, that was one small power. And in these days no one knew not to give one of the fae a true name.

For a spark to attach to a human was rare, but not unheard of. But more usually there was something about them – old blood or fae blood or some sort of gift. But no spark could make this mark, though its touch may have triggered its appearance. To be marked like this with the symbol of heaven, earth, human and fae, with the cross of the four races and the circles binding them together, to mark her with something representing all the planes of existence ...

The spark inside her made her a target, but this – this

marked her as something more.

'Who *are* you?' he asked again, more insistent this time. He stepped closer, using his frame to intimidate her, as his anger, defeat and horror, as the sense of being trapped by her, spilled into his voice.

She paled, her breath quickening. But she still didn't back down.

'Isabel Gregory.'

And there he had it. Gregory. *Grigori*. His head sank like a millstone. Was she even aware that he bowed? Did she know he had no choice?

She bore the mark of a Grigori, and the name too. He'd had no idea. The Council had even tried to warn him. But he thought the Grigori was older, a man. He thought— Well, what did it matter now? What did any of it matter? He was lost already.

'And what would you have me do now?' Whatever she said, he was bound to obey. And Holly would take her vengeance for that. She'd enjoy it, make sure she took her time. It didn't matter. His geis had made him someone else's slave. He couldn't bring Izzy to Holly now. Not unless Izzy told him to; the prophecy Brí had laid on him with his name left him no choice. Izzy had saved his life.

Bands of iron tightened on his mind, on his will.

This was what it felt like to be collared.

And by so gentle a saving hand.

She sighed again, weariness marking her face, darkening the

shadows under her eyes. She didn't even know. 'I came for answers. But I want to go home, Jinx. I just want to go home.'

He nodded and that was that.

Holly would give him an eternity's worth of pain in return for this.

But what choice did he have? The geis compelled him. His life belonged to Isabel Gregory, and hate it all he might, there was nothing he could do about it.

A peal of laughter made Izzy jump out of her skin and inwardly cringe all at once.

'Sheesh, I thought you'd gone.' Marianne. She'd never thought she'd be quite so glad to see Marianne, even if Mari herself didn't look thrilled to see her. 'Oh, well, I guess we can share a taxi or—'

She broke off, staring past Izzy at Jinx, who was still rearranging his clothes.

Irrevocably, Mari's gaze slid to Izzy. Her eyes turned knowing, teasing. 'No way,' she mouthed.

Izzy just wanted the ground to open up and swallow her. She felt her face flare with heat. *Why* did it have to be Marianne? And at the same time, she kind of wanted to throw her arms around the other girl and hug her. Mortifying though the moment was.

'What?' asked Clo, stumbling out of the club, a bottle of

overly bright alcohol still clutched in her hand. Dylan and the blonde singer followed, standing too close together.

'Izzy?' Dylan started forward, but the singer moved too and he hesitated. 'Izzy, what happened?'

'Oh, Jinx.' Underlying laughter rippled through the blonde woman's voice. 'What have you done?'

Jinx scowled at her and ran his long fingers through his hair. 'Saw off the Magpies. That's all, Silver.'

The steel in his eyes made Silver's smile fade away. 'You're all right?'

'Izzy? Did you've a problem?' Clo slurred a little and shook her head, as if trying to clear the slightly dazed expression.

Oh, good, she was going to have to get a tipsy Clodagh home on top of all… all this… But at least that didn't venture beyond the realms of normality.

'No. Jinx—'

— turned into a giant dog-thing and almost got killed anyway —

Not something you could say to normal people. And her mind stumbled over that thought a moment too late, filling her with dismay.

Was she not *normal people* anymore?

She tried again, needing it to be no big deal. What could she say? She kept her voice nonchalant. 'Jinx sorted it out.'

'Go home.' His voice rumbled through her. She could feel him, standing right behind her, the warmth of his body, the hum of his anger. 'That's what you wanted. They'll go with you.'

She glanced at him. No matter what she wanted, there were things she needed as well. And the real world, the *normal* world, wasn't going to give them to her. 'I still want those answers.'

To her relief, he nodded. Something in his face changed – it didn't soften, it was more like a wave of sorrow passed through him so strong that he couldn't shield himself from it, or stop his expression betraying him. 'And you'll have them. I will find you.'

Logic told her to give him a phone number or her address. Yet a more rational form of logic, laced with her mother's voice, insisted that giving strange men contact details was something only an idiot would do. She hesitated too long.

'Awk-ward,' Mari chimed, leaning in against Dylan. 'So, are you heading home or ...' She glanced at Silver, unable to keep suspicion out of her glare.

Silver had already stepped away from them, leaving Dylan behind her. Izzy watched in dismay as she slid her hand up Jinx's broad shoulder. It was too intimate a gesture to be a comfort. Her own reaction surprised her. Why should she care? What did it matter to her? And yet somehow it did. She shivered, reminding herself that she didn't owe him anything. She'd saved him. Jinx hung his head and the concern on Silver's delicate features grew even more pronounced.

Dylan's face flinched with a sudden shock of an emotion far stronger, one that looked a lot like jealousy. And something else. Self-disgust? Emotions in conflict played out over his features and Izzy could read them all, just for a moment.

She didn't like what she saw.

'Let's go,' he snapped, turning away as fast as he could. 'Izzy, come on.' He'd never talked to her like that in his life. But her surprise was overshadowed by another concern.

'How do we get out of here?' asked Izzy, her hands balling at her sides.

Jinx pointed down the alley behind her. 'Just head straight that way. Don't stray from the path, even if the alley seems to turn about on you. Head straight.'

She nodded, but Dylan was already off, heading down the alleyway with angry strides, his head down.

'Dylan,' Silver called after him and he jerked to a halt, as if her voice tripped him. 'My offer still stands.'

He didn't give her an answer.

'What offer?' Marianne demanded, hurrying after him.

Dylan didn't pause, just started marching forward again. 'It doesn't matter, Mari. Just music stuff. Like a gig. I don't need her anyway. No more than Izzy needs the Hulk back there.'

The Hulk. Yeah, funny. Don't get him angry.

'*Hunk* more like,' Clo grinned at Izzy. 'And as for you, sneaking off with him to do dark deeds in an alley, no less.' She slid her arm around Izzy and before she knew what was happening Izzy was all but holding her friend up. 'Oh, wait until I tell everyone.'

She ought to be irritated, but somehow she couldn't keep hold of the emotion. Relief at being back with them again kept washing it away. 'It wasn't like that.'

Her protests fell on deaf ears. 'Oh, yeah, sure.' Marianne gave a chuckle as they caught up. 'His shirt just fell off. And what else?' The dirty grin should have seen her locked up by the thought police for public indecency. 'You picked an awesome time to start building a reputation, Izzy. Just awesome. I wish my phone had a signal here. I really do. Freaky blackspot. Come on, Facebook's calling!'

They sped her away, towards the real world, to their Dublin far from Sídhe-space. Back to safety, she hoped. It felt safe with the three of them and she could breathe again, try to forget everything she had seen, all the madness. If she hadn't been afraid of dropping Clodagh, or of looking even more of a fool in front of Mari, she would have run. She didn't want to look behind her, but couldn't help herself.

Jinx and Silver were nowhere to be seen.

The cab dropped her about ten minutes from home. No way was Izzy going to drive right up to the house, despite Dylan's arguments. Since when had he got so protective? Besides, the meter was about to tick over. He'd been as communicative as a stone all the way home. Sulking or lost in thought. Once he'd checked that she hadn't been hurt, that was that.

She walked the last part quickly enough, her hands shoved deep in her pockets, her mind on Jinx and the Magpies. On the things they had said. On Jinx's transformation and all the weird shit that seemed to have attached itself to her.

And on Jinx's horror when he'd heard her name.

The mark on her neck started to tingle again as she turned into her street. Another warning? She faltered, looked up and saw the cop car parked outside her house.

Oh God, no. Something had happened. She knew it. Something terrible had happened.

Izzy broke into a sprint, tore a path up the gravel drive and scrambled to open the door. She almost fell inside and her mum burst out from the living room, pale, red-eyed, far too thin and drawn.

And yet the arms that seized her might have been made of iron.

'Where the *hell* have you been? Oh my God, Izzy, I thought ... I thought ... both of you. I went to wake you, but you weren't there and I thought—' She drew in a shuddering breath that shook her whole body against Izzy's. 'Both of you in one night. Where on earth did you go?'

Her voice broke. Helpless and desperate, her mother who was always so cool and collected could no longer heave words into her mouth. She choked and pulled Izzy against her hard and held her there, shaking like she stood in the midst of an earthquake.

Over Mum's shoulder, Izzy saw two police officers rise to their feet, their faces all solemn and filled with disguised pity.

'I was— I just—' Damn it, who cared right now? Mum

wouldn't believe her anyway. 'What happened, Mum? What is it?'

'Your dad, love. There was an accident on the way home. Another car hit his. He's in hospital.'

The icy flood of terror filled her again. There was nothing she could fight here. Nothing to run from or to. Nothing she could do. She was just a child.

'But he's okay, isn't he?' She looked from one grim face to the next. And finally to her mum again, to the bleak emptiness in her eyes. 'He's okay. Isn't he, Mum?'

Her mother broke down into tears and strangled sobs.

CHAPTER NINE

The Knot

The stab of raw agony brought Jinx up from his seat, almost to his feet, the instinct to fight, to protect, driving him up, though he didn't know what or where the threat was. The club was almost empty now, piped music driving out the late revellers and Silver curled up beneath her tree, nearly asleep. At the movement, she opened one eye like a sleepy cat.

'What is it?'

'I don't know.' He clenched his hands to fists of frustration. The pain simmered in the pit of his stomach. Not physical. The Creator knew he could handle physical pain. He'd been designed to completely change his physiology at will. If he couldn't stand pain, he'd die every time. This pain was emotional; the fae relied on their emotions, so heightened, so all-consuming. Physical pain was nothing. Emotional pain was a torture beyond bearing.

Silver pushed herself up, her feet tucked neatly beneath her. She held out her hands to him, but Jinx didn't touch her. Didn't dare.

'What happened with the girl, Jinx?'

He wasn't in the mood for this, for exposing his shame, for demonstrating what a fool he was. 'What happened with the boy?'

'He's not a boy, Jinx. You're not that much older than him yourself. He's a young man, and a gifted musician. I could make him great. Besides, I like him. There's something else, an unrivalled talent, a potential for so much more. He heard us from the street beyond the gate, followed the music.'

'I don't understand. He's just a human.'

'Just a human,' she laughed. 'You really *don't* understand. Potential is everything. He heard my music, a boy with no fae blood, nothing magical at all. No one has done that for forty years. He's special. Really special. But that isn't troubling me. You and the girl ... What happened out there?'

She gave him that resolute look. She wouldn't back down. She'd keep on asking until she broke him. It was her nature, the nature of most of the women of his kind. They wouldn't ever back down. And that thought chilled him to the bone.

'She's the one Holly wants,' Jinx said. 'The one who saw the angel and who now carries the spark.'

Silver frowned, a small, subtle line marring the perfect skin between her eyebrows. 'And you let her go? But Holly told you—'

'I know.' He all but barked the words, his composure slipping fast. He struggled to control himself again, ashamed at the outburst. 'The twins attacked us. They're after her too for Amadán. I fought them off. We did, I mean. She tried – God love her, she tried with an old bit of wood and nothing else. I got there just in time, but Pie had that bloody knife of his and he – he stuck me with it.'

He hung his head. As he said it, gave voice to the dreadful words, all the rage drained out of him, leaving only grief and shame, pain behind, his loss and something else. Something he couldn't name.

'She pulled it out, Silver. She healed me.'

Silver swallowed hard. Her throat worked too fast, as if she struggled to find words and the breath to say them, her whole body tightening.

'Jinx, what are you saying?'

'She pulled iron out of my body. She saved my life.'

Silver knew Jinx's geis as well as he did. She'd been with him as his witness and his friend when Brí handed it down. He'd been too young to represent himself, to take in any of it, and there hadn't been anyone else willing. But Silver had taken his hand, so small in hers, and told him to be brave. That she was there. That a geis meant he was Aes Sídhe and that was important. Of all people, Silver knew that those words bound him as tightly as any oath, words that sealed his fate. She had heard them laid upon him by Brí.

'*You'd hold Silver's hand for support?*' Brí had said. '*You poor fool. I'll give you your geis now and remember, it binds you forever –* '*No hand but your own can save you, or it will hold you fast.*'

'But—' Silver began now and stopped, her mouth closing to keep in unspeakable words.

Izzy owned him, all of him, body and – if only he'd had one – soul.

Silver regained some control over what she might say. 'What about Holly? All her wards and charms on you, all those spells ...' The pain of it, yes, pain she'd make him endure a hundred times over. Every bit of silver she'd forced on him stung. Every tattoo that constrained his form with a spell was agony.

'I had to let her go.'

'And now?'

'I can feel Izzy's grief, her pain. Something terrible has happened to her.'

'Then go to her.'

He shook his head. 'And lead the fae world right to her door? Silver ... she called herself "Gregory". Isabel Gregory.'

It was the final nail. Silver's face turned white and she gave a low moan of dismay. She knew. She understood what it meant. Grigori were different – watchers, balance-keepers, weapons, soldiers and custodians, tied to the horizontal plane, but beyond the petty rivalries of creatures like Aes Sídhe – and Izzy didn't even have a clue what she was. She couldn't know anything to be acting the way she was.

'You have to find her, guard her. She's so young. Maybe she

hasn't been told. She's going to need protection, Jinx. What if the Magpies track her down anyway, or if Holly sends someone else? She will, you know. What if she tasks Osprey next? What if Brí gets involved? If you're tied to this girl, this Grigori with a divine spark … Jinx, if anything happens to her—' her voice sank to a harsh whisper '—it could kill you too.'

'If I'm lucky. It will draw down the wrath of the actual Grigori, perhaps even worse than that. We have to stop Holly.'

'I'll talk to Holly.' If Holly would listen to anyone it would be Silver. Many Sídhe thought Silver should have stood in Holly's place by now. Her power was enough and she was beloved by all. She might be able to work out some sort of accommodation. Diplomacy was Silver's strength.

'Are you sure?'

'Yes. If Izzy is in such pain now that you can feel it, she needs you. Go to her and guard her. Keep her safe. That's what Cú Sídhe were created for.'

He got to his feet, but the sickened feeling clung to him like a stench. 'We were made to hunt, to kill.'

Silver shook her head and her smile was tinged with heartbreak. 'No. That's what was made of you. What Holly wants you to be. But you weren't meant to kill. The Cú Sídhe are born to protect, to be guardians. Now go reclaim that.'

On the night before her sixteenth birthday Izzy had

dreamed of a fish, leaping from the water of a fast-flowing river, swimming against the tide, determined, in spite of every bit of logic the world around it dictated, to make it upstream. A salmon. The Salmon of Knowledge who had eaten the Nine Sacred Hazelnuts which fell into Connla's well. When she was a kid Dad used to tell her the story so she knew it at once.

The next morning he gave her a necklace, a silver salmon in Celtic knotwork, and made some crack about it helping her through her exams. A charm to help her in her impossible task, he'd called it with a smile.

Exams seemed so very far away right now. Something that belonged in a normal life, where everything ticked over from one day to the next. Like the life she used to have.

The cold efficiency of the hospital moved like a machine around Izzy. She sat in comfortless chairs and waited. Time advanced strangely, in fits and starts, dragging out minutes like the drip of golden syrup or letting hours race by like water through her fingers.

It was late morning. The sunlight told her that. Mum hadn't even asked again where she had been. She was too distraught. Neither had the cops, which was another relief. Izzy fell asleep in the car and woke with a taste in her mouth as if something had died in there.

The thought made her cry, but she did it in silence, for fear of setting Mum off again.

The hospital wasn't far from home, small and compact, an

old-style hospital rather than one of the new modern ones like cities in their own right. A country hospital, swallowed up by the edges of the ever-expanding city.

A nurse brought her a cup of tea at some point. Izzy drank half of it, but the rest went cold when she wasn't paying attention.

She waited until nine to ring work from the payphone in the corridor, but there was no answer so she rang Marianne instead.

Dylan answered.

'It's me.' Her voice shook like a reed in the wind.

'Izzy? You okay? Last night was—'

'Forget about last night.' Her voice threatened to betray her entirely. She managed, just in time, to get it under control. It still shook. 'Dad was in an accident. He's ... he's in the hospital.'

There was a moment of shocked silence. 'Shit, I'm sorry. Izzy, I— is there anything I can do?' His voice was a rush of empathy, her friend. It made her eyes sting, her throat tighten as if in a noose.

'I've got a shift in the coffee shop and I couldn't get hold of them. Could Marianne cover for me?'

'I'll go get her. Hang on.' He hesitated though, not leaving the phone line. 'Izzy, are *you* okay?'

'I guess. I— I don't know. Can you ask Mari? Or get her to call in for me? Or something?'

'No problem. Don't worry. We'll sort it out. I hope— I hope he's okay. Give your mum my best ...' He trailed off with the awkwardness of someone who had no idea what to say. 'Izzy, I ...'

'I know. I'll talk to you later. Promise.' Her voice came out strangely high, strangled. She hung up before she started to cry again.

Sometimes Mum stayed with her, talking on her phone, sometimes she paced the corridor outside or talked in hushed, urgent tones with the doctors. Izzy wished she had her mobile. She wished she'd never gone out yesterday − was it only yesterday? − wished she'd never seen the wonders and horrors only to come back to this.

'How are you doing?'

A woman hunkered down in front of her. Late afternoon sun slanted through the blinds. When had it got so late? Time twisted around them, impossible to follow. Her face was strangely delicate for one so old. Not that she looked old, not really. Mum's age, perhaps. But her eyes were the soft blue-grey of rainclouds, and they looked ancient. Her skin was smooth and wrinkle free, so pale, like fine porcelain. Her hair, by stark contrast, was a bright, unnatural red.

'Um, okay. I guess.'

'Your mum's in with your dad now, Isabel. You can go in for a moment, if you like.'

'How is he? Is he okay?'

'He's sleeping just now.'

It was the way she said it that made Izzy frown. 'Sleeping? I'm not five.'

It was a stupid thing to say, thoughtless and bitter. But she didn't feel like being condescended to any more. She'd fought one monster, saved the life of another. Fire had danced, if only for a second or two, on the end of her fingertips.

And it was only after that her world had turned into this nightmare.

The woman gave her an odd, understanding smile.

'He's in a coma, dear. It's his body's way of giving him time to heal. Do you understand?'

Gratitude washed right through Izzy, taking the pain with it. 'Yes. And is he— Will he—?' Her voice threatened her as she tried to say it. All she could hear were the words she wanted to let spill out of her – words that begged, pleaded for him to be okay, for a miracle, for this to be just another nightmare like everything else seemed to be. Because it had to be. This time it had to be.

'Time will tell. Do you want to go in? Here.' The woman handed her a thin plastic cup half full of water. 'Why not bring him a drink? Help him get better. Talk to him. Offer him water from the cup.'

The plastic crinkled beneath Izzy's too-firm grip. It seemed like the most bizarre request ever. She followed the red-haired woman down the corridor to a private room. Mum sat there, sleeping gently, while on the bed lay the shell of a man.

Her father. Or what was left of him.

Mum didn't respond as Izzy entered. Her head was inclined to one side, her eyes closed and her chest rose and fell with the same gentle rhythm as the machines that quietly monitored Dad. Careful not to wake her, Izzy crept forwards, aware that the nurse hadn't followed her inside. She waited by the door, watching closely, too closely.

Izzy's hand shook, water slopping over the rim of the cup. She took her own shaky breath and forced herself to look at him.

If it wasn't for the machines, Dad would have just looked like he was asleep. She'd seen that often enough, on Sunday afternoons like this, stretched out on the sofa when they'd planned to watch a movie together. If it wasn't for the machines … But that was an awfully big 'if'. She'd never seen his face so blank. He was a man who smiled, who laughed even in his sleep, who rolled his eyes when Mum gave out. Now he was just … so still.

Izzy put down the cup on the cabinet beside him and took his hand. He didn't respond. His skin was cool to the touch, soft. Even his breath didn't alter.

'Dad?'

No response. No grin, no laugh. No Dad.

'Dad, I … I met a guy.' She frowned, trying to imagine a way to describe Jinx. She gave up. 'I don't think you'd approve.' But her own smile forced its way out at how formal that sounded. 'But I think you'd like him.' Shaking her head slowly, she settled his hand back down on the cover where it look comfortable. 'Did I mention he turns into a dog?' She almost giggled but then, too late, remembered the nurse.

She was still there, glaring at Izzy, her mouth a hard line.

Good, maybe she hadn't heard. That would be tough to explain.

The woman cleared her throat and Izzy remembered the cup, the water she'd been given to bring to him.

'Do you want a drink?' Izzy's voice came out as a hoarse whisper and she felt the air around her tighten. It was as if everything held its breath. Even Mum's stilled for that moment. The world teetered on the edge of something. Something incredible.

Izzy reached out for the cup, but as she did so something flitted across the corner of her vision. A shadow, a twist of black smoke, there but not there. Other.

The mark flared against her skin, like phosphorous burning into her. A cry of alarm filled her head, deafening her. Bewildered, Izzy cried out and knocked the water over with her flailing hand. The shadow rushed at her, vanishing under the bed, and Izzy staggered back, crushing the plastic under her feet with too loud a crack.

A terrible shriek filled the room, a scream that could not possibly be human, but neither was it natural. Izzy's head throbbed, her eardrums straining, her throat tightening. She whirled around and saw the nurse, screaming at her in despair.

Alarms went off on four different monitors. Izzy staggered back in horror as the nurse raced into the room, so fast she blurred. She moved like the Magpies had moved, faster than the eye.

Others followed, in slow motion when compared with her. Normal, natural, their faces white with concern but hard with determined professionalism. But the first one, the one with the cup of water, the one with the hair that was far too red, bore down on Izzy like some kind of monster.

'What did you do, you stupid girl? It's gone now, wasted! The moment's lost!'

'It wasn't my fault. I saw—'

What? Something that wasn't there. Again. They'd lock her up.

'What the *hell*?' It was Mum's voice, Mum, rising like an avenging angel in the midst of the other nurses who didn't even notice her. 'Don't you *dare* talk to my daughter like that! Where's the consultant? Who's your superior?'

Izzy's stomach lurched and she put out her hand to balance herself, bringing it down in icy water, water that pooled on the cabinet top and dripped down the side to spread across the lino at her feet. She tried to grab a towel from the washbasin to mop it up and bumped into the bed, dislodging Dad so he slumped to one side.

Not this. Not Dad! She tried to grab him, to pull him upright, and that was when she saw it. With alarms blaring and everyone shouting, with Mum and the red-haired nurse screaming at each other like they had some ancient grudge, with the others trying to reset the monitors and calm the situation, Izzy saw the edge of a mark on the base of Dad's neck. Just for a moment, before someone else caught him, forcing

Izzy away so they could lift him and settle him into the nest of pillows. She saw it and knew it.

Dad had a mark on the back of his neck, at the base, above the spine. Exactly where hers was located. It was the same colour and although she only saw the tiniest part for a moment, she knew that the interior was filled with intricate lines of knotwork. And she knew its shape.

It was a Celtic cross, in every way the same as the one that now marked her.

CHAPTER TEN

Messages

The coffee shop was almost empty when Dylan got there. Marianne didn't look impressed. Tips had obviously been bad. When Dylan ordered an Americano she just glared at him.

'Any word from her?' he asked.

At that, Marianne's face softened. 'No. We chipped in, sent flowers to the hospital.'

Dylan tightened his jaw and closed his eyes in despair. 'It's like last night changed everything. From the moment we heard that music—'

She slammed a tray down on the counter a bit too hard. '*You* heard that music.'

He narrowed his eyes. 'You heard it, didn't you? I know you too well, Mari. You're my sister. If I heard it so did you. Why lie about it?'

She glanced around, checking that no one was close enough to overhear them. 'Because it's *weird*, that's why. And I don't want to be weird, Dylan. No one wants that except you. Now go away and shut up about it. I'm working.'

A couple came in to get take-away lattes and Dylan took his coffee to the uncomfortably stylish brown sofa by the window. He perched there, watching his sister nervously as she clattered around ungraciously behind the counter, refusing to even glance in his general direction. She'd heard it too. He knew she had. And if what Silver had said about blood making him special, well ... she was his sister after all. There was no one closer to him than that. She had to have heard it.

But she didn't want to be weird. So very Mari, denying the amazing to be one of the fine young things, to be cool, or even just to fit in.

Taking out his phone he checked for missed calls or messages, but the screen was stubbornly uninformative. Izzy hadn't called again.

He wished he'd handled her brief phone call a hell of a lot better than he had. But how did anyone handle something like that well? It wasn't possible. Weirdness he could do, but reality? That kind of reality sucked.

The little bell over the door jangled merrily and he looked up to see a girl in biker leathers come in, helmet under her arm, her hair in a single long braid that snaked down her back. It was jet black and glossy, odd in its perfection. She leaned on the counter. She might have been pretty – high, slanted cheekbones, narrow jawline – but with her flat dark eyes and too-small nose and mouth it was more like the face of a python.

'I'm looking for someone,' she said to Marianne, who appeared to be less than impressed. 'Isabel Gregory.'

Marianne faked a smile. 'I'm afraid she's not here today. Family matters. Can I help?'

The biker stretched her neck in a serpentine twist and Dylan winced as the cartilage cracked. 'I doubt it. When will she be back?'

'I'm not sure.' Dylan could tell his sister was trying to be polite – even Marianne cared about keeping her part-time job – but it was a close-run thing between that, impatience and immediate dislike. 'Maybe I could take a message?'

The biker leaned in and eyed her carefully. 'Yes. I could leave a message.'

The incipient threat in those words made Dylan's blood chill. He put down the coffee mug and started to get to his feet. None of this felt right. It was like last night in the club, like hearing the music, like meeting Silver. But that had been wonderful. It had stirred dreams and desires he'd never really let himself count on before. This didn't. This was ... wrong.

'Mari?' He took a step forward. Marianne's gaze flicked towards him and she smiled. Just for a second. A tight, impatient smile, but a smile nonetheless.

The door behind him opened again, the bell jangling fiercely, and a pair of small but incredibly strong hands grabbed him.

'Get down!' Silver yelled. 'Cover your ears.' She slammed her hands on either side of his head and pulled him down as the biker opened her mouth impossibly wide. A scream wrenched its way out of her, high and wavering, like nails raking down a blackboard. Dylan hit the floor hard, Silver on top of him, pinning him there.

Pressure surged inside his head, and in the air all around him. He couldn't draw breath. The sound went on and on, spiralling higher and higher, a deafening shriek.

With a crash, the windows shattered, raining glass down on them. The display case exploded, as did the glass door of the fridge. Cans of fizzy drinks sprayed their contents all over the shop.

And then all was silent.

The biker walked out again, her boots crunching on the debris. The alarm whimpered, trying to go off, a weak and pathetic broken thing.

Dylan sucked in a desperate breath as Silver released him, carefully standing up. He scrambled to his feet.

'What the *fuck* was that?'

'A banshee,' she groaned, taking out a handkerchief and wiping sweat from her face. 'Someone sent a bloody banshee. Holly, no doubt – most of them work for her.'

'And what were you doing here?'

'I was keeping an eye on you of course.'

'On me. Right.' He shook his head. 'Why?'

'I told you last night, you're special. You heard my music

and came to me.'

He almost laughed at the ridiculous nature of that state-ment. 'I'm special. You hear that, Mari?'

There was no answer. The adrenaline and relief faded away to sickening dread.

'Mari?'

He threw himself towards the counter.

His sister was sprawled on the ground behind it, glass scat-tered over her. Blood trickled from her ears and she lay far too still, eyes staring at the ceiling.

Jinx didn't know where to find Izzy, but his instincts did. He could feel her location, like a golden thread strung between them. He only had to veer off course and it was there, tugging him back onto her trail. He followed it now, trusting in the magic in a way he never had before. He didn't want to. The last thing he wanted was a bond such as this. It had destroyed his father, cost him his family, his life, everything. But what choice did he have?

Besides, if he followed it and found her, maybe Holly could free him of these bonds. Maybe. It had to be worth a try. That way everybody won.

Well, everyone except Izzy.

The air shivered over him like static as he stepped out of his Dubh Linn and into her Dublin. One world to another in a single step.

He stood on the verge of a dual carriageway, traffic roaring past him. He stepped back as the wave of exhaust fumes and chemicals almost swept him to his knees. It was too easy to forget, to fail to prepare. The human world – her world – he didn't belong here. None of his kind did. That was the deal made millennia ago, to cleave the world in half, half for his kind and half for hers. Who could have guessed that the human enchanters meant to trick every magic being into a shadow realm? They were cunning. More cunning by far if the truth be told, though he wanted to believe the propaganda his people put out. The fae were faster, stronger, more beautiful by far, wickedly clever ... and yet, they'd lost.

Minds like their own iron. Never underestimate them.

His father had said that, or at least that was how Jinx remembered it. Perhaps the last words he'd said to his son. There had been no goodbye, not from his father ... Jinx couldn't even remember his face. Just his words. The words were imprinted on Jinx's heart. Burnt there. Etched in acid.

The golden wire that tied him to Izzy burst right through it, overruling them and forcing him around, turning from the road so he faced instead the whitewashed front of a cottage hospital.

Another place of modern man and death – the two went hand in hand – a far cry from hedgerow healers and fairy doctors.

Shadows clung to the doorway, shadows that seethed and

curled around the corners. As Jinx watched, one of them detached itself from the others and slid inside the building.

Damnation. They were already waiting for her. Ahead of him.

Shades were not the brightest in any sense, but if someone needed following, if someone needed frightening, there was nothing so effective. Raised in the Halls of Hell itself, he'd heard it said, and then sent forth to do a demon's bidding.

The shades shuddered in alarm as he approached, or in warning, recognising his otherness. They knew he saw them then and readied themselves to attack.

'Well, now, who sent you here?' Jinx asked them idly. No need to ask why. They were all on the same page as to why.

A man in ruffled scrubs stepped out of the doorway, glaring at Jinx with eyes that lacked white or iris but were all pupil. Black as oil. All shade. It lodged inside him, filling him with shadows, a man no more. Possessed.

The shade curled his upper lip and reminded Jinx of the angels in the alleyway where he had first met Izzy. Shades weren't angels. And though demons made them, they weren't demons. They were, however, as supremely arrogant as either. Jinx sighed. He'd had enough of the other planes' interference in this matter.

'I'm here to help her,' Jinx said. It was ... not quite a lie.

The shade snorted out a laugh and the other shadows surrounding him echoed it. Their mimicry wasn't perfect through. The sound quickly devolved to a hiss.

'Of course you are, faeling. So are we. And we were here first, sent by our Master to guard the spark.'

'Like good dogs,' said another voice, one which chimed like a bell. It came from behind Jinx and he turned sharply, a curse on his lips. An angel, one of the pair from the alley no less. The blonder, paler one, the one that had even then seemed far more dangerous.

'Well, if they're dogs and I'm a dog,' Jinx said in as calm a voice as he could muster, 'what does that make you?'

It happened so fast he couldn't fight it. How could he fight what he couldn't see? An invisible force slammed into the bend of his knees, knocking him to the ground. It snatched the air from his lungs and left him helpless in an instant.

Fantastic, Jinx. Piss off both sides.

'I am Haniel,' the angel told him, anger never marring the melody of his voice. 'I seek my fallen kin. I seek her lost spark. You know this. And you know where it is, don't you?'

The shades hissed and surged forward, only the one possessing the doctor standing his ground. Teeth flashed in the shadows, eyes flared red, like hounds indeed, like creatures of nightmare.

And that was when Izzy ran out, tears silvering her face, her grief-stricken features freezing with shock when she caught sight of him and his predicament.

She skidded to a halt. Confused, terrified, her eyes wide and desperate.

'Jinx?'

'Run,' he tried to tell her, but the word just rasped between his clenched teeth like a stunted growl.

The shadows around the door stretched towards her, heedless of sunlight or obstacle, reaching for her, ready to seize her.

Haniel's hold on Jinx collapsed. 'You? It cannot be.'

'Izzy,' Jinx yelled, trying in vain to push himself up off the ground. He had to get her away from here, from them. 'Run. Now!'

The shades fell towards her, spilling over the ground, crooning in triumph. Haniel stretched out his hands and spoke a secret word.

Light erupted around them, blinding, bright as a supernova. In the midst of it, Jinx heard screams, one of them his own, and Izzy's hand closed on his, pulling him to his feet and into a sprint. How she saw, how she was still able to move, was a mystery, but one he didn't have time to question now. He risked a glance at her and saw her face, determined, her eyes hard as stones, fixed ahead as if the light didn't affect her at all. The look in them almost sent the panic welling inside of him out of control. They ran, and the urge to transform rose within him, almost overpowering. An instinct for survival, a need to protect. It burned beneath his skin, slicing through him like dull blades.

Izzy must have sensed something, a tightening in his grip perhaps, or a change in his skin against hers. She squeezed his hand, pulling him onwards.

'Stay with me,' she said, the words harsh on her laboured

breath, and in an instant she looked like herself again, her blue eyes wide with near panic. A trick of the light, that fearsome angelic light. It had to be. 'What were they? What's going on?'

'Shades found you first. I guess the angel followed them.'

'Angel?' The word was high and wavering, terrified, appalled. They dodged through the parked cars and headed for the more modern block on the south side, as far away from where Haniel and the shades were locked in combat. '*That* was an angel?'

'Yes.' Humans always thought that angels were peace-loving ambassadors of goodness. Having met more than his fair share, Jinx could never figure out why. Good PR, perhaps. He almost laughed, giddiness fuelled by hysteria. The best PR, he supposed. The highest authority. 'We need to hide. Need to find somewhere safe.'

'Safe,' she panted. 'Yes, safe is good.'

Safe, Jinx thought to himself, *is subjective*. She was following him. She'd follow him right to Holly, and Holly could set him free of her. He just had to get her there before anyone else found them.

He fixed his mind on the nearest opening to his world. Not near, unfortunately, not as near as the one that had brought him here, but to go that way meant retracing their steps and he wasn't keen to run into anyone back there or to try to skirt a battle that might end at any second. His body still ached from the touch of the angel's power.

It didn't matter. None of it mattered if he could get the girl to Holly and be rid of her. He couldn't afford to think about what might happen next. To either of them.

Pulling her to a halt beside a black Prius, Jinx pressed his hand against the handle. The metal made his skin crawl for a moment, but he pushed the sensation aside, accustomed to living with the metal in the modern world in a way his ancestors never were. If he couldn't shrug off the pollutants in the air or the metals all around him daily, he might as well go and live in the last remaining patches of trees in the middle of nowhere. Besides he lived with silver every day of his life, punching through his skin. If he could stand that, he could stand anything. He exerted a little energy to spring the locks, which opened with a satisfying clunk.

'What are you—?'

'Climb in,' he told her. 'We're getting out of here.'

'But you can't just—'

He couldn't? Of course he could. He was Sídhe. Thieves, charlatans, tricksters, every one.

'Watch me, Izzy. Now get in the car before someone sees.'

She jerked open the passenger door and slid inside, even as he slammed his own and jerked the seatbelt into place.

'What if we get caught?'

Jinx glanced pointedly the way they'd come. 'If you mean by the cops, they'd be the least of our worries. But we won't. They won't even see us. I promise. Put your belt on.'

She fumbled as she obeyed him, her hands shaking so hard she could barely do it. He felt a moment of sympathy for her, an urge to tell her it would be all right. In short, to lie. He didn't though. He was feeding her enough lies already.

Jinx shoved the car into gear and they sped off. He liked it, liked the way it handled, liked the feel of it around and under him. They pulled out onto the dual carriageway, heading for town and home.

He glanced at Izzy to say something, but then caught sight of her face, the pain and horror etched there, the silvering of tears, the redness of her eyes.

The flippancy left him. 'What happened?'

Izzy ground the heels of her hands against her eyes. 'I just … I …' Dragging in a juddering breath she struggled to bring herself under control. If she started hesitantly, in moments words flowed from her like a gushing wound. 'It's my dad. He was in an accident and he's in a coma. And there was this woman who said bring him water and I … I don't think she was a nurse. But I screwed it up and spilled it and she went mental. And she and Mum were fighting and all the alarms …' Her voice trailed off. A strange twist of sympathy wrung at his heart. He gazed at her. She was dangerous. She had no idea how dangerous. But right now all he wanted to do was make the pain and fear stop. He almost reached out to her, but when she spoke again, common sense slammed back into him. 'Jinx, my dad had the same mark on his neck. I never saw it before, but he has it.'

'The mark?'

'This mark.' She twisted around and jerked down the neck

of her top.

Jinx almost crashed the car. Locking his arms on the wheel, he brought it under his control once more. 'Cover that up!'

She glared at him, the Celtic cross hidden again. Her eyes flashed with anger. 'What is it? What the hell happened to me? I want an explanation, Jinx. I want answers. What is going on and how is my father tied up in it?'

Grigori … damn it. This wasn't just about her and the council wanting the angel's spark she held.

Her father and Izzy, someone – or something – was after them both.

CHAPTER ELEVEN

Balance

I zzy waited, watching Jinx fix his jaw and concentrate all his attention on the car. She shouldn't be here. She knew that. A voice seemed to whisper it over and over inside her head, a voice like a memory or an echo in the back of her mind. Shouldn't be with him. Shouldn't be in a stolen car. Should never have left Dad. Shouldn't have run off when Mum was arguing with that bitch. *'Should just do what you're told …'*

But she'd panicked, she'd been terrified, she'd needed to get away from them. And outside …

Outside she found Jinx, and demons, and an angel. And all that madness again.

I want answers.

She still did. She just wasn't entirely sure if she would like them when she heard them.

He turned off the main road, heading towards the coast instead. Killiney Hill jutted from the landscape and press of houses up ahead of them, a cluster of green topped with the brilliant white point of the Obelisk. 'Where are we going?' she asked.

'There,' Jinx grunted and nodded towards the hill. 'It's green, natural forest – as much as you get around here anyway – and there should be a gate there.'

'A gate?'

'A way to Sídhe-space, back to Dubh Linn along the Sídhe-ways. And even if there isn't, it's safer. If nothing else it'll help me think more clearly.' He said that like 'green' was something special – like air, food or water.

'There will be people everywhere. Do you know how many people walk their dogs up there? There's a freakin' children's playground. What if those ... those things come after us up there?'

People didn't walk their dogs at night though, or let their kids run through forests in the dark. And it was growing dark. How had it got so late?

Jinx didn't answer at first. His dark eyes hardened to stones. 'They will. You need to prepare for that. They don't stop once they have a trail. None of them. Neither the demonspawn nor the angels.'

Another angel. But she'd seen the look in his eyes, the murderous look, and witnessed the pain he'd caused Jinx.

'I thought angels were meant to be ... good.'

Jinx snorted and changed gear with some feeling. 'They think they are.'

'Well ... kind then. Gentle?'

'Do you know what angels are?'

'God's messengers?'

He laughed, a low unsettling chuckle. 'Well, yes. Sometimes they carry messages. But as you saw, those messages are usually along the lines of *'do as I say or else'*. Don't you understand yet?'

Izzy's temper bristled. 'You don't scare me.'

'Don't I?' he shook his head, like he was too grand to argue with her and for a moment she hated him for it. 'I should, Izzy. *Something* should.'

'So what are they then? Angels?'

He didn't answer for a few minutes. Izzy stared out of the window as quiet suburban houses flashed by them.

'Soldiers,' said Jinx at last. 'Soldiers in a war that never ends. Assassins. Hunters. Killers.'

He turned up the road leading to the car park and Izzy let the feel of the green world wash over her. She'd spent most of her childhood playing up here. As had most of the local kids. They still did, running through the trees, climbing the rocks and cliffs, swarming over the playground, dangling off the monkey bars, laughing, shouting.

She had never felt so old in her life.

Nor so *other*. She carried a spark, or so they all said. And that voice ... that distant, commanding voice in her head that she couldn't quite accept as real, but couldn't deny either. All those ... *things* ... that hunted her.

Jinx included, of course. Damn it, she had to remember that. He was as bad as all the others. So why did she want to trust him?

And how was she going to explain all this to Mum? She had run away twice in less than twenty-four hours, and now she was in a stolen car.

Being followed by creatures from heaven and hell. But if Jinx was always there too, always leaping to her rescue, whenever one of them had her cornered or lay in wait ... what did that make him?

'Not to be trusted.'

Yes, the voice probably had that right.

Izzy studied him with a dubious gaze. Jinx manoeuvred the stolen Prius into a parking space and turned off the engine. Silence settled over them both.

'Why my dad?' Izzy asked at length.

'I don't know.' Well, at least he didn't pause. His features tightened. 'But the mark on you came from him, not from any angel.'

From Dad? How on earth—

It was growing darker outside now. Izzy had no idea what time it was, but she'd lost a day in the hospital. A whole day ... And it was meant to be the fairies who altered time.

She gave Jinx another suspicious look, wondering if he had a part in that, and rubbed her aching head. 'What now?'

'Now ...' Jinx sighed. She wished he sounded more determined, more self-assured. But he didn't. A line formed between his eyebrows which crept down to shadow his silvery eyes. 'Now we try to find someone to answer your questions.'

'Why are you doing this? Any of this?' Her voice shook, but she pressed on, unable to stop now she had asked. 'What do you get out of it?'

He looked less human here, in the growing dark. Not that he was ever entirely human in appearance anyway. But here, now ... His eyes glittered, his bone structure was sharper, his skin so pale it was almost tinged with blue. His many piercings caught the last of the light, and the lines of the tattoos darkened.

Jinx swallowed hard, as if he knew she was watching him without having to look at her. Of course he did. What self-respecting fae wouldn't know when he ... when *it* ... was being watched.

'I get nothing. I get nothing at all.'

'*Liar.*' The voice was growing stronger. Each time it spoke her heart stuttered in protest. She couldn't ignore it anymore. It compelled her attention, no matter how much she wanted to pretend it wasn't real.

A lie? No. It didn't sound like a lie. His voice sounded dead, and helpless. Defeated.

'Nothing?'

'Yes. Nothing at all. I don't want to be here, Izzy, but if I don't keep you safe, if one of them takes you ... then my life won't be worth living. Holly doesn't care for failures.'

'Who is Holly?'

'You'll see.' She wished that sounded comforting, but it just sent chills right down her spine. 'We should go. We're sitting in stolen property, you know?'

'One more question, Jinx. Can she help me? Can she get the spark out of me?'

Izzy winced at the blaze of protest in her mind – it was sharp and sudden, a spike of anger. Spiced with something else too. Fear. *Don't ask that!*

Jinx looked up sharply, his eyes wide, his features stricken. She'd hit a nerve – with both him and the voice – that was for sure. He looked ... she couldn't quite define it. He looked like she'd asked him to kill for her.

No. Given what she'd seen him do, killing would be a small matter.

But death was a shadow in his eyes. Painful death. 'Yes.'

'Jinx? Would you lie to me?'

'You know I would.'

'Because of Holly?'

'Because I'm *fae*. None of us can be trusted unless we have a deal. Unless we are bound.'

'He is bound.'

Izzy shook it away, refusing to respond to the disembodied voice dogging her thoughts.

'I saved your life.'

He flung the door open and threw himself out of the car.

For a moment Izzy sat there, shocked by the brightness of the cabin light, by his abrupt departure. Then she fumbled with her own handle and scrambled out, following him across the car park and onto the grass.

'Jinx!'

He stopped at the sound of his name – a tall silhouette, little more than a shadow in the dark. Waiting, tense and angry. And defeated.

'I saved your life, didn't I?' He'd been dying with that iron-bladed knife embedded in his body. And she had pulled it out. Catching up with him, she grabbed both his arms and pulled him around to face her. He towered over her, much too big for her to fight, for her to control. But he didn't move, not to attack or flee. He just stood there, lost. 'You owe me, Jinx. You owe me for that.'

His shoulders stiffened, hard, hunched lines, and for a moment she thought he'd grab her, or hit her. But he didn't. He just stood there, his head bent over hers, his eyes closing over in pain.

Izzy pushed at his chest. She barely made an impact. His skin felt warm beneath the material of his shirt. Somehow, she couldn't pull her hand away. 'Say something.'

Jinx's upper lip drew back to reveal sharp white teeth, a silent snarl, and his eyes snapped open. 'What would you have me say? I owe you. Do you have any idea what that means for one such as me?'

'No.' The mark on her neck warmed and a wave of pain

hit her, his pain, a tumult of emotions, all his. Her abdomen tightened sharply. Something like desire.

But it couldn't be.

He was handsome, true. Beyond handsome. Beautiful in a way nothing human could be. And that was the rub.

Jinx wasn't human.

Before she knew what she was really doing, Izzy pushed herself up on her toes and planted a kiss firmly on his mouth. She kissed him and Jinx let her. Shock perhaps. Or horror. He certainly didn't return the gesture. He just stood there like a statue, hard and cold and she kissed his stony mouth until her heart petrified as well. Stone, like him.

A fire of embarrassment crept up her body, desire burned to ash by this humiliation. She released him and turned away so quickly that her stomach almost lurched back up her throat.

Jesus Christ, what had she done?

Jinx's hand closed on her shoulder, his touch tentative, so delicate she thought for a moment she could detect a hint of trembling in it.

'I owe you,' he whispered and his breath played against her hair, his touch remained on her shoulder, reluctant to let go. 'I do owe you. You saved my life. But Izzy ... I owe others as well. I am tied in so many ways. Over so many years. I couldn't hope to explain them all to you.'

'To Silver?' How she managed the words without bursting into tears, she didn't know.

'Yes. And to Holly. And to my people. I said the angels were soldiers in a war. So are the demons and their spawn, like the shades you saw at the hospital. And so am I. Albeit, a poor one.'

'You're … you're like angels?' He didn't seem very angelic at the moment.

'My people *were* angels, long ago. When the war came to heaven and angels rose up against angels, some of them didn't take a side. Some refused to fight, and when it was all over found themselves banished, tasked with an impossible burden, here on the horizontal plane, bound to the earth.'

'And my father and I? How are we involved in this?'

'Your father is …' He paused, uncertain. 'He's safe for now.'

She pivoted to face him as her anger surged again. 'He's in a coma.'

'Yes. And as such he isn't a threat.'

'And am I? A threat? Look at me.' She meant it to mean she couldn't possibly be; she was just a girl, a human.

To her further embarrassment, he really did look at her, a long, considering look that seemed to bore into her eyes and beyond. His gaze trailed down her body and left her longing to fidget or run from him, but she couldn't. The alien cast in his face was even more pronounced here in the darkness on the hillside.

'You are changed. I don't know if that makes you a threat or not. But others think you are. Shades and angels follow you. Holly wants you too, as does the Old Man.'

'Then what can I do? Help me, Jinx. Explain it to me.'

'Your name ... your father's name ...' He trailed off, his brow knotting.

'David Gregory?'

'*Grigori*. It's an old name, older than human time. It means "Watcher", and sometimes "Shepherd", one who keeps watch, who guards. It's a powerful name.'

'It's just a name, Jinx.'

He took her hand, his grip warm and comforting. She shouldn't find it so. She knew that, but her body was determined to make an idiot of her time and again when it came to Jinx.

Leading her with him, Jinx made his way across the grass to the path that sloped up into the trees. He spoke quietly as he did and she had to hurry to match his long strides if only to catch every word he said.

'No such thing as *"just a name"*. Names define us. They make us what we are. It's a vocation, a bloodline. You should have been dormant for years yet, until your father explained it all, until the time came for you to join him or take his place. But something happened and it triggered the power within you, changed you.'

'The angel? The spark?'

'Probably. The most likely explanation. The mark appeared on your skin, the mark which should protect you, the mark as old as ... But what happens when a Watcher is also the bearer of a divine spark?'

How would she know? She wanted to whip out some quick and cutting remark – something clever to cut him down and make her feel in control again – but her voice lodged in her throat. Dad had known? About all of this? And he'd never said a word. And why would he? She was just a girl, just a kid. Dad wouldn't have told her anything that might put her in danger.

'That woman at the hospital ... she was one of you, wasn't she?'

Jinx shook his head. 'I don't know. Maybe. Or maybe something worse.'

'Not human, I mean. She was not human.'

He shrugged. 'Everything's so black and white for you, isn't it? What's *human*?'

'Me, for one. Is she like me?'

Jinx laughed. He actually laughed. It wasn't a particularly joyful sound but it was a laugh nonetheless. 'Like you! Well, it would help if I had seen her. Or even knew who she might be. So perhaps she is like you and perhaps she's just a nurse who you pissed royally off. It's been known to happen, darling.' The last word dripped off his tongue, honey-coated and malevolent.

'Yeah, well, you'd know all about pissing people off, you arrogant git,' she muttered, stumbling along behind him. The trees leaned in close over the path but as they rounded the bend, Jinx stepped off the tarmac too, into the woods themselves, into the deep darkness.

The world fell away to whispers and shadows. Izzy didn't want to say another word for fear of what she might disturb.

Because if he was right, there would be Sídhe here as well. And other things.

God only knew what.

Izzy held on to Jinx's hand, grateful for the contact. He might be only doing it to help her keep up with him, or even to keep her on her feet, but that didn't matter. It made her think of Dad, the one man she knew she could rely on, the one man she really could trust.

She remembered sitting in the long grass bathed in blazing sunlight, looking up at the High Cross of Clonmacnoise. Last summer, one of the good days, one of the best. She didn't have a job and could mooch around the country with him, visiting jobs in progress, travelling to meetings for new ones. Of course, she didn't attend the meetings. She'd find a coffee shop and wait, sit in the car and read or whatever. But afterwards, when he'd finished they'd head off, just the two of them, and explore. It was their very own adventure.

They bought sandwiches from the little café and cans that dripped moisture down the sides and made their hands cold and wet. They'd laughed as they'd shared crisps. She'd felt both very young and an adult at the same time.

And they'd looked at the cross.

'It's all about balance,' Dad said.

'Balance.' She squinted at the worn-down carvings on the stone. This was a replica. They'd seen the real one in one of the round rooms of the visitors' centre. But the weather and modern pollution had conspired to make this one look even older.

'Balance in everything. Look at it.' He pointed up. On top of the main column, depicting half-recognisable scenes from the Bible, the cross dominated the entire area. A circle, cut into four quadrants by the cross shape. In the centre was a figure, his arms reaching out to each side, head and feet touching top and bottom. There were other things there, just within his reach, above and below, on either side.

'Heaven and hell,' Dad pointed to the top and bottom. They did look a bit angelic and demonic, Izzy thought, if you narrowed your eyes so you could barely see. 'Humans,' he pointed to the right.

'And what? Fairies?' She meant it as a joke, but her laughter died in her throat when he glanced at her. A flat, unamused glance. The kind she never normally saw from him.

'Maybe. Who knows? There are more things in heaven and earth ...'

'Oh, no, not *Hamlet*! You're not allowed to torture me with *Hamlet*.'

That made him smile. 'The supernatural then, how about that?'

'Fine, Dad,' she groaned and then drained the last of her coke. 'So where are we in this grand scheme of yours?'

He grinned at her, like a big kid with a secret to tell.

'That's us in the middle, of course. Keeping it all together. Watching over the world. You and me, kiddo.'

'Yeah.' She lay back in the grass and closed her eyes. 'That's us. Fundamental to the universe.'

'Maybe,' he whispered fondly. 'Keystones.'

She cracked open one eye. He watched over her, with a funny expression on his face. He looked so out of place here, in his suit and crisp white shirt when all the tourists wore t-shirts and shorts. Like he never stopped working. 'Not everything is about architecture, Dad.'

'Of course it is. Balance. Harmony. Equal and opposite reactions.'

She pushed herself up on her elbows. 'Like what?'

He closed his eyes this time, tilted his face up so the sunlight covered it. So strong, so finely carved a face. She had his eyes, and something of his nose. Where her red hair and pale complexion had come from, she didn't have a clue. Poor Mum didn't get a look in at all.

'Sometimes we do things we think are for the best and terrible things happen. Sometimes ...'

'What terrible things have you done?' She asked in jest, but suddenly it seemed a dreadfully serious question. A deep silence fell over them both as if the world was determined to listen in on their conversation.

'Some pretty terrible things,' he sighed, still not looking at her. 'I've made my share of mistakes. A long time ago. Everyone does. But now I have you and your mum.' His eyes opened, sharply focused on her, intense and filled with an emotion she didn't know. It was fierce and a little frightening. 'Good things can come out of bad. Equal and opposite.

Balance. Look at you.' For a moment neither of them moved. Then he laughed and the spell broke. 'You've got crumbs all down your top.'

Izzy still remembered it, so clearly. He'd been about to tell her something. Something important. And then, she was certain, he had chickened out. But he had tried. And somehow he'd known about the fae, about this world she now found herself stumbling in and out of. 'The supernatural' he'd called it.

And he'd told her that they stood in the centre of it all. *Watching over the world. You and me, kiddo.*

Not anymore. Now there was just her and Jinx. A creature, a monster. One of those things Dad mentioned that he should never have known about.

They climbed up the rough path, and into a clearing where the trees opened out. By day it might be covered in flowers, but all she could see at the moment were dark masses that could be bushes and a tangle of shadows underfoot. All along one side, a wall rose out of the undergrowth, a wall built with spaces for doors and windows. But it was not a building. There was nothing on the far side. The hillside had once been part of an estate and the owner had carried out a series of works up here, ostensibly to help the poor learn trades during the famine. But the things they built were ... strange. Like this, a wall to a building that didn't exist. Elsewhere there were coffin-like structures, sarcophagi for giants. Not to mention the Obelisk itself, a white building right on top of the hill like a witch's hat and a smaller one a little further off marked with the owner's name.

And the Wishing Stone. It had come later apparently, though no one knew for sure. 1852 or something carved into the top stone on a step pyramid overlooking the sea. She'd heard stories – wild stories, of devils, black dogs and monsters, of a battle on the hilltop and fire that walked like a human. Old stories, like the Dalkey Gold Rush when the seaside town went mad, digging all over the hill until ghosts and demons drove them off. Stories that everyone laughed at now. Izzy shook her head. Why not? It suddenly seemed no stranger than anything else in the world, in *her* world anyway.

In this new world anything was possible. And that seemed both a blessing and a curse. With a fierce yearning, she wished for normality again, wished for the world where she didn't have to think such thoughts. It had been so much simpler. And she'd thrown it all away with one wrong turn.

Jinx stopped, pulling her out of her thoughts, his body stiffening. He lifted his head, scenting something on the air. They stood on the edge of another path, one that was not man made, but worn into the stone of the hill.

'Let go,' he whispered.

Izzy released his hand and watched as he slid into his hound form, a pained expression flickering over his face. For a moment he just stood still, then shook from head to tail, as if he was drying himself, or ridding himself of the last vestiges of his almost-human form.

Jinx lifted his head to the night's sky and howled.

And from the shadows amid the trees there came an answer.

CHAPTER TWELVE

Hounds in the Night

They glided through the night, black as the shadows that disgorged them. Not shades, thank the ancestors. They were like him, or almost like him. Close enough as damn it anyway. Not actually black, but a deep green just a touch away from it, the perfect camouflage for the forest at night.

Cú Sídhe.

Whatever Jinx had expected, it had not been that.

Their scents filled his nostrils – a thousand extra bits of information that his eyes would never have picked up – a pack, a community, male and female together, strong, eager to hunt and determined to protect.

So familiar.

The nearest male crept forward, hackles raised, asserting territory and mating rights, warning Jinx away as only one of the Cú Sídhe could. Anyone else would have fled like a cur.

Damn, he'd been away from his own kind for far too long.

Izzy's fear drenched his nose. She moved closer, trying so hard not to show it, unaware that the others could smell it from her as clearly as he could. And that scenting it, they would see her as prey.

And prey was to be hunted.

The need to protect her shivered across his skin.

'Don't run, Izzy. Whatever you do, don't run.'

Her hand reached for his shoulder, fingers burrowing into his fur. Comfort, strength. Had she heard him? No, that was impossible. But somehow, she knew anyway.

'What do you want here? This is our domain. You don't belong.' The nearest male lifted his upper lip in a half-snarl and all Jinx could do was lower his head. The hound was right. He accepted that. The diplomacy of Cú Sídhe was pretty basic.

And hopelessly elaborate if you didn't know what you were doing.

'We seek safe passage, that is all. We don't mean to trespass.'

A female approached from the right, haughty this one, proud. Their commander. *'Who are you? Identify yourself. What kith? What kin?'*

It was a traditional challenge and all the identification anyone needed as far as Cú Sídhe were concerned. Kin, he couldn't give them, his blood, his history, his parentage – they'd never understand or accept such a tangle of deceit. But his kith – his loyalty and sworn obedience – on the surface, that was easy enough.

'*I'm Holly's kith. My name is Jinx.*'

A murmur ran through the pack, an unsettling sound. Jinx didn't like it. Didn't like the sound of it at all. Surprise. And suspicion. No. This could not be good.

'*Jinx by Jasper?*'

The shock of it made his fur bristle. *Jasper?* It was a name he had not heard in a lifetime. Since childhood in fact. Holly had forbidden all references to it. The name he had thought forgotten.

'*How do you know that?*'

A long howl went up from one of the pack still hidden, followed by another. Jinx edged back, bumping Izzy's legs. Anyone else would have panicked and run by now. And she wanted to, he could tell by her scent, but she didn't. Her fingers tightened against the skin beneath his fur.

'What is it?' she asked. 'What's wrong?'

He growled, unable to answer her. He brought up his hackles and squared his shoulders, making himself as large and aggressive as possible. Whoever this pack was, they weren't taking him. And they weren't taking Izzy either. Not while he breathed.

'*Stand down, Jinx by Jasper,*' the female warned. Her voice rippled with power. But she had no power over him, not with Holly's wards wrapped around and through him. '*Blight, stand down. We mean no harm. Talk to us, Jinx. How did you come here?*'

She shifted, one minute hound and the next woman. Izzy

gave a small whimper of alarm, but the female didn't seem to notice.

It must look so strange to the girl, he thought, raised on a diet of werewolf horror stories. None of which were any preparation for what she now saw.

Naked and beautiful, the female approached them, her subtle markings almost iridescent on her deeply tanned skin. Not like his tattoos. Hers were natural; his were not. His had been designed to bind the powers of the Cú Sídhe. No such taint marred her skin. She was sublimely beautiful, the epitome of what a female of his kind should be.

'I'm Blythe,' she said. 'And these are my kindred. Blight, my twin, Freesia, Gun and—'

'I don't know what the problem is,' said Izzy quickly, 'but I'm sure—'

Blythe glared at her, eyes flashing with the metallic stain of magic. Fae and non-human through and through. But she did nothing. She didn't even attempt a glamour. 'I wasn't talking to you.'

Jinx slid back to human form, as heedless of his nakedness as Blythe. Izzy snapped her hand away from his skin and stumbled in a vague attempt at retreat. One of the other Cú Sídhe moved in behind her, growling softly – not actually a threat, not really, just a warning to a child – and she stopped her retreat.

'Jinx ...' she whispered.

'Stay still,' he replied curtly. 'Don't run.'

'She isn't going to run.' Blythe almost purred the words. 'She wouldn't be so silly. But what brings you both here? And *what* is she?'

'She's no one. Just a mortal.'

He said it too quickly, too earnestly. He knew it as soon as he saw Blythe's gaze fix on Izzy. Fascinated. Almost hungry.

'I see,' the female Cú Sídhe said and smiled slowly. 'Well, then, you two had better come with us. I afford you safe conduct until our kith leader says otherwise. I can promise no more, Jinx by Jasper.'

Jinx inclined his head in acceptance and with a series of yaps and snarls the other Cú Sídhe fell back. Only Blythe remained, watching as he gathered his clothes. When he struggled into them, a smiled played across her perfectly formed mouth.

'Interesting,' she murmured and strode away, naked in the night.

What a bitch, Izzy thought.

'*Quite literally*,' that newly active and all too rational voice in her brain supplied unprompted. Izzy didn't want rational right now. She was too scared and angry.

Story of my life since I met him. She wasn't expecting a reply, but she should have. Of course she should have.

'*Then maybe you shouldn't trust him so readily.*'

Izzy missed her footing as it commandeered her thoughts

for a moment. The urge to just let it, to do as it said, was like a dull toothache, wearing her down. She pushed it away again, refusing to acknowledge it, refusing to believe it was real.

Jinx glanced at her, though he showed not a glimmer of concern. Oh, yes, that would be far too much to expect.

She cursed herself and her imagination as she followed him through the trees, the other Cú Sídhe herding them like sheepdogs. This was wrong. On so many levels. But Blythe ... God, the way she looked at Jinx, the dismissive way she hardly glanced at Izzy herself. How could she fail to be angry?

'You're jealous. You're afraid and now you're jealous. It's perfectly reasonable.'

Go away! The thought roared out in her head, her own thought, *Shut up and go away!*

Izzy tripped on nothing and nearly went down. She had to face the fact that sometimes it *wasn't* her voice she was hearing; since the night when the shadows had moved, the other voice in her head had been growing stronger all the time. It wasn't her voice at all. Too musical. Too melodic. Alien to her mind.

Oh God, now I'm going mad? Now? After everything so far?

She tried to focus on the creatures surrounding them, the hounds. The area was rife with black dog legends, she knew that much. So this could be the origin, these fae creatures up here on the hill. Another part of a world she knew nothing of until now. Another aspect to it that terrified her. One of the Cú Sídhe brushed against her leg, a mass of warmth and muscle, and she shied away, bumping into Jinx.

'What's wrong?' he asked, none too kindly. Like she was an irritant, a pain in the ass brat he had to look after.

'Nothing. I just ... I thought I heard something.'

'Focus. Don't let anything lure you off the path.'

She looked around, half expecting to see the bobbing lights of a will-o'-the-wisp or hear the cry of a banshee tearing through the silent sentinels of the trees.

'I'm not a child, Jinx.' The words were out before she could stop them. Snappish, petulant, asking for a slapdown.

Instead, he took her hand in his, enfolding her freezing fingers in the warmth of his. He squeezed ever so gently. He didn't say anything though, just pulled her along beside him.

'Listen to me,' said the voice in her mind that couldn't be her own. *'You can't trust them. None of them. They're little more than animals. Listen to me, Isabel.'*

Well, why shouldn't she? Why not listen to the disembodied voice in her head?

Because that was never the safest option, was it? Even if it made as much sense as anything else right now.

Remember normal? she thought to herself, wishing she could have it back. *Remember what that was like?*

Once again Izzy wished she'd stayed home last night, wished she'd never gone into town in the first place the previous day. Wished, and wished, and *wished* ...

By the time they reached the top of the hill, stepping from

the forest walk past two flat-topped stone structures, she was almost dead on her feet, moving like a zombie with her bleary eyes half-closed and her body aching right through to the bones.

Blythe didn't hesitate, leading them on, with the Wishing Stone on the left and the Obelisk on the right. As they reached the foot of the Obelisk's mound, she turned towards the sea, following a path through the gorse and stepping out onto a flat area of granite. Cliffs dropped away from dizzying heights, only a few yards ahead.

The wind whipped at their clothes and hair, a cold wind coming straight in off the sea. Blythe walked to the southern end of the flat granite where an iron ring with the remains of a massive chain and a bolt had been driven into the rock. Red with rust, they still looked formidable. Blythe knelt between them, pressed her hand to the surface and with an agonising groan the stone split open to reveal a narrow passage leading down. Darker than the night around them. Darker than anything Izzy had ever seen.

One of the native Cú Sídhe gave a sharp yap, followed by a growl. Blythe turned to stare back towards the forest, her eyes just slivers of grey.

'Hurry up. Inside.'

'What's happening?' Jinx asked, his body tensing.

'Can't you smell it? We have visitors.'

His hand tightened on Izzy's, not so comforting now. Almost painful. 'Demons?'

'From the stench, yes, or shades anyway. Did they follow you? Inside.'

'Wait,' Izzy protested. It was futile. Jinx was too strong. She was surrounded by Cú Sídhe. But she didn't want to go in there. Not into the dark. Not like this. Every instinct she possessed told her not to. Every single atom that formed her. 'Please.'

She wished ... *Wished, and wished, and wished ...*

'*I remember,*' said the voice. '*I remember this place.*'

And suddenly she saw it, as if old film was playing before her, projected onto the air itself.

Monsters indeed, and a fire that walked like a woman ... the Cú Sídhe attacking at all sides while men armed with pikes and cudgels tried to drive them back inside the doorway. The iron sank into the stone and the hill rocked in rage and impotent defiance.

A shadow fell over the land. Night walked, cloaked in shadows. Mankind tore stone from the hillside, and for a while it seemed that the madness fell on them all as they dug for treasure that wasn't there.

Until the chain broke. Until the monsters escaped and brought ... sanity?

Izzy turned sharply. She could only see the top of the Wishing Stone from here. A hunger deep inside her called to it, longed for it. A fire. She almost started back towards it, but Jinx's hand stopped her. He stared into her face, searching for something. She didn't know what. But there was something horrified in the look he gave her.

'Are you okay?' He said the words too clearly, as if talking to an imbecile.

At a nod from Blythe, two of the Cú Sídhe backtracked along their path, passing into the shadows and out of sight. 'They'll buy us precious minutes, but we've got to move. Jinx, now! Bring her or leave her.'

Before Izzy could protest again, Jinx scooped her up in his arms. She struggled, but he quelled her efforts without any trouble. 'Hush,' he whispered. 'Hush, you'll hurt yourself.'

'Please, don't.' The cramped darkness rushed up to swallow Izzy and her voice rose, her heart hammering away inside her. She couldn't go in there. Not into the dark, into such an enclosed place. She needed to go to the stone. She needed ... needed to climb it, to use it, to make it open a way ...

'I remember,' said the voice. *'This place. I know this place. I need to be here.'*

This wasn't her. Somewhere, logically, she knew it wasn't her. Couldn't be. This need, irrational, overwhelming, but she only wanted to tear herself out of his arms, to throw him off the cliff if necessary and get to the stone. She had to get to the stone! The mark on her neck burned like molten metal, like acid in her skin. Warning her. Such a warning.

'Something's ... happening to me.' She had to force the words out. She was losing control of her body. Whatever it was sweeping through her, demanding that she go to the stone, and she couldn't fight it. She was fading, burned away by the frenzy inside.

'Close your eyes,' Jinx told her, his voice rumbling through his body and into hers. 'I've got you.' She clamped her arms around his neck, sucked in a breath to keep from screaming, clenching her teeth to keep from sinking them into his flesh. Jinx tightened his hold on her and stepped into the opening. As Blythe followed, it snapped shut behind them.

Izzy dug her fingernails into Jinx's skin, right through the shirt. She pressed her eyelids together, until sparks of white light danced before her.

'It's all right, Izzy,' Jinx whispered. 'I'm here. You're okay.'

Then the darkness took her consciousness as well.

CHAPTER THIRTEEN

Voices

Jinx carried Izzy's limp body through the dark passageway leading to Blythe's hollow in the hill. So afraid, so very afraid. He'd barely known what to do with her. That she passed out was a blessed release for both of them.

Had it been a spell of some kind? A curse or enchantment to keep her out of Sídhe-space? But she'd had no such problem in Silver's hollow. No. This was different. Not something to keep her out, but something else, designed to compel her, to control her. Something within. As if the spark had more sentience than he'd given it credit for and sought ... what? To influence her? It certainly didn't have the scent of fae magic. It clung to her, but also came from her. Something other. The look in her eyes – that flat, cold stare – had returned and he had barely known her.

And in her eyes, in the predatory gaze, something was

changing. Like a growing fire, a wave in the air, a glow rising along the horizon heralding the breaking of dawn. Not the spark. It was far more than the spark. He couldn't identify it and that made him very nervous indeed.

What had his option been, though? Stay behind and face demons while trying to control her ravings? Besides, Blythe and her kin had hardly given them an option. They were not guests here, no matter how civilly the Cú Sídhe pack were prepared to treat them for now.

But she had been so scared. He had felt it inside him as well. Terror. Fear of confined spaces, of darkness beneath the ground, of being shut away. Fear so great that she passed out rather than face it. But even her fear didn't quite feel like her own fear.

Her breath played on his neck, soft and regular, a delicate caress.

Jinx drove the thought from his mind with brute force. He couldn't even consider that. Her kiss had been an invitation and only shock had stopped him returning it. But he couldn't. Not now, not ever. She was Grigori, of a bloodline that stretched back – well, forever! And she carried a spark. A divine spark that was already changing her. He didn't entirely know what that made her.

Aside from untouchable.

As if she sensed his thoughts, Blythe glanced at him. 'Who is she?'

He almost barked out his answer. 'No one. Just a girl.'

Blythe gave a soft chuckle which spoke volumes about disbelief. 'Few people react so strongly to our wards. And she didn't look right, up there. It was like she was fighting off some sort of enchantment. Is she possessed? What are you doing with a human?'

'Nothing.'

'Nothing.' She twisted the word with amusement. 'I've seen people look at one another that way before and it's usually far from *nothing.*'

'Shouldn't you be worrying about your pack-mates out there, fighting demons?'

She shook her head, her silky black hair shimmering as it moved across her naked shoulders. Her scent was intoxicating and she was beautiful. It had been so long since he'd seen one of his own kind, let alone a female.

So why could he only think of the girl in his arms now?

Blythe watched him with far too knowing eyes. 'You may be young, but you're old enough to know the fae motto when it comes to humans, Jinx – *fell it, feed on it or fuck it.* Which is she to be?'

'Leave be, Blythe. It's none of your business.'

'You're here, trespassing on land I protect. That makes it my business. And the business of my matriarch. She's not going to ask so kindly.'

'And who might she be?'

'Oh, surely you know her. Her name is Brí.'

She could have had the same effect by dousing him in cold

water. Brí? He was in *Brí's* domain?

Jinx stopped in his tracks, pulled Izzy close against him. The urge to slide to hound form and run reached up in a stranglehold, crushing the breath from his lungs. He couldn't. It would mean leaving Izzy. But of all places to end up, of all people whose homes he could have stumbled into ... Brí? Fate wouldn't be that cruel.

Blythe turned to face him, her face harder, more calculating than before. 'Now what are you thinking? There's nowhere to go, Jinx by Jasper. You came from this hollow, from this pack. Whether you claim us or not, we recognise you. And she already knows you're here. Besides—' her eyes trailed down to Izzy, disdain and disbelief warring in their depths, '—she has a vested interest in your little human charge.' Her smile was cold, never rising beyond the corner of her perfect lips. 'Run and you'll have to leave her. You can't carry her in hound form. And you won't leave her. Will you?' Blythe laughed, a sound which did nothing to comfort him. 'Well, if you aren't going to cooperate ...'

She snapped her fingers and the Cú Sídhe of her pack materialised out of the shadows behind them. Jinx was seized from behind and Izzy taken from him. Freed of her, he twisted around, ready to fight, ready to pull her from them, when something hard and heavy came down on the back of his head and he sank to his knees.

The shadows of Brí's hollow danced with coloured lights and laughter. He slid to the cold stone floor and knew no more.

Izzy woke to darkness, unsure of where she was or how she'd got there, and almost fell off the low divan on which she lay. She cursed to herself and sat very still on the edge. She could make out only a little of the room, but a light came from under the door and gradually her eyes adjusted to it.

She got up and stumbled across the room until she found the door. With a shaking hand she tried the handle. When it didn't work, she rattled it.

'Hello?'

No answer. Of course there was no answer. Why had she dreamed there would be a freaking answer?

'Jinx? Hello?'

Nothing from him either.

She let out a long breath and tried to force her racing heart to a calmer rhythm. The last thing she remembered was the rock opening, Jinx picking her up and carrying her towards it. Into the dark. Then nothing. Frightening dreams, horrific images, and the overwhelming need to reach the Wishing Stone. It didn't make sense.

Then again, nothing made sense any more. So nothing new there.

Izzy swallowed painfully on a dry mouth. The room was bigger than the tunnel, but she was still shut inside. In the dark. The walls felt smooth, like polished metal.

'Hello? Somebody? Hey, you can't keep me in here. Let me out or I'm calling the cops.' If she had a phone. One that worked underground. As if she wouldn't have done that right away.

'Stay calm. You are quite safe.'

And right on cue, she was hallucinating again. That voice in her head, fan-*bloody*-tastic. Never a good sign. With a strangled cry of frustration, she kicked the door so hard it rattled and her foot began to throb with pain.

'You're going to harm yourself,' said the voice, with obvious concern.

'Who the hell are you and why do you care?'

'I care because I always care. Angels care, Isabel. Despite what Jinx believes.'

An angel? Oh, that was all she needed. And why not? Why should the angel get left out? It was only her mind. 'You're the one who fell, aren't you? Who left the graffiti angel and the spark.'

'I am.'

Izzy sank onto the narrow divan. 'This is all your fault then. Why me? Why involve me?' Her hand touched material, a rich velvet, fold upon fold of it neatly positioned at the edge. She pushed it off because it was about the only thing she could control anymore.

There was a long pause. Trying to figure out an answer no doubt. One that might make sense, hopefully, although she sincerely doubted it.

'You were the one. I sensed you nearby and knew you would come. And my enemies were closing in on me.'

'Demons?' Even in the warm stillness of the room, she shivered. 'There are demons?'

'Yes, you saw one of them. And his shades. They followed you home. They were outside your house. I sent them away.'

Of course you did, Izzy thought and then wondered if an imaginary angel had a sarcasm detector.

'Can you get me out of here?'

There was a moment's pause. Then a sigh. She felt it run through her body as if it was her own. The angel spoke again. *'No. I have grown weak. Like the spark, I am melting into you. Soon we will be part of you and I will be no more. It has been hard to even communicate with you.'*

For a moment Izzy almost felt sorry for her. But sitting in the dark, lost in a nightmare, sympathy only went so far.

The angel didn't sound upset, just despondent. They weren't the same thing. Well, boo-hoo. It wasn't as if she'd given Izzy any choice in it either. 'Do you have a name?'

'No longer. I gave it up to fall.'

'How did you fall?' That was serious, right? Falling. That was like being expelled for sin. It had to mean something really bad.

'I lost someone, long ago. Someone I loved. I … I made a mistake.'

A mistake. Right. Izzy knew all about mistakes. Mistakes had got her here, locked in a room in the dark. Underground. Alone. Or rather not alone, but talking to the fairly useless and rather pathetic angel lodged inside her head. A whole series of mistakes. Starting with going into that alley to look at a bit of graffiti in the first place.

Dad had mentioned mistakes too. Mistakes of long ago. Like not telling her everything when he still had the chance, she supposed. But thinking of Dad, especially thinking of him in anger, didn't help. It left a hollow ache that gnawed at her heart.

'*Don't blame him, Isabel,*' the angel whispered and deep inside her something warmed, comforting and calming.

'I don't. Not really.' She only whispered the admission. It wasn't the type of thing she could say out loud. How could she blame Dad when she could lose him at any second? But the angel, at least, seemed to understand that. Even if Izzy didn't.

She didn't hear footsteps in the passage outside, but the lock turned and the next thing she knew, the door was open, spilling light into the room, illuminating the figure of Blythe. Light bounced off the polished bronze that lined the walls. This wasn't the cell Izzy had taken it for, or at least if it was, it was a comfortable one. More like a waiting room. The divan, a soft chair, even a fireplace, though it was cold and empty. A table in front of it even had some food and wine. Her stomach rumbled loudly at the thought that it had been there all this time and she hadn't known.

Not that she would have touched it. She wasn't a fool, even if she was starving. If she was away with the fairies, she wasn't going to be taking their food and wine so they could keep her there. She remembered that much from the stories Gran used to tell her.

'Good, you're awake. Talking to yourself?'

Izzy ignored the jibe. 'Where's Jinx?'

Blythe just raised her eyebrows. 'He's safe and sound for now. Don't you worry about him. You didn't eat?'

'Bit hard when you can't see it.'

Blythe frowned at her and then gave a groan of dawning realisation. 'Oh, of course. Human eyes.' But instead of getting a lamp or something she just shrugged, 'You should be getting dressed. You have an audience with the matriarch, girl. She's very interested in you.'

Bristling again, Izzy pushed her irritation away. If Blythe was trying to get her to lose her temper, she had a long way to go to reach the Mari-standard of pointed remarks. 'Getting dressed in what?'

'That would be the dress, duh,' said the Cú Sídhe. How could she look like something out of a medieval fantasy and talk like she'd walked out of the shopping centre a few minutes ago? What dress, anyway?

The folded material on the foot of the divan. Izzy had forgotten about it. She picked it up from the ground and lengths of green velvet fell from her fingertips. 'You're kidding, this?'

'Not every day you're summoned to see a living goddess, little human. Might as well look your best.'

A goddess?

'*There is only one God. This is an impostor. One of the lost.*' The gentle, soothing voice was gone. The fallen angel's anger flared in the back of Izzy's mind – righteous indignation, divine rage. It left her stunned for a moment.

Soldiers, Jinx had called them, assassins and killers. From the tone of the voice in her head, his description had fallen short of the mark. Zealots and fanatics, more like.

She took a breath to calm herself and then found the strength to glare at Blythe. 'Well, if I'm going to get ready I need privacy.'

Without another word, the Cú Sídhe walked out, slamming the door behind her.

Damn, thought Izzy. *I should have asked for some light as well. Bitch.*

But what good would it do? The only way out of this was to go through with it. And hopefully find Jinx again.

She slid out of her clothes and into the dress. They hadn't thought of shoes. Or underwear, of course. Well, she'd have to do. Goddess or not, whatever she was. Thank God she still had her boots. They might not go with the required masquerade costume, but who gave a toss about that?

'*You're unarmed. You're walking into danger.*' The angel's voice softened to gentleness. Genuine concern coloured the words.

Izzy turned to her clothes and pulled the iron knife from her jacket pocket. She wasn't going anywhere without that. It might not be much, but it was iron and that counted for something. She slipped it up one of the long, close-fitting sleeves and it rested there, very cold, against her skin.

'How's that?'

There was no reply, but she sensed the angel's satisfaction. It purred like a cat at the base of her brain.

Izzy unclipped her hair and shook it out but before she could put it up again the door re-opened.

'Good,' said Blythe, examining her with a single glance. 'Let's go.'

'I will be with you. Where you walk so shall I, to shield and comfort. Do not fear, Isabel. I am with you.'

Sure. Just like that. It sounded like the angel was singing the words. Izzy swallowed down fear. 'Let's go.'

CHAPTER FOURTEEN

Collared and Bound

Izzy's footsteps echoed down the corridor, though Blythe moved without a sound.

'Where's Jinx?' Izzy asked again. She didn't get an answer. Blythe wasn't in a talkative mood. Maybe she didn't approve of Izzy getting this so-called audience. She didn't seem to approve of anything connected with humans at all.

The ceiling opened out above them, and they stepped into a cavern, deep inside the hill that Izzy thought she knew like the back of her hand, a vast chamber like a bronze dome, the walls hung with heavy drapes and portraits, with burning torches. Between the tapestries, and behind the torches, the walls were lined with the same polished bronze. It reflected the light, casting an infernal glow back again and again, illuminating everything in the chamber. Positively medieval. Nothing like the modern nightclub that Silver had made of her hollow. A world away. Millennia away.

Izzy could only stare. She tilted her head to look at the vaulted ceiling, high above them. Lanterns hung there, like stars in the sky. She didn't want to think about how they were lit. The idea made her dizzy.

All around her, Sídhe of varying natures gathered, like any crowd in a large space, clustered in groups, lost in their own conversations with no single focus for them. That all changed as she passed. The voices fell silent, and eyes as sharp as any thorn latched onto her. Hair, skin, eyes and clothes varied through every colour imaginable, and they were taller and smaller than any human. These fae were less human-like than any she had seen so far. Izzy held her head up high. No matter what happened, she wasn't going to be intimidated by them. She thought of Mum, of the way she held herself, of Dad's calm self-assurance. And she walked past them without giving them the benefit of seeing the nerves rioting inside her.

She wished Jinx was here, and quickly shoved that need aside. A weakness she couldn't afford, one that might leave her helpless.

Up ahead, the patterned marble of the floor came to a halt and a pool spread out. The water came right up to the ground, a smooth line unbroken but for the soft ripples that every so often shook the surface. It looked like a mirror. A dais rose from the centre. A throne dominated it. And in front of the throne, a flame.

It burned brightly, without any source or fuel, but it hung

there, incandescent in the still chamber. It joined with the torchlight and amplified it.

Blythe stopped at the water's edge and Izzy came to a halt beside her, staring into the brightness.

'Bring him out,' Blythe called.

A scuffle heralded a group of warriors bundling a shackled prisoner between them. Izzy's eyes widened as she recognised Jinx, but she held herself cautiously, careful not to react. He looked wretched, but when he saw her, pulled himself upright and tried to shake them off.

Proud, she thought. And strong. Noble, even in captivity.

And really, really stupid.

He had fought them. That much was clear. Bruised and battered, his body had taken one hell of a beating. A collar circled his neck, ornately decorated silver, and chains ran down to similar cuffs at his wrists. Beneath the skin was red and raw, as if the metal had burned him. Izzy's stomach tightened just looking at him. Pain was a constant ghost in his steely eyes. Not the after-image that always lingered there. This was fresher, stronger. Agony.

What had happened? What had he done? Last time she saw him, Jinx and the Cú Sídhe seemed like long-lost friends.

Jinx and his guards stood behind her and Izzy had to fight the urge to turn around and hurl a hundred questions at him. He was in no position to answer them. Her heart beat faster. This was wrong. So very wrong. All her instincts were screaming at her. Everything had gone wrong.

'You must not panic.'

Shut up, she thought desperately. *I don't need you distracting me now, mad voice in my head.*

'I can help you.'

No. Shut up and go back to being imaginary.

A curious sense of the importance of this moment spread over her, as if so much hinged on what happened here, as if a mistake now could cost lives – namely hers and Jinx's. She felt like someone else. Not a teenage girl whose biggest worry was upcoming exams and whether she'd still have a job at the coffee shop come Monday morning.

Her dad's life was tied up in this too. Had it really been an accident? Or had it been deliberate? She didn't know, but someone did. Someone knew what this was all about, why she was so important that an angel chose its moment to fall so it would be near her, so important that every supernatural thing seemed to want her, so important that the spark was eating into her. She caught her train of thought and almost laughed. *'Important'* wasn't a word for her. *'Cursed'*, perhaps, but not *'important'*.

She was never going to be normal again.

Izzy closed her eyes tightly and forced her breath to calm. In through the nose, out through the mouth, a wave on the beach, just like the mental yoga-pimping drama teacher at school liked to say. The shock was that it worked. Would she get a surprise when Izzy told her in September? If they made it to September. Next week was looking decidedly dodgy.

And as for tomorrow ...

Izzy opened her eyes again and allowed herself to glance at Jinx. He'd fallen, or been beaten to his knees. The glare he gave her wasn't exactly friendly. She knew it though, the same way he'd looked at her in his Cú Sídhe form, before she'd pulled the knife out. He wanted to change. But couldn't.

The silver collar. It was something to do with silver, the way it burned him. But he wore silver studs and rings, didn't he? He touched silver every single day.

This couldn't be good. It couldn't be good at all.

'We're here, Matriarch,' said Blythe, her voice measured with respect and more than a little fear. That worried Izzy more than anything. If a bitch like Blythe was afraid, what was the matriarch going to do?

Breathe in. Breathe out. Wave on the shore. Calm, calm, freaking calm.

Her hand shook and for a moment she worried that the knife would fall out. She bent her elbows slowly, carefully, and clasped her hands in front of her.

The fire flared, even more brightly, the warm gold bleeding to the edges while the centre turned white hot.

And in the middle of the inferno, a figure formed, slender and flame-haired with piercing eyes. The woman stepped forth, formed of fire itself, and smiled victoriously at Izzy. She wore an elaborate necklace like a swirl of gold, set with a huge chunk of amber which flickered like a flame.

She didn't look quite as she had. There was nothing human

about her at all now. All the same, Izzy couldn't help but recognise her – the nurse who wasn't a nurse. The woman from the hospital.

'You!' Izzy cried, before she could stop herself.

Blythe hissed at her and Jinx paled, but the woman – the matriarch of the Hill Sídhe – just laughed. It wasn't a comforting sound.

'Yes. Me. You left the hospital so quickly I didn't have time to introduce myself.'

Anger replaced shock. So much anger she thought that she might burn with incandescent flames as well. 'What did you do to my father?'

'*Do* to him? What did I *do* to him? Nothing, you stupid child. But together we might have healed him. You spoiled that. You and that bitch he calls his wife.'

That did it. Izzy snapped. 'Don't you dare talk about my mother that way!' she screamed.

Blythe raised a fist ready to strike, but the matriarch let out a snarl of rage. The Cú Sídhe fell back, her face startled and confused. And more than a little afraid.

'Never harm what is mine, Blythe. Never raise a hand to her. You are nothing compared to her. Remember that.'

Deathly silence fell across the hollow. All Izzy could hear was the sound of her own breath, heaving in and out of her body, waves on the shore beaten by a hurricane.

The matriarch stepped forward, onto the pool of water, but she didn't sink. Her feet touched the water's surface and it boiled beneath them. Steam flared up around her and her flame-red hair billowed out in her wake. Izzy took an involuntary step of retreat as the woman approached, but they still ended up standing face to face on the edge of the water.

'She isn't your mother, foolish child. I am.'

Izzy's body spasmed, ice cold with shock, rigid with rage. It wasn't true. Couldn't be true! She opened her mouth, struggled to find the right words. Only one came out.

'No.'

Her mother? It wasn't possible. Her mother was Rachel Gregory, neat and exact, far too intelligent for a daughter's peace of mind. Her mother ... her mother was nothing like the almighty bitch in front of her.

'No?' The matriarch sneered. 'Your father is a Grigori. A Watcher. He knows his duty and his place. He didn't argue. He was a dutiful lover.' Izzy's stomach twisted and her disgust must have shown on her face. He'd never do that, never betray Mum like that. Of all the things Izzy knew to be true and real, her parents' relationship was the strongest of all. The matriarch flapped a hand at her, dismissing of her reaction. 'Oh, he talked about his young bride, his love and all those other things men say, but in the end he did his duty. We needed a warrior, a vessel for divine power, and in time a new Watcher to take his place. Someone stronger. The mortal blood was thinning down the Grigori. It had made him weak. I was the best option and as part of the Grand Compact I complied. He obeyed. And what did it get us? *You.*' Loathing riddled the word.

It was like a physical blow, but Izzy stood her ground. What else could she do? Run now – not that she'd get far – and she'd never find out the truth.

Dad's mistake, his terrible mistake ...

Mum – would never look at Izzy like that. Mum who had held her and sung to her, soothed her or scolded her. Mum of the plasters and the kid's cough syrup, the hugs for no reason. Mum who turned up on Sports Day in the rain with a massive umbrella and a flask of hot chocolate. Mum who took her to lame Irish attempts at theme parks and woeful movies where they should have served the adults neat vodka instead of popcorn. Mum, who encapsulated the word.

This ... *thing* ... was not her mother.

'Who are you?'

'My name is Brí, I guard this place, stand vigil over the weak points in the world. I was once held to be a living goddess. I guard your whole line, the Grigori, the Watchers. I am one of those who see to it your family does their duty. And duty overrules everything else.'

'And what's our duty?'

'To maintain balance, of course. Balance in all things. Except, it seems, you.'

Balance, that's what Dad had been on about, last summer at Clonmacnoise. Tears stung her eyes like acid.

'You could have healed him, Isabel,' said Brí, her voice so soft and warm it drifted on the air around her.

'And when did you give her that option?' Jinx asked, his eyes still wild with pain, his teeth clenched.

But it struck Izzy in another sickening wave of realisation. 'At the hospital.' Her voice grated on her throat. Her chest ached. 'You gave me water at the hospital.'

'You're meant to be a grail bearer. It's in your blood.'

'What grail? It was a plastic cup!' Izzy yelled.

Anger fired Brí's voice. 'It was water, blessed by me, carried by you. It was a grail, no matter what it looked like. Do you think I could just walk into a hospital in the human world with a magic cup and go unnoticed? I cloaked it, disguised it as something mundane. You have no idea how much power it took, how much time … And what does it matter? It's gone now, destroyed, lost. It would have healed him, woken him, but what did you do?'

She could see it now, the crushed plastic cup, a pool on the lino, dripping down the side of the cabinet. It might have woken him?

'I spilled it.' All she could manage was a whisper, and a broken one at that. The fight died inside her. It had been a chance, a test perhaps, and she'd failed. Failed utterly.

'Spilled it,' Brí echoed, her voice strangely flat. 'And crushed the grail underfoot. Well done. You're useless. All of you. Self-ish, petty creatures with no vision beyond your own needs. I have done with you all. I have done with humanity.'

'Can't you do it again? Can't I try again?'

'What, just like that? Just pull another grail out of the air for you? And have the spark you carry destroy it again?'

'Destroy it? How could the spark destroy it? There was a shadow …'

'It's too late now. Besides, I don't have the power anymore. My grail is gone.'

'Please, help me. For Dad.'

Brí's mouth twisted into a bitter smile. 'Do you think he means something to me? He's just a tool. As are you.'

'So that's it?' Jinx interrupted again. 'She fails you by accident and that's all her chances. There were shades all over that hospital, and angels outside waiting for us. But you blame Izzy. Some mother you are. Not so much a mother as a motherfu—'

Brí flung out her hand and Jinx arched in agony, his voice choked to silence, his muscles ratcheting as the silver heated to white at his neck and wrists. A strangled cry forced its way through his clenched teeth and his nails sliced into his palms as his body tried to shift to hound-form in vain.

'Stop it!' Izzy yelled, but Brí ignored her.

'Sometimes the only way to shut up a barking cur is to teach him a lesson.' But she didn't look happy about it. If anything Izzy thought for a moment that Brí's gaze was regretful as it lingered on him. But she didn't look away, and she didn't do anything to ease his pain. The Cú Sídhe around them moved restlessly, clearly unhappy. Blythe raised her upper lip, baring her teeth, giving a low growl.

Brí released him and Jinx slumped to the ground, breathing

hard, his chest like a bellows.

'The spark,' said Izzy, terrified now, so afraid she couldn't let herself think about what was happening, what she was doing to Jinx. 'How do I get rid of the spark?'

Brí's eyes widened for a second. Just a second. Then they narrowed to slivers of ice. 'Get rid of it? Oh, my poor dear girl, that's why they want you. The angel's spark.' She laughed. 'Holly and the Old Man will be more than willing to help you 'get rid of it'. The power that thing offers … You can't let them do that. Really. But if you really want to do it yourself, you'll need another grail.'

'A grail?' Izzy's eyes opened wide and inside her the angel stirred, fluttering against the back of her mind, in equal fear. 'The Holy Grail?'

Brí shook her head and closed her eyes in exasperation. 'No, child. There are many grails. It means cup. A healing cup. They will only heal once though, and only the people they choose, or those who can find them. Fickle as the Sídhe. But a grail will indeed free you from the spark, and all those who hunt you.' She paused, giving Izzy a long stare. 'Or you could use it to heal your father. Or maybe that leech inside you will help. But you'll need the spark to work that miracle and if you were to use it that way, it will become part of you for all time. Bound to you until death. A bit like Jinx.'

'Don't listen to her,' Jinx warned, his voice still scarred with pain. 'She's playing with you.'

'I'm telling her the truth, raw though it may be. Unlike you, hound, who have told her nothing. So be silent.'

'Jinx? What haven't you told me?'

So much, her instincts warned. She'd been far too gullible. She didn't want to know the answer, but the words were already out there.

He hung his head, refused to meet her eyes.

'Why do you have him in chains?' Izzy asked Brí.

'When one of my enemy's kith, her would-be assassin, *wanders* into my realm, I'm hardly likely to let him have his liberty, am I?'

Assassin? Jinx? But they'd spoken of assassins and wars that never ended. She should have guessed. Which meant he'd killed people, he had blood on his hands. Izzy stared at him, but Jinx didn't look up. Like he knew she was questioning him, that she wanted answers.

'He said Holly could help me.'

'Help you by carving it out of you, perhaps. Holly kills angels. Their broken after-images are burned into her walls. That's how she holds her power, the way she thrives, filling her touchstone with stolen power. She can destroy lesser gods. I doubt you'd be anything like a challenge. But he can't allow that to happen now anyway, can you Jinx?' To the surprise of them both, Brí knelt down in front of him and cupped his chin, lifting it so she could look into his eyes. 'I gave you that geis for a reason, boy. If you'd but stayed true ...'

'Then why trade me away to Holly, Brí?' It came out like a plea, a lament. It was almost the voice of a lost child.

She smiled, a gentler expression. The words she said however were harsher. 'What choice did I have?' she asked. 'The
position your mother and father left us in … Look at you, with
her charms and wards all over you, entangling every atom in
you. Poor beast. And now, to make matters even worse, you're
well and truly tied, aren't you? Enslaved not to Holly. But to
her.'

To Izzy's horror, Brí looked up and their eyes met. She
looked away and found Jinx watching her too, his expression
haunted, desperate.

Izzy took a step back from them. 'I don't want a slave.'

Brí shook her head, amused. 'You don't get a choice. This
is old magic. You save a life, you own that life. You drew iron
from him, the very iron you try to hide from me now. Don't
look so guilty. At least you had the sense to come armed. Jinx
belongs to you now. He'll die at your command, he'll kill at
your command—'

'That's outrageous.' Izzy swallowed hard on the bile rising
in her throat.

'Any of the Sídhe would kill to have the power you don't
even know how to use. Let me guess, you've been running
since you first met Jinx? Shadows that move by themselves.
Angels dogging your footsteps. Monsters left, right and
centre. I ought to cut the spark from you myself, feed it to
my touchstone and draw on it myself. And maybe I would, if
you weren't my blood. A geis is a geis and they bind all the
Aes Sídhe, irrevocably. They're important. What else can hold

my kind to account? Your father should have prepared you for this, but no. They wanted you to be "normal". They wanted a human life. I've tried to keep watch over you, to guard you and shield you within my realm. And still they wouldn't listen to me. That woman—'

Izzy narrowed her eyes. 'What did my mother ever do—?'

Brí surged to her feet, her eyes blazing with sudden anger. 'I *am* your mother!'

'Really?' Izzy stuck out her small pointed chin and glared at the former goddess, seeing for the first time a reflection of her own bone structure, her own stubbornness. 'Where were you when I broke my arm? Who nursed me through scarlet fever? Who made my Halloween costumes and sat through endless clarinet recitals? Who was there with breakfast and supper and everything in between? If we're talking genetics then I don't know, maybe you are. But if we're talking about my life then you're no mother of mine.'

'You will acknowledge me as your mother one day.'

'Never.'

'Yes, you will. And come the day, what will you do if I refuse to answer?'

'I'll never have cause to need you. I'm leaving this place and Jinx is coming with me. Get those chains off him. We're going!'

'I'm afraid not,' said Brí, drawing back her shoulders and looking over Izzy's head, every inch the goddess she claimed she once was. 'You're both far too dangerous, and far too attractive to any number of people who would cause you untold harm. You're staying here. Indefinitely.'

The air grew chill around them, as if Brí had sucked the warmth from it, and Izzy shivered. 'You can't do that. I need to get to my parents, back to my dad.'

'Take them away,' Brí told Blythe and the Cú Sídhe. 'Put them somewhere … safe.' But before Izzy could argue or Blythe could act, another runner came from the shadowy tunnels and prostrated himself before Brí. She leaned forward and spoke to him in rapid undertones. Her features hardened. 'Very well,' she said at last. 'Bring her here. Unarmed. And if she raises even a glimmering of power, I'll have her head.'

The Cú Sídhe surrounded Jinx and Izzy, some in hound and some in human form. They herded the pair of them together and Izzy was able at last to hunker down beside him.

'Are you okay?'

'As "okay" as I might be, given the circumstances.' His voice was a bitter growl and he refused to meet her eyes. She reached out and brushed her fingertips along the line of his jaw nonetheless. Jinx flinched away, almost knocking himself over in his haste to get away from her.

'I didn't know,' Izzy protested.

'How could you know about Brí? If your parents didn't tell you—'

'About you. About you and me.'

She reached out and touched him again, his jaw hot beneath her fingertips. He closed his eyes, his mouth hardening. 'What does it matter? We have greater things to worry about.' But he didn't mean that, couldn't. Izzy could tell. He was bound to her. And hated her for it. A shard of guilt stabbed through her. But what could she have done? Left him to die in that alley?

The knife felt like ice against the skin of her arm.

He was an assassin. He'd killed people. The thought made her cringe inside. What was worse, he didn't try to deny it. The voice of the angel had warned her he couldn't be trusted. Was this why? Because how could she trust a killer?

The hall fell silent but for the delicate tap of a pair of heels crossing the marble. 'You're so good to see me, Lady Brí. My Lady Holly sends her most respectful greetings.' Silver's musical voice rang like bells of morning off the high ceiling.

Jinx's head came up so quickly, his lips brushed up against Izzy's palm and she felt the sharp edge of his teeth beneath. She turned, just as surprised to see the slender form of the singer standing only a couple of feet away.

And beside her, dressed in his customary black, his appearance unbelievably haggard, as if he'd gone through hell since she last saw him, Dylan.

CHAPTER FIFTEEN

Payments Past and Payments Due

Silver had spoken to the cops while ambulance crews scoured the scene of the disaster and whisked Marianne's body outside. Dylan shuddered and clamped his eyes shut, trying to make it be a lie, a nightmare, a terrible, terrible mistake.

'Dylan!' Silver rubbed his shoulders gently.

'I'm okay.' His voice sounded much brusquer than he intended, but that didn't seem to upset her.

'They think it was a gas explosion.'

'And what was it? What was that — that thing?'

She settled down beside him, feet in the gutter next to his. 'Banshee. Never had much time for them myself. Nasty cows.'

'Is Marianne—?'

Silver took his hand, her grip gentle but firm. 'Mari wasn't meant to be here, was she?'

'She's dead.' Saying the words just made it worse, even more unreal. Jesus, what was he going to say to his parents? He'd been sitting there. He'd been sitting right there!

The shock made his breath come in short gasps, made his body tremble uncontrollably. He clamped down on it with an iron will he wasn't aware he possessed.

'Oh, Dylan ...' Silver murmured helplessly.

'Who sent her? Who did this?' He wanted to find them, to break them, to make them pay. Suddenly nothing in the world seemed so important as that. His sister was dead.

'I don't know. But I mean to find out. Come on. Izzy has blundered into something far more dangerous than I thought.'

Mention of Izzy's name was like being doused in cold water. Blundered? That didn't sound good. 'What's wrong? What happened?'

'They've gone somewhere they shouldn't. Annoyed someone they shouldn't. I need your help to get them out. You're a neutral party. Well, pretty much.'

'A what?' This time he couldn't stop the words. He didn't feel neutral. He felt out of control.

His sister was *dead*. That creature had killed her while looking for Izzy. His parents didn't even know yet. How was he going to tell them?

Silver sighed, her voice dropping as if she was explaining something to a relatively dense child. 'We Sídhe have our own rules. One is safe conduct for the sake of negotiation. But to do that I need a neutral party. What do you say? I can elaborate on that offer I made. Maybe even give you a sample or two?'

What the hell was she on about? Didn't she realise what had just happened? Mari was dead. His sister ... His mind shied away from that thought, like a horse refusing a jump and galloping out of control. 'Silver, is Izzy still in danger?'

'That sort of depends on your definition of the word.'

So yes. When you got down to it. Yes, she was.

And whoever was after her had killed Mari.

'We have to tell the police, Silver. I have to go home. My parents—'

Her eyes narrowed, taking on a cunning glint he wasn't sure he liked. 'You can't, not now. You'll bring this down on them as well.'

'Why? Why would anyone follow me?'

'Because the person who sent the banshee doesn't know where Izzy is. But they know you and your sister have a connection to her. They could follow you. Think, Dylan. They've lost one child.'

He ripped himself away from her with a snarl, but Silver was quicker than him. In a rush of air, she was standing in front of him, stopping him in his tracks. She looked ferocious, terrifying and far too alien to be a part of his world.

But she was.

'They killed your sister trying to take Izzy.'

Red rage flared behind his eyes, rage like physical pain. 'Who did?'

'I'll tell you. But first, I need you to help me retrieve Izzy and Jinx. He's my family, Dylan. I want him back before someone does something equally fatal to him.'

'Tell me now.'

She shook her head, a small smile lifting the sensuous corners of her mouth. She already knew she'd won. And that made Dylan even angrier. 'After. I promise. And a Sídhe can't go back on that.'

Jinx's body raged with the need to change to his hound form, and with the pain that such a feeling always brought. Izzy and Silver stood in Brí's hollow, at her mercy. Worse yet, Silver had dragged Dylan along as well. He didn't give a damn about the human, but this was no place for him. No place at all.

In spite of what she'd said about the human's talent, she probably saw him as no more than a shield of impartiality right now. One she desperately needed to stand in Brí's hollow.

'I come as an emissary,' said Silver. 'Holly feels that this enmity has gone on long enough. You have taken one of her kith. She wants him back.'

'He trespassed on my land,' Brí replied, with a haughty tilt of her chin. 'And he's not so much "kith" as pet assassin. That's what she's made of him. That's all she sees the Cú Sídhe as — hunters and killers. Pretty though you make them, let's not mince words, Silver. For all I know she sent him to kill me. It's her way, is it not?'

Silver stood very still, and her voice was pitched so carefully that only those closest to her could hear it — Brí, Dylan, Izzy, Jinx and Blythe. 'With respect, Lady Brí, perhaps you should ask that of Jinx's father. But you can't. You sent him to Holly's Market, if I remember rightly, for much the same reason. Shall we make that public as well?'

Brí scowled and Blythe recoiled from her with a hiss of rage, but Silver didn't flinch. Even Dylan stood firm, his gaze determined, his mouth hard. Something was wrong there. He looked different. Dangerously different. Like something had broken inside. He wasn't charmed or bound to Silver, but something had happened.

Jinx's mind reeled sickeningly as it tried to tackle what they were saying, make sense of it all. He'd always thought he was just an honour payment for Holly's daughter's elopement with one of Brí's kith — and a hound at that — for the shame of their forbidden union. But if Brí had sent his father there to kill Holly, then he understood Holly's hatred. He hated his matriarch all right. Hated and adored her. She'd woven enchantments beneath his skin, punched silver through him and made him her own. She'd taught him to fight, to kill, and to hunt. But never to turn on her. Holly was his matriarch. She held his life in her hands.

Silver had been the one small element of kindness in his entire life. Until he met Izzy. He struggled to rise, but Izzy stopped him, her hand on his shoulder far stronger than he would have thought possible. She stilled him, with just a touch.

Silver smiled, a carefully designed smile that married triumph with reconciliation. 'Shall we instead work out a mutually appealing solution? As we did before?'

'When you *stole* my prize pup? Supposing I just take him back now …'

Stolen was different from a gift. So what was he? They talked such rings around each other, he couldn't follow all the undercurrents.

'I never stole him, Brí. He was a gift. An honour payment. And to return him now?' She laughed. Such a carefully modulated laugh. Calculated just enough to charm, but not to enrage. 'I'm afraid Holly would never agree to that. He is our blood kin. Belladonna was my sister. Besides, with so much of Holly's magic wrought around him, it would be impossible.'

'Well, then, we'd need to find something else, Silver. Something as valuable.' Brí glared at Blythe and the hounds, who were staring at her in a mutinous way, still surrounding Jinx and Izzy, but with a more protective stance than before. 'I told you to get them out of my sight. They don't need to hear these negotiations. Take them away. And make yourselves scarce.'

The Cú Sídhe weren't gentle, but Blythe was less aggressive as she led them away. Jinx kept as close to Izzy as he could, determined to protect her in any way he could. And now he had Silver to worry about as well.

Damn it. She was more like an older sister to him than an aunt, had been ever since Holly had first claimed him. She'd loved him for her sister, Belladonna: an Aes Sídhe, the daughter of a matriarch, with the temerity to love something as lowly as a Cú Sídhe. But Brí had sent Jasper to the Market to begin with, to kill Holly ... And Brí had given Jasper and Belladonna's child up; she had paid the blood debt by sending Jinx to Holly, to be her servant, her kith. But she'd cursed him with his geis first ...

He'd never been given answers to his questions. Not even by Silver. Honour debts, blood debts ... it didn't really matter when you were little more than a chattel. And when magic bound more powerfully than anything else.

Had Brí foreseen Izzy saving him? Had she foreseen him being tied to her own daughter? How far ahead did Brí's machinations extend? She had sight, everyone knew that.

They were bundled into a small room, but Blythe and the other Cú Sídhe remained at the door, gathered like the pack they were.

Izzy sat down on the narrow bench-like bed and Jinx stayed where he was, barring the way, a makeshift barrier though he was. All the protection she had.

'Jasper, your father ...' Blythe began, but then stopped as if unable to finish the sentence.

Jinx drew his chin up, steeling himself for another slur, another insult. 'Jasper is dead. Weren't you listening?'

'Yes, but I knew him, Jinx, even if you did not. She never told us she sent him there. He vanished for months before he returned with you. I don't know where they hid. He went to retrieve your mother, but he never came back. He was pack. There are few enough of us, even here, isolated amongst other Sídhe. For the last twenty years we thought ...'

She refused to meet his eyes.

'You thought what? That he left? That he betrayed you? Hardly the act of a Cú Sídhe, is it?'

'Or the act of a father.'

Jinx just snorted. 'I wouldn't know.'

'We never saw her, Belladonna, but we were told she was beautiful.'

Jinx stiffened at the sound of her name, his mother, the woman by whose blood he called Holly grandmother, when he dared. He knew little enough about her. Just what everyone else did. They called her traitor.

'Ancestors, are you always this dense?' Blythe snarled.

'You have met him, haven't you?' Izzy supplied in a miserable tone. Not helpful at all. Luckily Blythe paid her no attention. Jinx wished he could do the same, but her pain and fear pulsed inside him, transformed to his own emotions by their connection.

'You're our kin, Jinx. And Brí sent you away. Just as she sent Jasper away. We thought he had left us for your mother, for an Aes Sídhe, and then abandoned their child. No Cú Sídhe would do such a thing. Never. But we thought the worst. And then Holly demanded you as well. You're our blood. One of us.'

One of us. Words he had always hoped to hear from others of his kind, though he'd never admit it. Nor would he now. They were a pack for sure, intimate and comfortable with that closeness, living in the company of each other, pining without it. He would never be like that. It wasn't in him. He had other blood too. Blood that couldn't bear to be a hound for long. Each part of his heritage loathed the other.

Cú Sídhe would never understand that. The very thought of trading one of their own away horrified them. They weren't Aes Sídhe, though they could look like them. They had a duality of nature that needed to live in both forms at different times and found harmony in their transformation. They switched from one to the other as easily as breathing and he envied them that. Silver had tried to explain, tried to help him understand himself, but it wasn't the same for him. Not when changing to hound form hurt so much.

But Aes Sídhe were different. They'd do anything to get what they wanted. The High Sídhe. The Lords and Ladies. The Gentry. Not a true heart amongst them. Perhaps not even Silver, who walked a different path. She might see humans as nothing more than a thing to be used and cast aside, but so did all the Sídhe. She was one of the few Aes Sídhe who didn't regard the lesser Sídhe in much the same way. To those she loved, she was a fierce protector, eternally loyal and kind. He trusted her with his life. She was the only one.

But he had never tested her. He'd never dared to. All he knew of the Aes Sídhe was cruelty and abandonment. If he pushed Silver, would he find that he was just a means to an end as well, a tool like Dylan?

He hadn't even dared to dream of being part of a pack.

'It's history,' he told Blythe and willed her to leave him. But Blythe didn't move.

'History repeats. History is always with us. The history writes the tale of the man to be.'

'And old adages don't solve anything. Certainly don't get us out of here. Or bring my father home. Don't try to excuse him. It doesn't make us family any more than it makes Brí and Izzy mother and daughter.' Misery dragged the words from him. Knowing more about what happened didn't help. Knowing that he hadn't been abandoned couldn't erase the years of believing that they hadn't wanted him.

'But their blood does.'

'No, it doesn't,' Izzy interrupted, her voice stronger than he would have imagined. 'She's nothing to me.'

To Jinx's surprise, Blythe gave a brief but respectful bow. To Izzy. If the girl noticed, she didn't react, too much anger running its course through her still, perhaps. Much as his own.

'Do you need anything, Lady Isabel?' Blythe asked.

Izzy stared at her. 'Yes. Obviously. We need to leave. And Jinx needs out of those chains.'

Yes, he thought. *Because then I can fight our way free.* For once they were of the same mind. The thought pleased him almost as much as the need to attack bit deep into his guts.

And at the same time … he didn't want to fight through *this* Cú Sídhe pack. Not now. Not knowing what he had discovered. Something unwound within him. Just for a moment.

If Blythe would just take the chains off …

'I can't,' Blythe sighed. 'Not without her command to do so. She is quicksilver, our Brí. For the last twenty years, she's been worse than ever. But she cares, deep down. Unlike Holly. She wouldn't have given you up lightly, Jinx. I know she didn't. If you can find it in your heart—'

'Weren't you listening to her back there?'

'Perhaps we heard different things. Perhaps you should think about it.'

'She bound me with silver. She tortured me.'

Blythe shook her head, her eyes coming back to his face as if she could see inside him. 'Well, you were about to say something terrible. And she is still a matriarch. We would have raised you better.'

'Well, you didn't. I don't have a pack.'

She reached out her hand unexpectedly, too fast for him to dodge out of the way. But instead of striking him, her fingers brushed against his head, stroking his hair so gently.

'Yes, you do. You have always had a pack. I'm sorry you can't see that. Truly.' She drew back, smiling at his stunned expression for a moment before she snapped her fingers and led the Cú Sídhe away, closing the door behind them.

Jinx turned to her, but Izzy just sat there, watching him

with a careful expression. 'You're her daughter,' he said.

'No.' The vehemence with which she said the word gave her the lie.

'Izzy—' he warned.

She wilted, in that instant, curling into herself, her hands covering her face and her shoulders shook as if she had a palsy. Guilt left him unmanned. He couldn't leave her like that. She was just a girl, after all, confused, afraid, and so far out of her depth now that she didn't know the way back to shore. Jinx knelt before her and took her hands as best he could, the chains hampering his movements. The fire of their touch seemed to lessen in her presence, or perhaps that was just wishful thinking, but she'd healed him before.

Her hands were very small in his and so cold. She blinked at him, her eyes so bright a blue they might have been sapphires. He could see Brí's gaze in them now, knowing what he knew, though there was nothing of the hatred and the disdain. Had Brí charmed her father so? She must have, but he couldn't imagine it.

Although, she could command too, and would. She was Aes Sídhe, just like Holly. Charm took too long.

'It can't be true,' said Izzy.

'What do you feel? Not think.' Humans were creatures of thought. Sídhe were different. Creatures of emotion.

'I don't know. Afraid. Confused. Lost.'

Lost. Yes, he could recall that feeling. It came back to him now. He had been four years old when Brí used him to pay the blood debt to Holly. He'd run through the hollow and the surrounding woodland like a feral child, more puppy than Sídhe, secure and safe in the midst of pack he barely remembered now. But then everything had changed. All that warmth and security had been snatched from him when Silver came to take him to Holly. And, just before they left, Brí had laid down that geis upon him. The one that now tied him to her daughter, Izzy.

Had she known? How could she have known?

Or was this just an elaborate trick of heaven, or hell? The angel had drawn her to him. She'd walked right up to the gate and the angel was waiting for her.

Waiting just for her, leading her to him.

Back to the world which she came from. To Brí.

To the ghosts of his past.

'It's going to be okay,' he told her.

She gave him a look like he'd said the sky was yellow. 'I'm going mad. Hearing voices, delusions, seeing things … it's the only explanation. I'm having a breakdown. Because of Dad. Because of … I don't know. But Jinx, this can't be true. None of it.'

'I know it might seem like that, but it is. You have to stay calm. We will get out. Silver will think of something. It's what she does.'

'Silver.' She sighed. 'Why did she bring Dylan?'

The thought had worried at the base of his brain as well. Why bring a human here? But Silver had. As if she needed something from him. A Leanán Sídhe had only one use for a human – the lover she inspired, the victim she eventually destroyed. But in between those two states—

Someone she could trust unreservedly. Or someone with a reason to be there of his own so powerful he didn't care about his life anymore. Who would protect her, who Holly couldn't touch, who could take care of her if anything—

His grip tightened on Izzy's hand and she winced. 'No,' he whispered and surged to his feet, just as an unnatural scream tore its way through the halls of Brí's hollow. 'Silver!'

Jinx threw himself at the door, slamming his shoulder over and over against the wood. Running footsteps on the other side were the only thing that made him pause. When Blythe opened the door again, he pushed past her, sprinting down the hallway. Even with the chains he was faster. Silver's scream cut off abruptly, but he kept going, pushing harder and harder, his body still struggling in vain against the enchantments of the collar.

The cavern opened up around him and he saw her, lying on the floor at the edge of Brí's pool, her hair spilling about her head like rays of light. Dylan held her, cradled her and tried slowly to lift her. He staggered, almost unable to do it, he was trembling so badly.

'What happened?' Jinx roared, baring his teeth. 'What have you done?'

Brí still stood there, holding something in her cupped hands, something bright and beautiful, an ethereal light. She

looked up, startled, and then smiled. The expression was glee-
ful, like a child with a new toy.

'Well, there you are. Just in time.'

Izzy joined him, her hand a light touch on his shoulder,
so small a caress, so welcome a comfort. 'What did you do to
her?'

Brí rolled her eyes and then drew the light to her chest. It
only took a moment before it was gone, absorbed in the lumi-
nescence of her own form. Around her neck, the huge piece
of amber in her necklace glowed like another sun. She opened
her mouth and sang, with Silver's voice.

'A deal,' said Dylan, his face like a death mask. His eyes
glistened and he pulled Silver closer. She was breathing, but
unconscious. She'd given up the bulk of her magical power,
all but the final shred that was currently sustaining her, giving
it to Brí. And for what?

Brí spread out her arms in a formal gesture of announce-
ment. 'You're free to go. I rescind all rights to you, Jinx. Again.
But don't let me catch you back here or I won't be so generous. Get out of my sight. And as for you, Isabel the ungrateful,
you're always welcome. On my terms. If you come here again,
be prepared to curb that temper and do what you're told.
Remember, there's much I can teach you. Things that no one
else can. You're my child, my blood. Not a firstborn, perhaps,
but special nonetheless. Child of a matriarch, which means
a portion of my power is yours. See you don't squander it as
Silver has. I don't expect you to be submissive – I never was

– but I do expect you to acknowledge me. Never forget that. And next time, ask nicely.'

'Wait!' Dylan's voice broke through the silence like a whip. They all turned on him, but he still sat there, cradling Silver. His face was white with rage, his eyes like stones. 'The banshee, who sent it?'

'What banshee?' Brí snarled at him. 'I have no filthy banshees in my kith.'

'There was a banshee. It killed my sister.' A flicker passed over his face, a tick in his clenched jaw. 'Who sent it?'

Something changed in Brí's demeanour. She stepped forward and Dylan gathered Silver closer in his arms. But Brí just studied him, her eyes searching his.

'It isn't my style,' she said more gently. 'Humans shouldn't play near us. It's perilous. Don't you understand that yet?' Dylan's jaw tightened still further, but he didn't answer, just held Silver and stared back, waiting. 'You shine. Enough to interest her. I suppose that's why she brought you. But even the pet of a Leanán Sídhe can't help her when she's lost her power.'

'Who killed my sister?'

Brí smiled, as if she'd suddenly solved a riddle. 'Is it revenge you're after, little man? Then it's a dark path you're walking. Maybe Holly can tell you, but it's not like you'll get out of the Market alive. The only soft spot she has for humans is over a pit of spears. Revenge changes a man, enslaves him. Revenge is the way of the Sídhe. Perhaps you've more Sídhe blood in you than anyone knows. Even a drop in the mix can transform the mundane to something special. Did she tell you that you were special?' Dylan glanced down at Silver and Brí laughed. 'Silver has been alive for thousands of years, human. More time than you can fathom. She's known rather a large number of "special" humans. None of them are with her now. Understand?'

'Are you trying to be cruel?' Izzy asked bitterly.

If anything, Brí looked surprised. Her voice sounded unexpectedly gentle. 'No, Isabel. I'm being kind. I'm being honest. Now go, all of you. Go on. I've had it with the lot of you.'

As if released from a cell, Jinx scrambled across the wide expanse of the floor, to Dylan. Together they lifted Silver and her eyes fluttered open. Her beautiful eyes.

'What did you do?' he asked, desperate. Afraid. 'Why did you give her your voice?'

'Had to,' she whispered, little more than a croak. 'We should leave. I need ... I need to rest. Recover. Take me back to my hollow. The tree will restore me. Please.'

'Did Holly send you?'

She shook her head and pressed her face into Dylan's shoulder.

Jinx gazed at the young man's stricken features. 'That's why she brought you. She can trust you. You're hers and hers alone.'

'I don't belong to her or anyone.' But he held her closer. 'They sent a banshee. They killed my sister. I can't—' He fell silent as Izzy approached and lowered his eyes. Couldn't bear to look at her perhaps. Couldn't admit to her what Jinx already knew. That whether or not he had consigned his soul to Silver's care, he was already hers. That the need for revenge had brought him here but he'd never suspected what he'd find.

'Take his chains off,' Silver tried to say, though it came out as little more than a whisper. 'You know what they do to him.'

They burned, like his studs, like every ring he wore. But the little points of pain were only there to remind him that Holly ruled him, that Holly preferred him in Sídhe form to hound form and to help him maintain it. The chains and collar ... they bound him with fire, a thousand times more powerful. He could endure it, barely, but the pain was boring away at his mind, at his will.

He recalled the first time Holly had marked him. It had been like this – searing, agonising, pain he thought would only end when it robbed him of his sanity or his life. But Silver had been there. She'd held him as he screamed, had soothed him as best she could. She had sung to him as he sobbed himself to sleep.

Brí gave a dismissive wave of her hand. 'Do you think I'm a fool? Once he's out of my hollow, they'll come off. Until then, the traitor-child stays chained.'

'Come on,' Jinx said, turning his back on her. 'We've got to get Silver out of here.' All of them, if the truth be told. And while the going was good. It was not beyond Brí to have a complete change of mind before they reached the doors. In fact, he was expecting it. 'Now!'

The single barked word did it, shocking Izzy and Dylan into action. Between them they supported Silver and Jinx fell in behind them.

It was Blythe who led the way, her fluid figure clothed now, but no less alluring. And yet still he felt nothing.

Surely that was wrong. But for the girl who had attempted to kiss him, the girl he had rejected, his heart beat stronger than ever.

And that felt wrong as well. She was the daughter of his former matriarch, and therefore the enemy of his current matriarch. She was half-blood, like him, Aes Sídhe and Grigori. She was forbidden in so many ways. And yet ...

He shook his head, fought the snarl rising up from deep inside him. Blythe glanced at them, her gaze passing from Izzy to him. She knew. The females always knew. Where one was tied, where a bond existed, even one he didn't want. Even one he hated.

CHAPTER SIXTEEN

Demons in the Dark

Blythe stopped at the door to the hollow, pressing her hand to the stones at its side. Nothing happened. Izzy felt Silver tense.

The Cú Sídhe leader just stared at them, studying each one of them with her piercing metallic eyes.

'She's unlikely to just let you go. Even if it looks that way now. She may still change her mind, or run out of patience waiting for you to return.'

Izzy swallowed hard, her mouth suddenly dry. 'Will she come after us?'

'She rarely leaves the hollow, not these days. But she'll send someone. Me probably. Like it or not she's your blood, Isabel, and—'

'Izzy. No one calls me Isabel.'

Surprisingly a smile tugged the corner of Blythe's lips. 'Izzy, then. You're her daughter. And as such others will hate you. She expects you to come back to her, you know.'

'I won't.'

Blythe nodded. 'We'll see. It's unlikely you'll have a choice in the end.' She slammed her hand onto the stones and the doorway shimmered and opened. The night air rushed in on them with the sounds of the forest and distant traffic. 'They're out there. I can smell them.'

Jinx took a step forward, his nostrils flaring. 'Yes. So can I.'

'You'd better be quick.' She stepped aside, clearing their way and the night, along with whatever waited out there.

They stepped through the doorway and Jinx stopped. The shackles and collar holding him restrained snapped open and fell. Blythe picked them up, her long fingers running over their shining surface. Pain crossed her features but when she looked at Jinx, Izzy saw only remorse.

'How do you bear it?' she whispered. She didn't mean the collar or shackles. Her eyes lingered on the silver still piercing him.

'I bear what I must. It's what we do, isn't it?'

Blythe reached out, her hand tracing his cheek, his jaw, his neck where the tattoos marked his skin. 'For those we love, yes. For those who love us. But for those who steal our shape and force us to look like them and then loathe us anyway? Who take our freedom out of spite? No, Jinx. You need to love where it's worthy, boy. Jasper knew that.'

Jinx shied away from her and Blythe let him go with a sigh.

He flexed his arms, stretched his neck and spine and grinned at Izzy, showing all his teeth. Not a joyful grin. More like a grimace.

'Give her to me.' He stretched out his arms and with only slight hesitation, Dylan and Izzy released Silver. He took her in strong and sure arms and Silver stirred, looking at him groggily.

'There are demons,' she whispered. 'Shades and demon-spawn. Close by.'

'I know. I know it well. Don't be afraid.'

Demons? Demonspawn? Izzy bit on her lower lip. 'What do you mean, don't be afraid?'

'They sent a banshee, killed the girl,' Silver went on. 'I couldn't stop it.'

Izzy looked to Dylan, his taut white features, the hard line of his mouth. His eyes glittered for a moment and he looked away. Mari? Izzy registered it. Oh, God! They'd killed her? It couldn't be true. Not Mari. She wasn't involved in any of this. Why? And now she barely knew Dylan. They had stolen them both.

She tried to breathe, tried to draw in air, and it wouldn't come. Her chest ached, tight and unforgiving. She burned inside, but there was nowhere for it to go. They'd killed Mari, to get to her.

'*And why not?*' said the angel from deep inside her. A sly whisper which knew her far too well. '*They don't care about humans. They never have. They're different, heartless, and think only of themselves. They have always been that way, since the first days.'*

Nowhere was safe. Not here on the hillside, not Dublin or Dubh Linn, not the hospital, not even the coffee shop set firmly in the human world where Mari had died. The Sídhe were taking everything from her, every last precious thing. And she didn't seem able to do a single thing to stop them. Her life as she had known it was running like water through her fingers. She'd been normal. Her life had been normal. And now ... now ...

'I know,' Jinx said. 'I'll protect you.'

But he wasn't talking to her. He was gazing only at Silver.

'All of us?' said Dylan, dubiously.

'Yes.' He glanced at Dylan and then nodded solemnly. 'Give him a weapon, Blythe.'

She offered him the long-bladed knife she carried. Dylan took it without hesitation, testing the weight in his hand.

'Can you use that? If needs be?' Jinx asked.

Dylan nodded far too confidently and Jinx seemed to accept that. Izzy studied her friend's face, trying to work out what had changed, where the brittle hardness had come from. Jinx's voice snapped her back to attention. 'Izzy, where is yours?'

She pulled it out of her sleeve and held it in front of her. All the fae regarded it with distaste. Good. It protected her from them, but she didn't know how it would help her. 'What are knives going to do against demons?'

'More than you know. Iron is of the earth, tamed by mankind. That knife is special. If they should come at you, draw a circle in the earth and bless it. Say a prayer, ask for protection, whatever words work for you. Understand. And don't cross that line. I'll come. It's not far, downhill all the way. You just have to run.'

Izzy tucked the knife back into her sleeve and looked up, catching sight of something in the polished bronze walls, something that startled her. It held her reflection, but she hardly recognised herself. Not a girl, not really. Something more. But not really a woman either.

Her fingers searched out the changes in her face, but found the same features she'd always known. 'What's happened to me?'

'You know what you are now,' Blythe replied. 'They say that when anyone meets Brí she changes them. That cannot be helped. Your blood recognised her, even if you deny it.'

'I know what I *am*?' She couldn't believe what they were saying. The casual way they discussed her. Dismissed her. 'What the hell do you think I am?'

Blythe's gaze didn't falter. She just stared off through the trees. 'You? You're one of us. Well, half-blood anyway. Half Aes Sídhe, the highest of us all. Not that it helps you really. And as for the whole Grigori thing ...' She rolled her eyes as if Izzy presented a puzzle she wasn't even going to bother to attempt. 'Most of the fae regard any kind of half-blood as tainted, so I suppose that puts you more at our level in the scheme of things. They don't love the Cú Sídhe as they should.' Her chin lifted and she inhaled, nostrils flaring. 'You need a decoy, Jinx.

May I?'

He just raised an eyebrow, a question Izzy couldn't read. But Blythe could. She rolled her shoulders and he nodded. 'Be my guest.'

She moved fluidly from Sídhe to hound shape, her clothes pooling behind her. Her dark skin transformed into sleek fur, so dark and deep a green as to be almost black, and her nails lengthened to claws. She gripped the ground for a moment, raking it slightly, and then sprang forward, into the night.

Jinx watched her for another moment and Izzy frowned as the bitter seeds of jealousy unfurled inside her.

'Let's go,' said Jinx and together they began the helter-skelter dash downhill, through the darkness and the night. For a moment she thought of the Wishing Stone again, the compulsion she'd felt to go there. And then she was past it, and she didn't have time to think any more.

Trees flashed by her, the ground leapt up to meet her feet, making her stumble and pitch forward. She almost tripped, and only just managed to catch herself before falling. Dylan appeared from nowhere, his hand out to stop her fall.

'Are you okay?' He wasn't even out of breath.

'Yeah, I'm – where's Jinx?'

'I'm not sure. I can see the path though. Come on.' He held out his hand and she took it gratefully. As soon as he held her he ran, pulling her along after him. Izzy had no choice but to run.

'Where are we going?'

'Your house. It isn't far. We'll be safe.'

'How do you know?' Panic was getting the better of her. The shadows were moving again and the mark on her neck was so cold it burned. The voice, however, was strangely silent. No bloody use to her now.

'Silver told me. Then we're going to find whoever sent that banshee.'

'What banshee?'

'The one that killed Marianne!'

The wave of pain in his voice hit her like a blunt instrument, the words, the wild emotions spinning around him, the chaos in his eyes. She turned to deny it, to tell him no, it had to be a mistake. But before she could do anything, darkness rose in a wave before them and Dylan ran right at it. The walls that went nowhere loomed out of the shadows. The shadows surged towards them.

'Stop!' Izzy yelled, throwing herself backwards. They both went down in a tangle of limbs and undergrowth. Pushing him off her, she wasted no time, digging the iron-bladed knife into the ground. 'Help us, please. Dear God, please, help us.' She dragged it into a rough circle and jerked her head up as something launched itself out of the shadows between the trees, a patch of darkness with points of red for eyes. She screamed as it bore down on her, teeth forming from the glinting light that slanted off it.

With a concussive chime and a flash of electrostatic, it glanced off nothing right in front of her and howled.

'Holy crap, it works,' Dylan breathed.

They huddled together in the circle as the shadows uncoiled from the ground and air, creeping towards them in silence.

A growl rippled through the air. Izzy shied back, bumping into Dylan and giving a startled cry. The growl transformed into a laugh, not a human laugh. Not one of the Cú Sídhe. Not even any type of Sídhe. And it certainly couldn't be called angelic, which only left one option.

The shadows boiled and writhed, sliding from tree to tree like oil until they halted, rising from the ground in a black and glossy wave, twisting in on themselves until they formed a figure.

He wore an ankle-length trench coat and the brim of a hat came down over his burning eyes. Shades darted around his feet like terriers, snarling and baring their too-white teeth. He stepped right up to the edge of the circle, gazing down on the pair of them. Even this close, Izzy couldn't make out his features. Only the general shape of his face and the cruel hint of a mouth. And the eyes. Like points of fire. But she had seen him before. Outside the house last night. Watching her.

'Well, now. That's a clever trick, little girl.' He walked around them, each step carefully placed to avoid touching the line she had made. 'If you're planning on sitting there for the rest of the night, it's going to get cold and pretty nasty out here. And if you think your dog's coming to the rescue … Well, I think you'll find he's occupied elsewhere.'

Jinx! Izzy jerked upright. 'What have you done to him?'

'Done to him?' He laughed again, the same sound, halfway between laugh and snarl. Dangerous. Knowing. 'Well, nothing. *Yet.* It's you I'm interested in. Or rather—' He tapped his temple with his index finger, '—your little hitchhiker.'

Izzy felt the angel stir, afraid, burrowing deeper into the back of her mind, digging in like an animal at bay. Great. So much help. 'My ... my what?'

He smiled his cruel smile, leaned in closer. This time he whispered. 'I think we both know what I'm talking about. Come out of there, and I'll show you.'

Dylan's hands closed on her upper arms, holding her back in case she'd momentarily lost her mind or something. Izzy couldn't shake the feeling of relief. Part of her wanted to move. Something primal which longed to obey. It terrified her, its strength, its bone-deep conviction.

She forced herself to speak. 'I don't think so. Who are you, anyway?'

'Azazel,' he said with a laugh lurking behind the name. 'You can call me Azazel. Or Uncle.'

'Uncle?' she repeated, staring at him, cold dread clawing at her. The fear leached away at her, paralysing her, making her heart thunder against her ribs.

He stretched out his hand. His fingers were too long, the nails sharp and yellowed like old bone. Though the gesture was full of grace, it held such a sense of threat that her breath caught in her throat, choking her. 'Sometimes it means "my father's brother", sometimes it's a term of affection for an elderly male relative. Sometimes it means "I give up". Which one is up to you.'

'Leave us alone,' said Dylan, before Izzy could formulate a reply.

Azazel's finger jerked towards him instead. 'You're walking a fine line, young man. You're going to end up burned. You've already paid more than most would dare. Or do you think your sister will be the last victim? We're watching you now. So very closely. Talent and luck won't save you, not from *her*. And they won't help you with her either. She's dangerous.'

'You leave Silver out of this.'

He grinned wickedly. 'Was I talking about Silver? She isn't here. Why should I include her?'

Dylan scowled. 'Who sent that banshee?'

Azazel smiled at him, a thin, unpleasant smile. 'There's a price to know that too. A price not even you're willing to pay. So shut up or your guilt will destroy you. Come out of the circle, Isabel. Come out and play.'

Izzy struggled to keep breathing. What else could she do? Stepping out of the circle would be suicide, that was for certain. And Azazel, whatever he was, wouldn't help her, no matter what charming promises he might make.

The mark on the back of her neck was so cold it burned. All her instincts screamed in warning. For once her Grigori mark and the angel agreed. The angel writhed, desperate to escape Azazel. But she didn't speak. Perhaps she didn't dare. Hadn't Jinx called them soldiers and assassins? Izzy couldn't believe it. Why did she have to get the cowardly angel?

Although the angel didn't seem afraid, not in the traditional sense. It felt more like she housed a hissing cat driven into a corner and ready to attack than a mouse frozen in fear.

'Leave us alone,' Izzy whispered, gaining a little strength from the angel. 'We don't want anything to do with you.'

'You've no choice. Listen, little girl, little Grigori mine, there's more to this than you could possibly know. More than you could hope to know. You're not getting out of this unscathed, unmarked. That angel is mine. When they fall they belong to me, understand? You're going to release her to me.' He pulled a knife from inside the coat. It was longer than the one Izzy held, the blade black like obsidian. 'Come out,' he told her. 'I'll make it quick, I promise.'

'*Never!*' The voice surged up within her like the waves on a shingle shore, driven by a storm's rage. Izzy bit down on her lip to keep from saying it out loud herself. The angel didn't seem weaker now. No, she wasn't weak at all. If anything she was getting stronger.

'Did she lie to you, Isabel? Did she tell you there was a way to be free of her?' He hunkered down again, gazing into her face with his burning eyes, running his discoloured fingernails along the edge of the blade. Face to face with him, she could only stare back, unable to see his features, just the hints of them, suggestions, flashes of nightmare. 'There's only one way out of this, Isabel. Only one way to escape. And you know what that is.'

He flicked the blade back and forth so the meagre light flickered off its polished surface.

Death. She didn't need to hear the word. He would kill her. The moment he got his hands on her. All she had to do was step outside the circle.

'Don't listen to him!' The voice was a scream, high pitched and terrible. The angel surged up like a wave of fire inside Izzy's body. For a moment she felt her grip on herself crumbling, like it had up on the hill at the Wishing Stone, and something else tried to seize control. She struggled to push it away, but claws sank into her flesh from within, and fiery wind tore through her. *'Listen to me and only me, girl. Do as I say!'*

'Izzy?' Dylan's voice was faint, but insistent, a whisper beside her ear. He hugged her closer and the voice in her mind subsided. His arms tightened, trembling. 'Don't listen.'

To which one of them? She felt tears sting in her eyes and her chest ached as if it would burst. Or did he mean both?

Azazel shrugged. 'Then don't. Listen, that is. But it doesn't change anything. Not a thing. The angel is mine. She fell. And I am here to collect, spark or no spark. Now, or in the future. It doesn't matter. But it will get worse for you. I will always be here. Waiting. You know what you have to do.'

Azazel rose to his feet with unnatural speed, spread his hands out to either side and the shadows swept towards him, gushing over the roots and brambles, seething around him in a twist of the night.

And he was gone.

The sound of breath, heavy, laboured, filled the air and for a moment Izzy couldn't figure out where it was coming from. Then she did. It was her breath. And Dylan's.

'Are you okay?' he asked, his voice strained and sore, tight with the fear she felt herself.

'Yes. I think so. Yes. Have they gone? Have they all gone?'

He looked around, but he didn't move. Nor did he release her. 'I don't know. Wait, stay still.'

'But Jinx ... and Silver.'

His grip tightened. 'She told me ... said to protect you. Even from him. Even from her. What did she mean, Izzy? Why are you so important to all of them?'

Her face burned, but the tears covering it were cold as ice. She hadn't realised she was crying. She thought of Marianne, of what Dylan had said, and suddenly she couldn't stop. Mari was dead. Not a demon or an angel, not any kind of Sídhe or fae creature. None of them had paid the price. It was Mari. And if it hadn't been for Izzy, they'd never even have noticed her.

'I don't know. Everything's changed, Dylan, and it's my fault. Everything's changed.'

To her surprise, Dylan wrapped his arms more gently around her and pulled her close. He was warm and careful. He was human.

God, it felt so good to be so close to someone human. She closed her hands over his, stroked the skin stretched over his knuckles. His hand shook and he tightened his grip on her.

'It wasn't you, Izzy. It was them.'

CHAPTER SEVENTEEN

Home Truths

Jinx lost sight of Izzy and Dylan far too quickly. With Silver in his arms, he couldn't shift to hound form and find them. He could sense Izzy though, sense her terror, her despair.

Something was terribly wrong.

'Jinx? Slow down. Please. Just ... just stop.' Silver's voice was weaker, her body trembling in his arms. He came to a halt and lowered her as gently as he could to the ground.

'Call Holly,' she whispered, looking up at him with plaintive eyes. 'Call her. You have to, Jinx. I'm fading. She's the only one who can stop it. I need to get back to my tree. I have reserves of power stored there. More than enough to make up for what I gave Brí. Holly will know what to do, how to draw it forth for me if I can't do it myself.'

Her tree was her touchstone, her greatest source of power

next to her voice and the place where the energy from all those mortals she had inspired now dwelt. She was fiercely protective of it. He couldn't imagine her letting even Holly near it. And Silver might think Holly would help her, but Jinx wasn't so sure.

Izzy's face flared in his mind, afraid, in pain. What would Holly do to her? 'I can't.'

Tears slid down Silver's pale cheeks, sluggish and plump, glistening. 'I'm dying. Without my voice, without something to ... to feed on ... I'm dying, Jinx. Holly knows what to do. She'll take me to the tree. You can't, I know that, and I'm not asking you to, but ... Please.'

'She'll kill Izzy.'

'We're still in Brí's territory, aren't we? Let Brí look out for the girl.'

'You know I can't.'

'Then don't tell her about Izzy. I thought you were going to hand her over anyway. Let Holly have her. I thought ...'

'I can't, not now. Give her Brí's daughter? Are you mad? Imagine what she'd do? Brí's content to rule her Hill, guard against whatever she imagined broke free all those years ago. Do you want another war? Izzy still has that spark. The power it contains would make Holly nigh on invincible. And she'd never be content to remain in the Market, never be satisfied with Dubh Linn. She'd go to war against the whole council first. Hell, she'd take on every fae on the island, and the hosts of heaven and hell beyond them too if it suited her. And that's the best we can hope for, a war. Imagine what she'd do just for a moment. Imagine what she'd do to the lesser fae, to the humans, to everyone. I know she's your mother, Silver, but I don't think any of us want that again, do we?'

Silver grabbed his leg, her nails like points of steel. 'Jinx. Please.' She was afraid. Terrified. Silver was old. He always forgot that because she never acted like the others. But she was old. The sudden reality of dying was destroying her – she wasn't equipped to face death. Silver was a creature of emotion, of creativity and self-belief. Without that, she was nothing. 'One of the banshees killed Dylan's sister. She was looking for Izzy. Holly's getting impatient. She won't wait much longer, do you understand?'

Dylan ... Jinx understood now. Dylan was after revenge, just as Brí had divined. Dylan had nothing else to live for, or so he thought.

Jinx stared at Silver, appalled. 'Did you make him yours? Did you use his grief?'

'No!' Outrage gave her a little fire. But it faded too quickly. 'I didn't. Of course I didn't. Please, Jinx. Please help me. I won't last much longer.'

He pulled the phone out of his pocket, the screen giving off an eerie glow, and brought up Holly's number. He didn't want to, but what choice was there? Silver needed Holly. Only her matriarch could save her now. Silver firmly believed it and so it would be true. Leanán Sídhe couldn't exist without love. And no one loved her like Holly did. Her mother.

No one hated her like Holly either. If Silver couldn't see it, Jinx could. Holly hated Silver too. For her power, for her beauty, for the ease everyone felt around her. She walked a fine line to keep Holly happy. She was useful. Not a threat. Certainly not right now.

But where did that leave Izzy? Hunted on all sides, banshees, the Magpies, angels, demons, shades ... Her world transformed. Treated like a bargaining chip. Abused to become what others would have her be.

He could recall far too vividly that sensation.

'Here.' He tossed the phone to Silver. 'But give me a head start.'

She looked stunned, her mouth open, her eyes wide. 'What are you doing?'

'Getting Izzy and Dylan as far away from here as possible before Holly comes. Deal?'

For a moment he thought she would argue, but then Silver's mouth hardened in determination. 'Deal. But hurry. Please hurry. I can't wait too long. Understand?'

Jinx didn't need another moment. He turned and ran. The urge to shift was powerful, but he fought it. Too many complications at the other end. Unless it was necessary, absolutely necessary, he'd stay in Sídhe form. He'd need to explain to them both. He'd need to—

The shades assaulted him on all sides, bringing him down in moments, pinning him on the ground. He waited for teeth, for the tearing claws, but nothing happened. If he struggled they contained him. But they did no more. Which could only mean they had instructions.

Which never boded well.

'This is a busy place tonight.' The stench that rose with the demon's approach made Jinx's stomach heave in alarm and disgust. 'You must be what the fledgling Grigori was so worried about.'

Sudden rage sharpened his vision, made his teeth ache to sink into whatever borrowed flesh the thing wore. It would taste of poison and decay, but he didn't care. Even if the demon would shake him off like a fly. Some instincts were too strong. 'What have you done to her?'

The laugh grated on his skin. 'Nothing. Yet. But I thought you might heed a warning she ignores. Ready to listen, dog?' The demon leaned in closer, flaming eyes too bright. 'We understand each other, you and I? Good. The thing inside her is dangerous. To you. To all of us. But most of all to her. The thing inside her is not what it appears to be, not what once it was. I want it. It is mine. You'll bring it to me.'

Reaching out, he pressed his fingertips to Jinx's forehead, pressed harder. Something gave inside Jinx, something which should never give, should never be asked to. Jinx screamed. He couldn't help it. Images slammed into his mind, vivid and sickeningly stark. Like film with the contrast turned right up, like the blast of feedback through an amp on ten. He screamed and the images filled him.

'Look at her. I know you can see. Really look.'

Through the trees he saw Izzy, huddled on the ground with Dylan. They clung together, trapped in their own circle. He almost called her name, but it wasn't Izzy.

By all that was holy, it wasn't Izzy. It couldn't be.

'*Really* look.'

And he did. He didn't want to, but he couldn't help himself. With the demon's power pinning him down, messing with his perception, the world shifted. Dylan was a faint shadow beside her. Fire billowed through her hair and skin, under the surface, illuminating her. It wasn't the glow he associated with her either. Nothing so soft and delicate as that. This raged out of control, like the fires of a million suns. She stiffened and turned, or part of her did. Not Izzy. Izzy was still blind in the darkness. She couldn't see him so far away. Something else turned towards him and looked. He had no idea what it was. Her eyes, when she looked at him, were cold and empty, the void of space, and just as desolate. There was nothing of Izzy in them, no sign of her soul, her humanity.

The black and endless eyes fixed on him and within them all eternity spread out before him. She smiled, not Izzy's smile, but something else. Ageless and horrifying.

The thing inside her is dangerous.

Someone shouted his name. Izzy. The real Izzy. Here and now. The reality of her brought him tumbling back to himself. He tore free of the shades and found the demon was gone. Vanished in the night. He stood there, breathing hard, teeth bared, a fraction away from changing, more animal than Sídhe.

Cú Sídhe eyes saw better than anything else – mortal, fae or beast – that walked the horizontal. And now he knew where Izzy and Dylan were. He picked them through the darkness, between the trees, huddled together. But something in the way they held each other made every hair on the back of his neck rise, as if he was already in hound form.

He leapt through the darkness, snarling.

'Jesus,' Dylan said on a breath.

The silver on his body sizzled. The tattoos tightened around his skin, forcing him to maintain his Aes Sídhe form. Like a slap in the face, driving him back a step with shock and pain, forcing unwanted control onto his nature. Jinx reined himself in, though his body wanted only to attack, and tear through meat until the blood ran over his face. But he was Aes Sídhe, not an animal.

The words he forced out scraped along his throat. 'We have to go. Now.'

Izzy scrambled to her feet. 'Is he gone? Is it safe?'

'Yes, he's gone. But it isn't safe. Holly's coming. Run.'

'Where's Silver?' Dylan asked.

Jinx swallowed a snarl of frustration. 'Waiting for Holly. Who will take great delight in killing you. Both of you. It's what she does. Silver will hold off as long as she can, but we have to run.'

The boy didn't move. 'But if this Holly is so dangerous, we can't just leave Silver to—'

Jinx snapped. He crossed the meagre distance between in

a heartbeat, seized Dylan by his coat and shook him. 'What do you think Silver is, to have the power she does? Holly's daughter. Her blood-kin. Her heir. Get moving. Both of you. There's no time left.'

He could feel it, a ripple in the earth itself. Holly was coming. The trees felt it and shuddered, the ground felt it and cowered in fear. Holly was coming and Brí's wards wouldn't hold her back, not when Silver needed her. Brí's domain this hill might be, but Brí was a being of fire. Holly was the earth itself and nothing could stop her. Eventually, everything broke before her.

'Now.' He dropped Dylan, pushed him into motion. 'Run.'

The house was dark and empty. The alarm beeped as Izzy let them in. She moved quickly, with practised ease, to disarm it, her fingers dancing over the keypad.

'Kitchen's this way,' she said to Jinx.

As she took a step her feet tangled in the length of the wretched dress and she almost went down. Jinx turned, moving so fast he blurred, and he caught her before she could hit the ground.

'You're exhausted,' he said, studying her face. The matter-of-fact quality in his voice made her grit her teeth. Yes, he was right, but how did that help? 'And probably starving. When did you last eat?'

Eat? When had she last had a chance to even feel hungry?

'At the hospital. Maybe. At the— Oh, no. Jinx, I've got to ring Mum. Oh, God, I've got to—'

Dylan passed the landline phone to her. 'Ring her. I'll get some food, and tea, yeah? A nice cup of tea.' He studied her as well. 'With sugar.' Yeah, give the hysterical female strong sweet tea. Right. Brilliant. A very male solution to all her problems.

But at least he was making tea.

Whenever he paused, the pain in his eyes threatened to make him fall apart. The mugs rattled against the counter as he tried to put them down.

She snatched up the phone and hurried to dial the number. The ring only lasted a moment and Mum's voice, exhausted and shaken, answered.

'It's me,' Izzy babbled, words tumbling out of her. 'I'm sorry, I'm so sorry. But it's me and I'm okay and I think I've found a way to help Dad. I think I can help. Mum, I'm sorry I left, but I had to—'

'Izzy, where are you? What happened? Where have you been?'

And the words, gushing forth just a moment before, failed.

'I ... I'm okay.' *Turns out you aren't my mum* – oh, yeah, that would be a spectacular opener. *A woman made of fire told me. And demons, angels and fairy creatures are chasing me, all because of the voice in my head.* All perfectly reasonable. Not.

And Mari's dead, Mum. She's dead.

The thought left her weak and trembling. Her stomach

turned and she had to lean back against the counter to keep from falling. She glanced at Dylan. He moved like an automaton, as if nothing was really impacting him at all anymore.

His phone rang and he grabbed it, almost dropping it in his haste to see who it was. But when he looked at the name, he froze. With a shaking hand, he killed the call.

'I've got to … I'm sorry. I need to …' He swallowed hard and hurried from the room.

'Dylan, just—' she began, but stopped because she didn't know what to say.

Then Mum said the impossible, grabbing her attention back to their call. 'Was it Brí? Did she hurt you?' Her voice changed subtly, harder, with hidden depths intimating an untold capacity for violence. 'Izzy, answer me. Are you hurt?'

'No. I … I'm fine. How … how do you know Brí? Mum? What's going on? Is this—' a dreaded word, a word she didn't want to use, couldn't use, had to. 'Is this real?'

Mum hesitated for a moment. 'Yes.' Her breath down the phone was uneven, broken. 'She was at the hospital. I didn't recognise her at first. And by then you were gone. What happened to you? Are you safe, my love?'

Izzy glanced around the kitchen – at Jinx, standing by the open fridge, draining the last drops of a two-litre milk carton.

'Yes, I'm safe. But Mum … I have the same mark as Dad. On my neck.'

'That's impossible.'

Izzy almost laughed. Of course it was impossible. It was *all* impossible. Of everything, Mum couldn't believe the tattoo. 'It's true, Mum. There was a fallen angel and they say I got its spark and I—'

'*Who* says? Who are you with?'

'Dylan and … Jinx. He's a … he's a …' Jinx caught her frantic gaze, still watching her like a scientist with an experiment, waiting to see how he was described. Izzy's face turned scarlet. 'He's a friend.'

Her mum paused for a long and painful moment.

'Is he Sídhe? Just say yes or no, quickly now.'

'Yes,' she whispered, terrified. How could Mum, of all people, know any of this? How did she know about the Sídhe? About Brí? She spent her life on spreadsheets and business plans, on accountancy software and in boardrooms. It didn't make any sense.

She sounded like a businesswoman now though. Every inch. 'All right, now listen to me. You can't trust him, not unless he's bargain- or blood-bound at the very least. Even then … I want you to go out to the garage and get some iron, the older the better, a horseshoe or—'

A horseshoe? Where in God's name did she think there was a horseshoe lying around the house?

'Mum, it's okay. Really. I think—'

'Go out to the garage. There's some under the tarp your Dad keeps beside his tools.' Mum's voice didn't lose any suspicion. 'Is he Brí's kith? Or worse, her kin?'

'No.' It felt like a lie, like a betrayal. Jinx was looking at her, silvery eyes never blinking. He looked more alien than ever. He still held the empty milk carton in his hand. He dwarfed everything around him.

'Izzy,' he said softly. 'Just tell her everything. I'm Cú Sídhe. I'm geis- and blood-bound to you, but I'm Holly's kith by right.'

Izzy repeated it, turning away from him as she did so. At Holly's name her mother sucked in a frightened breath.

'You still can't trust him. Izzy, no matter what. Cú Sídhe loyalty may be one thing but a matriarch like—'

'How do you know all this?' Izzy screamed the words. Tears welled up again and tumbled down her face. She dashed them away angrily with her free hand. All she seemed to do these days was cry. That and be terrified. And run.

'I haven't spent all this time with your father and not learned a thing or two, Izzy. Maybe we should have told you all along, but I wanted you to have a normal life for as long as possible. I wanted—'

'Is what Brí told me true? That you're not my mother?' The question came out before she could stop it. With it came rage, frustration and sheer terror, all the things she'd been locking deep inside her since her audience with Brí. It was brutal and harsh, like barbed wire cutting through to her heart.

'I will *always* be your mother.' Mum snarled the words. 'No matter what that bitch tells you. *Always,* Izzy. Don't forget that. My darling, you are my daughter even if she *is* the one who gave birth to you. And I'll kill her before I'll let her hurt you.'

Izzy sank down to the tiled floor. Her head was spinning. It felt better to be near the ground. There wasn't as far to fall. 'What do you want me to do, Mum?'

'I can't leave your dad, Izzy. He's vulnerable now and I have to guard him. But they know I'm here. And they know you'll come.' It wasn't an answer, not really. Izzy couldn't doubt that Mum wanted her close. But she was right. They'd already been at the hospital and she'd barely escaped. Only with Jinx's help.

'There's a way to cure him. Something I can do. I have to try, Mum.'

'No. I don't want you in any more danger. Find somewhere to lie low. Maybe ... maybe I can pull in a favour or two. Make a deal. Get in touch with your grandmother. Find someone—'

There was no arguing with her when she used that tone. Even if it was clear she didn't know what they could do. Didn't have a plan. Izzy, normally willing enough to oblige, felt a fierce rush of defiance. Mum couldn't leave Dad, couldn't go looking for a solution herself. Gran was on a cruise, too far to get home quickly. Who could Mum make a deal with? Given the deals Izzy had seen and heard of tonight – no. She couldn't let Mum do anything so stupid. But Izzy could. If she could just get to the grail. And if Brí was right, Izzy was the only one who could use it as well.

'Don't do anything. Please, Mum. I'll be in touch, okay. Keep him safe and I'll find the grail.'

The noise of shouted protests rang tinny and distant from

the phone as Izzy lowered it from her ear and hung up.

She fixed Jinx with what she hoped was her most deter-mined glare. 'What do you mean, "geis- and blood-bound"?'

'You saved my life, remember? You pulled the knife out. It means I have to help you, do what you want of me, in the simplest terms.'

'Have to?'

He looked tired. She hadn't noticed the weariness in his face before now. 'Yes.'

'Brí called you a slave.'

'It amounts to the same thing.'

'I don't understand.'

Jinx shrugged. 'There are many types of fae, most of them lesser — bodaich, merrow, leps and the like. And then there are Sídhe, the higher fae. But even there, we have a hierarchy. We're big into one-upmanship. At the top of the pyramid are the Aes Sídhe, so powerful a group of Sídhe that as soon as they're born, their ever-loving family lay some sort of riddling curse on them to make sure that they don't get more power-ful.'

'And Brí gave you one?'

'Not at first. She waited until she was sending me away.'

'Maybe ... maybe it was *because* she was sending you away. Holly wouldn't accept you as Cú Sídhe. Maybe she was trying to make you more Aes Sídhe.' Why she was trying to justify anything Brí did, she didn't know, but the Cú Sídhe they'd met seemed to love her. They'd been horrified by what had happened to Jinx. She didn't need any fae-sight to see that.

'*More Aes Sídhe* ... like they or anyone else would want that. They don't hand out geis for fun, Izzy. Some would argue I shouldn't even have one – Cú Sídhe blood being lesser and all – but Brí is an untrusting bitch who wanted me to suffer for my father's failure. So she cursed me with a geis that now makes me yours. Body and soul.' He grimaced.

'I'm sorry,' Izzy whispered.

His eyes widened just for a moment, surprise flickering through their silvery depths. 'That ... that means a lot to me. Your human heart is strong to say such words. The Sídhe can never say them. They choke in our throats.'

'We'll find a way to break it, Jinx.'

That almost drew a smile from him, but such a broken-hearted smile she almost wished it hadn't. 'No, we won't. Only death breaks a geis. But I thank you for the thought, Izzy. Really I do.'

CHAPTER EIGHTEEN

All the Freaks

Jinx paced the kitchen, wishing they had more milk with which he could regain some strength, wishing he still had his mobile, but most of all wishing for the thousandth time he had not left Silver up there alone to wait for Holly's wrath.

Family or not, Silver didn't stand a chance before the displeasure of her mother and matriarch. And Jinx certainly didn't; his slender blood relation to Holly was a frail thing indeed. His mother had betrayed her kith and kin for the love of a Cú Sídhe. He'd always thought Jasper had killed his mother. But even if he hadn't, loving him had caused her death, after all. Even the Cú Sídhe didn't really know what had happened. They'd believed the worst for years. Now he had the bones of the truth, if not the full body: Jasper had gone back to find Belladonna, leaving Jinx in the care of his pack. That it had all gone to hell wasn't Jasper's fault. His parents had broken all the rules of Sídhe society. An Aes Sídhe, the daughter of a matriarch no less, with a Cú Sídhe sworn to an enemy ... such things were impossible. Everything about their relationship was forbidden, on so many levels. And in the end, did it change anything? They were still dead. And he would be too, no doubt about that, one way or the other, and very soon. But he knew now that he hadn't been forsaken. His father had gone back into his enemy's hollow to fetch the woman he loved.

It's what he would have done.

Once upon a time.

The Aes Sídhe valued matrilineal line. His mother, his grandmother ... that was all they really cared about. That didn't make his father any less important to him though. The Cú Sídhe were different. Everyone said so, usually in terms not half so politic.

'Oh, for God's sake, stand still,' Izzy snapped at him. 'Or better yet, sit down.'

He didn't obey, not as such, but he came to a halt by her side. Even from there he could feel her body tremble.

'Where's Dylan?' she asked. They both made for the door at the same time, but as they reached it they saw him, sitting at the foot of the stairs. He was cradling his mobile phone in his trembling hands and his face was pale and drawn. He stared at it, but he wasn't using it. 'Dylan?' said Izzy tentatively.

'I ought to go home,' he replied, not to her directly it seemed, but to the air itself. 'They keep ringing. They must be terrified. But I can't.'

'Why won't you go to them when they need you so?' Jinx asked. Izzy sucked in a sharp breath at the question. Insensitive perhaps, in human terms. He was never sure of the nuances. '

'Mari died because of all this.' Dylan gestured towards the two of them. 'Mari died because she was standing on the edge. Not even involved, just … just stumbling behind us. You heard what that demon said, Izzy. He's watching us. He's waiting. He'll hurt my family too.'

'You don't know that,' she said.

Dylan surged to his feet, any last vestige of colour draining from his features as rage took hold. 'Were you listening to him? That's what he said! It's what Silver told me too. Or is it all about you, Izzy? Is everything about *you* now?'

Jinx slipped between them, reaching out his hand until it pressed against Dylan's chest. To his surprise, the boy didn't swing a punch or attack. He just froze for a moment and then wilted.

'Come,' Jinx whispered, taking the phone effortlessly from his clenched fingers. 'Sit down. You need to rest as well and there was mention of food.'

Sit down, talk, find a solution, explain – these were all good plans for people with time. For people who were not being hunted by demons, angels and the entire fae realm.

People whose world had not just been turned upside-down.

He steered Dylan into a seat while Izzy set a teapot down between them. It was covered with a knitted cosy, each stripe a more garish colour than the last. In the sleek lines of the stylish kitchen it spoke loudly of a family.

'Izzy made it,' said Dylan, in a small, broken voice. 'We have one at home too. Hideous, isn't it?'

No, it was strangely beautiful, though logic told him it shouldn't have been. But before he could say it, Izzy was defending it herself, sort of.

'We were nine,' she protested. 'Besides we had to. Mrs Mayhew got us to knit in Home Ec. while she staved off her hangovers. Mari's was lovely. She knew how colours worked even then.'

Dylan blinked – his face showed that school and teachers and knitting, of all things, seemed so alien to him right now. Jinx pressed his hand against the small of Izzy's back in what he hoped was a comforting gesture. She stiffened, her spine straightening, her body tightening. He started to withdraw, but her right hand caught his wrist, stopping him. The touch was electric, commanding, and he didn't dare attempt a withdrawal again.

'Where are your folks now?' Izzy asked Dylan as she shifted a little closer to Jinx. It was almost as if she wanted to hide from everything.

'I ... I don't know. They left a load of messages. I should call back, I guess.' He didn't sound certain. In fact he sounded more terrified of that prospect than anything else.

'They'll be worried sick, Dylan. First Mari, and then you vanish?'

Much as she had done. Yes, her mother must have suffered beyond imagining this night. Jinx swallowed down the words. They weren't for him to say.

'I will call them. I will.' Dylan fidgeted in his seat, examined his fingers. 'I promise.' His voice tightened and Izzy jerked forward, her hand brushing his shoulder. Dylan pulled back.

Embarrassed, the girl turned away from him. 'I'll go and change.'

She fled the kitchen, leaving Jinx alone with the silent Dylan. Uncomfortable, unsure. He said nothing, merely waited. It wasn't the way of his people to grieve. They rarely lost those they loved. So now, he really didn't know what to do or say.

'They said you're an assassin,' said Dylan, in a voice that was strangely without tone or inflection.

'That's what Holly wants me to be.'

'You've killed people then? How many?'

Uncomfortable was not the word for it. It fell far too short. 'It's not like that.'

'More than ten?' The boy was relentless.

'No.'

'More than three?'

Jinx frowned. He could explain. He could tell him they deserved it, that they were evil and had preyed on the weak. He could use a hundred thousand excuses. But Dylan wouldn't understand and it really didn't matter. 'Yes.'

But it hadn't been as black and white as that. Had it?

Neither of them spoke. Dylan just stared at him, and Jinx met his gaze, even though every bit of him wanted to turn away. That would be weak, implying he was ashamed. And he wasn't.

It was Dylan who broke the silence. 'Mari didn't stand a chance, did she?'

'Not against a banshee, no.'

Dylan chewed on his lower lip. 'And if I'd been faster ...' His voice trailed off. He couldn't finish the sentence.

'You couldn't have saved her. There was nothing you could do. You have to believe that.'

'How did you kill them? What's the best way?'

'There is no best way, Dylan.' That at least was true. Death was never something to be taken lightly. It was a deep and abiding thing, one that changed the killer as much as it took the life of the victim. Death lingered in the mind. It whittled away at the heart.

'The quickest then, the surest.'

Jinx studied him for a moment longer, wondering if he really should answer. 'Go for the throat,' he said curtly and closed his mouth again. Warnings would do no good. He wasn't going to listen anyway.

Dylan slid off the stool and made for the shelves where row upon row of shining CD cases were racked up. For a moment he just stared at them but then, slowly, he flicked one after the other over, looking through the titles until he selected one and put it in the CD player.

Guitar music filled the air, magically played. Rory Gallagher. Jinx knew it from the first chords. There was no mistaking it.

'Good choice.'

'Izzy's Ddd has the best CDs. He lends me stuff, lets me copy them. He's got ... he's got all the best. Loves his music. My folks don't get it, but he does. They want me to give it up and concentrate on college. Can you believe that?'

Maybe Jinx could if he had any idea what it meant. Giving up music for him would be like losing his sight or relinquishing a limb or allowing someone to cut out part of his soul. He suspected the same was true of Dylan.

'Silver taught you, didn't she?' Dylan asked.

He nodded. Silver had taught him everything. She'd been his only friend, the only one who cared. She'd given him the music. More than the music. She'd given him a reason to be something more than Holly's dog. 'You need to be careful of Silver, Dylan. I know she means well, but sometimes ... like all of us, sometimes she can't help herself.'

Dylan turned up the volume, closed his eyes. The music was sad, lonely, abandoned. It pulled at Jinx's heart and made him think of Silver, of the expression on her face when he'd handed her the phone and left her there in the darkness. He'd made a mistake. He knew that. And there was nothing he could do about it now.

'I should go back, look for her,' he murmured, more to himself than to Dylan.

'Will she still be there?'

Jinx pursed his lips and then shook his head. 'Holly wouldn't have left her out there in Brí's territory, alone and hurt. Not even something like Holly would do that.' *But I would*, he finished to himself. *I did. What am I? What have I become?*

'What do we do now?'

Rolling his shoulders, Jinx took comfort in the sound of the guitar, the plaintive song.

'We help Izzy find a grail. And help her learn how to use it.'

'She's different than she was, isn't she? Changed. More ... more ...'

Jinx eyed him suspiciously. That look was unexpected – the gleam of interest was for Izzy, and Jinx found, much to his surprise, that he didn't like that. He didn't like that at all. 'More. Yes. Izzy is *more* now.'

I don't have time for this, Izzy thought as she closed the door firmly behind her. She wriggled out of the dress and kicked it against the foot of her bed. The t-shirt and jeans she pulled on instead felt blissfully normal.

The only normal thing.

She had to turn away from the bed. The urge to collapse on it was far too strong. Tears misted her eyes, drove little needles of frustration into the bridge of her nose. The stupid teacosy, that's what had done it. Something from another world, another life. Something made by another person. And Mari had one too. She raked her fingers through her hair.

Someone normal. That was all gone now. The sooner she accepted it the better. Because she had been living a lie. Her parents had been trying to protect her, but still. A lie. Now all the stupid weirdness made sense, right down to the toaster the other morning. All the things that had clapped out when she touched them, or blew up, or simply closed down with a whimper never to start up again.

She had never been normal.

Her face, in the mirror, looked pale and strained. Too thin. The contrast with her red hair was too extreme. Almost – the thought made her stomach turn – almost like one of them. Sídhe lines in her bone structure. Her skin so white, her hair like fire, her eyes burning like a gas flame. Like one of them.

Which she was. Kind of. Mum had admitted it. Brí had claimed her.

Pale skin, red hair, blue eyes. Like it or not, she even looked like Brí.

Not entirely human. Half Sídhe. Other.

Freak.

She sucked in a shaky breath and tried to make her head stop spinning. It didn't work. If anything, the sickening reel inside her brain got even more hectic.

Reaching out a hand to the glass, she pressed her palm to the mirror. Her reflection looked human enough in there now. The coldness of the surface grounded her.

'If you're a freak, we both are,' said the angel.

Oh, good. The moment she started to deal with one night-mare change, another made an appearance. Hysteria bubbled up inside her. If it wasn't the Sídhe matriarch claiming her as a daughter, making her a half-blood monster, and her own mother confirming it, it was the thing in her head trying to comfort her. In its way.

'We both are.' That made sense. Didn't it? Sense from the disembodied voice in her mind. Joy.

Downstairs the sound of a Rory Gallagher CD reached her. Well, at least someone was having fun. Two someones. How could guys do that?

The doorbell rang and Izzy swore. 'Dylan, will you get that?'

No answer. Izzy opened the bedroom door. The bell rang again, more sharply.

It was morning, Izzy realised. Somehow it was morning. She's been running on empty for so long she couldn't even tell the time of day. The tea helped, but she should have eaten. She needed sleep.

Needed it, but didn't have time for it. Her leaden body protested as she stood there, swaying, her head feeling like the centre of a maelstrom.

And beyond it, the warning, the icy touch of the mark on the back of her neck. The cross tattoo burning with cold against ... no, *inside*, her skin. Something was wrong. This was dangerous. More than dangerous. She knew that feeling now. Not the voice, just the sensation of her tattoo, a warning of danger.

Izzy's stomach heaved. Downstairs the sound of guitars got louder, duelling, sound upon sound that tore through her agonised brain. The doorbell sounded out, shrill and harsh, someone leaning on the bell, determined to get an answer.

'Listen, Isabel,' said the angel. 'No one must answer the door. You can't let them inside. Let me help you.'

The voice felt more determined all of a sudden, and different. Not the sweet lullaby it had been before. This was something more, something ... eager.

Another chill ran through her. And another. So very cold.

'Let. Me. Help!'

The words rang through her brain with such force that they brought Izzy to her knees. It was wrong. She knew it was wrong. The angel had tried to force Izzy to do her will twice now. She hadn't asked or cajoled, or even demanded like now. The angel had tried to force her. If she had succeeded then, would she bother to ask now?

But the voice was that of an angel. Her angel.

Izzy whimpered, pressing her hands to her ears. She couldn't stand it. This was all too much. She couldn't fight any more. She didn't want to. For once, someone else could help her, was offering to help her. She couldn't fight anymore.

'Help,' she whispered, aware that she was giving in, that her weakness, or exhaustion, had the better of her. She wilted, letting the angel have her way.

Light engulfed her. It tore through her veins and arched along her spine, crackling like electricity, alive and vital, agonising. Light everywhere, blinding, burning, searing through her body.

Her hearing focused, tightened, and she heard the latch of the door being drawn back, heard Dylan's voice.

'What?'

She didn't know who it was, or what they wanted, but the angel did. The angel knew everything. She surged forwards, moving faster than a mortal could move, her body no longer her own, no longer human. No longer part-Sídhe, even. She moved beyond the realms of the earth planes, into a transcended state that knew only the threat at the door. That only knew Dylan was in danger.

CHAPTER NINETEEN

The Angels at the Door

Dylan opened the front door with a curt 'What?' just as Jinx stepped out into the hall from the kitchen. Instinct for danger flared in his chest, but it was too late.

Two men stood there, in identically sombre suits, two men who, even to Jinx's jaded eye, were the most beautiful things to grace the planet. He faltered, put out an arm to pull Dylan back, even as the screaming in the back of his mind identified them as angels.

As more than just angels. Haniel was there, sure, but the other one. The other one was an archangel.

Hair like beaten gold, polished by a loving hand. Eyes of the deepest sapphire, both blue and black mixed into one shade and altogether endless. One momentary slip and someone could fall into them forever, be lost in the glory they held. Even a creature without a soul, such as himself, struggled with the urge to leap.

'Have you heard the Word?' the archangel asked. His voice flowed like music, like the strains of lyric adulation, like the heavenly choirs he lorded over in the Holy Court had all sung in unison. In wondrous harmonies.

Jinx and Dylan froze. What else could they do? Haniel was a minion. This creature, this marvel of creation, came from a far higher rank.

Which meant only one thing. Heaven was done screwing around with second-rates. It had sent the big gun to claim the prize.

'Izzy,' Jinx murmured and his body tensed, readied itself. If he ran, if he changed as he ran, could he make it past them and up the stairs in time? Could he—?

The angels pushed past Dylan, and he turned to stare helplessly after them, stunned by the voice that still reverberated in the air around them.

There were angels in the house. Jinx knew he had to do something and quickly, but their presence stole all his strength, drained away his will. And that voice, that melodic, hypnotic voice … He could only stare at them, lost.

Was it really possible? That his people had been like that once?

But then another light dawned above them, brighter, deeper, more terrible by far. Where the archangel's light was sunshine through clouds, this was raw, the light of the sun in space itself – boiling fire, untempered by air. It came from the top of the stairs and a voice rang out, a voice that shook the house from the upper rafters down to the foundations.

'You may not enter here without leave, my brother.'

Izzy's voice. And yet not her voice at all. Something else, something other, something with no place here.

The light of the archangel dimmed, revealing their figures again.

'You are no sibling of mine,' said the archangel. 'The fallen do not command us. Rather you should come with us, and give yourself up for judgement.'

Izzy took two steps down the stairs and stood there, aglow from head to foot.

'This is a place forbidden to you, under my protection. I need not leave. In truth, I need never leave. Not while I am here.'

'Sorath, you overstep yourself.'

Her hair flared back from her face as if a hot wind fanned it and light spilled from her eyes instead of tears. 'I know no other way, Zadkiel.'

'This is not over,' Zadkiel growled, his mouth a hard line.

'Far from it,' the angel Sorath promised with Izzy's sweet lips. Jinx's heart lurched inside him. He should have kissed her when he had the chance. He should have taken that proffered moment of joy because now … now … would there ever be another chance? With an angel inhabiting her half-Sídhe body, having ignited from the divine spark she carried, a transformation was inevitable. She'd never be herself again.

Even if Sorath deigned to give up her form. Which was unlikely. Izzy was a vessel. That's what Brí had called her. A vessel for divine power. She could have been made for something like this.

And angels didn't tend to give back anything they took.

Jinx sucked in a breath. 'Izzy.'

She turned and looked at him with that endless gaze full of light. It was only a glance, only the briefest moment, but it almost felled him.

Nothing of the girl remained to be seen. Nothing at all but the vague suggestion of the outer shell.

But Zadkiel wasn't finished. He took a step back towards the door, towards Dylan, and a sly smile spread over his perfect features. Dylan didn't move as Zadkiel reached out – his grace like an unfurling wing – and rested two fingers on his forehead.

'No!' Jinx yelled. But he was too late.

Light filled the doorway, blinding, dazzling. It forced Jinx back, his instincts too strong, terror like a netted bird inside his chest. And at the heart of that light, Dylan gave a strangled cry of agony. His knees sagged, but he didn't fall. Zadkiel pinned him there.

Sorath took another few steps down to the turn of the stairs and rounded on the angels.

'Leave. Now!'

Another blast of wind ripped through the hall and the front door slammed shut, the glass shaking in the frame.

The light snuffed out like a candle and the house fell still.

Jinx forced himself to take another breath. Everything in him was screaming to change, to attack, to rip the thing out of Izzy. That he couldn't do it was beside the point. That she was now far stronger than he could ever hope to be, just an aside. The angel turned to him now, folded her arms across her chest.

'Get out of her.'

She tilted her head to one side and fixed him with an expression far more ancient and knowing than Izzy could ever have managed. Her eyes were flat as stones – polished and beautiful, but lifeless. A predator's eyes. He'd caught glimpses of those eyes peering out at him before, behind Izzy's consciousness, but now, to look right into them and see nothing left of her at all … Jinx could barely breathe. He choked on fear.

'She asked for my help. I gave it. I didn't even have to be bound to do so. Not like you, hound. I am a generous friend and a staunch protector. Isabel knows this to be true. She trusts me.'

He ground his teeth together, even as they tried to elongate and sharpen. Everything inside him screamed that he had to protect her, that the angel was beyond dangerous. 'Let her go. Give her back control.'

The angel waved one of Izzy's hands dismissively. 'It will happen. I'm not strong enough to stay. Not yet. And she is strong indeed. I chose well. I sensed her across the centuries and she called to me. I put game-pieces in play and mapped their course. I fitted moment and vessel together so well. Perfect, as in all things.' She stretched, her arms reaching out to either side like wings, tilting her head back so that her throat was exposed. 'But now, I'm tired. Catch me.'

It took an instant to register what was happening, what she was doing. She pitched forward, down the stairs, and that momentary hesitation made his heart lurch with panic. He dived forwards, catching her before she hit the ground. Izzy, his Izzy. She hardly weighed anything at all, but he held her close, the most precious thing on the earth. Or above or below it. Not because of her bloodline, or the angel, or because of the spark.

Because she was Izzy.

And for a moment he'd thought her lost forever.

The shocked realisation robbed him of breath. He cradled her close, growled in the back of his throat and fought the curious sensation of being whole at last.

'Jinx?' Her voice was hoarse, as if it had passed through razors to reach his ears.

'I'm here. You're okay.'

I should have kissed her. When I had the chance. And I should kiss her now.

But he didn't dare. Wanted to. *Needed* to. But didn't.

Her eyes fixed on his face, studying him intently. 'Are they gone?'

'Yes, for now. We're safe.'

'Dylan?'

He hesitated, unsure of the answer to that. Unsure of everything. Especially of the girl he held in his arms. No, not a girl. Not facing the things she was being forced to face. A woman. The one who now, somehow, held his heart as well as his freedom.

CHAPTER TWENTY

Aftermath

The first thing Izzy knew was that her head felt like something was trying to claw its way out. The second was the sound of someone crying softly, so quietly, because no one would ever hear, because no one would care even if they did. She struggled towards wakefulness, in spite of the lurching stomach and the throbbing at the top of her spine.

'Steady,' said Jinx's voice.

Strong hands cradled her, helped her to sit. So gentle. Touching her as if afraid she would shatter into a million pieces.

Which was just as well because just then she was afraid that she might.

Dylan sat on the sofa, his shoulders shaking, his face buried in his hands. As she managed, with Jinx's help, to drag herself upright, the memories flooded back – the angel, the deal, the fire and burning light. As if the sun had poured directly into her veins.

'What happened to Dylan?' she asked. Jinx had been there, she recalled, as she came back to herself, as she fell forwards down the stairs. He caught her. And she had felt – safe?

Safe. With him. A shapeshifting Sídhe hound serving as an assassin to a mistress who hated Izzy's biological mother – who only wanted to kill her for the spark inside her, to torture her for the angel she harboured. Jinx, who was only helping her because he'd been inadvertently bound to do so when she pulled the knife out and broke his geis. He didn't have a choice in this, did he?

So why was he suddenly being nice?

'What happened?' Her throat ached, like she'd spent the night screaming. Which wasn't far from the truth.

'The angel.'

'She said she'd help.' Izzy wilted against the warmth of his hard body. So close a contact, so warm, and that scent, that intoxicating scent – cinnamon and musk, heady. It made her shudder inside. 'What happened?'

'You don't remember?'

A swirl of light, of fire, filling her, consuming her, and a voice, not her voice. Her body no longer her own. Her mind burning.

'Sorath,' she whispered. 'Her name is Sorath.'

Jinx stroked her hair. The urge to lean in to him, to let him caress her made her tremble inside. Shivers passed over her scalp and down her spine.

'Dylan?'

'I'm here,' he said, his voice ragged. 'I'm okay.'

Izzy tried to stand on legs almost too wobbly to hold her, but made it the short distance to the other sofa. Kneeling down was easy. She just wasn't sure she'd ever be able to get up again. That didn't matter right now, did it? This was her fault. All her fault.

'He looked inside my head, rummaged around in there like it was a box at a jumble sale.' Dylan pushed himself up from the sofa and lurched towards the French windows. 'I need air. I'm sorry. I just—'

He didn't finish, just escaped from their company as quickly as possible. Izzy watched him go, unable to think of a single thing to say that might stop him.

'Then they know everything.' Jinx was pacing again. Like a caged animal. True to his nature, she supposed. Always moving, always watching, guarding her whether she wanted him to or not. They were bound, Brí had said. He was hers to command, her slave.

Her stomach twisted at the thought. Not in a good way. 'You don't have to stay.'

'Yes, I do.' He didn't even hesitate. He didn't pause. His eyes scanned the windows, the garden beyond.

'I mean, you don't have to if you don't—'

'Yes,' he interrupted, his voice more forceful this time, 'I do. You don't get a say, Izzy. You don't get to be the magnanimous lady of the Sídhe or whatever you imagine you're trying to be.

I have no choice. And neither do you. I must protect you. If I don't, your mother's revenge will be the least of my worries.'

Her reply was almost automatic. 'She isn't my mother.'

He ignored that, charging onwards in his explanation. 'If I do, my matriarch will never forgive me. And if I don't, even if I manage to evade both of these nearly all-powerful bitch-queens from hell with goddess complexes, if I don't protect you, fate itself will take a hand and feck me royally over. A geis works that way. It's like karma. Only much more of a pisser.'

'So you're protecting me because of what *might* happen to you if you don't?'

He studied her face and then looked away far too quickly. Hiding something else. Always hiding something. That was Jinx through and through. What was it this time? 'I'm protecting you, that ought to be enough,' he muttered sullenly.

Change the subject, she decided. Quickly. 'They were angels, at the door?' The question earned only a brief, silent, nod. 'And the angel in me—'

'Sorath.'

'Sorath. I ... I felt fire.'

'Yeah, angels are all about fire. Usually in the "razing things to the ground" with it variety. But that one, Sorath, she's retribution and anger burning with all the fires of the sun. She fell for a reason. And she chose you. She timed it so you'd be near. Which means she's up to something. I hate it when they're up to something.'

Like you are? Izzy didn't say it and it didn't seem quite fair.

But she couldn't help but feel it. Reason, that was what she needed to use now. Logic and reason.

The angel had helped her, though. She'd saved Dylan, had driven the other angels away. Just as she'd promised.

Outside, Dylan's phone rang. He answered quickly, his voice subdued. Jinx closed the door over to give him privacy. As he turned back, Izzy rounded on him.

'An angel who fell in time to pass her spark to me. Heaven, hell and all your Sídhe hierarchy after me. My dad hurt. And the only way to save him, or me, a grail. Where do I get a grail, Jinx?'

He shrugged. 'I think Holly has one.'

Izzy could only stare at him. 'You *what*?'

'It's not like a big deal or anything. Not the Holy Grail. The angels would never leave something like that kicking around, would they? But Holly used to have one. It's a cup. Very shiny. It heals people. She used to use it in battle. Any time some warrior of hers was hurt—' he snapped his fingers '—pow! Back and ready to fight again.'

'And this would be Holly who wants to kill me, and who will torture you as a punishment for helping me. The same Holly? Not some other psychopath of your acquaintance I haven't been introduced to yet?'

Jinx gave a brief laugh. 'The sarc becomes you, you know?'

A compliment? What the hell? Oh, no time for that, she decided. Not now, no matter how good it felt. An unexpected compliment, if it was truly a compliment, was no reason to get off track now.

Ah hell, she couldn't help it. '*Becomes me?*'

A smile crept across his lips – gentle, almost mocking but not quite, almost fond. 'It gives you fire of your own.'

Like Brí. Deny her mother as much as she wanted, she could see the similarities. And yet Izzy's fire was all her own. She could summon it at her fingertips. Sometimes. Not when she wanted to, of course. She sighed before returning the smile. Half-hearted though it was. Because even a mention of all this madness robbed her of wonder in it all. 'Sorath's too much. If she hadn't let me go, I'm not sure I would have been able to … I couldn't have …'

'Fought her?'

All fire and passion, anger and rage. There was no fighting that. It was like a tsunami sweeping over her, and nothing could stand against it. 'I wasn't strong enough. I was so scared. I couldn't help but give in and let her do what she wanted. And then … she was so … she consumed everything. I couldn't get away.'

Jinx reached out and took her hand, his long fingers wrapping around hers, his touch so tender. 'But she wasn't strong enough either,' he replied. 'She couldn't hold you. And she needed your permission, didn't she? She said you had to ask for her help.'

Izzy frowned. She *had* asked for help, he was right. But strangely that wasn't a comfort. She had known, as clearly as she knew her own identity, that something dangerous was coming, something none of them could ever hope to handle.

Izzy's strength had returned, the angelic energy dispelling her need for sleep, her need for food. Everything had changed. That, more than anything, confirmed what she already knew, that she wasn't entirely human.

But that was the problem, wasn't it? She wasn't entirely human anymore. She didn't know what she was right now. Was the angel changing her? Or was it her own blood, whatever made her Grigori? What was she becoming?

And while an angel didn't sound bad, the way Jinx reacted to the thought of one, of *any* angel, what she had felt when the angel possessed her … it was disquieting.

Dylan's voice rose from outside the door and Izzy winced at the pain riddling it. She could still see the phone clutched in his white-knuckled hand.

'So, this grail … where is it?'

A shadow passed over Jinx's expression at that question. 'Ah. Holly holds court in the Market. In Dubh Linn, you understand. Not here. In my city rather than yours.'

'Your city,' she sighed. 'How does that work? The two co-existing, the Sídhe-ways popping in and out of reality all over the place, and no one knowing about it all?'

He was still holding her hand. He didn't appear to have noticed that. She didn't want to stare at their hands for fear he would, but her skin tingled against his and the mark on the back of her neck made her feel like she was bathed in sunlight. It was blissful, like coming home.

God, I'm completely losing it. Answer the question, Jinx. Answer the damn question!

'It's a very long story. Your ancestors ...' He paused and then carefully disentangled his hand from hers. Izzy cursed inwardly, but pushed that from her mind, listening to the soft cadence of his voice instead, trying to absorb as much information as she possibly could. 'Your *human* ancestors, when they came here, found mine already occupying the island. It had been given to us, you understand, our one refuge in all the worlds. Exiled angels have few places where they can rest. But here ... here, we had a place, a place to fight for. Given all we had lost by not fighting, what other choice was there? It was a terrible war and many died on both sides. Our elders, who remembered the war in heaven, were sickened, disgusted to see such horrors again. Eventually a truce was called and it was agreed to divide the island between us. But the Sídhe hadn't reckoned on the cunning of humankind. We learned that from you, learned it all too well, sad to say. The enchanters divided the island all right, but on planes of existence rather than with borders. So you got the sunlit realm and we got the shadows. And while we can travel between the two, we don't belong in your world any more than you belong in ours.'

'Then how do I even exist?'

'Because your father is a representative of higher powers, an ambassador, if you will, a unique mix of bloodlines. There should only be one Grigori at any time, or so I understand. You're dangerous, all of you, a mix of all the bloodlines –

angelic, demonic, human and fae. A delicate balancing act which needs correction from time to time. That's why your father and Brí … Well, yeah.'

'Why Brí?' she asked, although the question wasn't really for him. But there was no one else to ask.

'Brí's … special. Old. The members of the council are the last, strongest of those cast out. But Brí stood highest amongst them when they were still angels. She might even have been a Dominion, highest of the second sphere, the kind that almost never come to the horizontal plane in case it sullies them. I can't say for sure. But powerful, much more than an angel or an archangel. But they never speak of the fall, not anymore. It hurts them too much. There are stories about her, about her home, about the Hill itself and why she stays there. That there's a thing of power buried there, that she's hunting for it, or guarding it, or … It doesn't really matter. She's Aes Sídhe now, one of the oldest and the highest among us. Her touch-stone – that thing around her neck – they say it was once fire from around the throne of heaven but she took it with her and turned it into stone. And fire dances to her will. No one knows her mind and she doesn't share. Her reasons are her own. And she always has reasons.'

His voice had softened to a murmur, as if he wasn't telling her anything at all but repeating fond stories to himself. His eyes filled with such longing that she wanted to tell him that everything would be all right. But she didn't know that. Not anymore.

This was her mother he was describing. Her birth mother. And if Brí could control fire, maybe she could as well. She remembered the sparks, the little useless flames that she'd conjured in panic. She stared at her fingers, willing it to happen now, but it didn't. If anything her hand felt even colder.

So much for maternal blood then. Her mother hadn't given her that much.

Strangely enough, it didn't matter. Not so much anymore. She knew it should and perhaps later it would. Later when she could talk to Dad, get his side of the story. Perhaps the fact that Mum knew helped. Perhaps the fact that Izzy wanted nothing to do with Brí made it easier to accept. Later, she promised herself. Later and later she would sort it out. If there was a later.

'It was Mum,' said Dylan, entering the kitchen and heading straight for the fridge. He pulled out a bottle of beer and opened it. Without a moment's pause he drained it and slammed it down on the counter. 'I need to go home. I need to let them see I'm okay.'

Jinx glanced at Izzy, but she didn't know what to say. Dylan looked far from okay. He looked like someone with a death-wish. And that thought alone terrified her.

'You should.' She tried the words even as she said them and found they didn't ring true. Some selfish part of her didn't want him to leave. But she didn't want him to be any more involved than he already was. The price was high enough already and Dylan ... she just knew he'd do something stupid.

Really stupid. He was in so much pain, and no one thought when they were in that sort of internal agony, did they? She ought to know.

Dylan chewed on his lower lip. 'I don't know what to do.'

The jangle of his ringtone cut the silence again and Dylan fumbled in his pocket, cursing it until he brought out his phone. He frowned as he flicked it open. 'Silver? Where are you?' The frown deepened as he turned to Jinx and offered him the phone. 'She wants to talk to you.'

Jinx took it from him, the size of the thing ridiculous in his large hand. 'Silver?'

They all heard her voice – unnaturally tinny and distant – but carrying so much pain and distress. 'I'm at our hollow. With Holly. She's furious, Jinx. I've never seen her so angry. I don't think I can reason with her this time. You're the only one I can trust, Jinx. The only one. You have to help me.'

CHAPTER TWENTY-ONE

The Merrow's Kiss

It hadn't taken Jinx long to find another gate to the Sídhe-ways.

'They stand out in your world to us,' he said, as he strode along the footpath. 'Like a patch of icy air in an otherwise warm room, or that sort of shudder you get when ... when ... how do you say it?' He fumbled for a phrase.

'When someone walks over your grave?'

'That's it. Yes. Morbid lot, humans.'

Well, Izzy thought, *if you had to worry about age and death maybe you'd be morbid too.* But she didn't say it.

Had Mari thought about death? Had she even imagined it might happen to her, years from now, let alone when it did? Izzy's chest squeezed itself more tightly around her insides and she tried to push the thought away. Maybe she was right to be feeling morbid. Maybe she should be thinking about death a whole lot more.

A short walk took them down through leafy suburbs to Sandycove, past the squat Martello Tower to a point where the rocks were swallowed by the angry sea. It was still early morning and there were no cars on the road, no sign of life at all. The real world was asleep and dreaming. Blissfully unaware.

Izzy trotted along beside Jinx, determined to keep up with his long strides. He didn't slow and that, as much as anything else, told her he didn't want her there. The kindness was bleeding away from him again. Frustration, fear and the nightmare of what might have happened to Silver had robbed him of that. The threat to her own family kept her going, made her stay with him, because he was the only chance she had to help them right now.

'You don't have to do this.' He used exactly the same words as he had the dozen or more previous times. She'd lost track of how often he'd said it, or how often she had given the same answer.

'Yes, I do.'

This time though, that wasn't enough for him. 'As Brí's daughter—'

'I am *not* Brí's daughter.'

'—you are Holly's enemy. She'll use you against Brí, or kill you, or ...' He broke off with a frustrated growl and picked up the pace, as if he could leave her behind by just outdistancing her, as if she wouldn't follow him. 'With both the spark and the identity of your mother, your blood-mother, Holly will do anything to take you. Please, Izzy, let me do this alone.'

'I need the grail. For Dad.'

He paused on the street corner as a car roared by them.

'And the timing of his accident doesn't bother you?'

The way he said '*accident*' told her he thought it nothing of the kind. And he was right. The one person she would trust to protect and guide her had been taken away at the very moment she needed him most.

She dug her fists into her pockets. 'I need the grail. More than ever. Don't you see? If I can heal him, he can explain, he can help, and he can—'

'Be your father.' There was a ripple of compassion in his voice. She reached out for his hand and he took hers without protest. Her fingers felt very small and cold in comparison to his. Her skin looked too pale against his patterned skin, marking him as Cú Sídhe and her as ... as what? Not like him, anyway. She glanced up. Silvery eyes glinted at her from beneath the black hair that had fallen over his face, and the metal piercings he wore – so much a part of him that she barely noticed them anymore – caught the sunlight, gleaming. He looked so fierce, and yet somehow not fierce at all. Vulnerable.

The sea crashed onto the rocks, a roar of invincible nature.

'What happened to your dad, Jinx?'

'He died.' His hand slipped rapidly free of hers and he stepped back. 'Come on then, if you must.'

'Holly killed him, didn't she?'

His shoulders stiffened and he looked into the distance, unwilling to meet her eyes as he spoke. 'He was Brí's man, trespassing in Holly's stronghold, probably with the intention of killing her. That's what they all say anyway. And he was a thief. He ran off with Holly's daughter. I don't know if that makes him a thief, but that's all they ever told me – a thief and an assassin. He went back for my mother. I don't know. I presume Holly caught him, executed him. And claimed me in recompense, as part of the *einechlan* due to her for the insult.' She stared at him blankly. 'The honour price,' he explained and then gave another of those little growl-like sighs of frustration. 'I don't remember much before that. I was too young. It's ancient history I've done my best to forget and I don't want to talk about it.'

Dylan's phone, tucked in Izzy's pocket, chimed, filling the silence and giving him an excuse to stop. Dylan had insisted she take it before he left for home, for a confrontation with his parents, for the grief that awaited him.

Mari's name came up and Izzy's heart nearly stopped. Her hands shook as she brought up the message.

'It's Dylan,' Izzy told Jinx as she read the text. He'd found her phone. Tears stung Izzy's eyes at the thought of what it might have taken out of him to use it. 'Are we there yet?'

'Yes. Over there.' He pointed towards the shore and when she squinted against the morning sun, she could almost make it out, like a heat haze around the top of a large boulder which loomed over a wide, shallow pool. The blue of the sky reflected in the water. The gateway shimmered, slightly distorting her vision, and around its edges faint sparkles crept outwards until they bled into the human world.

Izzy sent one word – *yes* – back to Dylan and tucked the phone away. 'Let's go then.'

It was further than it looked. They scrambled over rocks, skirting deep pools and the soft mush of stranded seaweed, slick and glossy, treacherous underfoot. The wind rose, pulling at their hair and clothes, and the previously fine summer's morning could have been a lifetime away. Jinx cursed almost continuously now, a litany of obscenities as they edged closer to the rock. The sea roared back at him.

'They're trying to stop us,' he told her as the wind rose to a scream around them. Back on the road, the trees barely moved and the sun shone. But here, at the foot of the boulder, they'd entered a localised hurricane.

'Who?' The sudden squall pulled her voice away the moment it left her lips, but somehow he heard her anyway.

'Whoever controls the gate. They're stirring up the elements against us to drive us off.'

'Not Brí?'

Under her feet, the rocks pitched sideways and she fell with a cry, landing hard on her knees. Jinx's hand closed on her upper arm, hauling her back up.

'Best not mention her here. She's not exactly a good neighbour.' He pulled her against him and the mark on her neck gave one of those shudders. Not a warning, or at least not a warning of danger. And not just the mark either. Her whole body. 'Not her. There are other factions in control here – sea fae who have no love for the rest of us, nor any reason to love us. Just stay close.'

Secure against him, his arms wrapped around her, Izzy closed her eyes and let the feeling wash over her. Safe, content, triumphant. Even if it couldn't last. For this moment, for just now ...

'Isabel, beware your feelings. He can't be trusted.' Pity stained the angel's voice. The sound turned whatever Izzy had just been feeling to ashes in the pit of her stomach.

'We'd better go on,' she whispered and Jinx released her, his withdrawal as reluctant as her own. Or maybe that was wishful thinking on her part.

He didn't let go of her hand though. More for balance and safety, certainly, but that didn't matter. She was ridiculously, and profoundly, grateful.

They stood before the shimmering gate and Jinx raised his free hand, tracing some sort of sigil in the air. Sparks of light followed his fingertips like scratches in reality.

Izzy swallowed hard until her ears popped as the air around was sucked away. 'What's on the other side?'

'Somewhere like this,' he replied. 'And not.' Without further explanation, he pulled her through behind him.

And not. That was the freaking understatement of the year. Though the basic landscape remained the same – the rocks, the sea, the hill rising in the distance, the shoreline to the rocky point of the Forty Foot and the wide sweep of Scotsman's Bay beyond it – the world around her had transformed.

The houses were gone, but that was the least of it. So were the roads, the walls and all the familiar landmarks of mankind. Flowers rioted along the edge of the dirt track leading inland. The sea turned calm, like a mirror, reflecting all around it in perfect symmetry. Too calm. Too quiet. Unnatural. Izzy turned around in a circle, staring with eyes too wide. She knew this place, knew every nuance of this land. And it was changed, swept away and replaced with something other. Like her life. Like what she had thought was her life. Replaced with madness.

The tide was further in too, surrounding the boulder on which they stood, cutting off the gate from the mainland. The sea whirled around them, deep and green, too dark to see the bottom. They were marooned.

After a couple of seconds studying the shore Izzy realised there were houses, but not as she knew them. Shacks hugged the shoreline, made of flotsam and jetsam – old spars and barrels, tin drums and buoys, ragged nets and something that might once have been a shopping trolley. They occupied a position half in, half out of the water, all but submerged.

She turned at the sound of a splash behind her, but the water was just as still as before. Dark shapes moved beneath the surface, shadows within the mirror of the sea. A head popped out, glossy mahogany, almost black. A seal. Izzy pushed back the sliver of alarm worming its way through her. Just a seal. It regarded her with eyes like obsidian marbles.

Another splash sounded, and another, and suddenly they were surrounded by dozens of seals, all of them watching the rock, studying Izzy and Jinx with calm, impenetrable eyes.

'Jinx?'

'Selkies,' he told her in a voice too calm for comfort. Purposeful, dangerously quiet. That *I-don't-want-to-worry-you-but* … calm. 'Just be quiet and don't make any sudden movements. Don't scare them off or make them angry. Just hold on to me. They can help us. I'm told their elder is the Oracle of the Sea. Maybe he can guide us.'

'How did the sea come in so fast?'

'Because they told it to. Don't insult them. What does *quiet* mean, Izzy?'

'But they're just—'

He swept her into his arms too fast for her to dodge him. His hand clamped over her mouth while the other pinned her against his chest again.

Seals, she wanted to scream at him. *Just seals.* You saw them all the time along this stretch of coast, especially near the harbours or fishing points. Anywhere they could pick up a free meal of fish. *Just seals.*

And then, from somewhere far off and unseen, a voice began to sing.

Jinx shuddered, a great quivering of his still, hard body that ran from his feet right up his legs and torso and along the arms holding her. Even his fingertips trembled. Izzy had never heard music like it, sweet and high, almost hypnotic in its beauty.

The selkies splashed in the water, which now rippled and moved like mercury. With no more than an agitated flip and turn, they vanished beneath the growing waves. Gone, as if they had never been there. The voice, however, sang on. Slowly, inch by inch, Jinx released her. She watched him, bemused, as he slid to his knees on the rock, using his arms to support his body so he could search the surface of the water.

'Jinx? You okay?'

He didn't hear her, or didn't react if he did. The urge to kick him rose inside her and she almost did it. Right square on that too-finely sculpted ass to send him face first into the water that captivated him so. But out of the corner of her eye, she saw something approaching and it drove all thoughts of petty vengeance and mischief from her mind.

Like seaweed, drifting towards their position. Green and gold tangles in the water. But seaweed didn't move, as far as she knew. It certainly didn't change direction, or speed up. The voice, weaving its charms and wiles, stole all sense of urgency from her. She stared at the something that moved through the water, its music twined around it.

Another voice joined the first, and another. She saw the splash of a tail, a flicker of iridescent scales touched by sunlight, and then – impossibly – a hand, a shoulder, the curve of an ear, an open mouth.

They sang in intricate harmonies worthy of a madrigal,

voices that bewitched and pleasured and made her mind wonder and her heart ache. Izzy found herself kneeling at Jinx's side. She glanced at him, to see if this music enchanted him as it did her.

The music stripped all the hard edges from his expressions, honed those sharp angles to untold beauty. He gazed in rapt wonder into the water. Izzy frowned as something inside her ate away at the periphery of the music's spell. He'd never looked at her like that. No one had. She'd never seen such adoration focused her way, and she wanted it. She wanted it more than anything else she could imagine.

From him.

Bile stung the back of her throat. The sweet scent on the air dissolved to the stench of seaweed rotting in a hot sun, and the sludge of decay, the scum of pollution that ringed the shoreline, the carcasses of dead things. She looked down into the water. Pale figures swept through the water, like bleached corpses, rising higher and higher, their mouths open in song. And in hunger.

The first one broke the surface just in front of Jinx. Golden hair spilled down her back, spreading out in the water like tendrils of sunlight. She smiled at his adoration, such a beautiful expression, until her lips parted and Izzy saw her teeth. There was nothing human about them. The only place she could recall seeing anything comparable was in the grinning maw of a shark. The creature's eyes were dull, opaque, dead eyes. Beautiful she might be, this mermaid, on the outside at least, but it didn't take a second glance at the seaweed tangled in her hair, at her dead eyes and the ragged and razorlike teeth to know that there was nothing Disney about her.

Lifting her long hands from the water, the mermaid reached for Jinx, tilting her face as if ready to receive a kiss. Between her splayed fingers, thin webs of white skin – *corpse skin, dead skin*, Izzy's brain screamed at her sluggish body – spread out as well, so tight that it might tear at any moment.

A second movement in the water beneath her revealed another face, hauntingly similar, beautiful and terrible. Dead and rotting, seeking sustenance, the hungry mouths of the sea.

'Jinx.' Fear made her voice thin and desperate, a harsh and reluctant thing. 'Jinx, they're—'

'Merrow,' he whispered and even the word sounded like a spell on his lips. He smiled, such a wistful smile, not marked by his usual cynicism and bitter doubt. This was an expression of wonder, of innocence she'd never seen in him before. He bent lower and the merrow's hand touched his skin at last. A sigh shuddered out of him as she stroked his cheek and jaw, leaving a trail of shining wetness behind. Jinx leaned in closer again, his lips parting, and his hand lifted from the rock, reaching out, over-stretching his balance.

Izzy whimpered in alarm as the merrow nearest her was joined by another. Dead things in the water, corpses, white and waxy of flesh, their beauty only a mask for the monster beneath.

'What do I do?' A whisper was all she could manage. Just

like Jinx, her treacherous body was leaning towards them, drawn by the song, lured towards the water. 'What can I do?'

'*Don't let them touch you.*' Sorath's voice tore up from the back of her mind.

A deep-throated groan of pleasure sent all thoughts of mermaids and danger from Izzy's mind. She stared at Jinx in abject horror.

The merrow was half out of the water, her catwalk-perfect upper torso pressed to the rock and her arms entwined around Jinx's neck. His hand tangled in her golden hair. Their lips met in a strangely savage kiss and slowly, so very slowly, she began to draw him forwards, over the edge of the rock and down.

'Jinx!' Izzy yelled. She grabbed his shoulders, tried to pull him back, but he felt like the rock that was their only hope of safety. 'Jinx, stop! Please!'

Bloody man! Stupid bloody man. Sure, he wouldn't kiss *her*, but give him some waterlogged dead thing, half-supermodel and half-Jaws, and it was tonsil-tasting time. She thundered her fists on his back, pulled at his clothes and hair.

The other merrows laughed. She could hear it in their song. They bared their teeth and the long, razor-sharp nails on their fingers, ready for blood, ready to kill, to tear him apart as soon as he was theirs.

'*Are you going to listen to me?*' Sorath said petulantly. '*Trust me, Isabel. I haven't failed you before, have I? Listen if you want to break the spell.*'

'Tell me!' Izzy screamed as Jinx edged nearer the water, as

the merrow pulled more insistently, as others joined it, their hands snaking up from the water to claim him. 'Tell me what to do!'

'Silver.'

'She isn't here!'

'The metal. You're wearing silver. Different fae creatures have different desires. Different addictions. Merrow love silver. Throw it into the water. As far as you can from here.'

Her necklace. The one Dad had surprised her with on her birthday, a little Celtic knotwork fish. The Salmon of Knowledge. She loved it and it was all she had of him right now. Wincing, she ripped it from her throat and dangled it out over the water. It glinted in the sunlight.

As if someone had flicked a switch, the merrow released Jinx. Izzy pulled him too hard, eager to get him out of their clutches, and he fell back against her. She went down on the rock beneath him, her hand flung out over the water clinging to the silver necklace. A merrow jumped, made a grab at it, but Izzy snatched it back just in time.

Their song stopped now and they hissed at her, milling about under the necklace like sharks in a feeding frenzy.

'Throw it, Isabel. As hard and as far as you can.'

She hurled the necklace away from her. It arced out over the mirror-like sea and fell. The merrow took off after it, pushing past each other, tearing skin and scale in the effort to get there first until blood stained the water. They plunged under the waves after the necklace, still fighting each other, ripping each other apart.

And everything went still again.

Jinx lay on his back, pinning Izzy's legs beneath him, dazed. He stared at the sky and gasped for breath like a drowning man. His face and hair were drenched. So were his arms and shirt, everywhere the merrow had touched him. He was half-drowned already before he'd even reached the water.

'Are you okay now?' Izzy asked, wishing she didn't sound so scared. She'd just saved him. She shouldn't sound terrified. 'Jinx, can you hear me?' She twisted around, pulling her legs out so she could bend over him.

His gaze moved to her, shell-shocked and unknowing. She tried to study his eyes, tried to see if his senses were finally returning or if the merrow had robbed him of far more than kisses.

Jinx surged up before she realised what was coming. His hand cupped her face, his thumb sliding along her jaw line until it settled at the back of her neck where the mark turned molten beneath his touch.

It didn't matter. Not when his lips brushed hers in as tender and tentative a kiss as she could ever have imagined. No boy's kiss this, fumbling and uncertain. No rude clash of lips and teeth. Even in this state Jinx knew how to kiss. It left her stunned.

The first kiss was a question. Too surprised to react, she let it happen to her. The second was an exploration, an elaboration on that first question, and when his lips parted, hers were compelled to mirror them. What else could she do?

Jinx kissed her, and all conscious thought fell away in shock as she found herself, impossibly, kissing him back.

CHAPTER TWENTY-TWO

Tears for a Selkie

Jinx tasted sweet and yet spicy too. A strange cocktail of maleness and the forbidden, which made Izzy's heart lodge at the base of her throat and beat a furious rhythm there. Blindly, her hands ranged over his shirt, across his skin, exploring in the same way as her mouth did, wanting, needing so much more from him, terrified that she might get it. But wanting everything nonetheless. She needed to remember this, to memorise every sensation, every millimetre of him because it couldn't last, it wouldn't. Eventually, inevitably—

He broke the kiss and she opened her eyes. Her face heated beneath his bewildered stare. When their eyes met, she saw the flood of shame wash the silver in them away to dull and horrified stone.

'Ancestors,' he breathed. 'Oh no, Izzy ...'

If he had other words to say, he didn't use them. He extricated himself from her, shaking himself free, and stood up.

'Merrow.' The word sounded like a curse. 'Damn it, I should have been more careful. It seems I owe you my life once again.' It wasn't thanks. Not exactly. It sounded more like an accusation.

His meaning dawned on her and Izzy closed her eyes, wishing the rock would just swallow her up. Bad enough that she'd saved him once and broken his geis, now she'd done it again. Just to rub in her ownership of him, she'd made him doubly indebted to her.

And that sparked off her anger. Well, hard luck. Would he rather be dead? Would he rather be merrow food?

'We need to get out of here, before they come back.' Her voice sounded far more self-assured than she felt.

'The selkies might help.' He couldn't quite hide the tremble at the heart of his voice. 'For a price. I was going to ask them before ...'

'What price?'

'Well, they like silver.'

Oh, he couldn't have told her that before? Or at least before she'd used the only bit of silver they had to save his miserable hide. And what right did he have to be like this now? He'd kissed *her*, not the other way around. Not at first anyway.

'I'm all out of silver.' She couldn't keep the coldness out of her voice.

He looked down as if to ask a question, but then seemed to think better of it.

'Tears then.'

She stared back at him, at the guilt that crossed his brow, wondering if the merrows had stolen his mind as well. He loomed over her, his shoulders pushed back, his arms folded across his chest.

'Tears?'

'It's what you do, isn't it? At the first sign of conflict, dissolve into tears. Any kind of danger, have a good cry until someone comes to the rescue. Don't get your way—'

Her traitor eyes stung as if he'd thrown acid at her. 'Wh— what?'

Jinx's mouth twisted into a sneer. That same mouth that just before now had been kissing her like all her fantasies had finally arrived. It was bad when she kissed him on the hill and he didn't kiss her back. This was a whole new version of hell.

She tried again, tried to make her voice strong. 'Jinx, what are you saying?'

'Only the truth.' Raw truth, just like Marianne had always said, hurt so much.

But Marianne was dead. And it was her fault.

The bridge of her nose tightened, stinging like needles thrusting into her brain. Tears made her vision blur. They gathered on her lashes and spilled down her face. She dashed them away, furious with herself, furious with him. How dare he be right!

He pulled her to her feet, holding her upper arms too tightly and shook her. 'Come on, Izzy,' he went on, relentless. 'This is how you deal with conflict, isn't it? Cry or hide. God forbid you'd ever fight back. It's not the done thing, not civilised. And that's all–important, isn't it? To be civilised. To be human. To be normal. Well, you're not. You're not normal at all. You're Aes Sídhe and Grigori, you're angel and shades, a half-blood, mixed-up freak.' He leaned in, face to face. 'Come on,' he snarled. 'Show me those tears.'

'Why?' She lashed out at him, struggling in his grip. 'Because you can't shed them yourself? Is it a purely human thing? Or maybe it requires having something like a heart and a soul to begin with.'

He froze, just for an instant, and she knew one barb at least had sunk in. Pain flashed like forked lightning over his face and then, just as quickly, he put it away and that hard mask returned.

'Oh,' he told her in arctic tones. 'I have a heart, little girl. And one that feels more than you could ever imagine.'

'Shame,' she spat back at him, ready to fight now, desperate to fight. 'You never show it.'

Jinx released one hand, still pinning her before him with the vice-like grip of the other. He was too strong for her to pull away. He gathered her tears on his fingertips as best he could and shook them out into the water. She gasped as he gently enfolded her in more careful arms. She could feel his heart beneath his chest as he pulled her to him, so fast, so angry, so hurt. Just like her own. His touch softened and he lay his head atop hers. 'Oh, Izzy,' he sighed. Pain filled his voice, the pain she was feeling, but she didn't care, didn't understand, didn't want to.

A seal head popped up out of the water, watching them with limpid eyes. Jinx let Izzy go and she slumped down, back onto the rock, her misery complete. He'd used her, said those dreadful things to get the tears he needed. She cried to herself now. For herself. Who would care if they heard her?

'We mean no harm,' Jinx was saying in calm, respectful tones. 'We just need to get to land and be on our way. It's Sídhe business and I have no wish to be here when the merrow return. Nor do you. Please. There's nothing in either of us to threaten you.'

Izzy's vision blurred as more tears poured from her eyes. The things he'd said – was that really how he saw her? Nothing more than a pathetic little girl? And how was she acting now, her own voice raged inside her.

'Hush, Isabel,' Sorath tried to soothe her pain and anger with soft words of comfort. *'Pay him no mind. He's but a fool. I'm here. Hush now.'*

The seal's face blurred, sank back beneath the water and when it re-emerged, it wasn't a seal anymore, but a man. A handsome man with the clearest brown eyes she'd ever seen. He reached up and touched her lips, and then her cheeks. He came away with her tears and rubbed his fingers and thumb together as if testing the liquid. He brought it to his mouth, his full, sensual lips tasting her pain.

'Why would you do this?' His voice resonated deep inside

her, like music, but he wasn't speaking to Izzy. All his attention was upon Jinx.

'It was necessary.' So cold, so formal, and withdrawn.

The selkie stroked Izzy's cheek again with his cold, wet hand. 'Many things are necessary, but this was not kind, Cú Sídhe.' He cast solemn eyes over Jinx's body, glinting as his gaze alighted on his various piercings.

Jinx hesitated for a moment. There was a hitch in his voice as he spoke again. 'But still necessary.'

The selkie pursed his lips as if he didn't quite believe it and wondered whether to call Jinx's bluff. 'Your names and your kin, if you will.' He looked back at Izzy again and she gazed at him, bewitched. She'd never seen anything quite so beautiful. Unless she counted Jinx.

Which she didn't. Couldn't. Not now.

'Jinx by Jasper, Holly's kith.'

The selkie's nostrils flared and he raised his perfect eyebrows.

'Your father means little to us, your matriarch less. We aren't dogs. Who gave you life, Jinx by Jasper?'

Again, Jinx hesitated, reluctant. This time even Izzy turned to stare at him. He looked like a child caught in a lie. He shifted his feet, knotted his hands together. 'Why does it matter?'

The selkie scoffed. 'Don't you know? Did she deny you? Are you bastard in fact as well as in action?'

Jinx snarled at him. 'Belladonna.' The word came out of his gritted teeth like a curse.

There was silence, but for the lapping of the sea against the rock and the rise and fall of their breath.

The selkie sighed. 'Ah. Son of a traitor then. Son of a turn-coat. Suddenly so much makes sense. And you, sweet one?'

Izzy opened her mouth but her voice failed as, unbidden, Sorath surged to the forefront of her mind.

'Tell them nothing. They'll use such information. Use it against us both.'

'Izzy?' Jinx prompted, his tone wary with concern. 'We need to get off this rock, remember?'

As if she'd listen to him after what he'd just done. As if she needed him. She didn't. She could make her own way to shore. In her mind's eye she could see it, standing tall and proud with her arms stretched out to either side while behind her eagle wings would spread out, wings spun of gold and light and divine will. Wings which would carry her aloft and beyond the realms of mortality. She could stand up now, take to the air and soar like an—

'Izzy!' Jinx's hand closed on her shoulder, fingertips brushing the edge of the mark which burst into incandescent heat. She hissed, recoiling from both his touch and the selkie.

She was standing on the edge of the rock, arms outstretched, ready to jump. The sea boiled beneath her. A step back put her right against Jinx's body. The heat, the hard lines of him, the scent – it was almost overwhelming. Her head lurched inside, as if something it couldn't hope to contain struggled to get out and then withdrew, to wait for another day.

Jinx slid his arms around her waist, held her loosely against him, and she shivered. Why did it feel good? Why when he could reduce her to tears with just a few well-chosen words? How did he have that sort of power over her?

Other guys had never made her feel anything at all. The guys her age, the older brothers of her friends ... sure, she knew the other girls fancied them, talked about them, but they left her indifferent. She'd wondered if she'd ever find someone to match her ideal, who could make her feel so strongly, so passionately, and now she had ... and everything was pain. It wasn't fair. It just wasn't fair.

'Isabel Gregory,' she told the selkie with more force than she thought left inside her. 'I'm just Isabel Gregory.'

The selkie frowned, his gaze lifting to meet Jinx's over her shoulder, and then returning to her face, to study her. 'Then you may go,' he said gently. 'But beware, Isabel, of a man who would use your tears thus. No good will come of it.'

She shook herself free of Jinx and stepped out of his reach, folding her arms tightly across her chest, hugging her jacket close around her. The slim shape of the phone in her pocket reminded her of Dylan and suddenly she longed to talk to him, even just to hear his voice. To reach out to someone normal and embrace reality again. To take back her normal life.

The selkie had fixed his attention on Jinx and after a moment he spoke again, his voice less kind, his words harder. 'And beware too, son of a traitor, for you will and must pay for your actions here today. In pain, in regret, aye, and in blood. It came too easily, didn't it? Cruel words. We Oracles speak cruel words and you've heard too many yourself. It's a small thing to turn them on another, but no less cruel for that. More perhaps, knowing their poisoned barbs so well.' He waved a hand and the sea withdrew from the shore like a time-lapsed film, sweeping him away in its embrace. 'You should tell her you are sorry.'

The Cú Sídhe hung his head. 'You know I can't. None of the Sídhe can. Our ancestors swore it when they were expelled from heaven. Don't you recall?'

The Oracle's voice drifted back to them across the water. 'What I recall ... you couldn't imagine.' Jinx and Izzy watched him go, until they could see him no more, and the rocks revealed a path to the shore. Jinx jumped down, testing the footing.

'Oracle of the sea, my arse,' he muttered and then held his hand out to Izzy, who stared at it as if it was poison. 'Let's go,' he snapped. 'You want to help your father, right? And Silver needs us.'

The sun shone on him, glinting off the silver piercings decorating his body, binding him.

Izzy's body froze there, trapped by what she saw, what she realised.

He'd had silver all the time.

His words still reverberated through her mind. Any tender feelings she'd been developing for him twisted in on themselves like a plant starved of water, baking in the hot sun. Was he going to pretend nothing had happened? That he hadn't kissed her like she was his only salvation? That he hadn't used her to call the selkie? That he hadn't said all those terrible things? When he could have just taken out one of the rings piercing his flesh and used that? She shrivelled inside.

'Izzy, we don't have time for this.' He thrust his hand at her again. 'What do you want, an apology? I'm Sídhe. Let's get moving.'

'The Sídhe can't say they are sorry for anything,' Sorath whispered. *'Not until they say it before the Creator, and they took blood oaths that none of them would ever do so. And because they can't say they are sorry they can never be forgiven. They are rebels, eternally cursed. Listen to me, Isabel and I can help you get the grail. We'll heal your father together. I can do it, if you let me take charge, just for a while. And perhaps … perhaps we'll make Jinx sorry.'*

'All right,' Izzy whispered to the angel, though the grim line of Jinx's mouth relaxed as if she had just agreed with him. If she couldn't trust an angel, who could she trust? So why did her stomach flutter in panic as she said it? Why did the mark on her neck turn to ice? Why did it feel wrong? It shouldn't. Sorath had driven away the other angels and saved Dylan, she'd shown Izzy how to get rid of the merrow, she'd told her the truth. Jinx wouldn't even apologise for using her tears to escape when he could have just used a single silver ring.

But she didn't just want Jinx to apologise. A desperate need burned in her. She wanted him to beg for forgiveness. And then she wanted to deny it.

Ignoring his proffered hand, she jumped down off the rock and skidded across the slick rocks, making her uncertain way towards the shore. She might have walked at Jinx's side, but she couldn't bring herself to look at him again.

CHAPTER TWENTY-THREE

Broken Branches

Dylan paced the upstairs hall, back and forth, unable to settle, unable to let go of the phone in his hand, unable to stop or leave his family. How could he? His sister was dead. They needed him.

But so did Izzy. He couldn't abandon her now.

Sure, Jinx would protect her, for as long as it suited him. For as long as whatever hold the geis had over him continued.

Dylan hadn't been able to help Mari, even standing a few feet away from her, but maybe … just maybe, he could help Izzy. He had to try.

And then there was Silver to think of. Part of him didn't want to. He knew she was dangerous. Especially to him.

Lost, alone, in pain. Dylan shuddered to think of it. Silver was in danger and there was nothing he could do about it. Nothing. Except send the others off and wait here in case they needed him.

The madness of it all swept over him in a wave of despair that robbed his breath and left him nauseous. Mari's face still hung in his mind's eye, staring at the ceiling of the coffee shop, shards of glass all around her. But then again, so did Silver's, weak and desperate, afraid in the dark on the hillside. Izzy, standing there pale and resolute, with more steel in her than he'd ever seen in anyone, had promised him, had sworn on her life, that she'd help him.

Dylan paced back and forth, pausing only to glance in on his mother. Sleeping tablets had claimed her consciousness quickly enough while downstairs his dad was drinking glass after glass of whiskey with Uncle Joe. His aunt and cousins clattered around in the kitchen, cooking enough food to feed an army. They didn't need him here. And he couldn't afford to involve them in the world that he'd stumbled into, the world that had taken Mari from them.

Azazel's words came back to him. The shades would follow him here. Maybe they already had. He couldn't risk his family. He couldn't lose anyone else he loved.

Ever since the music in the alley, ever since he had heard Silver's voice, he had changed. Izzy too. Changed beyond recognition.

Isabel Gregory shone with strength and determination. She was a good friend, loyal and kind. His friend. Izzy was brave too, braver than he'd felt, standing in front of Brí, facing Azazel on the hillside. Half-blood, they called her and couldn't see how that made her stronger than any of them.

Stronger than Silver, as it turned out. Silver without her power was helpless.

Silver ... the thought of her made something in his heart give a little twist. Where was she? She'd sounded so ... lost, helpless. And he'd handed the phone over to Jinx. Like Silver didn't matter to him at all.

Well, she shouldn't. If they hadn't met Silver, wouldn't Mari still be alive, irritating him and bitching behind his back? If he hadn't met Silver ... would he be happy?

He couldn't answer either question. All he knew was that Silver mattered. That he needed to see her again, needed to know she was all right.

He checked the phone again. Sent another message. Waited. No answer.

Fuck this, he told himself. Fuck all this.

He was out the door before he had a chance to second guess himself.

The alleyway leading to the hollow was deserted. It smelled of ashes and vomit and Jinx paused, experiencing an eerie sense of wrongness. The place felt empty. A cold breeze whistled against the ancient stone walls and he'd never heard the Sídhe-ways so silent. Not here, in the heart of Dubh Linn. Silver's hollow, small though it was, had always been a hive of life, a hub of chaos.

His home.

Now it felt dead and empty, and he hadn't even gone inside yet. Warning clung to the threshold, ominous with unspoken threats.

Izzy shifted from foot to foot. Her silence was unsettling him as well. Maybe that was all it was – her silence, her pain, and the guilt that gnawed away inside him.

They were never going to get off that bloody rock if he hadn't made her cry. So he had. And he hated himself for having done it. The silver piercing his body didn't come out, would never come out, because Holly had put it there. It was an enchantment. But Izzy didn't know that. And pride wouldn't let him tell her.

It didn't matter though. What was done, was done. He couldn't take back anything he had said. And she wouldn't forget it either. Which might offer her some sort of meagre protection at last. No 'sorry' could make it better, even if he could force the words from his mouth. The selkie had been right. What scared Jinx more was how easy it had been. Words like those that had been turned on him in childhood came too readily to his mouth. He hated himself for it, for becoming like Holly and her ilk. For using her cruellest lessons to his advantage.

What he'd done had been necessary. That didn't make him feel any less of a bastard. She didn't deserve that sort of treatment, no one did. He, of all people, knew that. But he couldn't allow her to get any closer to him. She was liability enough already.

'Aren't we going in?' Izzy asked.

He swallowed down guilt and anxiety onto a roiling stomach. 'Stay behind me. Get ready to run if anything happens.'

'Oh, don't worry about that,' she muttered as she fell in behind him. 'First sign of trouble and you're on your own. I just want the grail.'

'And you'll get it. But I need to make sure Silver is okay first. Like we promised.' He glanced back to meet her narrowed eyes, almost entirely Sídhe in the dim light, betraying her blood more than anything else about her. Where was the glow he'd seen in her that first day? It had dulled to no more than a flicker now. She gazed back at him with hard, untrusting eyes and looked so cold. 'Just do what I say,' he whispered, knowing she wouldn't, hating that he'd squandered her trust.

Then there was the matter of that kiss – forbidden, unwanted, intoxicating. Every time it flashed back into his mind his body reacted all over again. He wanted to grab her and kiss her, to take his time and do it thoroughly. But she was Brí's child. A half blood. And his mistress.

Jinx gritted his teeth and opened the door.

Nothing moved inside the hollow. The entire place was strangely silent. He tried the lights, but nothing happened. So still, so quiet.

Then the smell hit him, beyond the normal reek of the

place the morning after a night of revels. Something horribly familiar.

Jinx put out a hand to stop Izzy. When his fingers touched her arm, she shied back. Slowly he exhaled and then drew in the scent, studying it in the way only Cú Sídhe could do.

'What is it?' Izzy asked, but he didn't answer. How could he tell her that his home was daubed in blood and terror, that the very air stank of death and torture?

'Holly was here.'

'That's what Silver said.' Impatience tightened her voice. She didn't understand.

He felt the briefest itch against his skin as magic kindled behind him. Light blossomed in Izzy's outstretched hand, a little ball of flames coiling round each other, bound up in a shell of her will, like a miniature sun swirling above her palm.

'How did you—?' Brí's daughter, of course. Fire magic would come naturally to her, for all her human blood. The angel must have told her how. Who knew what Sorath or the Grigori side of her could make of that? Jinx knew nothing about them — human creatures, but not quite human. A hybrid? Was that what Silver had called them? A human-demon hybrid created long ago to ... to what? Damn, he should have listened. She'd tried to teach him more than music, but he'd never wanted to learn the lore and dry histories of the races. What was the chance *he* would ever encounter a Grigori?

Right. Hilarious now.

'Sorath told me how,' Izzy admitted. Of course, she had

that advantage too, though Jinx wasn't sure if that was the right description. The angel whispered in her ear, far beyond even his hearing. Jinx didn't like it, but sometimes he sensed it. He was certain that cold stare he occasionally saw was the angel looking out at him from behind Izzy's eyes. If he was in hound form his hackles would rise. There was more to this than a convenient accident. Had to be. Far too many coincidences were colliding – and he didn't believe in coincidences to begin with.

Izzy sucked in a tight breath and the fire flickered wildly. 'Oh, shit.'

In the moment it took her to regain control, the light flared more brightly and he could see in graphic detail what her mortal eyes could only begin to make out.

Blood indeed. And death.

Everywhere.

Bodies lay strewn over the dance floor. Not many, for not many would have been here. Most of them weren't intact, that was part of the problem. But there were glasses and bottles, all smashed, scattered like shards of ice amongst the corpses. Had they been celebrating Silver's safe return? Honouring Holly's presence? Every face was familiar..

Or had been.

And then the wrong word had been said, a piece of bad news imparted, one fatal mistake made. Or maybe Holly just took the opportunity as it presented itself. Maybe she had just been waiting for the right moment.

Holly had been here indeed. And only those she still needed would have left with her.

Sage slumped half on and half off the stage, his green eyes gazing endlessly at the ceiling. Most of his stomach had been torn out.

Panic seized Jinx. He had to find Silver. He had to know.

If she was dead … if she was dead …

But Holly was Silver's mother. Silver was so special she'd got her own hollow within Holly's domain. Every Sídhe wanted that. Holly's child. Holly's first child.

She wouldn't! She couldn't! Not even Holly!

Silver was no threat to her. All down the years she had never made a move, never brooked any mention of independence. She could have. It was her right and she was strong enough. But she didn't. She was so very careful.

Tearing through the curtain to the VIP lounge, Silver's little realm, Jinx wasn't even sure how he crossed the death-soaked club. The light, and Izzy, bobbed along uncertainly behind him, gradually illuminating horror after horror.

They had uprooted the tree, broken it, killed it. Silver's tree, which was her strength and her heart, the place she had poured all her power down through endless years, the place where she stored the memory and essence of those lovers who had served her as Leanán Sídhe.

They'd smashed it to matchsticks and firewood. The harp had been crushed underfoot.

'No,' he whispered, uselessly. Who was there to hear? Who

would care but him? And Silver, if she could possibly have survived this?

Silver had already been stripped of the power she had in her body by Brí. Could she survive this?

Izzy's free hand closed on his shoulder, a single point that wasn't made of pain. Her voice shook. 'What does it mean?'

'Silver lost her magic to Brí, that which she carried within her, but the tree could have restored it. She'd poured her excess magic into its branches and leaves over the years, and her heart and will too, as a safeguard against such a loss. When she took the life of a lover, at the end, this was where it went. It was her touchstone, the source of her magic, of her life.'

'And Holly ... broke it?' He just nodded. 'But you said Holly is her mother?'

'It's complicated, Izzy. Our ways of dealing with kin and kith, with family and bloodlines, with loyalties and duties, aren't the same as yours. As her mother, Holly is owed duty. She owes very little to Silver in return. But Silver owes every-thing. She's always been loyal, always!'

A new voice broke the silence. 'Holly's hardly the maternal type, is she, Jinx?' Mistle ambled from the shadows beyond the tree.

Jinx didn't think, couldn't waste the time. He leaped across the shattered room, seized the wretched fae and slammed him into the wall. 'What are you doing here? Picking through the debris? Out for a buck from the dead?'

Mistle turned his head to one side and spat onto the floor.

Coolly collected, far too at ease. Prickles of alarm raced up Jinx's spine.

'Waiting for you. Knew you'd turn up sooner or later. Holly trashed the tree and took Silver off. Ordered her guards to wreck the place and kill the others.'

'And where were you?'

'Hiding. What do you think? I amn't facing off against Holly, not even for Silver. Not for any of the bastards in there.'

He grinned and nodded back to the warren of rooms beyond, strewn with the broken bodies, the corpses of Jinx's friends. As near to friends as he had ever had, anyway.

Jinx let him go, dropping him like something diseased. Mistle cast his filthy and broken grin at Izzy. 'Nice to see you again, princess. You've turned out well, I see.'

Izzy had already drawn the knife, brandishing it and Mistle fell back. 'You stay the hell away from me,' she said.

Mistle dropped to his knees and bowed his head in perfect submission, his hands wringing together in front of his wizened body. 'No offence meant, my lady. I mean only to serve. No offence.'

Izzy stood there, trembling, light in one hand and death in the other. 'Then tell us where they've gone.'

'Jinx already knows that, don't he? He's kin, almost as strong as Silver is. Kin to her and kin to Holly, mistress, though they hate to say it, because of his blood. Because of what Belladonna did.'

'His blood?'

'Because of my father,' Jinx growled. 'And Belladonna ... my mother was a child of Holly's bloodline, like Silver, but younger, by hundreds of years. She helped my father, loved him, and ran away with him, or tried to anyway. She died for it. Holly doesn't forgive.'

Izzy stared at him as if he'd announced that he could fly. 'That's what Brí and the selkie meant?' Jinx nodded. 'Your mother betrayed Holly because she loved Jasper and Holly blames you. That's ... that's cruel. Oh, Jinx ... I'm sorry.'

For a moment he dared to hope that she meant it. She glowed again, a fair soft glow that could have just been the fire in her hands. But it wasn't. It was that glow again, one he hadn't see in her for some time. He'd missed it. Gentleness filled her voice, softened the strained lines of her face, and her eyes glistened with tears.

Tears like those he'd forced from her with cruel words earlier. Now she gave them willingly, for him.

Jinx's heart had never weighed so heavily before. He turned to Mistle, kicked him back from Izzy, but the old fiend still grovelled before her when he landed.

'Where's Holly taken Silver?' he snarled.

'To the Market. Where else? Plans to make an example of her.'

'Where's that?' Izzy asked. 'Is that where the grail is?'

Jinx bared his teeth, wishing she'd watch her words around Mistle, but it was too late now.

Mistle's head jerked up from the floor. 'Holly's grail? What would you need that for?'

'None of your business.' Jinx replied before Izzy could give more away. 'Just answer her.'

'Yeah, Holly's grail is at the Market. She likes to show off her prizes. You know that, Jinxy-boy. Showed you off enough while she had you marked and pierced, didn't she?' He'd stood there for days, on the dais in the middle of the Market right beside her touchstone, with them all gawking at him, tied to a pole so he couldn't hide, or change, her spells swirling beneath his skin, the silver burning him. Blistering tears had coursed down his face and the fae had laughed. They'd all of them laughed. Only Silver hadn't. Shudders ran through him at the memory.

Jinx turned his back on Mistle to shut out the words. They still reached him, but at least he didn't have to see the glee on the old fae's face. 'I know where it is, Izzy, but it's not some-where to enter lightly.'

She stepped up beside him, a warrior ready for battle, her jaw firm and her eyes blazing. She didn't touch him and for that he was grateful. He couldn't bear to beg her to go back home and forget all this. 'All this' wouldn't forget her, not now. It would be the action of a child, a soon to be dead child. But he wanted to. He wanted to make her run and hide, for once and for all.

But there was nowhere left to hide.

'Take me there,' she said.

CHAPTER TWENTY-FOUR

Into the Market

They crossed the city centre, flitting between his world and her own. Dubh Linn for some streets, and just Dublin for others. Izzy stared at the strangely dressed fae and Jinx stoically ignored the human eyes that widened as they passed over him. Izzy stood closer to him than she should. Time shifted as they passed from one to the other. She could feel it, like an after-taste in her mind, a sense of wrongness, the temporal equivalent of sea-sickness. It was later afternoon now, if the light was anything to go by.

Izzy itched to touch Jinx, to comfort him, even knowing that he would only hurt her again. All the excuses crowded her mind. It didn't matter. He'd still said what he said, used her to get them to dry land. The logic of it didn't make the facts any easier to bear.

Smithfield opened out from narrow streets and close-crowded buildings, a patch of first-world city that had been dropped into the remains of Georgian slums and warehouses. It shone with all the new-age optimism of the millennium that somehow completely missed the mark. Luxury apartments soared up to the sky, but at their feet, on the edge of the square, boarded up windows gazed at them like the eyes of the alcoholics who slept in the doorways at night.

Not all of them human, Izzy realised.

The old world clung to the human edges and waved at it through the ragged end of torn posters, leering up through the gutters amid the rubbish. They picked their way beneath brushed steel lamps and past the gaudy lights of the hotel and pub, avoiding the horse shit littering the square from the fair that no one seemed able to get rid of. Smithfield was as strange a mixture of two worlds as Izzy had yet seen. Old and new Dublin, like Dublin and Dubh Linn, didn't mix well, but somehow flowed together, each pointing out the flaws and cracks of the other.

'Stay with me,' Jinx said for the thousandth time. 'Try to keep out of sight. Don't accept anything offered, don't admire anything and don't even look at anything if you can avoid it, understand?'

'Am I allowed to breathe?'

He glared at her, his eyes like steel, his mouth a hard, unforgiving line. 'Not if you can avoid it.' He glanced at the ragged shadow Mistle made behind them and dropped his voice. 'We're here for Silver and the grail. In and out. Nothing more, get it?'

The urge to tease – or argue – rose again, but she pushed it down. For once even the angel agreed with him, so what was the point? He wouldn't listen anyway.

'Yes, Jinx.'

He paused, studied her a little closer. 'That's it?'

'Yes.'

What did he mean, *that's it*? Hadn't she just agreed with him? God, was he *never* happy?'

'No arguments? No opinions? No brilliant plans you haven't thought to warn me of?'

'Should I have some?'

'It never stopped you before. I'm not entirely sure I like your trust, Izzy. Makes me uncomfortable.'

'I didn't say I trusted you.' Hell, no, she'd have to be insane to do that. 'In and out. Silver and the grail. That's all I agreed to.'

'Oh.' To her surprise, he sounded deflated. Intrigued, she glanced up at him, but he refused to meet her gaze. Well, what did he expect? After everything that had happened. He was the most mercurial, maddening man she'd ever met.

And of course, he wasn't a man.

'Jinx—' she began more gently than she had thought she was still capable of. But Jinx wasn't listening again.

'Let's go. Be prepared though, you might see anything in there. At Holly's Market, anything goes. And usually does.'

In the centre of the square, between two of those ridiculous lampposts that resembled half-rigged sails, the world gave an odd sort of shimmer like a heat haze or the familiar sickening dread of a migraine aura. Points of light wavered around its edge, as if made of acid eating through the fabric of reality. Her reality, or what remained of it.

The phone chimed, Dylan again, checking up on them. It was only then she noticed about five messages, all saying roughly the same thing. *Where are you?*

Smithfield, she sent back. *There's a gate to the Market. We're going in.*

Her first thought was that the whole area was too quiet. The knife, tucked into Izzy's belt formed a cold line against her hip even through the jeans, an unbending block which made her movements feel awkward. But having carried it for days now, she couldn't imagine being without it. Her neck on the other hand felt curiously bare without the pendant. She missed it, in the same way she missed Dad – with a dull, hollow ache deep inside.

Walking through the gates was like walking through a wave of electricity. It danced over her skin, each hair rising in alarm, each follicle prickling – a brief moment of pain, of excitement and, yes, of fear too.

Izzy sucked in a shocked breath and Jinx caught her arm to steady her. Irritation rose again and she pulled free.

'I'm okay.'

'Of course you are. Take a moment.'

She shivered and fought not to throw up. 'What is it?'

'Just one of her jokes.'

He could have warned her, she thought. But then again she probably wouldn't have believed him anyway.

'No guards? Not even someone watching the front door?'

Mistle stepped through behind them, shaking himself off like a dog coming out of the water.

'She don't need guards, little angel. Not here. Everyone can come to the Market. Open to all, isn't it?'

Jinx exhaled in a long, impatient breath. 'Let's go.'

The square had vanished beyond the gate. A tunnel opened up ahead of them, broad and high enough to allow a bus to drive down it, lined with polished bronze. Light bounced from wall to wall, reflecting downwards. As they walked down the steep incline, their reflections followed them, hazy and indistinct in the metal. From the corner of her eye, Izzy saw other things too. Shadows that jumped from place to place in a way no shadow should. Points of light that crawled and scurried. Sometimes the reflection of Jinx flickered to his hound form and Mistle appeared smaller, horribly hunched, his eyes gleaming red. Worst of all, however, were the glimpses she caught of herself. She stood much taller in the curved bronze, her head held high and instead of her shoulder-length red hair, wave upon wave of golden locks tumbled down her back, where it was abruptly obscured by the sweep of feathered wings. Light swelled in a nimbus around her as she descended to the underworld, the light the bronze lined walls carried underground, but something else too, fiery and golden, like the sun, like naked flames.

She glanced over her shoulder to check once, twice, and again, to see if the feathers fell burning to the ground behind her, incinerated by the raw heat, but there was nothing. Only Mistle, leering at her. Her stomach clenched and she reached for the knife, still there at her hip, one small and cold comfort.

The noise grew as they descended, at first a vague murmur like the waves on a shingle shore, then the whispering breeze moving leaves in a forest. Finally it swelled into a swarm of life and activity. Hawkers' cries, accents that were pure Dub and lilting brogue and something else entirely, screaming, cajoling, and the ringing tones of many other languages, each more exotic than the last. Snatches of music drifted out through the vast cavern below ground. Laughter, anger, songs and curses, blended together in a riot of vitality. They stepped out of the tunnel's mouth into a cross between a carnival and rush hour. The force of the noise and the stench of the place pummelled Izzy's senses, driving her back a step or two. The sheer number of people surrounding her was momentarily overwhelming.

No, not people. Beings. Creatures. Fae.

Jinx locked his hand around her wrist, his touch strangely warm against her skin, impossibly strong, but by no means painful. He pulled her down the nearest aisle of stalls decked with by turns silks and velvets, fragrant oils, all manner of food and caged birds or lizards. Izzy tried not to stare as the fae tending their wares surged forwards in search of a sale. They weren't wearing glamours here. They didn't need to. Strange and beautiful, terrifying and bizarre, everywhere she turned ...

A girl whose pale blue skin was etched with lines of azure in some kind of delicate Old Irish script smiled as she held out a gossamer-fine scarf which shimmered as if spun with moonlight. A bull-shouldered man with the thickest neck Izzy had ever seen carefully handled tiny finches in fingers like sausages. He whistled softly and all the birds started to sing in harmony, just for him.

She stumbled past a stall where bottles of a thousand different hues gave out intoxicating aromas. Someone she couldn't see thrust a small cup into her hand. The liquid was icy cold inside, the exterior of the glass damp with condensation.

'Drop that,' Jinx barked and she realised she had already lifted it halfway to her mouth.

'But it's just a sample,' Mistle protested. 'And Hands makes the best vintages there are.'

Jinx pulled Izzy hard against him and snatched the glass from her fingers, deftly tossing it aside in the same movement. 'No such thing as *"just a sample"* with lilac wine. Drink that and you'd crave it for the rest of your short and bitter life. Keep moving.'

She ought to be offended, but he was protecting her. She knew that. She looked away, and more wonders were waiting.

At the far end of the aisle, a giant of a man was juggling fire. Not torches or brands, but balls of fire that burst from his fingertips and rolled up towards the roof. Izzy followed their path, dazzled. Could *she* do that?

High overhead, bronze plates shone with stolen light and licks of his flames, curved into a dome. The whole Market heaved and swarmed under the arc of that roof, and was reflected in it, in all its strange and wondrous glory. Too far away to make out details but all there. Every single one, playing out above just as below.

And in the centre was a column. It looked like crystal, sparkling in the borrowed light. The biggest she'd ever seen, thick as the trunk of an ancient oak.

'That's where Holly sits,' said Jinx, following her line of sight. 'Whatever we do, we stay the hell away from that.'

'And where does she keep the grail? Where is Silver?'

'The grail will be in her treasury, and Silver in her prison. Either side of the Market, deeper underground.'

'Should we split up?'

'Not on your life,' he muttered and his grip tightened still further.

Izzy pulled back, her free hand straying towards the knife. 'Jinx, do you think we'll be able to do both? Really?'

'We have to.'

She could hear it in his voice, how desperately he wanted to get to Silver, to rescue her, to help her. And she hated herself for what she had to say next. 'The grail first.'

His shoulders sagged and he turned away, setting off towards the nearest wall. He'd hoped she'd choose Silver. And she'd just commanded him to leave his only friend and help her instead.

Because according to his geis, Jinx had to do as she said.

Something twisted inside Izzy's heart, and the angel laughed.

Mistle stayed with them. Part of Jinx was relieved because if he was here, he couldn't be elsewhere making mischief, like telling Holly where they were. But it left him unable to argue with Izzy without giving his position away.

Argue? Who was he trying to kid? Plead was nearer the mark.

They skirted the edge of the Market, towards the entrance to Holly's treasury.

Suddenly, Izzy stopped, frozen in her tracks, right in the middle of the path.

'What is it? What's wrong?'

She stared at the walls and he followed her gaze to the after-image of a broken figure. It might have been painted there, might have been sprayed on the wall. The image of an angel. One of the ones Holly had killed whose sparks now fuelled her touchstone and lent her vast power.

'*What is that?*' She didn't sound like Izzy. She didn't sound like Izzy at all. Her eyes had that cold, flat look again.

'It's a ...' He grabbed her arm, pulling her away. 'Don't look at it.'

Nothing like the angel she'd described. This one was twisted, its face stretched in pain. Holly's favourite pastime.

'We have to go,' he told her. 'We don't have much time.' But she wasn't listening.

There would be guards here, of that he was sure, but if he could talk his way past them they might just make it. His plan was looking shakier by the second. Izzy followed him, her body stiff and unresponsive, her hard as stone eyes seeking out and finding other images now, fallen angels, bound and murdered by Holly. The glow in her had faded completely.

'Don't,' he whispered. 'You can't think of that right now. You can't let it throw you off, Izzy. Are you even listening to me?'

She looked at him like he was insane. Or a monster.

That look, he knew too well.

The doorway to the treasury was unguarded.

'Wait a minute.' He frowned at the entrance but nothing changed, reached out with his mind in search of something, anything that might denote a form of magic he couldn't see. None of his senses indicated anything at all.

'What's wrong?' Izzy asked.

'Nothing, I just ...'

'*What?*'

'I don't believe it.'

'Over there,' said Mistle, nodding back down the nearest aisle. Two of Holly's guards stood by the first stall, talking to the pretty little brownie tending it. They had mugs of something hot and fragrant in their hands.

'They're on a break?' Izzy's whisper shook.

'No. They don't get breaks. It's not like your average day job, Izzy.'

She stiffened, her eyes growing distant in an all too familiar way. Eyes like stones, so cold and hard. She was talking to the angel, communing with the serpent coiled inside her.

'It's Sorath,' she said on a breath. 'She's doing it. Quickly, Jinx. She says go now, before it wears off.'

He didn't stop to think about it. There wasn't time. Opportunities were to be seized when presented. All three darted into the inner warren of chambers that made up the treasury.

Chills ran with Jinx's blood at the thought of an angel, especially one like Sorath, lodged inside Izzy's mind. Right now it felt like several vital organs had encountered liquid nitrogen. Messing with other angels, driving back Shades, healing him, even seeing off an archangel – that was all well and good. He'd thought it was Izzy using the power of the spark, but now he wasn't so sure.

He didn't like it. Not at all.

Izzy moved on ahead of him, her neat little form radiating determination and something more. Excitement? Hardly the terrified girl he had first encountered in the alley with the graffiti angel. And Mistle.

Jinx glanced back at the old fae, but Mistle, tricksy as ever, had vanished.

'Damn. Hurry it up, Izzy. Mistle's gone.'

She swore softly in a language like church music, words he didn't understand, but that made his hackles rise. Enochian. How did Izzy know the language of angels? There was only one way and he didn't like that prospect either.

'Can you turn hound?' she asked, in a voice unlike her

own.

'Now? Why?'

'Your senses. We may need them.'

He wanted to tell her that they were as good in Sídhe form, although that wasn't strictly true. But he didn't want to be the beast now. Especially not now, when danger crept up on them. Illogical, sure, but mind and heart screamed it. Not in this place. Not with Holly so close.

Callous, vindictive Holly. Grandmother who should have been there for him, who should have cared. His first memory of her was of a woman far more terrifying than any demon, standing over him while those who served her marked him, ringed him, cut and beat him. It came back now, so clearly that the silver piercings sizzled with their freezing fire, and every tattoo writhed and squirmed beneath his skin in an effort to escape.

The grail, he reminded himself, shaking off the past, resigning it to the shadows where it belonged. Pain be damned. Get to the grail, get Silver, get out.

Those were commands a dog could understand.

He slid to hound form, leaving his clothes behind him on the polished floor. The world turned sharper. So much easier. Friend. Enemy. Everything made sense. Black and white — no nuances of understanding, no shades of grey. The silver in his body might burn and the markings rebel against twisting into this shape, but what did that matter? There was no balance to him, not like the other Cú Sídhe who inhabited both sides of their forms with ease. His duality was a mess.

Cú Sídhe preferred their hound forms, so everyone said. Blythe, along with all her kin, had been horrified by the charms Holly had woven around him. Charms to make him revert to Aes Sídhe, to be more comfortable as Aes Sídhe. To make him more Aes Sídhe than hound. To twist his nature. Being hound was his one rebellion. His only true freedom. Why else would he change, if not to assert his own will? That might have been why Silver had taught him music too. To give him something else into which to pour his frustrations and pain, a single echo of that true freedom.

He followed Izzy on silent feet, her scent wrapping itself around him, his loyalty secured by his geis and by her kindness. Those kindnesses he had repaid with cruelty.

She had saved his life. From the Magpies, from the merrow. He owed her everything. When she smiled the sun shone on him. He didn't deserve her, couldn't ever hope to be worthy. Not after all he'd done to her. She smiled less and less, her eyes held ghosts instead of delight. Her glow was gone. And it was his fault.

The air charged around them, electrifying with energy of another kind. Jinx's ears pricked up and his fur bristled. This was it. Ancient energy flowed out of the chamber ahead of them. Like a different kind of song. The sweetest song of healing and peace, of relief. Even for him.

Jinx nudged Izzy's side with his head, pushing her in the right direction. Her hand touched his head, caressed his long ears, her fingers so very cold now. From her pocket the phone rang, the jangly unnatural tune out of place here. Dylan again, no doubt, checking on her. But this time Izzy ignored it. She hadn't done that before. Never. Especially not where Dylan was concerned. It fell silent, forgotten, unwanted.

The cup stood on a pedestal in the centre of the little chamber. So small a thing, easily held in one hand. Plain gold, patterned with leaves and fruitful vines. Of another age. Of another world.

'Thank you, faeling,' she said and stepped inside.

Golden light formed around her in a nimbus and he knew it wasn't Izzy anymore. Not completely. She was Sorath as well. Perhaps Sorath more than Izzy at this stage.

A growl started in the back of his throat and then, from behind him, he heard a laugh. One he knew too well.

No. Ancestors, no!

He turned, too slow, as a silver-tipped crop descended, slicing through his skin and forcing him to the ground. Its stroke was expert, designed to hurt and humiliate all in one go. Well practised and as familiar as her voice. He changed as he hit the marble, back into Sídhe form, naked and helpless before her.

'Well, it's about time,' said Holly. 'I thought we were going to have to wait all day. Take her.'

Holly's guards stepped out from behind her and Jinx tried to move, tried to go to Izzy's aid. Holly's foot came down on his back, the sharp heel grinding into his spine.

'Oh no, boy. You should stay exactly where you are. We have quite a lot to discuss, you and I.'

CHAPTER TWENTY-FIVE

Holly's Web

Holly paced across the podium beneath the huge crystal, studying her iPhone and sneering at whatever she saw there. Izzy couldn't stop watching her, couldn't avoid the woman. Not when she couldn't move.

Wires of silver stretched across her body in a net that pinned her to some freakish kind of Roswell-esque examination table. It was like being wrapped in the web of a rather elegant spider. And there was no doubt that Holly was elegant. Part diplomat's wife, part supermodel, all psychopath.

'*She's dangerous,*' Sorath whispered. To which Izzy wanted to reply '*no shit*', but didn't dare in case the words came out aloud.

Jinx had been dragged off somewhere out of sight. There was no sign of Mistle and, but for the occasional, unhelpful murmur from the back of her brain, Sorath wasn't saying much either.

Izzy was alone. Completely alone.

Holly stopped her pacing and held out the phone until a servant scurried in and took it away. She studied Izzy with eyes of crystal blue, pale and frightening. And in all that time she didn't blink. She barely moved.

'Well,' she said at last. 'I can't say you're what I expected. Yet here you are – infiltrating my stronghold, stealing my belongings, beguiling my favourite hound and even turning my own daughter against me. That makes for a pretty impressive résumé, Miss Gregory. If I were looking to hire a spy or an assassin I might be impressed.'

'Look, I'm sorry,' Izzy tried, keeping her voice as calm and reasonable as she possibly could under the circumstances.

'Really? How very *human* of you.' Holly smiled an empty smile. 'That's nice. Polite and well said. Do we have a '*but*'?'

'I need the grail.'

Holly's eyelashes fluttered as she blinked. 'I beg your pardon?'

'I need the grail. For my father. That's all I want.'

'Oh, is it? My grail? This grail?'

She snapped her fingers and it was brought to her. Izzy's gaze latched onto it. It was her one hope. Maybe if she could just explain everything, just get Holly to see what the situation was, use reason, then—

'Please,' she whispered. 'It's my only hope for him. He's in a coma. It could wake him. I could—'

Holly's thin smile silenced her. 'Let me show you something, little girl, so you know from the outset what you're dealing with. I have three words for you – *I don't care.*'

With one hand, she crushed the grail. The metal twisted in her grip, folding in on itself; golden, molten drops dripped from it to the ground where it sizzled and popped until the stones swallowed it up like scraps from the table of its mistress. With impossible Aes Sídhe strength, Holly destroyed it. The grail, Izzy's only hope, transformed from a cup to an unrecognisable mess of twisted metal in her hand, spilling from her grip. Holly opened her fingers one by one until it clattered onto the stone floor. Then Holly brought her designer shoe down on it and crushed it. It remained on the floor for a moment, broken, until it lost all cohesion and leaked away into the rocks and the earth beneath.

'There now. That's that,' said Holly with a pretty laugh that made her think of Marianne at her most petty. 'No grail for you to fret over. There's nothing to bargain about, nothing to win. You aren't leaving here, Isibéal Ní Bhrí. So we'll move on, shall we?'

Isibéal Ní Bhrí – she didn't even need a translation for that. She'd learned Irish in school, enough to get that much. *Isabel, Brí's daughter.* Izzy's stomach opened up onto an abyss of pain and despair. This couldn't be happening.

'It's just a cup,' said Holly, gazing intently at her face, reading her emotions as they played across it. 'Just a vessel that can heal. So am I. So are you.'

'I can't—'

Holly laughed, cutting her off. 'Ah, it has a voice again, but not an angelic voice. Where is she? I want to talk to her before I crush you both like the cup.'

But Sorath remained silent, burrowing even deeper inside Izzy's mind. Afraid. Damn her, she was afraid.

And so was Izzy. More so than ever.

She marshalled what little bravery she had left. 'Where's Jinx?'

'Jinx?' Her laugh sounded again, a curiously joyless sound. From outside Izzy's field of view, other voices joined in. So many. Was the whole Market watching? Her stomach twisted as she cringed. 'Jinx,' said Holly. 'Come.'

In a silent moment, Jinx walked to Holly's side, his head bowed so his long black hair hid him from Izzy. His chest was still bare and the tattoos, like graffiti painted on his skin, stood out all the more starkly, their intricate patterns beautiful in their primal nature, horrible in their intent. His hands were clasped in front of him and he wore only a pair of black jeans. But his elegantly shaped feet were bare. It made him look so vulnerable. So defeated.

'Mistress,' he said. His voice sounded dead, empty. He refused to make eye contact with either of them.

'Our guest is worried about you. Show her you are unharmed.'

Then he did look up and it was worse, far worse. Hopeless eyes examined her face, not silver anymore, but the dull grey of an execution morning's sky. His mouth, his full and beautiful mouth, formed a line that showed neither joy nor despair. She watched his hands tighten their grip on each other.

'Jinx,' she whispered, even knowing that it would do no good, knowing that Holly would hear too and laugh at them. 'Help me. Please.'

He dropped his gaze, deliberately avoiding looking at her.

Izzy's heart cracked and cold pain flooded into the place where it should have been.

'Jinx,' she tried again. 'Jinx, please.'

'Mistress,' his voice rumbled from deep inside the shell of his body. 'Is this all? May I leave?'

Holly ignored him. She stepped right up to Izzy and reached out her perfectly manicured fingertips. Izzy tried to shy back from her touch, but slammed her head against the contraption holding her.

Holly just brushed away tears Izzy didn't even know she was crying.

Always crying. Just like Jinx had said. It was pathetic.

I'm not a child.

'He made you cry to escape the selkie's rock. He told me everything, not that he had much of a choice. But he's able to make you cry so easily. You care for him, even after so short a time. Or maybe because of it. The nature of youth, I suppose. A survival instinct, this need for protection, this need to mate. Your hormones rioting inside you just make it all the more intense.' She tilted her head to one side, catlike in her movements. 'So strange a thing to study. Humans. You always have been. I suppose you haven't truly experienced betrayal yet. You think you have, but no. Not in so brief a life. That makes this trust, this emotion, so much stronger. You haven't learned what others can do, the damage they can wreak on your emotions. You haven't learned fear. Like a baby. But you will, little girl. Before I kill you.'

'Mistress.' Jinx's voice made Izzy tremble. With Holly silent, he tried again, his voice hoarser than before. 'I've done all that you asked. I brought the spark to you intact. Silver needs me. May I go?'

'No, you may not,' Holly snapped. 'You will stay. And be silent unless I order otherwise.'

For a moment, he lifted his head and his eyes flashed – anger, defiance, rebellion – but then it was over in a instant and he dropped his gaze once more.

Izzy swallowed down a sob of frustration. 'Why kill me?'

Holly turned at the sound of Izzy's voice and a slow smile opened her full lips.

'If you want the spark, you can take it,' Izzy continued, helpless when faced with the silence and that dreadful, patient smile. 'I can't stop you. If you want Sorath, she's here. Why kill me?'

'Because I can. But first, to make sure my old friend Sorath doesn't think of going anywhere ...'

Holly's touch scraped like steel nails against Izzy's forehead. She squirmed in the tight bonds, trying in vain to twist away but it was useless.

'Just like you,' Sorath snarled with unexpected venom. *'I told you not to trust him. I told you! Why didn't you listen to me, Isabel?'*

But Jinx hadn't betrayed them, had he? He couldn't have. And yet he stood there now without making a sound or lifting a finger to help her. He hadn't fought when Holly had captured them. He just lay there at her feet.

'Jinx!' Izzy screamed as pain welled up from a deep, dark well and swallowed her. Lines like molten metal spilled through her mind, thundering along the runnels in her brain, searing the tendons in her arms and legs, coiling around her spine, crushing her vital organs and ratcheting her muscles, little barbs of fire hooking in all over her body. His name became inarticulate, a long roar of agony.

Holly stepped back, admiring her handiwork as Izzy blinked sweat from her aching eyes, and struggled to find breath again. 'There now, she's secured. Part of you. So when you die, so will she.'

The angel struggled inside, a bird in a net, desperate, enraged and terrified. Sorath was terrified. Izzy shook from head to toe, her skin crawling as if it could get away where she could not.

Holly pursed her lips. 'Never really thought things through, did you, cousin? Turned against me and mine readily enough when your lover failed and you were left alone. You should have gone with him, Sorath — the Dawn and the Morning Star together. You would have been happier.' She leaned in until her white teeth snapped in front of Izzy's wide eyes. 'We would all have been happier. Expelling the Sídhe gained you nothing but time. You still fell. And how you fell. Look at you!'

Another voice rose up in Izzy's throat, one that sounded different in her mouth to the one in her brain, but one she couldn't stop all the same.

'It gained me time indeed. Time for the right vessel.'

'This pitiful Grigori? Did you think I wouldn't touch their line? Did you think she was protected? Surely you know me better than that. I haven't changed that much. Her father isn't dead. He'll recover and become Grigori once again. That makes her eminently disposable.'

But Sorath wasn't listening. 'And it gained me choice.'

'Choice?' Holly shook her head in slow disbelief. 'You're an angel. You've no more choice than my hound there.' She nodded at Jinx whose shoulders stiffened. But he didn't move other than that. His eyes still downcast and beaten.

'Not at all. I chose when to fall. I chose here and now. I chose Isabel.' Sorath dropped her voice to a low whisper and Holly leaned in, intrigue colouring her eyes, a mocking smile painted on her lips. 'I chose,' said Sorath with Izzy's voice and her hand slid down beneath the wires holding her. The metal scraped across her skin, ripping, tearing, like cheese wire on her flesh. It didn't matter. Izzy couldn't stop the angel using her body to do its will. Tied together as they were with Holly's power, she couldn't fight Sorath's will at all.

It felt like drowning in oil, waiting for the touchlight on a fuse and then, in a roar, flames engulfed her. It billowed through her body, burning her away to ashes, the purifying refiner's fire, leaving Sorath and Sorath alone in control. The angel of the dawn, with all the intensity of the newborn sun and the fire-wielding ability in Izzy's Sídhe blood, tore through the net of wires, heedless of the body she wore. She seized the iron dagger at Izzy's hip, pulled it out so it sliced through the silver wires, and drove it straight at Holly.

But Holly wasn't there anymore. In a blur of motion, someone else seized the matriarch and thrust her aside, someone else who couldn't move himself out of the way as well, not in time. No one could move that fast. Someone else who stood there and took the full blade of the iron knife.

Jinx.

He shuddered as he stood before her, mouth open, eyes wide. He jerked, a spasmodic reflex, and one hand closed around her wrist, the one holding the knife. His grip was like the iron that penetrated his body.

'No.' Izzy's voice was her own, hoarse and broken. Her body was her own again. Every cut burned with pain and she trembled as she stared up into his eyes. Mist filled them, mist and rain, a sky rolling with darkening clouds. 'No, Jinx. Please.'

The same thing she always said. Her eyes burned, her tears like acid on her cheeks.

He pulled himself off the blade and opened his mouth again, as if to speak. But he didn't. He slipped to the ground at her feet.

Smithfield was empty. The square looked like a ghost town. Izzy's text had told Dylan where to come, but he found the gate himself. How he knew where to look, he wasn't sure. It was almost as if he remembered it. Or something murmured the information he needed at the back of his brain, like an almost forgotten song lodged in his subconscious mind.

It hadn't been there before, this curious music that he could only half hear. Not before the angels at the doorway. Something had changed, and that frightened him. But he knew that if he followed it, he'd find them. Music tied them together and he knew what he had to do. Find Izzy. Find Silver.

It stood between two lampposts, shimmering in the air like a heat haze, touches of light refracting from its surface. It wasn't real, couldn't be real, and yet there it was.

'Open to all,' said a voice. 'Anyone can go in or out if they know how.' Dylan turned to find a tramp sitting behind him, his ragged clothes only slightly more filthy than his skin. 'Thought you'd come looking for her. I hear them a-whispering to you.'

Them? Dylan didn't like the sound of that. 'Who are you?'

Fae, no doubt about that. Dylan could tell by the unnatural gleam in his eyes, the slanted bone structure and the malicious broken smile. 'Name's Mistle. Went in there with your friends. Came back to look for you.'

'Did Jinx send you?' There was no answer to that. Dylan

fought the urge to shudder. 'Do you know where Silver is?'

'I know it. Got no beef with Silver. She's a kindly one. But she's guarded.' Mistle got to his feet, leaned in too close. His stench almost made Dylan gag. 'Think you can deal with that?'

'I just need to get inside.'

Mistle shrugged. 'Badass attitude. Like I said, anyone can get in if they know how.' He turned away, stepped through the gap and vanished.

Anyone. Like him. Just anyone.

Dylan crept inside, through the field of static that made him think of school science experiments and 1950s sci-fi. There was nothing badass about him, no matter what Mistle said. His stomach lurched and tightened with every footfall, his whole body tense like twisted wire. But Silver was here somewhere. She had to be. And so were Izzy and Jinx. They hadn't called, or answered the phone. There was no sign of them at all. No way could this be good. No way at all.

The music was louder now, a raucous carnival tune, played on pipes and drums with some sort of accordion sawing away at the melody. It made him think of riots and clowns, of teetering on the edge of a precipice while a mob cheered and called for blood. The sound of shouts and hawker's calls wrapped through it. Noise and chaos and all the things in the world he didn't want to see or go near.

Someone, or something, lurched across the narrow corridor ahead of him, stinking of beer and piss. They laughed hysterically and fell face-first through a doorway. Dylan advanced again. Where had Mistle gone?

The crowd roared its approval and the music got even louder, the same rolling, seasick tune that pounded into his head. And through it came a scream. Terrified and desperate, scream after scream after scream.

He couldn't see where it was coming from, or who it was, so desperate, so afraid, in such pain, physical and mental. Skirting the edge of the Market, Dylan pushed it away and made himself continue on into the darkness of the nearest side where a tunnel opened in the bronzed walls.

'Where're you going, boy?' slurred a filthy voice. Beady red eyes peered at him from the opening. 'She's this way. No, this way! Quiet now.'

The rounded a corner and Mistle pushed Dylan back against the wall. 'You got a weapon, boy? You got something to fight with? You're going to need it.'

A woman stood by a doorway, a woman dressed all in black leather whose face Dylan would never forget. Never. The long braid of hair was flicked over one shoulder. She was pale and dark-eyed, snake-like. Just as he remembered.

The banshee. The one who had killed Mari.

Dylan stiffened, sliding his hand into his jacket pocket to pull out the knife Blythe had given him. It felt heavy in his hand. Right.

Go for the throat, Jinx had said.

'What you need is a distraction,' said Mistle and he stepped out, waving his hands. 'He's here!'

Dylan didn't have a chance to think or react. The banshee came at him, her mouth already opening, the scream that had killed his sister beginning to form. He hurled the knife at her, instincts and muscle memory he wasn't aware he possessed acting for him. The knife thudded straight into her throat.

She went down, convulsing, the shriek silenced as she fell still. Dylan heaved in a breath and his stomach churned.

The old man shuffled past him, stepping over the body. 'She's in there. Be quick. You haven't much time and neither do they.'

'*They*?' Suspicion vibrated through his body.

'Well, who did you think was screaming? I serve the angel and therefore Isabel Gregory. If you want the Leanán Sídhe, she's in there. But more guards won't be long in coming and then there will be blood. So hurry up, minstrel.'

Dylan knew he couldn't trust the wizened old fae. On some deep, instinctive level, it was blindingly obvious. But he also didn't have a choice. He'd just killed a living thing. A murderous, cruel and terrible thing. But he'd snuffed out its life in an instant.

A tremor of shock rattled through him. He stumbled forwards, looking for Silver. Hoping, praying, that finding her would make it all right again. He had his revenge for Mari's life. But it didn't feel good. It didn't feel good at all.

Silver lay in a small, dark room, no bigger than the guest toilet at home. She curled in on herself, her white hair splayed out like cobwebs in the shadows. Dylan knew her in an instant.

He also knew it meant Izzy and Jinx had failed. That they too were in here somewhere. *Who did you think was screaming?* That sound. That terrible, desperate sound. His gorge rose. Izzy would be scared, alone and lost in this nightmare.

What was Holly doing to her?

And Jinx? How did they even know if they could trust Jinx?

Dylan forced himself to focus. So why was he even here, standing over Silver? Why did he feel such a blind need to help her? Perhaps more than Izzy. Perhaps more than anyone. She'd saved his life, but hadn't given Mari a second thought. They hadn't made a deal. Not yet. She'd offered. He'd been tempted, but no words had been spoken. No agreement made. He owed her nothing.

She moved, just a brief intake of breath, and her whole body shook with the effort. It made his heart wrench in sympathy.

'Silver,' he whispered.

She rolled over, or most of the way, so she could open her swollen eyes and focus on him. Her parched lips opened in an 'o' of surprise and she said his name. Or tried to. She barely had the breath to form it. Dylan sank to his knees, reaching for her, carefully lifting her into his arms. She weighed no more than a child. She had faded away, far from the glorious, vibrant thing she had been.

'I'm here,' he told her. 'It's going to be okay. I'll get you out.'

'There's nowhere to go.' Her breath sawed against her throat. 'She uprooted my tree, broke it, destroyed my hollow. There's nowhere to go.' Tears spilled down her face, onto his chest, spreading out through the material of his shirt. 'My friends ... I thought I had friends but they ... She killed the others. All who stayed. Poor Sage screamed when she cut him open. He screamed and screamed. And she just stood there and smiled. Didn't even look at him. She only watched me. What's she done with Jinx?'

'Silver?' Dylan slid his hand up the frozen skin of her arm. She trembled when he touched her. 'Tell me what I can do.'

'Nothing,' she insisted. 'Nothing. Go away.'

Will you give me anything? She'd asked him that once, her eyes filled with laughter, with promises. It had all seemed like an enormous joke to her then. *Even if I ask for a piece of your soul? Even if you know I'd drink down your essence like sweet lilac wine?*

A different Silver, proud and strong, alive and giddy with that life. Now she felt too light and trembled against him – a bundle of rags.

'Will it help you live?' he asked. She knew what he was asking. She had to know.

Silver closed her eyes, a crease forming between her eyebrows. 'For a little while. Then I'd need more. And then more, until, in the end, there'd be nothing of you left. Why do you think so many of my lovers take their lives, Dylan? They're already dead, that's why.'

'But it would help.'

'Not in the long run. It would be futile. There's nothing for me now. No voice, no tree, no mother, no kin. I was always faithful. I never gave her cause to doubt me. I never gave her cause to *hate* me so.' Silver wasn't used to hate. She was a creature who thrived only on love, after all. Hate was a poison. 'Let me go. Let me fade into the air and be gone forever.'

No. He couldn't do that. He shook her gently. 'And what about Izzy and Jinx?'

A tear slid from the corner of her eye, trickling down her pale cheek like a jewel. 'Nothing but trouble, either of them. From the day I first saw him to the day he chose her over me. Just like his mother. When he was first born, while they were still in hiding, Belladonna put him in my arms and I promised ... I promised ...'

'To look out for him?'

She nodded and buried her face in his chest. 'To love him. To love him like she would have. She had the sight. She knew what was coming, though Jasper tried to hide Jinx from Holly, she knew. She'd seen her own death and Jasper's too. She'd seen his future, what Holly would make of him, though she wouldn't tell me everything. She begged me, my little sister, and I couldn't deny her. I could never deny her. Or him.' Her voice was lost in her sobs for a moment, but then she looked up, struggled to get it back. 'He loves your Izzy, you know that ,don't you? Can't help himself, poor fool.'

He wasn't the only one, Dylan told himself glumly. There were fools everywhere. But he couldn't say it. Not to Silver.

'Did he tell you that?'

'I still have eyes,' she mumbled. 'And I know hearts, both true and flawed. He'll betray her. He can't help it. Holly is too strong. She's spent years binding him with charms and enchantments. He's her creature, in spite of himself. Every tattoo she had them etch into his skin, every piece of silver she had him pierced with, they all make him her thing. Jinx doesn't even know how far it's gone. All his life, Dylan. All his life she's tortured him and bound him. Made him into… whatever it is she wanted him to be. She has plans, plans within plans. I did all I could to comfort him, to make it easier. But it was a pathetically small amount.'

Dylan rocked her against him, murmured her name, but she went on, tears and pain wringing the story out of her.

'And Izzy doesn't realise what's at stake. It isn't just about her anymore. Or about her bloodlines. The angels and the demons, the balance of power on earth, the creation of a new Phantom Queen to link them all … power beyond power… the divine in a single form … She'll walk again, and where she walks, unhindered by the constraints of heaven … There were other gods, you know? Other beings of such unimaginable power … Holly knows. She knows all about it. She would use the spark herself, to create such a creature to do her will, or to become one herself. But so will that *thing* in Izzy … We're lost. All of us. The angel will take it all, free her lover and break every plane to pieces. Heaven's war will come here with all the nightmares it entails. Everything will burn. It always burns. Do you know what angels are, Dylan?'

'Yes,' he said, trying to soothe her. 'Yes, I guess.'

'No, you don't. You think they're clad in white with feathered wings. Bringers of peace and light and all that other new-age crap. You can't imagine them as wheels of fire, razing cities to the ground, or creatures made of eyes and teeth, or swords that blazed white hot until nothing could look at them without being blinded. You don't know … No one can withstand them. And Sorath was one of the highest. It was like gazing into the heart of the sun. And then the sun would burn the eyes out of your head and consume you … Because it could. Because it wanted to. She'll walk again, like a goddess, and everything will burn. Good, evil, it doesn't matter to them. When they think you're tainted … I saw it, Dylan. I saw what they did in their war. That's why I wouldn't help. That's why I wouldn't join them. And they cast me out for it. It can't happen again. It cannot happen here.'

She didn't want to live, he realised. Not through that. Not again.

He knew it from the way she said it. He had no idea how old Silver might be. But if she was Holly's first daughter, she had to be ancient. Sometimes he'd guessed it, looking into her eyes, the ghosts of aeons drifting round the edges of her heartbreaking smile. But nonetheless, he didn't want to be without that smile.

'You offered me a deal once, Silver. I'd be your lover and you'd make me more famous than I could imagine, remember? You'd make me a legend.'

'There are better things to be. And only for a time. A terribly short length of time, Dylan. It will pass in the blink of an eye and you'll regret it for eternity. I should never have offered. It never ends well.'

'It's time enough to figure out a loophole, if you'll help me. Please, Silver. They need your help and you need mine. It's the only way.'

She sucked in a breath. 'The kiss of a Leanán Sídhe can hurt. It will kill eventually. If I were at full strength it might leave you a thrall. So many things can go wrong. As I am ... I don't know what it will do to you.'

'Then let's find out.'

Dylan dipped his head and brushed his lips to hers.

CHAPTER TWENTY-SIX

The Death Howl

Jinx had never known pain like it. Not like this. Sure, he'd felt the knife when he'd been stabbed before and she had healed him, but this time ... oh, ancestors, this time *she'd* stabbed him. Her face, her tears, her trembling hand and the blood that covered it, his blood, her blood. Pain danced in front of his eyes and all through his body, the poison of iron eating away inside him. The silver he wore was bad enough, but iron ... Iron was like boiling water poured on ice. Iron inside him, in his blood, travelling through his body destroying it from the inside out.

And he'd done it to save Holly.

From Izzy and her angel.

The sickening horror of it clawed at the edges of his brain and by turns made him want to laugh and scream. Old instincts got the better of him and he couldn't help it. He'd saved Holly when he should have let her die. He should have let her die a thousand times.

Izzy bent over him, shaking him, shouting, but through the high-pitched whine in his mind he couldn't hear her. It was the death howl, and though he knew the Cú Sídhe legend he'd only heard it once before. When one of his kin died … his father. He'd been too young to understand it then. And the others, Blythe's pack, had gathered around him. They'd all heard it − Blythe and her kin, the pack he should have been a member of if Holly hadn't demanded him. Like they'd all hear it now. They'd all know. They'd hear of his failure, his disgrace. They would hear his death. He only hoped they'd mourn him. Just a little.

He could only hope.

Izzy shook him hard, bringing his attention back to her again. He could see her saying his name, saw the shape it formed on her lips, almost a smile, but partly a grimace. She bore the pain and grief in a way worthy of her bloodlines. Bore it, but fought it and raged against it. He loved her rage, her refusal to accept the inevitable. Loved her stubborn, giving heart and the way she never seemed willing to accept her lot. She fought. He loved when she fought.

She was a mistake, a flaw like him. A crack in the order of the world.

Dying wasn't so difficult after all. He'd always imagined he'd fight. But now, he slid softly towards the darkness, grateful for the peace.

'No!' Izzy said, her voice finally reaching him across the abyss like a song. 'Come back to me. You have to. You can't die. I won't let you. Don't leave me.'

So sweet to hear her say it. She even sounded like she meant it. He wanted to tell her that she couldn't order him about anymore. Not now. She'd gained that power by pulling the iron out of his body. By putting it back in, she'd broken the spell somehow. He didn't know how it worked. But it did. He was free. Free of Izzy and free of Holly.

Finally free, for the first time he could remember.

Maybe dying was worth it after all.

Then he heard howls, a chorus of howls.

Something spoke to his hound-self from the recesses of his mind. It howled.

Blythe.

He opened his eyes to light. Light so bright it was like the end of the world. Or the end of his life.

And again, not very far away, he heard howls. Not in his mind this time. But all around him. So many howls.

Izzy jerked alert at the sound. Howls came from every-where, all over the Market, and Holly screamed for her guards. Izzy didn't care. It didn't matter anymore. Sorath might be here to kill Holly, or she might just have taken the opportu-nity as it presented itself. None of it mattered. Not now.

Panic engulfed the Market and Holly retreated. 'This isn't over! This will never be over, Sorath.'

'Cousin', she'd called the angel. The Sídhe had been angels once, wasn't that the story? Family feuds really could last for eternity. So why did Izzy have to get caught up in it. Why did Jinx? It wasn't fair.

She pulled him closer, but he was limp in her arms. He was bleeding, bleeding far too much and she was still holding the knife that stabbed him. She couldn't help him.

'Sorath,' she yelled. 'Help me. Please, now. You've got to help me. How do I heal him? How do I—?'

'Let me help you. Let me take care of it. I know what to do. Please, all you have to do is ask. Ask me in. Let go of your control, Isabel.'

Holly's guards circled her, weapons at the ready. It didn't matter. Only Jinx mattered right now. Jinx and Dad. If she could help them ...

'All right. Help him and promise to help my dad. That's all I want. Please.'

'Done,' said the angel and it sounded like a thunderclap.

Light flooded the place, light so bright Izzy had to close her eyes. She bent over Jinx's body, cradled him against her and prayed.

With a thud, a Cú Sídhe landed between them and the approaching guards. Its tail lashed back and forth and it snarled, hackles rising like spines all down its massive back. Another flanked her, and then one on the other side, surrounding her, cutting her off.

Protecting her. Protecting them both.

Izzy felt the angel inside her growing in power, taking control, like sunrise inside her, burning her own will away like morning dew. She – or Sorath, it was hard to tell anymore – lifted her hand and pressed it to the wound. Power rose in her and it wasn't like the time she'd pulled out the knife before. This was like a wave, crashing over her.

Jinx jolted up in her arms as if electrocuted. He sucked in a breath and his back arched, every muscle turning to steel. His hand closed on her arm, fingers digging into her like bolts. She sobbed in relief and pain, but clung to him, unable to let him go. Not now. Not ever.

'Let go,' said the angel. 'It's time now. Let go.' She tried to hold on. But she couldn't. Control was slipping away fast. The angel was too strong. 'We had a deal, Isabel.'

Silver stepped up onto the dais, her bare feet silent, her movements elegant and beautiful. She glowed with energy, with light and power. The air trembled around her.

'Silver, what do you think you're doing?' Holly snarled, advancing on her daughter, but retreated when the Cú Sídhe snapped at her.

'What I should have done a long time ago, mother. You killed Belladonna, as surely as if you'd taken her life yourself. I swallowed that down, but I never forgave you. You killed her when you killed Jinx's father, when you took Jinx. I'm setting him free. For her.'

'You have no right.'

The ground trembled. 'No right? I'm your first daughter. That gives me every right. All the times I bowed to your will instead of my conscience.'

'This isn't possible. I broke you when I broke your tree.'

Silver smiled, as chilling a smile as her mother's. 'Yes. Just like this.'

She reached out her hand to the column of crystal rising from the ground to the ceiling, the crystal that captured all the light stolen from the mortal world and bounced down here. Holly's crystal, Izzy realised. As powerful as Silver's tree had been. Perhaps even more so.

Silver touched a single fingertip to it and Holly screamed.

For a moment nothing happened, just the scream that went on and on, drowning the noise of the rapidly evacuating Market, the stampede of fae-folk up the tunnel to the outside. And then the crack appeared, a hairline fracture deep inside the quartz, reaching for Silver's finger with a sound like the demise of an iceberg. It spread, speeding through the crystal, branching out until it looked like skeletal leaves, racing through the stone.

Holly choked and her voice died in her throat. Silver opened her mouth and a pure high note rang out. It rebounded off the bronze walls and ceiling far away, echoed back in abstract harmonies and the crystal trembled. When Silver stopped singing, the voice went on, amplified to dangerous proportions.

'I found another source,' Silver went on, 'one more potent than any of us could have imagined. Will you?'

The crystal shattered. Shards rained down on them like hailstones. Holly gave a sob and fell back, into the arms of her guards. Surrounded, safe, but broken, as surely as her crystal was broken.

Silver shook her hand as if ridding it of something unpleasant. 'Now we're leaving. And you'll let us go, or I'll give Brí's hounds leave to do as they will.'

'Brí's hounds? *You* brought Brí's hounds here?'

The nearest one shook its head and slid to Sídhe-form. Blythe stood there. 'We came ourselves. We followed our brother and saw what you've done to him. Now we'll take him home.'

'Izzy?' Jinx whispered, his voice wretched, his eyes searching her face. 'Izzy, are you okay?'

But she couldn't answer him. She was just a spectator now. Sorath wasn't finished with her. And she'd given her word to allow it. Her struggle to resist the inevitable, this delay, had only made the angel furious. But she couldn't help it. She had to know Jinx was all right. She had to know that he was safe. Even as the flames boiled through her again, she kissed him. Kissed him and felt him kiss back, indulged in the wonder of that sensation, and felt herself bleed away, into the light, swallowed up by the being inside her.

Her last thought was that at least she had felt that final kiss. At least she knew he lived. And that Silver and Blythe would make him free.

That was enough. She could do no more. The angel took her.

Dylan lurched against the wall as he tried to stand and struggled for breath. The rough stone dragged at his jacket and his stomach roiled inside him, cramps shaking him like a terrier with a rat. Sweat stood out on his forehead, pinpricks of ice.

'Careful now, lad,' said Mistle, his harsh voice grating against Dylan's ears. 'Don't want to do yourself an injury now, do you?' Laughter hung beneath the words like a stench. Unpleasant, mocking laughter, the kind that made him cringe inside, the kind that sapped the will to do anything more than curl up in the corner and die.

What had Silver done to him?

He tried again, pitching himself forwards so his legs had no choice but to keep up or let the rest of him fall. The edge of the cell door gave way to smooth bronze and he slid more comfortably now, his vision blurred and indistinct.

Mistle's hand came in to support him. 'Steady. You don't want to break the connection, not if she's facing off against old Holly right now. She needs you calm. Think of the music, the songs you want to make up. Let it fill you.'

And there is was – music. All around him, flowing through him, music that shivered across his skin and twined itself around each heartbeat. Music, the thought of which brought tears to his eyes and a smile to his lips. It had colours, shades and textures, layer upon layer of harmonies combined in a wondrous whole. He could feel each instrument, the way the angles and plains interlocked, the colours and shades merging in the glorious whole.

His body ached for this music. He needed to capture it. He needed to cup it in his shaking hands and share it, let others know its wonder as he did. He needed—

This was her promise, he realised as he forced himself onwards. And if he allowed it, he knew it would swallow him whole. Hearing this – *feeling* this – he'd never be the same. This was her promise and her curse, the reason one didn't seek out a Leanán Sídhe and the same reason to think not twice but three times before kissing one. Before accepting any deals.

Silver had tried to stop him. He sobbed, but in time and harmony with the melody of that marvellous music.

Part of him wished he had listened. Because the music was almost too much. The prospect of trying to capture it daunted him. And thrilled him.

Dylan's consciousness reeled inside his skull.

Silver appeared as if from nowhere and caught him before he could fall.

'I'm here,' she said, as if speaking to a child. 'Shh, don't be scared. I'm here.'

She kissed him again and drew the music from him. The world shuddered back to normality. Weaker, drained but himself once more, the music fading to memory, a dream. Dylan drew in a breath and found every atom of his body transformed.

'Silver, I ... I heard ... I saw ...' She rested her forehead to his, holding both his shoulders, and she stared deeply into his eyes, studying him as if she could see into his soul. Perhaps she could. He would put nothing past her.

'I know,' she said on a sigh heavy with regret. He could still feel it, the connection between them. Another kiss and it would reignite, he would hear that symphony again and be lost in it, in her. The music wasn't gone and neither was she. A surge of relief swept through him, followed by one of fear, almost as powerful. He had agreed to this. To give up his life for the wonder of being with her, of hearing the music she heard. It had been his choice. It was terrifying, but glorious. Just like Silver. 'But now, we have to go.' She took his hand possessively, drawing him after her. 'Stay with me, now. You can't afford to get lost.'

'Did you find them? Are they safe?'

She stopped and looked back over her shoulder, impossibly beautiful but alien, impassive.

He heard Jinx's raised voice before Silver could answer. 'Back to Brí's domain, are you crazy?'

'It's the quickest way out of here,' another woman replied, just as stridently. 'Besides, I can offer safe passage.' It was Blythe, he realised. But how was she here? Everything had changed while he'd been ... what? Away with the fairies? Insane laughter bubbled up inside him.

'For a price,' Jinx growled. 'The last price nearly killed Silver.'

They stood at the mouth of the broad tunnel leading back to the gate to Smithfield and the human world. Dylan's world, the one he desperately wanted to see again. The Market was deserted, stalls and goods scattered, the traders and buyers fled. There was no sign of Holly either. Nothing but an eerie silence. And still the Cú Sídhe argued.

Izzy stood to one side, holding her arms tightly across her chest. Mistle hunkered down in front of her, his head bowed, breathing hard. Dylan couldn't catch a word, but he was sure Izzy spoke to the fae. Not in English though. The language sounded so strange, lyric and unreal. Mistle's eyes glowed with something like adoration. Weak though he felt, Dylan made straight for her. 'Izzy, you okay?'

Mistle shuffled back, muttering angrily to himself. Izzy stared at Dylan, as if trying to place him. Blood ran down her arm, her skin torn, her sleeve ragged. And she held a knife. It too was covered in blood. Then she glared past him at Jinx.

She tightened her grip on the knife in a way that sent ice through Dylan's veins. Then she seemed to see him for the first time and tucked the knife away behind her back. 'You look like hell.'

He caught her arm and pushed up the blood-sodden sleeve to examine her shredded skin. She didn't even wince. 'Not as bad as you.'

Blythe and Jinx circled each other and the black dogs surrounding them cowered and snarled. Silver stepped into the middle of it, aglow with light.

'Enough!' Silver cried. 'We don't have time. We've just declared war and struck Holly hard. She won't take long to regroup. And we cannot afford to be here when she does. Come with me.'

Her voice shook them all into action. Before Dylan could shout a warning, Jinx took off after Mistle, the other hounds breaking into a run behind him, running for the sheer joy of it, until Blythe called them back, a curse underpinning every word she used.

'You're looking at her a lot,' Silver teased, without any real malice. Amused desire coloured her voice.

Yes, he'd been staring at Blythe. The naked woman with the exotic patterns marking her skin like pale scars.

'There's a ... a lot of her to look at,' Dylan replied as smoothly as he could.

Silver smiled at him and it was a smile that chilled him to the core. It knew far too much. 'Get Izzy out of here,' she said. 'She needs you. She's been through a terrible ordeal. Go.'

He nodded and caught Izzy's uninjured arm. She didn't fight him, didn't argue.

Like a sleepwalker she followed him, and together they ran from the Market while the hounds formed a line behind them, a retreat line of military precision, with Blythe holding the centre.

The gate shimmered ahead of them, like a moonlit pool, capturing the light from the other side, natural and man-made. Distorted shapes moved beneath the surface, and the lights, so many lights swarmed across the surface. Too many. Dylan hesitated, but Izzy didn't stop. He tried to pull back, tried to stop, but in the last moment her fingers dug into his arm and with inhuman strength, she dragged him after her.

'They followed you,' she hissed in a voice that wasn't her own. 'You idiot. They've been whispering to you all along, directing you and tracking your every move. The angels planted a beacon in your brain and then just followed you right to us.'

CHAPTER TWENTY-SEVEN

A World Away From Help

The air rushed over Jinx as he crossed the threshold of the gate in pursuit of Mistle. Fresh, cool and charged with ozone. He shuddered, shaking off the transference, and the silver carriages of a Luas tram slid along the bottom of the square, cut by the intervening trees and then swallowed up behind buildings. It was a momentary distraction, but he cursed it as all around him, host upon host of slender, beautiful figures closed in. Angels. Everywhere. All their attention was fixed on the gate, on the girl just now emerging with Dylan at her side. On Izzy.

With a brief intake of breath, Jinx tried to fall back, to put himself between her and them.

Mistle barrelled into him, pinning him down. The old fae

brought a knee up into Jinx's stomach and with surprising strength, wrapped his hands around Jinx's throat.

'You should have died. You should have died.' Spit speckled Jinx's face. 'I took care of her father, just like she told me. And I'll deal with his wife too, if she gets in the way. I didn't kill him but I could have. *I could have.* For my angel. The Grigori do nothing for us, nothing at all. They've abandoned us all. Why should we protect them and hold them inviolate? Sorath's need is greater. She is greater. Brí isn't enough to hold the girl here. If you'd only died there'd be nothing to hold her here at all.'

The grip tightened, closing off his airway. Jinx twisted, marshalled his strength and flipped Mistle to one side. They landed heavily and even as Jinx tried to right himself, Mistle was on him again.

Three blows, face, stomach, face again and Mistle went down snarling and spitting, crawling across the paving stones towards Izzy.

'Izzy!' Jinx yelled, scrambling up from the ground and trying to reach her before the angels. They'd take her and tear her to shreds in order to get to Sorath. They'd destroy her to take back the spark. 'Get back, get inside. Run!'

But Izzy didn't move. Not even when Dylan tried to break free of her, Dylan who up to that moment had been apparently supporting her. Her hand locked onto his arm and she pulled him against her, locking her other hand around his throat. Silver gave an outraged cry.

Light burst from the air around Izzy and Dylan, flames rained down on her and around her. Izzy smiled, her eyes blazing with an incandescent glow, and she raised one hand, her fingers splayed out like a shield.

Angelic voices rose in song, in a war chant that assaulted Jinx's ears and drove him to the ground, but Sorath – it had to be Sorath ... No way Izzy could stand before it, holding Dylan and facing down a host the like of which Jinx had never heard of on this plane or any other.

Not since the war in heaven. Not since the stories only the oldest fae told.

'Go back?' The angel's voice made the ground shake. The paving stones shattered, cracks spreading out from her position like the fingers of her hand. 'No. I shall go on. And they cannot stop me. No one can stop me. He shall be freed. He shall be freed and we shall be together again. A soul and a body is all I need.' She shook Dylan like a rag doll. 'And here it is. You have no power over me, not anymore.'

The angels took a step forward, Zadkiel and Haniel at their fore. Their mouths opened and their song rose, worse than a banshee, more beautiful and terrible by far.

Mistle dropped to the ground, little more than a yard from Izzy, grovelling and crying out Sorath's name. 'I did everything for you, my angel. Everything. Please, don't leave me here!'

The song swept over them. Dylan screamed, wilting in Sorath's grip, her hostage, her failing shield. Silver cried out, stumbling forward to try to save him, but the song robbed her newly regained strength. The Cú Sídhe howled, whined, and dropped to the ground. All the Sídhe, no matter what their power or nobility of birth, were felled in a single stroke.

But Sorath, in Izzy's body, stood firm.

'Would you have them all die for you?' Zadkiel asked, breaking off his song. 'Does your pride extend that far?'

She cast her eyes around the square where fae and human alike toppled whether they could see the angels or not. 'What are they but beasts that walk the horizontal? Lower plane creatures. They are nothing. You know the truth, Zadkiel. You know what we are. Feel this power. Revel in it. Come with me, share this.' She stretched out her hand, the one she had previously used to threaten Dylan, and beckoned to the angel.

To Jinx's amazement, Zadkiel hesitated. He felt it too, the sheer desire to fall at her feet, to worship and love her. She gave off the imperative to everyone there and he saw them waver. The Dawn herself, most beloved, the angel who heralded the new day and the joy of morning, queen to the Morning Star ... who could fail to love her, to want to please her?

Zadkiel shook her off. An archangel, made for war and inured to such enchantments, he stood straighter than those around him who failed.

'Give back the spark and accept your fate,' he declared, his voice ringing out through the night. Across the square, the street lamps flared and exploded, bursting for a moment with power. 'Sorath, you are fallen. You will burn. Accept it!'

The spell she wove shattered. Jinx felt its tendrils slither off him, freeing him. Too long under the bonds of a desire to please, he welcomed the release, shook himself free with relief and joy, but others all around him wept with grief – human, fae, and even angel. Haniel dropped to his knees, burying his face in his hands, all his pride wiped away as he sobbed her name.

'I accept nothing,' Sorath snarled, her hatred transforming Izzy's pretty face to something snide and detestable. 'I *will* burn. That is what I do, you fool. That is my strength. You cannot take me. Not in this form. It is mine. She has agreed.'

No! Jinx dragged himself up on his arms, his body shaking as he tried to fight off the massed powers of the heavens who strove to drive him down. How could Izzy have agreed to let Sorath possess her? Why?

And he remembered the iron in his belly, the sense of drifting away to peace, to darkness, to another side of existence before he was drawn back, before the light. Light like the dawn.

'Izzy,' he breathed. 'You didn't.'

Sorath cast a glance his way and she smiled. Not Izzy's smile. There was no joy, no innocence, no love in that smile. His heart stuttered to see it and he shied back. She couldn't have done it for him. She wouldn't have. She wasn't that much of a fool, surely. No one was. Even Izzy wouldn't have given that much for another, for someone who had hurt her, betrayed her and let her enemy take her. She couldn't be such a naïve child.

But she could. He knew she could. And it wasn't naivety. It was part of the reason he loved her.

Sorath raised her hand a third time and fire billowed forth from the gate. Without a moment's hesitation, she stepped back into it, pulling Dylan with her.

And the fallen angel, the young man and the girl who had given herself to save him were gone.

Without hesitation Jinx dived after them.

She had twisted the Sídhe-way beyond the gate. He felt it the moment he passed through its burning embrace. Her fire had scorched the Sídhe-way, making it writhe from its intended course and twist to a new destination. Nature shrieked at such an offence and travelling along this new, unnatural path, even Jinx's body rebelled. His mind squeezed on all sides within a migraine-inducing vice, his teeth aching from pressure, his lungs straining to breathe air that should not be there at all.

But he forced himself onwards, following Sorath and her path cloven through reality using her power combined with Izzy's fae and Grigori blood. He should have known, or at least have guessed that Izzy herself was the goal. All planes met in the girl; Grigori blood was demon and human. Add to that Brí as her mother, and she became as potent a blend as might be found. Sorath – and Holly for that matter – had called her a vessel, and so she was, one designed to hold an angel. One designed to survive as a human. A creature of magic with a soul, possessed of the divine spark. Sorath may have fallen, but she herself admitted she chose the time and the place so Izzy would be there.

She'd even put Mistle in place to ensure the girl touched the after-image so the transference could take place. She was cunning and she'd had millennia to plan this. The thought sent a tremor of fear through him.

What else had she done? Izzy's father's accident – Mistle had all but admitted causing that. It was too convenient to be an accident. Jinx didn't believe in coincidences. And the rest of them? Lives ruined, lives changed forever, lives lost, lives so readily dispensable. What did it matter when you were older than the stones, older than the stars? What did it matter when all that you thought of was heaven and hell, with humans and fae just an irritating infestation of the horizontal plane?

Angels and demons never saw the whole. Sometimes he thought the Creator had made them blind to it deliberately.

It had worked. Until now.

So why did he still live? Why save him? Unless it was the only way to ensure Izzy's cooperation. She had saved him once, healed him using the spark. Now that Holly had bound them together, Sorath needed Izzy's cooperation. Had that been the angel's plan all along? Or had she simply played Holly when the opportunity arose? A dangerous game. Holly loved nothing in the world so much as to kill, and nothing to kill so much as angels. She'd tied Izzy and Sorath together so Sorath would die when Izzy did. But if that was Sorath's plan, so they could not be parted ... Izzy would be hers – heart, body and soul.

But why?

He sensed the break in the Sídhe-way and reached for it. It was a ragged tear, with no grace or elegance in its formation. The angel had simply ripped her way through, the opening malformed and higher, it turned out, than the ground on the other side.

He fell.

The earth, grassy and damp from the late-night rain slammed into his body. He rolled onto his back, unable to stop the groan that the impact wrenched out of him. No way of knowing how much time had passed, how much redirecting the Sídhe-way had disrupted the world around it. It was dark, cold and he'd have to deal with it. The time was of no importance. Now was all that mattered.

Another body lay a little way off, at the foot of the slope where the ground flattened out before falling away to gorse and rocky cliffs. The dark expanse of the sea beyond reflected the low moon. Jinx knew this place.

The body stirred and gave a similar groan of pain. It was Dylan, Jinx realised, the music he made silent now. He lay very still and pale, his chest moving only a fraction of an inch to betray the fact he still lived. Such a waste. Such a senseless waste of a life of talent and promise. He'd heard Silver's music, followed her call. And look where it had led him.

Beyond Dylan, a stone structure rose from the ground, man-made, modern, especially by Sídhe standards, but shaped like something older and alien to these shores. A stepped pyramid, topped with a single square block. It was a folly, out of place and out of time, locally beloved. They called it the Wishing Stone.

He stood up, stretching out his aching body. This was Killiney Hill, in the shadow of the white Obelisk, right above Brí's hollow. Close to Izzy and Dylan's homes.

And a world away from help.

Light blossomed out of the darkness, dawn breaking, or so he thought at first. But this light came not from the horizon, but from the Wishing Stone. Sorath walked around the base, took the first step up onto it.

'I know what you're doing,' Jinx shouted.

She didn't respond, just kept walking on, circling the first level anticlockwise until it was complete and she stepped up to another.

'I won't let you take her,' he marched towards the steps and felt the power imbued in the stones. Not magic, not angelic or demonic, but something else. Something he'd never felt before.

Human?

As he tried to step up, the power in the stones rose up, lashed out, flinging him backwards. He took a glancing blow off the boulders, gorse and brambles behind the pyramid and landed heavily.

Sorath's laughter, so like Izzy's, and so unlike it too, rang out over the hilltop.

'Jinx,' Dylan whispered, struggling up from the ground.

'Jinx, it's the stone.'

Jinx shook his head, trying to clear it of the high-pitched whine drilling into his brain, trying to force himself up. 'It's magic.'

'It's the Wishing Stone. Wishes. Human belief. Human dreams. That's what she's going to use. She has everything else already. You have to stop her.'

He seized Dylan's shoulders and shook him. 'How, when it won't let me set foot on it after her?'

Dylan gasped for breath, breath he couldn't quite draw. Jinx released him in shock. His ribs were cracked, a lung punctured. It would kill him, slowly and painfully, without help. 'She made the same mistake at first.' He wheezed out the words, each one an agony. 'Made me tell her. You have to follow the rules, circle each level of the stone before climbing to the next. Then face the sea, the island, to make your wish. Did it a thousand times as kids, Izzy and I ...'

'Lie still. You'll make it worse. Help will be here soon.'

What help? Help was too far away.

Dylan sank back onto the ground. He knew. He understood. 'Tell Silver ...'

'I know. I will.'

Jinx turned to the stone. Sorath was on the third level already, almost around to the steps. It was magic indeed. Human magic, and like all magic the rules were everything. He sprinted for the stone and this time, once he'd circled it, he could step up onto the first level.

Wishes, human magic, like prayers, like faith, all the intangible things his kind could never really understand, so called by other names.

'Sorath,' he shouted, 'don't do this.'

'It must be done, faeling. I swore it long ago, when I cast your ancestors out, when the Morning Star fell and I was parted from him. I swore it. I've planned for so long. Why would I stop now when I've given everything to be here in this time, this place, with this body?'

'Let her go.'

'Why when she's mine? She wouldn't exist without me. The blood of the Grigori, her family line, Brí's obsession with her father, even Brí's own expulsion from heaven for the sin of refusing a side ... who else could have done all this? I designed her to be my vessel.' She stopped, towering over him, the wind whipping Izzy's bright hair back from her face, her eyes aglow with all the fire of the sun. 'Is she not perfect? The fire is part of her, you see. Brí's blood welcomes me, recognises me, as like knows like. Fire is an integral part of us both. You've felt drawn to her from the moment you first interfered. So come, follow us now and see it to the conclusion. Come, Jinx, and try to take her back.'

He pushed on. Sorath reached the top ahead of him and stood there, arms outstretched, facing the waters. Light formed around her, a circle of light, a nimbus glow, and the hill quaked beneath them, nearly throwing Jinx off the steps altogether. He grabbed her, wrapped his arms around her waist and tried to topple her, but it was like trying to uproot a mountain.

Sorath laughed. 'I would have used Dylan as a host for my lover. But you'll be so much better. So much more stable – Aes and Cú Sídhe combined. Holly prepared you so well as a vessel, with all her spells and charms.'

'Izzy,' Jinx shouted. 'Izzy, listen to me. Whatever she's promised, she's not going to do it. Whatever she said to you, it's all lies. She's not going to save me, or your dad. She's not going to help anyone. She's going to destroy us all. She's going to break the world apart!'

'Of course I am. I'd tear the universe and all its realities apart to be with him again. And you're going to help me, faeling.'

She grabbed the back of his head in her hand, the grip impossibly strong, inescapable, and pulled his mouth towards hers. Jinx tried to shout, but his voice was snatched away as fire consumed him, fire the like of which he'd never seen or felt, brighter than magnesium, devouring more quickly than acid, acrid like brimstone.

'Izzy,' he managed to whisper. 'Forgive me.' He'd thought it so many times in his heart, wanted to say it, wanted to tell her. Time for her to actually hear the words the Sídhe couldn't say. He forced them out, tumbling from his lips. 'I'm sorry. I'm so sorry.'

CHAPTER TWENTY-EIGHT

Swimming Upstream

Deep within the fire, Izzy opened her eyes at the sound of his voice. Jinx, so lost, so far away, penitent. Desperate.

He had to be, to ask her forgiveness.

The fire surrounding her didn't burn. It didn't even hurt. She knew it intimately now, was as much a part of it as it was of her. It was easy to fall back into its eddies and flows, to forget and be at peace. It seemed so long since she had actually felt at peace. And yet, she burned.

But why did Jinx need her forgiveness? After all that had happened, all he'd done, she would have thought he'd be grateful to be rid of her.

But instead he called her name, held her, kissed her. Refused to let go.

She could feel it. The first sensations to touch her for what

371

felt like years. Sorath didn't know desire, or love, or not on a level Izzy could comprehend. Everything burned so brightly within her. Love was obsession, desire was pure craving. But Jinx made her feel ...

Like a salmon swimming upstream, Izzy struggled back to herself as he spoke of lies, of her father, of betrayal.

Where was she?

A cool breeze touched her face, lifted her hair. Blissfully cool. She saw the sea, and the beam of the distant Kish lighthouse. Endless points of cold, manufactured brightness. Just for an instant, as if she saw them while she blinked her eyes, instead of the darkness she expected.

Sorath's fire reared up again, not a comfort now, but a wall of rage intent on pushing her back, quashing her.

The salmon swims against the river, Izzy. She could almost hear Dad's voice. *It has to. No matter what. That's part of its destiny, to struggle, to overcome. That's knowledge. It's easy to give up, to be mundane and never try to rise above the flow. But that's not our way. We study, learn and understand. We must know. We're like the salmon. We're stubborn.*

'I threw it away, Dad,' she murmured. 'I had to. To save us both.'

The spell Sorath wove faltered and her wish ... Izzy could feel it brewing within her, within the stone on which she stood, potent but not yet strong enough. It used the power imbued in this stone of more than a hundred and fifty years of hopes and dreams, tapped into desires and prayers. It fed on those wishes to serve Sorath's will.

In a glance, Izzy saw what the angel wanted to set free. It wasn't real. She knew it wasn't real – it was more like looking at a scene projected on the scenery around her, as if she was looking at the present and the future at the same time.

A figure strode from the hill with Sorath at his side. Wings of smoke and fire spread out behind him, and the ground withered where he walked. She saw the scorched earth that would follow, the death and destruction as the angels went to war against this creature, fallen from their number so very long ago and trapped in stone, in nightmares. In hell. She saw the death of countless humans, demons and fae as they were used as cannon fodder in an impossible war. He looked like Jinx. But he wasn't.

And it wasn't real.

Stronger now, she tried to recall what had happened since they left the Market.

Nothing.

Where's my father? she asked. *You promised to heal him. Where is he?*

'In good time,' Sorath replied, her voice just a touch too soft and cajoling to be believable. How could anything want its mate with such a passion and be prepared to consider anything else before it? Not even for a promise. Not with the controlling obsession for the Morning Star Izzy had seen in the angel.

The Morning Star. She knew that name. Remembered

it from Religious Education classes. From brief snatches of Milton and *Paradise Lost*. Lucifer. That was what she'd seen in Jinx's form, wasn't it?

And all it would take to bring him through was a crack in reality, a flaw in the world. Like she was. Something that shouldn't be, but was nonetheless.

'Forgive me,' Jinx had said. A plea. A different kind of love in his voice, one strained with regret. She tried to find him, but she met his pain first. It speared her mind and made her gasp in shock.

Elsewhere Dylan struggled to drag himself towards them and keep on breathing. But he didn't give up. Couldn't give up, even if it killed him. She could see into his mind, could read his determination that what was happening before him had to be stopped. And further off, amid the trees, shadows moved, terrified like children when they should have been fierce like monsters. Beneath her hill, locked in the hollow by Sorath's spell, Brí raged impotently.

There had to be a way to stop it.

'There is no way. Give up your fight, Isabel. It's senseless. You're just a child, too weak, too helpless. And look at him. Look how magnificent we will become.'

Jinx lifted his head, drunk with pain, and his eyes burned even brighter. His mouth twisted to a cruel and heartless line. He closed his hand around Sorath's throat and squeezed. But the angel just leaned into it and gasped as a surge of ecstasy made the fire even more fierce.

No. It's my throat, Izzy thought. *My throat, my body, my life she's stealing, and Jinx's she would sacrifice to Lucifer.* Her skin burned under his touch and her heart skipped as it tried to beat too fast. Darkness broke through from the place behind the fire. A darkness terrible and eternal. It sought its way out, through her, into Jinx and into the world.

My body, Izzy told herself. *My life. My blood. No more lies. No more tears. No more other people coming to the rescue. It ends here. It has to.*

Her hand flexed, fingers curling according to her own will at last. It moved spasmodically, jerking out and in again, closing around the iron knife.

'Go on,' Sorath sneered. 'Kill him again. It won't matter now. It's his body we need. It doesn't have to be alive.'

No. Not him. She'd never hurt him again. He had saved her, even from herself. But she had Sídhe blood too, right? Brí's blood. Anything was possible with Sídhe blood.

And from a distance she imagined she could hear Brí. *Yes my daughter, my child, my blood kin.*

She thought of her dad, lying helpless in the hospital bed and Mum by his side, curled up like a child against him, sleeping fitfully. What would happen to them if this nightmare broke free? What would Sorath do to rid herself of Izzy's last connection to the world?

Can't allow it. Just can't allow it.

Her fingers locked around the hilt and she pulled it free.

'No, Izzy!' Jinx's voice rang out. His own voice, the horror in his face real. He knew. Somehow he knew.

But she didn't – couldn't – hesitate.

And she didn't aim for him.

She drove the knife up to the hilt into her own body.

Sorath screamed and an answering cry tore up through the earth, through the Wishing Stone and through her, a howl of thwarted rage.

There was a soft whoomph, like an exhalation of air. Wind lashed the hilltop as figures appeared from nowhere, angels. Angels everywhere.

And the sudden cold, crisping the grass with frost, infecting the evening with winter's chill. The shadows deepened, writhed with sudden sentience. The shades and their masters were here too. So many of them, swarming from the shadows with glowing eyes and gleaming teeth.

Angels and demons, all over the hilltop.

Izzy's legs buckled, but Jinx caught her, his arms trembling. His body felt feverishly hot, his skin slick with sweat. He shook as he tried to hold her. But he didn't let her fall.

'What have you done?' he shouted. 'Ancestors, what have you done?'

Jinx lowered her to the top of the pyramid, lying beside the topmost cube. The knife jutted from her stomach. But it didn't hurt.

Izzy stared up at the stars. They seemed awfully close all of a sudden. As she watched, they spun above her, revealing wave upon wave of colours impossible to define, like one of those space telescope pictures seen through the naked eye. So beautiful. So cold. Fire in the heavens.

There was music, voices, harmonies, sweet and moving. They echoed through her, through the air and through the earth. They rippled up through her, rained down upon her, and the voices of the angels and demons seemed to join in.

'Izzy, talk to me. Please, talk to me.' Jinx's voice shook and the urge to leap into the sky above and swim against that current of light and sound faded a little. She focused instead on his face. He might have been carved from marble, he looked so pale. The tattoos stood out in sharp contrast to his skin. So beautiful. He didn't even realise how wonderful he was. No one had ever shown him that he too was beautiful, a wonder. A glorious never-should-have-been, like her. 'They're here. They're just watching. What are they waiting for?'

'For the end.' Her voice grated against her throat. 'They need to know, to be sure. And if we didn't do it—'

'Why did you do it?'

'Had to do it,' she sighed and the stupidity of the whole situation flooded through her.

Something filled her throat and she coughed, a violent racking movement. Then there was pain, pain like she'd never imagined, and blood filled her mouth. She gagged and spat it out.

Shit. That couldn't be good.

Sorath stirred, as angry as a wasp in the back of Izzy's mind.

Tied together, Izzy thought triumphantly.

'You idiot,' Sorath said. 'You've killed us both. I'm an angel. I don't die.'

'Yes,' Izzy whispered, resigned, determined. 'Yes, you do.' She closed her eyes. 'And if you don't, they'll rip you out of me and we'll die anyway. So what does it matter?'

'Izzy!' It was Jinx again. 'Izzy, don't you dare go and die. Talk to me! We can get help!'

'No. Too late. Doesn't hurt.' A lie, but as she said it the lie became true. It didn't hurt.

'But you're a grail. Can't you ... can't you heal yourself?'

She blinked tired eyes open, glared at the concern in his face. She wanted to laugh bitterly, but didn't have the breath.

'Obviously not. You're a moron, you know that?'

And God, she loved him for it.

'I should have kissed you when you first kissed me, Izzy. I should have seized every moment. Izzy ... Isabel.'

'Don't. Not Isabel. I hate Isabel.'

'Tell me what to do.'

Yes, definitely a moron. 'Kiss me now. And pull the knife out.'

'It'll kill you.'

She smiled. That hurt, though it shouldn't. 'Yes. Your kisses are bloody awful. You need to practise.' What did it matter now? She might as well say what she wanted. What she felt. She might as well tell him, before it was too late for words, before—

Tears hit her face. Not hers but his. Jinx was crying? Not

possible. Must be rain. Jinx the cruel, Jinx the caustic ... How could Jinx cry for her?

The angels stirred expectantly, the shades murmured on the edge of hearing. They moved forward, but only to the foot of the pyramid. No further. Izzy frowned, feeling the pressure building in the air around them. Tightening around her skin, squeezing her, until she thought she'd pop. But all she could do was lie there and wait.

'Isabel Gregory,' said a new voice, one she had half been waiting for. Hoping for. He would have killed her the last time they met, but only the angel interested him. Now she had done the job for him. She was dying and here he was. Come to collect. With the sound of a billowing black cloak, or the unfurling of great wings, Azazel appeared from a twist of shadows, standing on the next level of the steps. The magic warping around the pyramid didn't hold him back, she realised. Because she was here. And so was Sorath. He held a gold-rimmed crystal bottle in his hands. 'Are you ready?'

Information filtered directly into her mind and she knew what had to be done. The spark couldn't stay here. This was the only way to get rid of it and rid of Sorath too. She wasn't afraid of Azazel, not this time. He had what he wanted, or would have it shortly. She gave up the fight.

'Pull out the knife, Jinx.'

The angels and the shades hissed, a low-level sound that rippled across her senses like sandpaper. He had to do it. When Jinx didn't move, she closed her own hand around the hilt. But she wasn't strong enough. It hurt to try, each effort wrenching an agonised cry from her. She twisted in Jinx's arms.

He held her still and then closed his hand over hers.

'Just remember I love you,' he told her. Perfect words, words she'd longed to hear from him. Suddenly nothing seemed to hurt any more.

The knife slid out of her flesh and with it a golden mist came too. It floated up into the night air and Azazel quickly gathered it up in the bottle and sealed the lid in place. It floated there, like pollen on a breeze, like plankton in the deepest ocean. A perfect element of creation, a primal being.

Sorath's voice was gone.

'Where is she?' Izzy asked.

There was a susurration of relief from the creatures watching them, infernal and divine alike.

Azazel tapped the lid of the bottle. 'She's in here, where she belongs.' He glanced up, surveying the attending crowd. 'Angels are dangerous enough without allowing fallen ones to run amok. You did well, little Grigori. Very well.'

'So well she's dying for it?' Jinx growled.

Azazel shook his head and smiled as he tucked the bottle inside his cloak, out of sight. 'Always so angry, Cú Sídhe. I sometimes think your first fathers were crossed with a pit bull. The heavens know, you're ugly enough.' He snapped his fingers. 'Well, you've work to do, girl. Get up.'

Izzy shook her head. 'Dying, remember? Stabbed myself.'

Azazel stuck out his lower lip. 'Oh well, in *that* case, don't listen to your great-uncle. I'm just a foolish old man who was there when your line first came to be. Who has watched and guided your family every step of the way down the long years. We put the mark on you all for a reason, you know. By all means, lie there. But others might have something to say. I think we're about to find out.'

A strident voice rang out across the hilltop, getting louder as it approached. A female voice that sounded like she'd just found her best flowerbeds desecrated, or the wrong cutlery used at dinner. A beautiful voice, a stolen voice, and one Izzy had hoped never to hear again.

'What are you doing here? All of you, go away. You've no place here. Even setting foot here constitutes an act of war. Before I lose my temper, you'd better—' The shades were gone in an instant, though the angels lingered. Izzy tried to smile. Even angels wouldn't last long against Brí. '*Get off* my hill!'

The same soft displacement of air. And they were gone at last.

'And what do you think you've been doing, young lady? Jinx by Jasper, you put my daughter down. Who locked me underground? Not *them*. They'd never dare. I broke out before and will again and again. No one chains me inside my own hollow. Where is Blythe? What is the meaning—?'

She must have seen the blood. Or Izzy's pallor. Or the grief that transformed Jinx's face into a death mask.

'Get out of my way, demon,' Brí hissed, passing through the

space between them in the blink of an eye. Azazel obliged, stepping back with a gracious bow. Brí ignored him completely. 'Who did this, Isabel? I'll eviscerate them. Was it Holly? Was it *him*?'

She turned on Jinx, but Izzy stayed her hand.

'It was me.'

Brí let out a long breath, studying Izzy's face. The resemblance was there when Izzy really looked. Like it or not, she could see herself in this fairy woman, this matriarch of the Sídhe.

'You foolish child, what were you thinking?'

Izzy almost laughed, but it made her mouth fill with blood and she choked instead. Now Brí sounded like a mother. Izzy wondered if she realised that.

But Brí wasn't in the mood for listening. She bent over Izzy, intent on her injury. 'Hold still. Stop wriggling about.'

Yeah, like wriggling was on her mind right at the moment. Any kind of movement at all was agony.

Brí pressed her hand to Izzy's side, just as Izzy had done instinctively to Jinx so long ago. It felt natural as breathing – something that suddenly Izzy found she could do again. The pain ebbed away and she sat up in Jinx's grateful embrace. He buried his face in her hair, breathing deeply.

'Dylan,' said Izzy. 'We've got to help Dylan.'

'What do you think I am? One of your plug and play contraptions?' Brí scolded.

'Please,' Izzy said. Brí's gaze hardened. 'Mother.'

For a moment Brí froze and then her features softened, just for a moment, before the gruff bluster returned.

'Very well, but just this once. You'll have to sort out your father by yourself. I'm not wanted there and you're well able to do it. I showed you before. Those doctors – those *so called* doctors – have done nothing for him and *that woman*—'

'Rachel,' Izzy corrected her with a gentle note of warning in her voice. 'His wife. My mum. Please, Brí, help Dylan.'

Best not to remind her that she'd met him before, who he'd been with. Best not to mention Silver at all.

Brí bustled over to him and they followed, Jinx never once releasing her, his arms forming a shield around her whenever he could.

He'd said he loved her. The thought of that made her glow inside. Not with the fires of Sorath's obsession. This was warm and natural, a comfort. And so much stronger.

Dylan had made it to the foot of the pyramid. He leaned against it now, breathing hard without ever getting enough breath. His ribs were broken, Izzy realised, and one at least had pierced a lung.

'You tried to save her, even hurt like this?' asked Brí in a low voice. He nodded, staring at her in awe and more than a little fear. He knew what she was and what she could do.

Brí frowned and recognition swept her face.

'You're the one who was with Silver. But you're not as you were. You're full of power … What did she do to you, boy?'

'She… she kissed me.'

'Oh, she did much more than that. You're a touchstone, a living touchstone. I've never seen the like.'

'That's not possible,' said Jinx weakly. 'Nothing mortal can be a touchstone. That's the whole point. To endure.'

'Are you calling me a liar now? What was that tree of hers originally?' She glared up at him before turning her attention back to Dylan. For a moment she just stared, shaking her head softly. 'You won't last long like this. They'll be after you like junkies. You'll only be safe with her. And only for a while. Here, I'll see what I can do.'

She bent over him and whispered in his ear as she pressed her hand to his chest.

Dylan leaned back, stunned, but then nodded. Brí stepped back with a dismissive snort and he struggled to his feet, healed. Or at least mostly healed. He was still bloody and bruised, the gashes still livid on his skin, but he was breathing again, standing, almost himself.

And he was changed. Completely changed, somewhere deep inside.

Brí turned away, muttering about the idiocy of people, Silver in particular, and the violation of her home and vanished into the trees without so much as a goodbye.

Not that Izzy wanted one. It just would have been nice to have an acknowledgement or something. But that was Brí, she supposed. It would take some getting used to.

Azazel had vanished too, all trace of him and his shades wiped away. He'd taken Sorath's spark with him.

They were alone, the three of them, on the top of the hill.

'We need to get to the hospital,' said Izzy. 'Get you looked at, Dylan. And I need to see Dad.'

'What about you?' Jinx asked.

She ran her hand down to the bloody tear in her shirt, through to the smooth skin underneath. No sign of a wound there. Not even a scar.

She took Dylan's hand, and interlocked the fingers of her other hand with Jinx's, leading them both down the hill. 'I think I'm going to be okay.'

'Does she always give so many orders?' Jinx asked Dylan.

'You've no idea, mate.'

'Well, I wouldn't get cocky. If you really are Silver's touchstone now, she's going to murder you for almost dying.'

The amused expression faded from Jinx's face. If what Brí said was true, Izzy figured, he was in a lot more trouble than that.

They picked their way through the dark woods, past walls to no buildings and paths that led nowhere until, almost at the bottom of the wooded area, Jinx called for a halt.

Shadows moved amid the trees. Not shades or demons. Not now. Cú Sídhe. A bark went up and a young man rose up from the bushes. Izzy grinned as Jinx pushed her behind him. She was becoming incorrigible with all this new-found confidence.

'Blight?'

'Jinx by Jasper. We've found you at last,' Blythe's brother said, bowing his head respectfully. 'We've been searching for you everywhere.' He spoke briefly to one of the other hounds, sending word to Blythe no doubt.

'Brí isn't happy. She wants to know where you were. Sorath locked her in the hill to stop her interfering.'

'Did it work?' Blight asked, surprised.

'Only for a little while.'

'They tried that a hundred and fifty years ago and it didn't work then. But yeah ...' He ran his hand through his hair and breathed out in a long exasperated sigh. 'Yeah, she's going to be well angry.'

The largest of the black hounds loped into the path, growing as she circled Jinx. Blythe clawed the dry leaves and then changed into her Sídhe form, standing with her hands on her hips.

'Where the hell have you been? We thought she'd killed you, or that the angels had tracked you down. They all vanished. Just like that. One minute Silver and I were facing them down and the next they were gone. What happened?'

'It's over,' said Izzy. 'They came here, but in equal numbers I think. And we'd already taken care of Sorath. So I imagine they had nothing to stay for. She's gone.'

Taken to hell where she belongs, Jinx wanted to add, but he didn't.

'Blythe,' Dylan interrupted. 'Where's Silver?'

'Ah, looking for you, I'd imagine. Although if you'd like to stay lost—'

'That might not be a bad idea, Dylan,' said Jinx. 'Really. You should go home.' Dylan looked away, his shocked expression fading with exhaustion and defeat. Clearly his instincts agreed, but something else made him hesitate. All that Brí had said, no doubt. Jinx couldn't offer comfort though. He wouldn't know where to begin. There had never been a human touchstone before. Rocks mainly, plants that had been magically transformed, things like that. Not people. Definitely not humans.

'I should …' he began, then nodded. 'I should go.'

'We'll see him safe home,' said Blight.

Dylan stiffened and glanced at Izzy. For a moment their eyes locked and something passed between them. Jinx frowned, and then recalled what Brí had said. That they'd all be after him as Silver's touchstone, the source of her power. There was only one person he'd be safe with, and that wouldn't last very long either. Silver needed her magic.

So should Jinx bring him to her? Or help him get as far away from her as possible? He didn't know anymore.

'No,' said Dylan. 'Not home. Not yet. I need to talk to her first.'

Blythe glared at Jinx. 'And you … don't leave it so long to visit again.'

'Not sure Brí would like that,' Jinx said, recognising the threat in her voice as only superficial. It was more affectionate than that, the tone someone would use to a disruptive pup.

'She'll put up with it, for us. You are kin, after all. You proved it when you died. We all heard you. That's what brought us to your aid. Even Brí couldn't deny that.'

'She didn't try to stop you?'

Blythe stared at him. 'She's our matriarch, Jinx. She would never deny us what we want. There's a gate over there. It'll take you to the hospital. That is where Izzy wants to go. Kin being kin. Just remember, Jinx, you have a duty to her now. More than kith. More than kin.'

He bowed his head to his fellow Cú Sídhe. 'I understand that.'

Izzy hugged him and he only just managed to stifle a smile.

The hospital grounds were empty, even the dual carriageway outside was desolate. The streetlamps fizzed and hummed as they walked up to the entrance. Izzy's heart shivered with every sound.

Silver leaned against the security desk. On the far side the guard snored noisily. The Aes Sídhe smiled as she saw them and it was as if the fluorescent lighting flared briefly overhead.

'I was wondering when you'd get here.'

Dylan hesitated, hanging back between Izzy and Jinx. 'Silver …' he said carefully.

Her expression changed as she took in his battered face, the dried blood on his clothes, the mess the angel had made of him. '*What* happened? What did she do to you?'

She strode forward, her eyes blazing as she examined him, turning his face to one side as if he was a possession damaged by some careless handling. He pulled back sharply, irritation marking his features.

'I'm okay. Really. Brí sorted it.'

'Brí,' she snorted brusquely. 'You're lucky she didn't drain you dry.'

'Like you will. She told me, Silver.'

'*I* warned you. Right from the start. That's how it works until eventually you're gone. Your life force goes into my touchstone.'

'The tree. But there's no tree anymore. So what is there, Silver? What's left? Apart from me.'

She snarled, baring her teeth, but it wasn't an entirely aggressive expression. There was desperation in it as well. 'What do you mean? You're just a human, a talented one no doubt but you're just—'

'I'm the only touchstone you have.'

'No!' Silver turned away, every muscle tight with alarm, poised for escape. But she didn't go. She looked back at him, shivering from head to toe. 'Dylan ... this isn't what I intended. I swear it. I would never have done this to you if I'd ... I don't even know how it happened.' She looked like she wanted to beg forgiveness, but naturally, the words stuck in her throat. Izzy saw tears well up in her pale eyes. Terrifying or not, Silver had never intended this.

Dylan caught her arms, pulling her back to him, a surprisingly gentle gesture. 'There's a way to control it. To work this out, so we both can live. It won't be easy, but there is a way.'

Silver slipped free of his arms, staring at him in confusion. She'd stopped retreating though. 'There's no way to break the spell of a Leanán Sídhe, Dylan. I warned you of that too.'

'And no way for you to survive without a touchstone. That's what they say. You should have died back in that cell. But Brí says differently.'

Silver's expression froze. 'And why would Brí share her secrets?'

'Because Dylan tried to save me,' said Izzy.

'I *failed* to save you.' He said it with half a laugh. 'Jinx did that.'

'No,' Jinx admitted. 'That was all Izzy. She saved herself, and us. All of us.'

'Silver,' Dylan murmured and held out his hand. 'There is a way, and I will find it. It won't be easy, it won't be painless, but we can do it. If you'll help me.'

She hesitated – how could she not? What he had said was probably an understatement of epic proportions. But here he was, a human, who should be her thrall, asking for her help. Holding such power over her, and not wielding it like a whip. Izzy could see the conflict in Silver's beautiful eyes, but then she took his hand in hers. 'Tell me what Brí said. We'll work it out together. Then we'll see what's possible.'

Izzy watched them go, hand in hand, heads bent together as

they whispered of secrets.

Mum was asleep in the chair at Dad's bedside. She looked childlike, all petite build, hair like gold. The differences between her and Izzy now stood out starkly to Izzy's eyes. So clear that they weren't related, now that she looked. Really looked. It didn't matter. Mum was, and would always be, Mum. Izzy hesitated by the door and put her finger to her lips so that Jinx wouldn't make a sound. Foolish really. He could move more quietly than any cat if he wanted to. But still, he smiled and nodded his agreement. He leaned against the door jamb, waiting for her.

There was a cup of water waiting on the locker. Izzy sat on the edge of the bed and picked it up. With her other hand, she steadied her Dad's head and tipped the plastic cup until the water moistened his lips. No more than that.

If she needed a grail, she had to look no further than herself.

The effect was instantaneous. He grumbled something, in that indistinct, sleeping-Dad kind of way, like when she caught him nodding off in front of the news or halfway through the Sunday afternoon DVD he'd promised to watch with her. Izzy lowered him back down onto the pillow and his eyes flickered open.

Dad smiled weakly at her. 'Well, now,' his voice sounded rough and strained. But it was his voice and it was wonderful to hear. 'You look like you've been in a war, sweetheart.'

'Just a small one,' she conceded.

His eyes narrowed, hardened in a way she wasn't familiar with. The expression looked strange on his face, but at the same time clearly belonged there. 'What sort of war?'

She surprised herself when she found a smile. 'One you neglected to tell me about.'

Dad sighed, closed his eyes. 'I never could find the right moment. How did you find out?'

She sat down on the edge of the bed, took his hand. His grip closed around her fingers, reassuring, secure. 'It found me. But I managed.'

'I see that. It doesn't go away, Izzy. It never goes away. I guess we wanted to spare you for as long as possible. To give you a normal, happy childhood.'

'And you did.' Tears stung her eyes and she squeezed his hand. She didn't feel like a child any more, but with Dad, that didn't matter. She would always be his daughter. 'Brí isn't best pleased.'

He let out something like a sigh, which was more than half a groan. 'Brí is *never* best pleased.'

'Yeah, I got that much. My mother? Really?'

For a moment she wished he would say 'no', at the same time knowing he wouldn't. But just for that second, she wondered if he would make that go away with a word.

He went white and then the shame in his face was enough of an answer. 'Yes. It was ... I'm sorry, Izzy, I—'

Izzy panicked, not ready to hear this, not ready for any of

it. He was still her dad. He was a Grigori. Part of her couldn't bear for him to be human too, to admit failings and weakness, mistakes and regrets.

'It's old news,' she said, cutting him off. 'And it doesn't matter. Not really. I've made peace with it, with her, I think. You're my family. You and Mum.' She looked over her shoulder to where Mum slept. She knew too and had said nothing. But it was in the past.

'And him?' He nodded towards Jinx, standing just beyond the doorway. Dad didn't miss a thing. And Izzy wouldn't have expected any less.

'He's good. I promise.'

'If you say so.'

'I do.' As she said it, Mum murmured something, almost waking, and Dad's attention shifted slightly. Torn. The adult thing was to take pity on them, give them the space they needed. And though the childish part of her didn't want to, Izzy smiled. 'Later on, you can tell me everything. I'll hold you to that. I'll be outside, if you need anything.'

She kissed his forehead and Dad wrapped his arm around her, his embrace so strong that she knew she'd never need to fear anything with him watching out for her. But just occasionally, if needs be, she could look out for him as well.

Jinx stepped back to let her out, her shadow, her guard and more. Izzy wrapped her arm with his and led him away as her father softly called her mother's name.

'Rachel?'

Izzy kept walking. Away from the exclamations and the endearments, away from the two people who needed just each other right now.

She'd go back later, she promised herself.

But for now, they deserved to be together. Jinx stopped at the end of the corridor, pulled her into his arms and kissed the top of her head. She nestled against him, her cheek pressed to his chest while his heart thundered away like a stampede.

She knew the sound. Hers was doing the same thing.

A long way from an alley with an angel painted on a wall. A long way from the girl who had first met him.

The mark on the back of her neck warmed again, and this time it wasn't frightening. It was the sense of coming home.

Words & Phrases

Aes Sídhe: (Ay Shee) The highest caste of the Sídhe, most angelic in appearance, the ruling class.

Amadán: (Am-a-dawn) meaning Fool, also known as the Old Man and the Trickster. Member of the Council.

Brí: (Bree) meaning Strength. Member of the Council.

Cú Sídhe: (Coo Shee) Shapeshifting Sídhe who sometimes take the form of a large hound. A lower caste of the Sídhe.

Dubh Linn: (Dove Linn) The black pool, original name for Dublin.

Einechlan: (I-ne-chlan) Honour price.

Geis: (Gaish) A taboo or prophecy, like a vow or a spell, which dictates the fate of a member of the Aes Sídhe.

Íde: (Ee-da) meaning Thirst. Member of the Council.

Leanán Sídhe: (Lee-ann-awn Shee) Fairy lover, the muse, Sídhe who feed from the magical lifeforce of others, but can inspire unbridled creativity in return.

Sídhe: (Shee) Irish supernatural race.

Seanchaí: (Shan-a-key) Storyteller. Member of the Council.

Tuatha dé Dannan: (too-atha day dan-ann) The people of the Goddess Danu, or the people of God, the Irish fairies.

Coming soon ...

A Hollow in the Hills

BY RUTH FRANCES LONG

When Holly unleashes an ancient and forbidden power, Izzy and her father must prevent the war in heaven spilling across the earth. But when Izzy refuses to sacrifice Jinx, she sets in motion a chain of events which will see them hunted through the Sídhe-ways, across the city and into the hills, where Izzy will face the greatest challenge of all. In the deepest and darkest Hollow, an angel of death is waiting and the price he asks for his help might be too high.